CRASH
THE
THUNDER

JEFFREY POOLE

Jeffrey Poole's Epic Fantasy Books
Bakkian Chronicles:

The Prophecy
Insurrection
Amulet of Aria
Disneyland Debacle (short story)
Winter Wonderland (short story)

Tales of Lentari:

Lost City
Something Wyverian This Way Comes
A Portal for Your Thoughts
Thoughts for a Portal
Wizard in the Woods
Close Encounters of the Magical Kind
The Hunt for Red Oskorlisk (short story)
May the Fang be With You (Pirates trilogy #1)
The Hammer is Strong with This One (Pirates #2)
These are Not the Stones You're Looking For (Pirates #3)
Blast from the Past

Dragons of Andela:

Harness the Fire
Strike the Spark
Crash the Thunder

Mysteries by J.M. Poole
The Corgi Case Files Series
19 delightful cozy mystery novels featuring corgi
sleuths, Sherlock and Watson

CRASH
THE
THUNDER

Dragons of Andela, Book 3

JEFFREY POOLE

Secret Staircase Books

Crash the Thunder
Published by Secret Staircase Books, an imprint of
Columbine Publishing Group, LLC
PO Box 416, Angel Fire, NM 87710

Book layout and design by Secret Staircase Books
First paperback edition: April, 2025
First e-book edition: April, 2025

* * *

Publisher's Cataloging-in-Publication Data

Poole, Jeffrey
Crash the Thunder / by Jeffrey Poole.
p. cm.
ISBN 978-1649142184 (paperback)
ISBN 978-1649142191 (e-book)

1. Andela (Fictitious location)—Fiction. 2. Epic fantasy fiction 3.
Dragons and mythical creatures—Fiction. I. Title

Dragons of Andela : Book 3.
Crash the Thunder
Poole, Jeffrey, Dragons of Andela epic fantasy series.

BISAC : FICTION / Fantasy/Epic.

813/.54

For Giliane —

Even when you argue with me about a title for my own book,
I'll love you always & forever!

Table of Contents

Prologue

The campfire flickered, casting long shadows across the beach as waves lapped gently at the shore. Zeira's scales glimmered a dull red in the firelight, her wings folded tightly against her body. She stared into the flames, lost in troubled thoughts. Across from her, Gocri's white form seemed to glow ethereally, while Sif's smoky gray coloring blended into the gathering darkness. Jerica sat cross-legged on the sand, her blonde hair whipping in the sea breeze, the beautiful green jhorium goblet clutched protectively in her hands.

An oppressive silence hung over the group, broken only by the crackle of burning driftwood and the mournful cry of a distant seabird. Zeira's chest felt hollow, aching with the absence of Skellig. His dry wit and flashes of lightning were sorely missed. And now the valthans ... Word had come to them that the water dragons were captured, suffering who knew what horrors at the hands of the Thunder King.

She clenched her talons in the sand, fighting back a surge of despair. Some leader she had turned out to be. Letting one of their own be taken, unable to protect innocent creatures who had done nothing to deserve such a fate. The weight of responsibility pressed down on her, threatening to crush her entirely.

"I can't do this anymore," Zeira blurted out, her voice cracking.

Gocri's icy blue eyes fixed on her, concern evident in his gaze. "What do you mean, Zeira?"

She swallowed hard, shame burning in her chest. "I'm not fit to lead us. I'm weak, unworthy. Skellig is gone because of me. The valthans ..." Her voice trailed off as grief closed her throat.

"That's not true," Sif interjected, her smoky form rippling. "You couldn't have prevented what happened."

But Zeira shook her head vehemently. "A true leader would have found a way. I'm no Fire Lord Darazok, no Queen Freriss or Lady Chrys. I'm just ... me. And clearly, that's not enough."

She looked at each of her companions in turn, seeing the worry on their faces. Even their human companion, Jerica, seemed to sense the gravity of the moment, her fingers tightening around the goblet's stem.

"I want to step down," Zeira said quietly. "Someone else should take charge. Someone stronger, wiser."

The words tasted like ashes in her mouth, but a small part of her felt relief at finally voicing the doubts that had been gnawing at her for days. She wasn't cut out for this. How could she, barely more than a hatchling herself, hope to stand against the might of the Thunder King?

Gocri shifted, his massive form casting new shadows as he leaned forward. "Zeira, you're being too hard on yourself. We all believe in you."

"You shouldn't," she stated, averting her gaze. "I'll only lead us to ruin."

As the others began to protest, Zeira tuned them out, sinking deeper into her spiral of self-recrimination. She thought of her mother, Gynnyth, and the legacy of the Phoenix caste. What would they think of her now, cowering on a beach while evil threatened to consume their world?

She exhaled sharply, a few sparks escaping her nostrils. If only she could ignite a fire within herself, burn away this paralyzing doubt. But the embers of her confidence had been all but extinguished, leaving only cold ashes behind.

Suddenly, a commotion erupted at the water's edge. Nuri, who had been silently observing from the shallows, thrashed her blue serpentine body, sending sprays of seawater hissing into the fire.

"You all will have to sort this out. I can't stay here any longer," she declared, her voice tight with barely contained anguish. "My people, my kin—they're suffering under that tyrant's rule. I have to do something!"

Before anyone could react, Nuri plunged beneath the waves, her sleek form disappearing into the inky depths with startling speed. The abruptness of her departure left a palpable void, the air thick with unspoken fears and mounting urgency.

Jerica stood, sand clinging to her legs as she stared out at the turbulent sea. "Nuri, wait!" she called, but her voice was lost to the crashing waves.

Gocri rumbled uneasily, his wings rustling. "This doesn't bode well. If Nuri acts rashly ..."

"She could expose us all," Sif finished grimly.

Zeira's heart raced. She wanted to dive in after Nuri, to stop her friend from potentially endangering herself and their cause. But what right did she have to make that call? She was no leader. And, unlike Nuri, she was no water dragon.

As if sensing her inner turmoil, Jerica turned to Zeira, her eyes reflecting the firelight. "What do we do now?"

Before Zeira could formulate a response, the air shimmered, and a spectral image materialized above the fire. It was Queen Chrys of the Smoke Dragons, her ethereal form rippling like a mist.

"Hear me, allies," Chrys's voice echoed, tinged with steel.

"The dragon realms are mobilizing. From the icy peaks of the Frost dragons to the molten caverns of Blaze, we prepare for war."

The projection shifted, revealing glimpses of dragon armies assembling. Armored scales glinted, wings unfurled like battle banners, and claws were sharpened to lethal points.

"We must end the Thunder King's tyranny before he decimates us," Chrys continued. "We march as one, united against this threat to all dragonkind. Our diversity is our strength. Fire and ice, earth and air—all elements are within our power."

Zeira watched, transfixed, as the image showed Lord Myrdaynth of Gale rallying his Spark dragons. She caught a glimpse of Dym, Skellig's sire, his jade green scales crackling with barely contained energy.

"But we cannot succeed alone." Queen Chrys's voice grew solemn. "We need the aid of our human allies, those who remember the old bonds between our races. Zeira, Jerica—your roles in this conflict may prove pivotal."

The projection faded, leaving only the crackling fire and the reminders of expectation hanging heavy in the air.

Jerica broke the silence, her voice barely above a whisper. "It's really happening, isn't it? All of Andela is going to war."

Zeira nodded numbly, her mind reeling. The gravity of their situation crashed over her like a tidal wave. This was no longer just about rescuing Skellig or freeing the valthans. The fate of entire realms hung in the balance.

"We need a plan," Gocri rumbled, his eyes gleaming. "If the dragon armies are mobilizing, we must find a way to coordinate our efforts."

Sif nodded in agreement. "And we can't forget about Nuri. She's out there alone, potentially heading straight into danger."

Zeira felt all eyes turn to her, awaiting her decision. She looked at the faces of her friends, saw the trust they placed in her, and her doubts returned.

Gocri's icy blue eyes flickered between Zeira and Jerica, his voice soft yet resolute. "Zeira, you've led us admirably, but perhaps … perhaps it's time we consider a different approach."

Sif nodded, her smoky form shifting slightly as she added, "Jerica has shown remarkable courage and ingenuity. Her connection to the jhorium goblet and the oron stone gives her unique insight and powers beyond our own."

Zeira's head snapped up, surprise etched across her features. She hadn't considered this possibility, but as she pondered it, relief washed over her.

Jerica's eyes widened, her hands instinctively clutching the goblet at her side. "What! Me? Lead?" Her voice quavered. "But I'm just a village girl. I don't know the first thing about war or strategy."

Gocri's tail swished, unleashing a small flurry of icy crystals across the sand. "None of us were born leaders, Jerica. Leadership is forged in the crucible of necessity."

Jerica shook her head vehemently, blonde hair whipping about her face. "No, you don't understand. I can barely manage my family's shop without messing up inventory. How could I possibly lead a group against the Thunder King?"

Zeira watched the human girl, noting the tremor in her hands and the fear in her eyes. But she also saw something else, a spark of fortitude, buried deep beneath the doubt.

"Jerica," Zeira said gently, "your ability to craft the jhorium goblet was no accident. You have a connection to these magical forces that none of us fully understand."

Jerica's fingers tightened around the glowing green chalice. "But that was just luck, wasn't it? I didn't know what I was doing."

Sif's form coalesced into a more solid shape as she leaned toward Jerica. "Sometimes the greatest leaders are those who don't seek power but rise to meet the challenges before them."

Jerica's thoughts formed a chaotic whirlwind of doubt and possibility. Their expectations pressed down on her, as heavy as the jhorium goblet in her hands. She gazed into its ethereal green glow, searching for answers that refused to materialize.

"I ... I want to help," she whispered, her voice barely audible above the crackling campfire. "But what if I make the wrong choices? What if I lead us all to our doom?"

Zeira's massive red form shifted closer, her scales

reflecting the firelight. "We all face that fear, Jerica. Even I, as a dragon of Blaze, have doubted my every decision, especially since Skellig's capture."

Gocri nodded, frost forming around his snout as he spoke. "It's not about being perfect. It's about doing what you believe is right, even when you're terrified."

Jerica's fingers absently traced the shape of the goblet. "But how can I lead dragons? You're all so much more powerful, so much more knowledgeable about this world."

Sif's smoky form swirled around Jerica, a comforting presence. "You bring a unique perspective, Jerica. Your human ingenuity, your connection to the jhorium—these are strengths we need."

As the dragons spoke, Jerica felt a small ember of courage ignite within her. She thought of her village, of her family, of all the innocent people threatened by the Thunder King's tyranny. Could she really stand by and do nothing?

"I'm scared," Jerica admitted, her voice growing stronger. "But I'm also angry. Angry at the injustice, at the suffering. If there's even a chance I could make a difference ..."

Zeira's eyes gleamed with approval. "That's the spirit of a true leader, Jerica. Courage isn't the absence of fear—it's acting in spite of it."

Jerica took a deep breath and straightened her tunic, her hand tightening around the jhorium goblet tied to her belt. The green glow pulsed in time with her heartbeat, as if sensing her acceptance. She stood, facing the dragons gathered around the campfire.

"Alright," she said, her voice wavering slightly before steadying. "I'll do it. I can't promise I'll always make the right choices, but I swear I'll give everything I have to rescue Skellig, to stop the Thunder King, and free the valthans."

Gocri rumbled approvingly, a plume of icy mist escaping his nostrils. "Well said, young one. Now, we must plan our next move carefully."

Jerica nodded, her mind already racing. "The Thunder King—Emerus Dinty—he's after the jhorium. It was his whole purpose in building that horrible Cerebus machine, to mine every scrap of the valuable mineral he could find. We know that much. But why? What does he hope to gain?"

Zeira's tail lashed, sending sparks dancing into the night air. "Power, undoubtedly. But the specifics elude us. Jerica, what can you tell us about the properties of jhorium?"

Jerica frowned, recalling her father's teachings. "It's incredibly rare, and it has ... a sort of resonance. When I worked with it, it felt alive somehow. The goblet often feels like it's responding to my thoughts, my emotions."

Sif's misty form coalesced into a more solid shape. "Perhaps that's why he seeks it. To harness that responsiveness, to bend it to his will. The goblet and the oron stone are powerful, Jerica, and you possess both."

"But for what purpose would the Thunder King want them?" Jerica mused, unconsciously reaching into her pocket, her fingers tracing the shape of the oron stone there. "A weapon? Some kind of magical amplifier?"

Gocri's ice-blue eyes narrowed. "Whatever his intentions, we must act swiftly. The longer the valthans remain under his control, the greater his power grows."

Jerica nodded, her mind whirling with possibilities. "We need more information. Is there any way we could infiltrate his stronghold? Or perhaps find someone who's escaped his clutches?"

Zeira considered, "A direct assault would be foolhardy. But ... there are whispers of a resistance movement forming among the humans in Spark. Perhaps we could make contact, gather intelligence."

"It's risky," Jerica said, her voice tinged with both excitement and apprehension. "But it might be our best chance. I could go—I'm human, after all. I might be able to blend in certain places where you couldn't."

Gocri growled, frost forming on his scales. "Absolutely not. It's far too dangerous to send you alone into enemy territory."

Jerica felt a flash of frustration. "But I'm not helpless! I have the goblet, the oron stone. And isn't this what a leader is supposed to do? Take risks for the greater good?"

Sif's smoky form swirled agitatedly. "Perhaps a compromise. Jerica could go, but with one of us in disguise as a companion. A protector, should things go awry."

Jerica considered this, her heart pounding. "That ... that could work. But who? And how would we disguise—?"

They all turned to look at Sif, the one with the ability to take on any number of guises. Jerica smiled.

Then her mind drifted to the Thunder King. She imagined his cruel face, twisted with the lust for power. The thought of confronting such a formidable enemy sent a chill down her spine, but she pushed the fear aside. They had to act, and soon. The fate of dragons, valthans, and humans alike hung in the balance.

Zeira's voice cut through the debate, her tone soft but resolute. "We're stronger together. Whatever we decide, we should face it as one."

The young dragon's words seemed to settle over the group like a warm blanket, easing the tension that had been building. Jerica felt a swell of gratitude, realizing how much she'd come to rely on these extraordinary creatures.

"Zeira's right," Jerica said, her fingers reaching out to stroke the red dragon's left talon. "We can't afford to be divided now. The Thunder King wants this goblet and the oron stone. He wants to crush the dragons and enslave the valthans. But we won't let him."

Gocri nodded, a low rumble of approval emanating from his chest. "Well said, little one. Your leadership already shows promise."

Sif's eyes gleamed through her smoky form. "We may be few, but our bond is strong. The Thunder King cannot hope to match the power of true friendship and loyalty."

As night deepened around them, Jerica felt a curious mix of emotions. Fear still gnawed at her belly, but it was tempered by a growing resolve. She looked around at her companions— Zeira's gentle strength, Gocri's fierce protectiveness, Sif's unwavering loyalty. They were an unlikely group, thrust together by circumstance, but united by a common purpose.

"Tomorrow," Jerica said, her voice steady despite the butterflies in her stomach, "we begin our journey to the heart of the Thunder King's territory. We'll face whatever comes, together."

The dragons murmured their agreement, and Jerica felt a surge of warmth that had nothing to do with the flames from their campfire. As she gazed out over the dark waters, the role of leadership settled more comfortably in her mind. She thought of Nuri, out there in the sea, setting out alone.

Chapter 1 — Unmatched

Deeper and deeper Nuri dove, navigating through the murkiest of water with the ease of someone who felt no fear. Strange and spectacular marine life, the likes of which were rarely seen by the surface dwellers, darted away the moment her presence was discovered. At a depth of nearly a thousand meter, she leveled off her descent and surveyed her surroundings. She had arrived at the sea floor, following a lead, hoping to find traces of Skellig, while investigating the news that valthans had been captured by the Thunder King.

An underwater field of thick seaweed, swayed back and forth with the currents. Running her forked tongue across her fangs, she briefly wondered if she had the time to stop for a bite to eat. As if in answer to her unspoken thought, a large grouper, easily two hundred pounds, lifted off the seabed and appeared less than ten meters away. The grouper didn't wait for an introduction. It immediately turned and fled.

Nuri flicked her tail and shot forward. One snap of

the jaws and it was over. Hunger abated, she continued her search. However, one thing became abundantly clear: they had been misinformed. Again.

Nuri sighed. This wasn't the news she wanted to relay. It had been two days now since Skellig had been taken, and they were no closer to discovering his location than at the instant he disappeared.

Anything? Jerica telepathically inquired, sounding hopeful.

I've arrived at the floor. There's no shipwreck here, or anything else that looks like it was created by one of the tribesmen. Er, humans. I do believe we were led astray.

Nuri felt her kai's disappointment before it could be acknowledged. Find the shipwreck, they had been told. Buried within the captain's quarters was a chest that was supposed to contain correspondence between the Thunder King and the people of an as-yet unidentified kingdom. But, what did she find? Nothing but seaweed and oddly glowing fish that Nuri refused to touch, which was surprising. Normally, she would eat practically any fish from the sea. After all, Nuri was a valthan.

Being a water dragon, over forty meters long from nose to tail, meant her domain was the water. Unlike Zeira, or Gocri, or any of her other companions, she alone did not have to worry about the Fade. Her home element, the sea, stretched for many thousands of kilometers in all directions. Then again, it also meant that, should any of her friends have to battle the evil, maniacal human, it would more than likely happen on land.

Although she had the ability to venture out of the water, movement on dry land was cumbersome and inconvenient given her ridiculously small legs. Obviously, she spent as little time away from the sea as possible. Since bonding with the human kai, she had willingly ventured out of the water far too many times for her liking. But it was for her kai. She'd do it again, if the need arose.

Do you really mean that, Nuri? her kai asked.

I do.

Prior to meeting us, another voice chimed in, *how many times had you pulled yourself out of the sea?*

The voice belonged to Zeira, the young fire dragon

from Blaze, another along for their excursion with the intent to make the world a better place. After all, when one unscrupulous biped rises to power and threatens the world you call home, how could one *not* act?

Zeira had taken it upon herself to see if she could bond with a kai. The riders were selective, and not all were compatible, but sure enough, when they found Jerica, she not only bonded with Zeira, but also with Gocri, a glacial dragon from the far north, Sifula, a smoke dragon from Rokke, and Skellig, a Spark dragon from Gale. Oh, and then there was Othos, the sol. An actual, honest-to-goodness sun dragon.

Nuri shook her head. To think that one of the genesians, a celestial, was looking out for them was mind boggling. Despite the power he had, he looked, and acted, like any of her other companions, and ...

What is it? Zeira's thought came, worriedly, as she and the others circled above the sea.

I'm not sure. I taste ... oil. I hear the creak and groan of wood. If I didn't know any better, I'd say ...

Nuri's eyes widened with alarm. She knew *exactly* what was nearby: a sailing vessel, and a large one at that. Its existence and proximity to her friends was too much of a coincidence.

She swam off. Two sets of fins, one larger and one smaller, unfolded themselves from her body. A series of spinal plates appeared along her back and tail flaps, usually only found on aerial dragons, appeared on the end of her tail, one on either side. Due to her extreme velocity in the water, evolution had utilized every possible method of giving her control over her great powers.

The valthan shot upward faster than her winged cousins could dive through the air. Nearing the surface, she slowed and adjusted her body so the wake she generated didn't create any tsunamis. Carefully, she allowed the top of her head to breach the waves. Her instincts were spot on. There, floating less than a hundred meters away, was a vessel Jerica referred to as a war galleon. Its gunports were open, cannons pushed forward, and if Nuri didn't know any better, they were preparing to belch forth spherical chunks of iron—at high velocity.

What was it aiming at?

Nuri paled. There, two hundred meters to the south, was a small, deserted island. Jerica was there, probably alone, as the dragons patrolled the air.

They're going to fire upon Miss Jerica! Gocri roared. The ice dragon's emotional outbreak was rare. *Nuri, are you there? Can you deal with this?*

Are you sure we want to sink this ship? Zeira asked, growing nervous. *We don't want to draw any more attention to ourselves.*

And you think the Thunder King doesn't know about us? Nuri pulled her head below the surface and watched the large vessel begin its turn south. *We both know that isn't true. It's turning. In just a few moments, the ship will be able to fire its weapons. I won't allow it to harm Jerica.*

It's appreciated, came Jerica's shaky reply.

Can you destroy it in such a way that you won't harm the humans aboard? Zeira wanted to know.

Nuri hesitated. If she targeted the lower cargo hold areas only, and seeing how most of the bipeds were crawling about on the top of the boat, human casualties should be practically nil. Then again, take away their floating contraption, thus forcing the bipeds into the water, where would they go?

Straight to the island, where Jerica is hiding.

I hear you, Zeira told her. *I just retrieved her. Jerica is safe. Nuri, would you do the honors?*

Gladly.

She swam to the ship to see for herself just how much of it sat below the surface. In this case, over six meters. The valthan rolled to her side, allowing her to extend a leg and caress the hull. Good. Solid wood. This would be easier than she thought.

She knocked softly as she explored. Her eyes followed the shape of the ship as they traveled up the hull, to the surface. There. Just above the keel at the front sounded hollow. That would do perfectly.

She backed away, then pushed herself forward, lashing out at the forepeak as she sped by. Her strike punched through the hull and framework. Water poured in through the two-meter hole, and the ship groaned, tipping forward.

She waited a few moments for the bipeds to go topside, then unfolded her fins and raced out to sea. One kilometer away, Nuri turned, sighted the galleon, and accelerated.

The ship didn't stand a chance.

The surface turned frothy as water rushed into the hull. Listing badly, the three-masted brigantine shuddered under the second strike, and with its keel broken by the valthan's furious assault, it quickly sank into the depths of the sea.

Four skiffs were all that was left. For the next twenty minutes, crew members fished the survivors out of the water before turning their attention on the small island. Jerica's island. Shouts were made, and oars were manned.

Nuri's head surfaced. She turned to face the closest boat. The first mate let out a squeal of surprise before turning pale and fainting. She addressed the remaining humans.

"*I* am the one who sank your vessel. Leave now, while I still allow it. Proceed toward that island, and I will personally make sure it's the last thing any of you ever see."

There was more shouting. Four prows were immediately reversed. The skiffs slowly—but steadily—rowed in the opposite direction, toward the coast visible in the distance. Nuri made certain the survivors were headed in the right direction before turning to make for the island.

"Were there any problems?" Jerica asked. "No one was hurt, right?"

"They all survived," Nuri confirmed. She checked the skies overhead. "Where are the others?"

"Gocri said something about making certain the lifeboats made it to shore. Zeira went with him."

"And Sif?"

Movement on Jerica's left side drew her attention. A small lizard, no bigger than her kai's hand, scurried down the teenager's arm and the moment it touched ground, swelled in size until a form so big that it dwarfed even Gocri, stood before them. Sifula's smoky body rippled and waved in the wind.

"I refused to leave. I do not trust humans to keep to their word. Oh! I am so sorry, Jerica. I did not mean that as harshly as it sounded."

Their rider waved off the insult. "I've heard worse, and you wouldn't be wrong."

Moments later, Gocri and Zeira landed, taking up the better part of dry land the island offered.

"What are we to do?" Sif asked.

"We've searched tirelessly," Zeira said, sighing. "We haven't discovered a single clue which can tell us where poor Skellig is being held."

Gocri's great white head shifted. "We're not giving up, are we? He would keep searching for us, should his fate have befallen us."

The dragons looked toward Jerica, who seemed thoughtful.

"I'm not giving up," Sif vowed.

"None of us are," Nuri said. She unfolded her front legs and took a few steps onto shore. "I think we have to become … *choosier* when deciding where to look next."

All eyes focused on the valthan.

"Explain," Gocri rumbled.

"This world is too big to search," Nuri began. "We could spend the rest of our lives—searching separately—and still not find our friend. We simply do not have the time to search."

"We *have* to rescue him," Sif insisted.

Jerica nodded. "And we will. However, we're going to need help."

"What kind of help?" Zeira asked.

"Information," Nuri suggested. "Anything that will help pinpoint where we need to look. Ideally, we should confront Skellig's sire, Dym, and force him to tell us what he's done."

"I'd help you do it," Gocri vowed.

"As would I," Sif added.

"We all would, if we knew Dym's location," Jerica pointed out. "Can you think of no one to ask?"

"If this were for any other matter, I'd suggest we contact my king," Zeira said. "He always knows what to do."

"A monarch," Nuri repeated, thinking hard. "If anyone might know where the Thunder King would hold a prisoner, it'd be one of them. What an excellent notion, Zeira!"

"Er, you're welcome? So, if the decision is to confront

one of our kings, or queens, who would be closest?"

"Perhaps mine?" Gocri volunteered. "We're not too far south. My glacier lies to the north. But ..."

"But *what*?" Jerica pressed.

"She and I ..."

"You have a history together?" Nuri asked, shocked.

"It's not what you think," Gocri sighed. "She and I don't really see eye to eye."

"What could she possibly have done that you disagreed with?" Jerica asked.

"Her Royal Majesty decided it'd be easier if we just attack the humans."

"Well, that's one way to deal with the Thunder King," Zeira decided.

"*All* the humans," Gocri clarified.

Jerica's mouth opened with surprise. "Oh. Er, I guess I should thank you for not following her orders?"

The ice dragon shrugged. "It was the right thing to do."

"Then, perhaps I should ask mine," Nuri suggested.

"You say that because you're the fastest?" Jerica asked.

Nuri shrugged, which created a ripple, extending from the back of her head to the tip of her tail. "Just a happy coincidence."

Sif turned to Gocri. "How long would it be to reach your king?"

"Queen," the ice dragon corrected. "At least a day. Perhaps a day and a half?"

"And you?" Sif continued, addressing Nuri.

The valthan shuffled backward, toward the water. Once Nuri was under the waves, she sampled the water. She hummed a few bars and waited for the echolocational information of the surrounding area to appear. Once it did, she saw that they were nearly four hundred leagues west of Cael, Jerica's home village. She also knew her home waters were in the same direction.

"No more than four or five hours," Nuri finally answered.

Gocri nodded. "You are the logical choice."

"I wish you didn't have to go alone," Jerica said.

"She won't be," Sif said, drawing everyone's attention. "I

will go with her."

"How?" Nuri wanted to know. "We're not talking about a different home element. The problems you'd face accompanying me are more of a life-sustaining nature."

"Being able to breathe," Sif agreed, nodding. "If you can do it, then so can I."

Nuri's eyes widened. "You're suggesting you become a valthan! Have you ever been one before?"

The smoke dragon shook her head. "How hard could it be?"

"More than you probably realize," Nuri pointed out. "Be that as it may, I can give you some pointers. This is wonderful news, Sif! I was dreading being alone, something that has never bothered me before."

"I'd like to go," Jerica stated.

Conversation came to an abrupt stop as all four dragons stared at the lone human.

"We already confirmed that, while I'm on Nuri's back, I can breathe underwater," Jerica pointed out.

"True," Zeira said, nodding, "but that would mean you wouldn't be able to leave her back. You'd have to be in physical contact with her at all times."

"It shouldn't be a problem," Nuri decided.

"*At all times*," Zeira repeated.

"No harm will befall her," Nuri promised. "Sif, we should be going. Let's see how you do as a valthan. Zeira, Gocri, what will you two do?"

"How long will you be gone?" the fire dragon asked.

"No more than a day. Less, hopefully."

Zeira looked skyward. "We will resume canvassing the area. Somewhere out there is Skellig. I personally won't stop until we find him."

"I'll be right there beside you," Gocri promised. The great white head fixed Nuri with an appraising look. "Protect her."

"I will," Nuri said.

"I will," Jerica echoed.

Valthan and human eyed each other, smiled slyly, then turned to Sifula. The smoke dragon had approached the water's edge and was already shifting. Her wings folded against her back, shimmered, and were absorbed into her body. Her forelegs shrank, her neck stretched to three times its length, as did her torso.

"You'd better get in the water," Nuri advised.

By the time Sif was bobbing in the water, she was a mirror image of Nuri, all the way down to her coloring. Sif noticed Nuri's frown and correctly guessed that the valthan didn't want *every* detail cloned. Still, her vaporous friend had done a remarkable job in shifting forms, down to the dual curved horns, body-length spinal ridge, flared tail wing, and the two sets of fins that Nuri was certain no one else had ever noticed before.

"Jerica, climb aboard. Sif, keep close. That way I can … where'd you go?"

Nuri felt a blast of water surge by her. Without realizing what she was doing, she used her fins and her body to make subtle adjustments to the wave. Moments later, it lost power and rapidly dissipated.

A second valthan appeared by her side. Sif nodded, executed a rapid spin around, and wriggled with excitement.

"This is so much fun! It's exhilarating! I see now why you love the water. I never knew it could be like this."

"Be careful of rogue waves," Nuri cautioned.

"Rogue waves?" Sif repeated.

"If you move too fast through the water, you *will* create a wake. You need to prevent such a wave from occurring."

"How?" Sif wanted to know.

"Too long to explain. Fear not. I will be by your side. If you accidentally create one, I can nullify it."

The light began to fade as they swam deeper. Nuri felt Jerica fidget in place, and checked on their shape-shifting companion. In valthan form, Sifula was a natural. She had acclimatized incredibly fast, and needed virtually no explanation on how to swim or rapidly accelerate. Swimming comfortably side by side, the two of them descended deeper into the darkness.

"How are you faring?" Nuri asked.

"I, er, am good," Sif answered.

"Jerica?" Nuri called. "How about you?"

"It's so weird that I'm surrounded by water, I can feel the water, and yet I'm fine. But, I'd be better if I could see where we're going."

"We've barely left the surface behind. We have to go much deeper before we'll reach Hythos."

"Hythos?" Jerica repeated. "Is that where your queen lives?"

"Aye."

"How much farther is it?" Sif asked.

Nuri smiled. "We've a ways yet."

"How are we supposed to see?" Sif wanted to know.

"I'd like to know, too," Jerica added.

Nuri looked up at the distant surface. The sea morphed from dark blue to black, reducing visibility to zero.

"This is going to be a problem," Jerica reported. "Nuri, can you see in the dark?"

"In a manner of speaking, aye. We'll wait here for just a moment."

"What are we waiting for? Is there someone who ... oh!"

Everything had become illuminated! From the multitude of fish swimming by, to the rock formations jutting up from the sea floor, and even the floor itself: everything sparkled with tiny bits of light.

A sea serpent, nearly ten meters long, kept its distance from Nuri as it passed. Dark blue dots, mixed with a few intermittent green ones, glowed brightly as it swam. A patch of anemones, some only a few inches, to other gigantic specimens easily a dozen meters tall, shone a soft orange light, lit from within.

Everywhere Sif and Jerica looked, they could see a strange, ethereal ecosystem thriving.

"It's so beautiful," Jerica remarked. "Nuri, is this what your home looks like?"

"No," the valthan replied shaking her head. "This is nothing compared to my home waters. I know you may not think so, but there still is a significant amount of sunlight here, enough to affect how your eyes see. Actually, as my kai, now you're using *my* eyes. Once we're another several hundred meters down, the sea will become so dark that all the colors you see now will become magnified by a hundredfold. *That* is something no outsider can imagine."

"I cannot wait," Jerica said, sighing with contentment. "I would have said my own home in Cael was the best, but I think you win."

"Sif," Nuri called, "are you alright? You should be able to see everything I can."

"Oh, I can," their vaporous companion confirmed. "Don't mind me. I'm trying to process what my eyes are seeing. Jerica is right. Your domain is much more beautiful than ours."

"What is Rokke like?" Jerica asked.

"Mountainous. Hot. And cold, I guess, if you go high enough."

"Where do you build your nests?" Jerica asked.

"Caves work the best for us," Sif said, as she flicked her tail to pull ahead of Nuri as they swam, "but they're not easy to find. Many of us choose not to bother with them at all."

"What? Why not?" Jerica wanted to know.

"We spend little time in the nests," Sif explained. They swam in silence for a few moments before she continued. "As you may imagine, my kind do not have many offspring. Lacking physical bodies, how do you think we procreate? Jerica, I am so sorry. I feel your embarrassment. I wasn't trying to make you feel uncomfortable."

"Smoke dragons do not hatch from eggs?" Nuri asked.

"Correct. Two smoke dragons will take a small piece of their substance, swirl them together, and wait to see if the mixture gains consciousness. Once it does, the donor dragons determine their duties have been fulfilled, and will depart and go their separate ways."

"How horrible," Jerica breathed.

"I had no idea," Nuri added.

Sif shrugged. "It is what it is. It's what I've known my entire existence, so there is no reason to feel sorrow on my behalf. Nuri, what's that glow in the distance?"

"We approach Hythos," the valthan reported, turning in all directions watchfully. "You will see an increase of activity as we near. Do you feel that gentle rocking motion?"

"It feels like waves on a beach," Sifula reported.

"Exactly. What you're feeling is the arrival and departure of the others. Do you see the concentric circles of violet light about fifty meters away?"

Sif nodded. "I do."

"That is where I hope we will find Queen Salenthina."

"Ooo, tell me she's nice," Jerica pleaded.

"Nice? She's the queen."

"That really didn't answer my question," Jerica pointed out.

"From a certain point of view, it did," Nuri argued. "My queen is tough, experienced, and feared by all. But my biggest fear is that the stories of the valthans' capture is true and we are entering a trap."

"I'm getting a bad feeling about this," Jerica mumbled.

Nuri continued to scan each area they passed. Nothing seemed out of place. Yet.

"We'll be fine with the queen," Nuri promised. "I've had dealings with her before. She's fond of me. At least, I like to think so."

The city of Hythos was alive with normal activity. Rock spires a hundred meters tall were festooned with twinkling lights. The surface of the sea floor was covered with a crushed white shell, making it appear as if they were swimming over a beach of pristine sand. Other valthans became visible, zipping by almost faster than their eyes could track. That is, until one of them caught sight of Nuri and the rider she carried on her back.

The valthan pulled itself up. Its coloring was dark green on top, and a rich coral for the lower half. Both sets of its fins were engaged, and the enormous tail wing was extended, fanning the water behind the magnificent fellow. It flicked a fin and almost immediately appeared at Nuri's side.

"Nuri! You're back! I don't want to alarm you, but you appear to have picked up an infestation. Isn't that a human on your back?"

"Greetings, Finnry. I must speak with the queen. Is she available for an audience?" Nuri relaxed slightly. Nothing in the other valthan's demeanor suggested a tragedy.

"Did you not hear me? You have one of those pesky bipeds on your back. How you did not detect it is a wonder. How is it even still alive? I would have thought it should've drowned long ago."

"You'd think so, wouldn't you?" Jerica asked, popping up and giving the strange water dragon a wave. "And there's no need to be rude about it."

"It speaks?" Finnry exclaimed, concerned. "Have they always?"

"What a silly question!" Jerica said, giggling.

Not for us, Nuri silently told her. *Valthans and humans have never interacted in such a manner before. I will admit to not considering how we would present ourselves.*

Is it a problem? Sif asked.

Actually, no. This might work to our advantage. Say nothing until we're in the presence of the queen.

Understood.

They arrived at the source of the violet rings: a large plaza, more vast than anything either Jerica or Sif had seen before. The illuminated rings had been set into the floor, slabs of Nurimarine marble, which glowed brightly enough to illuminate the surrounding area. The three companions made their way toward an arch set into the side of one of the larger rock formations. The cool, blue light from the opening mixed with the teal and violet from the surrounding area and presented a soft, welcoming sensation. However, stationed on either side of the opening were two dark valthans, much larger than any of them. They quickly spun in place, flinging their tails directly in front of the entrance. With the way effectively blocked, the three of them were forced to stop.

"No one enters ..." the valthan on the left rumbled.

"... by order of the queen," the right guard finished.

Nuri placed herself before the two guards and raised her head high. "I am Nuri'gulipidus Chunris, holder of the sacred Diamond Scale of Yor. I have been on a secret mission for my queen. You may tell her I found one."

"One *what?*" Left Guard asked, using a suspicious tone.

"That information is not for your ears. Now, you can announce my presence yourself, or she can find out when

I swim in on my own accord. How do you think she'll react when she learns of your inability to follow simple protocol?"

"No one sees the queen without being first approved by ... did you say *Chunris?*"

Nuri nodded. "I did, aye. You surprise me, golstan. Not many know that name."

Golstan? Jerica repeated. *What's that?*

It means soldier, Nuri translated.

Surprisingly, both guards suddenly couldn't get their tails out of the way fast enough.

"My sincerest apologies," Left Guard sputtered. "You may enter, Nuri Chunris."

Say nothing, Nuri ordered. "Thank you. Can Queen Salenthina be found at the Farandole?"

Both guards nodded and returned to their posts. Nuri glanced over at Sif and, verifying she was watching, beckoned with her tail.

"Shall we go meet the queen?"

"Uh, sure," Sif answered, almost hesitantly. "I trust you know what you're doing."

Swimming through the archway revealed that the huge formation, which resembled an underwater mountain, was essentially hollow. Valthans were everywhere: some resting on the floor, some swimming in circles high above their heads, while others floated motionless. Nuri verified Sif was following before flicking her tail to start rising to the top.

Less than fifty meters from the highest point inside the queen's palace, a smaller opening became visible on the left, glowing green. Nuri slowed her pace until she was creeping along no faster than her kai could walk. After all, the queen was notoriously *anxious* about her security. Guards could be waiting in the shadows.

"What is farandole?" Jerica asked.

"It's more of a place. It's where Queen Salenthina keeps her supply of wistning." When there was no further response from her kai, Nuri turned. "You do know what wistning is, don't you?"

"I'm not a valthan," Jerica pointed out. "I've never heard of it."

"What about you, Sif?"

"What does it do?" the smoke dragon countered.

"It gives the user sight beyond sight. She can … I'm not describing this very well. I can just … no, that'd be rude. Jerica, may I search your memories for a better explanation?"

"Thank you for asking, Nuri. Of course."

They slowly swam through the tunnel, watching as various valthans quickly drifted up from their prone positions on the ground. One look at Nuri was all it took for them to quickly nod and back away.

"Wistning is a substance available only to the valthans," Nuri began. "It's first harvested from mastons, but only those that have achieved great size. Then, the wist undergoes a very lengthy process to convert it to its liquid state. After it has been purified at least nine times, it is ready for use."

"At least?" Jerica repeated. "Can this thing be purified more than nine times? And why would you want to?"

"The more it is purified, the stronger it becomes," Nuri explained. "But, each consecutive purification takes nearly three months. And, before you ask, I have no idea why it has to go through the process nine times. After eight, the wist has become a liquid, but is inert. But the ninth—full strength."

"Wist," Sif said. "Harvested from a plant?"

"Mollusks," Nuri corrected. "Ah, here we are. Your Majesty, I have returned."

Mollusks? Sif's voice echoed. *Jerica, are you just as confused as I am?*

More, the girl admitted.

The three companions had reached the end of the hallway and emerged into a vast chamber decorated with more of the marble. This time, the marble on the floor was a deep purple, with white marble traveling up the walls and across the ceiling. Faint veins of gray created random patterns all across the walls and ceiling.

Nuri watched Sif closely to see what her reaction would be. She also kept her senses shared with Jerica, since this would be the first time a human had ever beheld the valthan queen.

Queen Salenthina was shorter than Nuri, by nearly a

dozen meters. She was covered head to tail in shiny blue scales of a hue like the bluest of skies. The valthan queen watched them approach. Nuri saw Queen Salenthina's eyes open wide, so she knew her kai had been noticed.

"I don't know what I was expecting," Jerica whispered, "but that certainly wasn't it."

"My queen." Nuri dipped her head. "I am pleased and relieved to find you safe and the city unharmed. The rumors we heard from the outside were worrisome."

The queen nodded but remained focused on Jerica's presence. "Explain yourself. You bring *that* here?"

Nuri bowed. "I am fulfilling my vow. I promised I would search for a means to help. As you can see, I found myself a kai. She …"

"No valthan can have a kai," the queen stated. With a flick of her fins, she closed the distance between them. Salenthina lowered her head for a closer look. "How is it still alive underwater?"

That's not the first time I've heard that since coming here. Jerica laughed.

Sif snorted once, a stream of bubbles escaping through her nostrils. The queen noticed.

"And who are you? Why aren't you bowing in my presence?"

"She—" Nuri began.

"Do not speak for her. You. What is your name?"

"Sif."

"Sif? What kind of designation is that? What's your full name? Who are your parents?"

"Oh, my apologies. Sifula. As for my parents, I never knew them."

"No valthan has such a short name," the queen insisted. "And I'm sorry. Did a catastrophe befall them?"

Nuri shook her head. "No. I know this will be difficult for you to understand."

"I've never seen her before," the queen insisted. "And stop speaking for her. She has a tongue, does she not?"

"I do," Sif confirmed.

"Then speak, valthan. Why do I have no knowledge of

your existence?"

"Because, she's not a valthan," Jerica said, drawing the queen's attention to herself.

"The biped speaks? What manner of sorcery is this?"

"I hate to break it to you," Jerica said, leaning forward on Nuri's back, "but we humans have always been able to speak. Granted, many of the things we say may not be the nicest, or the smartest, but we do have our own voices. Take me, for example. Ever since we began this adventure, I never would have imagined having such a diverse group of friends. But, you asked about Sif. She's not a valthan. She's a smoke dragon. Wait. What did you call yourself?"

"Drifter," Sif answered.

Queen Salenthina's head jerked up, as if suddenly discovering her tail was on fire. "A drifter?"

Nuri sighed. "She's a ..."

"A smoke dragon," the queen breathed, amazed. "What are you doing here, drifter?"

"I volunteered to accompany Nuri, and to be there to render aid to Jerica, should she need it."

"And Jerica is the name you've given the human?" Queen Salenthina asked.

Nuri nodded. "That's her name, yes, but I didn't give it to her. Like us, she's given her name by her parents."

Salenthina shook her head. "Fascinating. I never knew. Well, why do I have a human and a drifter in my presence? What are you doing here?"

Both Jerica and Sif pointed at Nuri.

"We're accompanying our friend," Sif answered. "We need some information on the human known as the Thunder King."

Salenthina gave a visible jerk.

"Do you know him?" Nuri asked.

"I have ... *dealt* with him on more than one occasion," the queen admitted.

"It didn't go well," Jerica guessed.

"He tried to mandate what I tell my valthans," Salenthina said, lifting her nose. She emitted a low growl. "He wanted my allegiance. I made it clear that at no time would he have any say over my subjects. We would *not* be doing his bidding, and we would *not* follow his mandates."

"What did he want you to do?" Jerica asked.

The leader of the valthans stared at her for a few moments before shaking her head. "I am not used to having bipeds address me in casual conversation. Very well, let's do this. I'll agree to answer your questions if you agree to answer mine. Do we have an accord?"

Jerica, she's trying to wheedle information about how you're able to be my kai, Nuri told her.

Do I tell her anything about being a kairie?

You can trust my queen. If she's willing to help us, then we should reciprocate.

Thanks for letting me know.

"Your Majesty, it's a deal."

Salenthina nodded. "Excellent. Now, to answer your question, he wanted valthans to patrol the sea and prevent any human vessel from reaching destinations of his choosing."

"Nobody should hold that much power," Jerica said, sighing.

"There's more," Salenthina said, growing angry. "There was something he wanted, something unspoken. When pressed, he wouldn't admit anything and became very irritable."

"I'm glad you refused his proposal," Sif said.

"It wasn't a difficult decision," the queen answered. "Now, answer me this, human."

"My name is Jerica."

"Very well. Jerica, how is it you are here? You are an air breather."

"I'm also her kai," Jerica pointed out. "I'm protected in whatever element I happen to be in. What? Why are you shaking your head?"

"Do you think we have not tried to find our own kais?" Queen Salenthina argued. "Year after year, we look for compatible bipeds. None has ever been found. What makes you so different?"

Jerica sighed, unclipped the leather band on her right arm, and presented the concealed mark to the valthan queen. She explained the significance of the mark, and the simple fact that she had bonded with not one, nor two, but *five* different dragons.

"Incredible," Salenthina breathed. "So, you could probably bond with me, too."

Jerica shrugged. "More than likely."

"And your powers—have you really created new abilities?"

"I have."

Another twenty minutes passed as Nuri recounted their experiments, and all the unique powers that manifested.

"The ramifications of this are monumental," Salenthina said, as she stared hard at Jerica. "Valthans can have kais!"

Sif gave a cough. "In this case, a kairie. I do not believe any kai would work."

"Acknowledged. I commend you. All of you. You three are attempting to save our world. My valthans and I will be at your disposal. Ask of us anything you require, and if it falls within my power, I will grant it."

"One of our companions was taken," Nuri began. "He means a great deal to us. We've been searching tirelessly for him for three days, and have been unable to find any traces. You've met the Thunder King. Do you have any idea where he'd hold a dragon against its will?"

Salenthina fell silent as she considered.

"Skellig was battling another Spark dragon, and that dragon, Dym, did something to him," Sif recalled.

The queen perked up. "Spark? You travel with a Spark?"

"And ice, and fire," Jerica added.

"And sol," Sif said.

Queen Salenthina paled. "Othos! You travel with a sun dragon?"

Nuri nodded. "Yes, he wanted to help."

"Incredible. What I can tell you is the Thunder King is from Gale."

"Makes sense," Jerica said. "Dym is a Spark dragon."

"You're saying we should travel to Gale?" Nuri asked, growing despondent. "It's a long journey and we are rapidly running out of time. There's no way for all of us to get there and back, before the Thunder King destroys our world."

"And we're fresh out of huge bugs," Sif added.

The queen gasped again. "An archyx? You know about…?"

Nuri nodded. "Yes, yes, we used one to travel to another continent, since we didn't have a choice in the matter."

The valthan queen beamed her approval. "Exactly. You're familiar with the portals. Excellent. Therefore, since you need to make another such journey, your next course of action should be easy enough."

"I do *not* want to ride on a giant bug's back again," Nuri proclaimed. "It was very uncomfortable the first time."

"No archyxes are needed," the queen promised.

"Where's the closest portal?" Jerica asked.

"In six hundred meters of water," Salenthina answered. "It's not far from here."

"That is much shallower than the first portal," Nuri said, nodding, "but it doesn't change the fact that my companions are air breathers. They will not be able to dive that deep."

The queen turned her gaze on Jerica. "With *her*, they don't have to."

Nuri and Sif turned to look at their kai.

"Umm, could you explain the *how* part for me?" Jerica asked.

"You, kairie. You're in physical contact with Nuri. Your magic is protecting you while you're here."

"And?" Jerica prompted. "This helps me *how*?"

"You described similar experiments when you were trying out your new powers. What happened when you remained in contact with one another?"

"We could all contribute power," Jerica breathed, growing excited. "You're saying that, if we all remain in contact with one another, we could all make the journey to the portal? Safely?"

"I am."

"Did you know that?" Jerica asked Nuri.

"I didn't think of it, but it does make sense."

"It's not going to be easy," Sif said. "All of us? In physical contact with one another as we swim to a depth of six hundred meters? Gocri and Zeira aren't going to like that."

Nuri felt a tap on her back. She twisted her neck around until she was looking at her rider. Jerica, in turn, pointed up.

"We should test this, Nuri. If it works, then we could make it to Gale before the day is done!"

"I'll give you directions before you leave," the queen promised. As the visitors prepared to depart, Salenthina used the tip of her tail to tap Nuri on the top of her head. "I wanted to tell you something, Nuri'gulipidus Chunris."

Nuri turned to face the queen. "Yes?"

"I'm proud of you."

Nuri nodded. "Thank you, Mother."

Chapter 2 — Cursed

The following sunrise found the team huddled together on shore. The five of them stared, in silence, at the gentle lapping waves. Gocri was the first to turn his great head and stare at Nuri.

"It was bad enough that time Skellig and I had to fly together, holding talons. I can't think of a worse way to swim, not that I even want to get my wings wet."

"He'd do it for you," Jerica returned.

Gocri returned his gaze to the sea, and let out a sigh. "We might as well get this over with. What do we have to do? Where is this portal?"

"Before we do anything," Nuri said, as she swished her tail noisily through the water to get everyone's attention, "we must test this. It was suggested Jerica could allow everyone to be safe underwater. I, for one, would like to see if this is true before we risk anyone's lives."

Zeira nodded. "Agreed. I shall volunteer to …"

"I'll go," Gocri interrupted. "Miss Jerica and I will see if this theory is true. Nuri, I trust you'll come to our aid if we are not?"

"I'll be by your side at all times," Nuri vowed.

Gocri turned to their kai. "Miss Jerica? Are you ready to try this?"

"Let's give it a go. Zeira, could you put me up there? I'm sorry, Gocri, but you're too big."

Once Jerica was situated on the glacier dragon's back, gripping several of his smaller back plates in anticipation of what was to come, Nuri levered herself back into the water. Gocri took his first step into the sea, looked down at his leg as if he had just stepped in something unpleasant, and hesitantly took another step.

"I cannot remember the last time I took a bath," Gocri grumbled. "I do this for you, Miss Jerica."

"I appreciate it. I really do."

"You're not afraid?" Gocri asked.

"I was on Nuri's back for the better part of the day yesterday. We were submerged deep beneath the surface. Once that shock wore off, I was fine. In fact, I don't feel any fear whatsoever. I know you will not willingly hurt me, and if something happens, Nuri will be close."

Gocri faced the water and sighed. "Very well. Let's do this."

"Er, can you swim?" Nuri asked. "I'm sorry, I should've asked that earlier."

"I can," Gocri confirmed. "It's just that I prefer not to."

Nuri watched the huge white dragon stride into the water. Taking uncharacteristically small steps for a dragon Gocri's size, they slowly sank into the sea. Keeping a close eye on them, Nuri positioned herself next to her friends.

The surface was now over their heads. Jerica, for her part, appeared to be unaffected. She waved, smiled, and gave Gocri a few reassuring pats.

All is well? Nuri inquired.

It's just like before, Jerica said. *I can feel the water on my face, and even in my mouth, but for some reason, I am still able to breathe just fine. I love magic!*

Nuri's long tail whipped around, making a circling motion. *Gocri, try swimming around.*

Why?

I'd like to see how you're able to handle yourself. I need to know how fast you can swim, turn, and so on.

Oh. Very well.

Ten minutes later, they returned to shore. Zeira and the others were anxiously waiting for the final decision.

"And?" Zeira prompted.

"It worked!" Jerica proclaimed, as she slid down Gocri's back to land in the sand. "It was just like riding on Nuri, except …"

"Clumsier," Gocri finished. "It's all right. You can say the word. I am not nearly as adept as I thought I was."

"No one is," Jerica said, smiling. "I never would have imagined swimming with friends could be so much fun!"

Zeira nodded. "Now that we've verified Gocri and Jerica both remained safe, we need to add a third. We need to see if the dragon without a rider will be safe. Therefore, I volunteer. Nuri, please be ready to assist should I embarrass myself and panic."

"You'll be fine," Nuri assured her. "We won't be going very deep."

After another ten minutes had passed, they surfaced. Sif, the only one who elected to remain on shore, was anxiously waiting.

"Well? You were gone long enough. How'd it go?"

Zeira nodded. "We're all fine. We swam to a depth of one hundred meters. It's a very strange sensation when your senses are telling you to breathe. I had to fight my instincts to *not* kick away from the others and make for the surface."

"It'll be very important to maintain contact," Gocri rumbled.

"This really isn't too bad," Zeira decided. "Sif and Nuri will already be valthan. Gocri, Jerica, and I will be the ones who need to be careful. Wait a moment. What about Othos? Should we wait for him?"

"We'll probably return before he does," Sif said.

Jerica shrugged. "A fair point. He's always disappearing.

Well, time is of the essence. We can't wait for him."

Nuri extended her fins and pushed herself away from shore. "Shall we? The sooner we do this, the sooner we find Skellig."

Gocri nodded. He reversed course and returned to the water. Nuri watched as ice and fire hooked wing talons together and then dipped below the surface. Movement caught her eye. Turning, she saw Sif—in valthan form—nod once and disappear beneath the waves, leaving a trail of bubbles.

Nuri had no idea if the portal they were looking for was identical to the one they previously used when they fought the djinn for its piece of the oron stone. None of them had ever physically seen one. The last time they attempted this, they were safe beneath an archyx's wings as it dove down to depths even deeper than the valthans deemed safe.

The sea floor sloped away, descending into a darkness that became blacker with every passing moment. Nuri felt her eyes close of their own accord and allowed her parietal eye to see every speck of visible light. Then, an alarming thought occurred.

Gocri? How are you faring?

I've been better.

Are you able to see?

Yes. While not ideal, I am able to see enough to keep moving.

And you, Sif?

I'm fine, Nuri. I can see everything you can.

Your abilities are certainly envied, my friend.

As are yours.

Do we know where we're going? Zeira asked.

Of course, Nuri said. *I located the portal shortly after we left Hythos, exactly where my queen said it would be. I had a feeling we'd have to do something like this, and I wasn't about to risk any of you. We already lost Skellig. I'm not losing anyone else.*

He was taken from us, Jerica corrected. *Consider him temporarily misplaced. And, we're going to get him back.*

Nearly half an hour later, they arrived on the sea floor. This time, there were no plants or signs of life, only barren, rocky ground which stretched away endlessly in front of them. There, less than fifty meters away, was a wide, jagged crack in the rock. Nuri knew, from having explored it before, that it was wide enough for everyone to fit, and yet it was not very deep.

We have to go in that? Jerica asked, growing fearful.

It's perfectly safe, Nuri assured her. *The crevasse extends another hundred meters before widening. The portal is located inside the wider section.*

It'll be a tight fit, Gocri observed.

Flatten your wings as much as possible, Nuri instructed. *There. Perfect. Zeira, you and Gocri must remain in contact with one another. Perhaps hold his tail?*

This just gets better and better, Gocri grumped.

The less said about this, the better, Zeira agreed, as she reached for the white tail in front of her. Once she was holding the tip, she unhooked her wing talon from Gocri's and folded her wings. *How far is it? I will admit to not being fond of this tight area.*

It's worse for me, Gocri called, as he carefully picked his way through the narrow confines of the crevasse.

We don't have far to go, Nuri reported. *There. Do you see the light?*

A bright blue glow shone directly in front of them.

I see it, Gocri said. *How do we proceed?*

In contact with one another.

Like you could pull all of us behind you, Gocri scoffed.

Their valthan smiled and proved him wrong.

The first thing Nuri noticed, after swimming through the portal, was that the water tasted different. The salinity had changed, which typically meant the depth had changed. She could only hope it was shallower, not deeper. She didn't know how much longer Gocri could remain underwater. Her glacial friend was fidgeting, his eyes kept darting toward the surface high above their heads, and he was uncomfortable remaining in physical contact with someone else.

We're all through, and you'll be pleased to know we're much closer to the surface. We're about to start our ascent. How's everyone doing?

Eager to see the sun, came Gocri's response.

We're almost there. Fear not. Just another twenty meters.

Four reptilian heads broke the surface of the water. Gocri

roared with approval. His head slowly rotated until he located land, which was less than a hundred meters northwest. The glacier dragon checked on Jerica, saw that she was alive and well on Zeira's back, then met the fire dragon's gaze.

Zeira let go of his tail with a sheepish grin on her face.

"Sorry. Let's make for shore. I'd really like to feel solid ground under my feet once more."

Gocri nodded. "Agreed."

Soon they were all standing, dripping wet, at the water's edge, looking out over the open expanse of water behind them. Gocri gave himself a solid shake, sending droplets of water flying. Sif's valthan body turned smoky, then shifted into a replica of Zeira, complete with matching colors. Perfectly dry, too.

Zeira was too tired to protest.

Jerica was about to suggest they take to the air, to locate Gale's king, but a rumble from the skies grabbed her attention. One by one, her companions lifted their gazes to the overcast sky. Heavy cumulonimbus clouds rumbled overhead, moving in rapidly while flashes of white and yellow briefly illuminated the clouds from within.

Seconds later, it began raining. Hard.

"Just what we needed," Jerica said, adopting a bright and cheery tone. When no one said anything, the kai continued. "Well, we wanted a way to wash the sea water off, so this is a good thing! Er, right?"

A flash of light and a crack of thunder caused everyone to jump.

"That was close," Jerica whispered, awed. "We need to find shelter."

"Lightning strikes are not something I wish to deal with," Nuri agreed.

"Perhaps we should dive deep and wait for it to blow over."

"What if it doesn't blow over?" Gocri wanted to know. "This is Gale, home of the Sparks. Would that not suggest that lightning strikes are prevalent here?"

"Which suggests this storm might not ever blow over," Zeira said, sighing.

"How *do* valthans live here?" Sif wanted to know. "I'd think it would be too dangerous for them."

"It is," Nuri confirmed. "I don't sense any others like me anywhere in these waters."

Lightning flashed again—thunder rumbled high above their heads.

"Skellig thought this was paradise?" Zeira demanded. "It's dreary and gray and pouring rain. And the winds—I'm not sure how a dragon could even fly here."

"Well, it *is* called Gale," Jerica reminded her.

"You want to see a proper home? Look no further than the comforting lava fields of Blaze. That's peace and tranquility. That is bliss."

"No, Bliss is the northern ice fields," Gocri corrected.

Zeira nodded. "I apologize. Poor choice of words. We need to find the Gale king before the weather becomes even worse. What was his name?"

"Myrdaynth," Nuri responded. "I remember it because Othos said it with such indifference that I had to force myself not to laugh."

"And yet Skellig told us the king is two-faced. Pretends that he cares, but has little interest in helping his subjects," Jerica reminded her. "This may be an impossible mission."

The winds suddenly doubled in strength. Thunder shook the heavens, and the flashes of lightning became brighter and more frequent. Nuri looked up at the sky and switched to their silent communication.

We should get moving. I shall scout out the shoreline. Don't fly unless the circumstances become dire.

Zeira nodded. *Agreed.*

Nuri rapidly dipped below the waves. The others dashed for the shelter of some nearby rock formations.

Nuri sped through the unfamiliar waters, exploring a large swath of the sea floor. Resurfacing, she spotted something on the shore nearly a thousand meters away. She cast a quick look to verify her friends were all right, which they were, before swimming to the water's edge to get a closer look.

We have a problem.

All four of her companions came to an abrupt stop.

Zeira's head lifted and sought out hers.

What is it?

There's something you need to see. It's down the beach from your position.

Is it something bad? Jerica wanted to know.

It certainly isn't good, Nuri replied.

She was waiting on the beach by the time everyone else arrived. Luckily, the wind and rain had abated somewhat. They quickly gathered around her and stared at her discovery. Nobody said a word until Jerica steeled herself for a closer look.

It was a figure of a dragon, sitting on its haunches, wings partially extended, facing backward as if it knew something was behind it. The dragon appeared gray, the same color as the nearby boulders and the clouds overhead. The statue was so realistic that everyone knew they weren't looking at a carved block of stone.

Is he still alive? Sif asked.

Nuri shrugged. *I wish I could say.*

Gocri reached his neck out and inspected the prone figure. What might have befallen the unfortunate dragon? Nuri saw Gocri's mouth open, but the words were lost as the wind began to howl again.

It's a Spark dragon, obviously, the glacier dragon announced, switching to their shared mental communication. He poked a talon at the immobile Spark and grunted. *The flesh is hard as stone. It could easily be taken for a statue.*

Is it? Jerica inquired. *Could we not be looking at some strange sculpture?*

Out here, where there's no one else around? Zeira asked. *I'm inclined to agree with Gocri. This is a denizen of Gale. Something has happened to this poor fellow.*

I trust this not, Gocri announced.

Perhaps there are others? Zeira suggested.

And if there are? Nuri wanted to know. *What are we supposed to do about it?*

Be certain that whatever befell them doesn't happen to us, Gocri answered.

Nuri paused. *I can agree to that. Should we split up and investigate?*

No separating, Jerica ordered. *If someone is responsible for this, I'd like to think we have a better chance at survival if we all stick together. Nuri, keep as close to us as possible.*

I will.

The group of friends headed north, following the shoreline. Faster than the others, Nuri had ample time to explore the surrounding sea. Notably, there were no schools of fish, no underwater flora. No kelp forests or seaweed-covered floors. There were no coral reefs or fields of anemones. No comforting songs of the cetaceans could be heard, either. She reported all this to the others.

Is that a bad thing? Jerica asked.

It's ... unusual. I don't see any devastation. It makes me think that this area has been devoid of life for quite a while.

You might want to come up here, Jerica suggested.

I feel a growing sense of panic, Nuri said, becoming alarmed. *I'm on my way. What's happened?*

We found another one.

It was the same as before: a hyper-realistic figure of a winged dragon. This time, the poor fellow was depicted scratching an errant itch on his front leg.

The poor thing, Zeira lamented. *What could cause something like this to happen?*

That's what we have to find out, Jerica said. *Something tells me that the rest of Gale is going to be like this. I can only hope their king has been spared.*

Why would the king be spared? Gocri wanted to know.

Most likely as a message.

The Thunder King, Zeira said, horrified.

Jerica nodded. *Precisely. I hate to say this, but the only way we'll find the king is to split up. I ... What's the matter?*

Four sets of reptilian eyes latched onto their kai. Jerica slid off Sif's back, to the ground. She cautiously approached the immobilized dragon and laid a hand on its leg, whipping it off instantly. With her eyes wide, she replaced her hand and kept it there.

He's still alive!

The dragons crowded close.

You can sense that? Zeira asked.

Well, no, but he did tell me he wasn't a statue and that his name is Draig.

Nuri pulled herself out of the water and rested a dozen meters of her torso on the shore. *Did he say what turned him into a statue?*

Jerica shook her head. *No. Draig could only tell me he landed to feast on a … a … I'm sorry, what did you call it?* Their kai fell silent as she gazed at the stricken Spark dragon. *A cremp? Does anyone know what that is?*

It's a mollusk, Nuri reported. *I've eaten hundreds.*

Describe them, Gocri requested.

About a meter wide, half that high, and extremely tasty. Crunchy on the outside and chewy on the inside!

Let's find the king and then we'll see about locating something to eat, Zeira suggested.

He knows! He knows where to find the king! We have to … no, slow down. You're going much too fast. Your king is where?

Everyone turned to their kai and waited.

He says we need to look for a single peak higher than the others, with three others close by. Two peaks, less than half the height of the king's lair, will be to the north, and a fourth peak, also the same size as the smaller ones, will be to the south.

Sounds very specific, Sif decided. *I'm sure we can find out. Does he know whether or not the king has suffered the same fate?*

He's certain the king was spared, Jerica relayed.

What better way to make an example of someone and send a message at the same time?

Who said that? Zeira asked. *You or him?*

Him.

Ah. Very well. Can he hear us?

Draig, all of us thank you.

He knows we're trying to help, Jerica relayed. *He says it's all the thanks he needs. We should go and find the king now.*

I believe I've already found his lair, Nuri suddenly reported. *I remember seeing a series of mountains like the ones he has described.*

How far away? Gocri asked.

Less than twenty leagues. Inland. I'm unable to approach too closely. But, I can get within visual range.

This time, Jerica chose to accompany Sifula. The smoke

dragon had elected to shift into the form of a winged dragon the same size as Zeira, but with two sets of wings.

How many forms do you know? Gocri finally asked.

Sif shrugged. *I have never counted. At least a hundred, I believe.*

Nuri retreated into the sea.

From the air, the others followed her trail of bubbles through the water, and by the time the winged dragons and Jerica arrived, Nuri's head was visible above the surface. She gave a nod toward a range of mountains to the north. The king's lair was in there, somewhere.

"I shall wait here, in case there's trouble." Nuri dipped below the surface once again.

And do what? Jerica wondered. But she didn't voice this to the others. They needed all the confidence they could muster. She nudged Sif into the lead, toward the single highest peak, as Draig had described. Within ten minutes, they were circling the base of the mountain, scouting for signs of an entrance.

The craggy peak was riddled with ridges and crevasses, where rivers flowed toward the sea, carrying runoff from the massive rains.

The king will surely live in a cave with a sheltered entrance.

Agreed, Jerica. Sif's voice came through, despite the whoosh of the wind.

Zeira dipped a wing and edged closer. *I have some experience with mountains. Well, volcanos. I suggest we fly to the eastern face. It will be the leeward side.*

Good idea. Lead the way. Jerica still felt a little uneasy in the leadership role. Asking Zeira's help would help ease it for both of them.

It didn't take long to spot the rift that concealed an entrance to a large cave. The dark hole in the mountainside, with two Spark dragons crouched on the ledge in alert position—it was a dead giveaway.

Sif, as the largest of them, led the way with Zeira and Gocri to her left and right. She landed on the ledge while the others circled within sight. The Spark guards stood and spread their wings, blocking the way to the entrance.

"Who goes there?" one of them demanded.

"Queen Salenthina of the valthans sent us." Jerica hoped it sounded at least halfway true. "Your dragons are being attacked near the beaches. We come to assist."

She wasn't sure if one of those statements did the trick, or if it was the unbelievable sight of a human riding a smoke dragon that caught their attention. Whatever the reason, the guard dragons stepped aside. Jerica slid to the ground and Sif transformed into a quarter-sized version of herself.

Zeira, come and join us. Gocri, stay in flight. If we are not back within the hour, notify Nuri and find help.

The two dragons and their kairie strode through the mouth of the cave, following a series of airlock-style turns, until they emerged into a central chamber. Unlike the home of the valthan queen, this place had no beautiful colors, no twinkling lights. A few torches cast a gloomy light. The walls were rough-hewn rock, the ceiling an uneven surface of stone. Had Sif walked in here at her full size, she would have taken a nasty bump on the head.

A black dragon stepped forward, straightening his back to appear larger, flexing his yellow wings slightly. "What is your business with the king?"

Jerica repeated what she'd told the outside sentries, edging slightly sideways to catch a glimpse of the dragon at the end of the long chamber, which was lit by two posts that gave off flashes of electrical energy for light. The elder Spark dragon sat on his haunches on a nest of cushions, a wiry, almost shrunken version of Skellig. She could tell where their friend got his looks. But that was where the resemblance ended. The old king was far more wrinkled and there was a gray tinge around his jaws.

The king held his head at a haughty angle while minions circled with platters of fresh meat and a bowl of some type of beverage. As soon as she spoke, his attention focused on that end of the room.

"The queen of the valthans cares about us?" he bellowed, the strength of his voice belying his fragile, elderly appearance. "I highly doubt that. We each look out for our own. No more."

The black dragon who had approached them stepped

aside, and the small group approached carefully.

"Your Majesty." Jerica approximated a little curtsy, then introduced herself and her companions. "Our dear friend, Skellig, is a Spark dragon and he is missing. We come in search of him. Queen Salenthina believes you can be of help to us."

"And why would I?" Myrdaynth practically sneered.

Skellig was right. This king cares not for his citizens.

Careful ... Jerica had no idea whether the Spark King could tune into their mental conversation without their knowledge.

"We would be happy to help, to provide something you need, in return," Jerica offered.

Myrdaynth gazed around the chamber, cocking his head, thinking. "Perhaps ..." He shifted in his seat. "You will notice that my staff has been greatly decimated. My food gatherers have almost nothing to offer me."

"Is it because of what's happened to the dragons outside? We saw several, near death, on the beach."

Myrdaynth's expression darkened. "The work of the Thunder King! Our storms have increased in intensity, and now there is some type of spell on our dragons."

"The Thunder King caused this?" Zeira moved slightly forward, her red scales gleaming in the torchlight.

"That miserable biped who thinks he will rule the entirety of Andela—yes, he's the one."

"We have come across Emerus Dinty, um, this Thunder King, already," Sif offered. "Jerica, our kai, has—"

Jerica laid a hand on Sif's nearest talon. "Let's listen to the king, shall we? King Myrdaynth, what can we do for you, in exchange for our friend, Skellig?"

"Remove the spell that miserable human placed on my citizens." He met her gaze straight on.

"I ... I'm not sure how to—"

"She'll do it," Sif promised. "Give her a little time."

Jerica stared up at Sif, who suddenly seemed busy scratching an itch.

"Send one of my dragons to me, one who was caught in this suspended animation spell of his, as proof that you've upheld your bargain. You are dismissed." And with that, Myrdaynth turned away and left the chamber.

"Okay, what now?" Jerica asked, as the three of them emerged into daylight.

"You healed Gocri's wing using a portion of the oron stone," Zeira reminded her. "He called you a wizard when you did that."

"Uh, right. Okay. Let's go." Jerica climbed onto Zeira's back this time, and the two dragons launched themselves off the mountainside.

Gocri quickly spotted them and soared to join up. While Zeira used their mental connection to fill him in on the mission, Jerica closed her eyes and went deep inside her memories to recall various spells. There weren't many.

But by the time they landed on the beach where they'd found the barely conscious Draig, she'd thought of something. Pulling the oron stone from her pocket, she carried it to the inanimate dragon and knelt beside him. She tucked the stone under one of his wings and said the words she'd used to heal Gocri's wing.

Well, why not, she told herself. Broken wing, disabled wing ... It might work.

As she held the stone in place she began to feel the dragon stir slightly. His thoughts were coming through clearer, too, and he told her he could feel energy coursing through his entire body. Within minutes, he began to move. Jerica felt her heart lighten, and she actually cheered when Draig got to his feet and stretched his wings.

Now, how to work the spell on the rest of the dragons of Gale without taking the time to visit each one individually? She looked toward the sky, saw the roiling thunder clouds. A bolt of lightning struck a tree about a hundred meters away, and Jerica chanted the words of her spell as she took back the oron stone and held it up.

A crackle split the air. The stone tingled with energy, sending sparks toward the rocks on the beach. At once, as if magnetized, dozens of rocks bounced in place.

"They're glowing!" Zeira exclaimed. "Blue, red, green— just like the oron!"

"Quick! Gather some," Jerica instructed. She ran to the nearest ones and picked one up. It was warm to the touch.

Spinning around, she spotted another of the statue-like dragons. She ran over to it and applied the stone, as she had the original oron to Draig. It didn't take long for the second dragon to regain motion.

"Draig, take these," Jerica instructed, giving him the words of the short spell. "You and …"

"This is Drakkin."

"You and Drakkin can take these enchanted stones around to the rest of the affected dragons, say the words, and get everyone moving again." She turned back to her friends. "We have an appointment with the king. And he owes me one."

She was about to climb onto Zeira's back once again when Gocri intervened.

"Jerica, there's something I didn't tell you." His frosty breath came out in little puffs. "It's Nuri. She received a telepathic message while you were in that cave with the Gale king. There's trouble in the valthan regions, and this time it seems to be for real."

Chapter 3 — Ravaged

The waves crashed against the shore, their constant rhythm keeping with the chaos of the rumbling thunder around them. Jerica stood at the water's edge, her boots sinking into the wet sand as she gazed out at the horizon. The usually calm sea churned with an ominous energy; dark clouds loomed in the distance.

Suddenly, Nuri's voice came into Jerica's mind, clear and urgent. *Jerica, can you hear me? It's ... it's worse than we feared.*

Jerica's heart pounded. *I'm here, Nuri. What's happened?*

The storms ... they've ravaged everything. It's as if the elements have turned against us.

Jerica's fists clenched at her sides, her nails digging into her palms. *How bad is it?* she asked, dreading the answer.

A lump formed in her throat as Nuri told her of coral reefs being obliterated, shifting currents that disrupted migration patterns, and many valthans missing and injured.

What about the other realms? Is there news?

Reports are coming in from all corners of Andela, Nuri continued. *The fire dragons' volcanic sanctuaries have been flooded by unprecedented rainfall. It's … it's as if the world is coming apart at the seams."*

Jerica tried to comprehend the scope of the disaster. *This has to be the work of the Thunder King,* she stated, more to herself than to Nuri.

It is. He's using a magical talisman called the Eye of the Storm. They're saying an evil sorcerer created it for him.

We need to gather the others. Now.

As if on cue, Jerica heard the sound of approaching footsteps. She turned to see Gocri and Zeira making their way down the beach, concern evident on their faces.

Jerica faced them grimly. "Nuri just contacted me. It's worse than we could have imagined. As soon as we retrieve Skellig—" Her attention was drawn to movement in the air. Sif.

"Bad news." The smoke dragon landed next to Jerica, with Draig beside her.

"Tell us."

"I've just come from presenting Draig to King Myrdaynth, as proof that we upheld our part of the bargain …"

"He's reneged? *No!*"

Sif nodded. "He told us Skellig is imprisoned. He won't say where, and he's leaving it entirely up to Dym to release him."

"But Dym is to blame." Zeira paced, her tail flipping in agitation. "He's the one who kidnapped his own offspring in the first place."

Gocri blasted a breath of icy fury. "Show me this king. I shall teach him—"

"It won't help. Myrdaynth cares nothing about his own subjects." Draig wore a resigned expression, then he brightened. "But, for that reason, I can recruit others to help."

"We need to act fast," Jerica announced. "The Thunder King's power is growing by the minute. If we don't stop him soon, there might not be a world left to save."

As they spoke, a cold wind whipped across the beach. Jerica shivered, not just from the chill but from the ominous feeling that settled in her gut.

"We need to confront this Eye of the Storm," she said, her voice barely audible over the howling wind. "It's the source of the Thunder King's power. If we can somehow neutralize it, we might have a chance of stopping this madness."

Sif's wings rustled nervously. "But how do we even reach it? The storms have made travel nearly impossible, both by air and sea."

Jerica's mind searched for a solution. She thought of Nuri, swimming through the treacherous waters, and an idea began to form. "We need to use every advantage we have," she said slowly. "Nuri can navigate the underwater currents. And Gocri, your icy abilities might be our key to piercing the heart of the storm."

The Frost dragon's eyes widened. "You want me to … what? Fly into the eye of a magical storm?"

"Not alone," Jerica assured him quickly. "We'll find a way to support you. But your ability might be our best chance at disrupting whatever dark magic the Thunder King is using. And if we can get close, we've got the oron stone and the jhorium goblet. *Something* has to work."

"It's risky," Gocri mused, "but it might just work. We'll need to coordinate with Nuri and the other dragons to create a diversion, draw the Thunder King's attention away from the Eye of the Storm."

As they spoke, the sky darkened further; night was coming on. Jerica couldn't shake the feeling that they were running out of time. The responsibility of their task settled heavily, but she refused to let it crush her. She raised her eyes to the sky, where a single star appeared at the edge of the ferocious clouds. *Oh, Othos, what can we do?*

As if in response to her thought, a massive wave crashed against the shore, spraying them with salty mist. Jerica wiped the water from her face, and there on the sand stood Othos, the celestial dragon, the all-powerful sol dragon. His massive size obscured the rugged mountains behind him.

"You called?"

Despite the dire situation, Jerica nearly laughed at the celestial dragon's light tone.

"Uh, *yeah*. Got a little emergency here," Zeira responded. She waved a claw skyward at the threatening clouds.

Othos listened, in his patient way, as Jerica and the dragons recounted the situation. When they were finished, the sol dragon nodded thoughtfully. "The third continent. I believe you may find what you seek. None of this drama has reached there yet."

"But we don't need to escape just to save ourselves. We need to figure out this Eye of the Storm thingy and get rid of this pompous human who thinks he can rule the world."

Othos's attention was drawn to an especially loud thunderclap. "Seems like he's doing more than simply thinking it."

"And you're saying the answers are on the third continent?"

A nod.

Jerica's eyes scanned the tumultuous waves, her mind racing. "So, we need to reach the third continent, but it takes months to get there …" She trailed off, watching as another massive wave crashed against the shore.

Othos, his enormous form hovering protectively over the group, rumbled thoughtfully. "There is one who …"

"*Anahita!*" Zeira breathed the name reverently.

Jerica's heart leaped at the mention of the sea spirit. "Can you summon her, Othos?"

The ancient dragon nodded, his eyes glowing with an otherworldly light. "Stand back," he warned.

As the group retreated, Othos raised his massive head to the stormy sky and let out a reverberating roar that seemed to shake the foundations of the earth. The sound echoed across the churning waves, and for a moment, everything fell silent.

Then, with a sudden rush of water, a figure emerged from the sea. Anahita, beautiful and terrible, rose before them, her form shimmering between that of a woman and a great serpent.

"Othos, old friend," she greeted, her voice gentle. "What brings you to call upon me in such desperate times?"

Jerica stepped forward, her hand unconsciously moving to the jhorium goblet at her belt. "Great Anahita," she said, her voice steady despite her pounding heart. "We seek your aid in crossing these treacherous seas to reach the third continent in search of our friend, Skellig. The Thunder King's storms have wreaked havoc, and we must stop him before it's too late."

Anahita's gaze fell upon Jerica, and the young girl felt as if the sea spirit was peering into her very soul. "And what makes you think you can succeed where others have failed, young one?"

Jerica lifted her chin, meeting Anahita's eyes. "Because we have no choice. Because if we don't try, all is lost."

A smile flickered across Anahita's face. "Well spoken, child of Cael. Very well, I shall grant you safe passage through my domain."

Relief flooded through Jerica, but before she could express her gratitude, Nuri appeared at the shore. "We thank you, Guardian of the Seas," the water dragon said, her sinuous form coiling with anticipation. "But we must do more than simply cross. We need to navigate the depths themselves."

Anahita's eyebrows rose. "A bold request, young valthan. The depths are not kind to surface dwellers."

Gocri stepped back, his fear evident. "I, um, I'm not a great swimmer ..."

Zeira's expression mirrored his. Sif nodded, as well.

Anahita regarded them with kindness. "I propose to transport those who wish, to the third continent instantly, without swimming."

"With that special medium Othos told us about?"

"Aye, Frost dragon. Any others?"

Jerica stepped closer to Nuri, drawing strength from her friend's presence. "We're connected. I can breathe underwater, share Nuri's senses."

The sea spirit studied them for a long moment, her expression unreadable. Finally, she nodded. "Your bond is strong. It may indeed be enough. But be warned, the journey ahead will test you in ways you cannot imagine."

"Guardian, I wish to show the kai the extent of the devastation below the surface. It will help her understand what must be done to defeat the Thunder King. Please transport the others safely. We will join them."

"I stand ready to carry both of you to the third continent, as well, should you need my assistance." She pointed to the brilliant green jhorium goblet. "Call my name if you need me."

As Anahita began to weave her magic, calming the turbulent seas, Zeira, Sif, and Gocri joined her at the water's edge. In an instant, all four were gone. When Jerica spun around to face Othos, he, too, had vanished.

"That was quick." Jerica turned to Nuri. "Well, my friend," she said, a nervous smile playing on her lips as she climbed on the sea dragon's back. "Shall we take a swim?"

Nuri's answering chuckle reverberated through their shared consciousness. *Indeed. But brace yourself, Jerica. What lies ahead may not be so wondrous.*

Within minutes after they descended, the pristine waters began to darken, and Jerica's heart sank at the sight that greeted them. The once-vibrant coral reefs lay in ruins, shattered and bleached, their brilliant colors reduced to ghostly shadows of their former glory.

"By the gods," Jerica whispered, her words emerging as a stream of bubbles. "It's worse than I imagined."

Nuri's sleek form glided forward; the dragon's eyes filled with sorrow. *The storms have ravaged more than just the surface world.*

They swam on, navigating through a graveyard of broken shells and churned-up sand. Schools of fish darted past, their movements frantic and erratic, as if still fleeing from the chaos that had torn through their home.

Suddenly, Nuri tensed. *Look, there,* she directed, her mental voice tight.

Jerica followed her gaze and gasped. A group of merfolk struggled to clear a massive pile of debris from what appeared to be the entrance to an underwater grotto. Their faces reflected exhaustion and despair.

We should help them.

Agreed, Nuri replied, propelling them toward the group.

As they approached, one of the merfolk spotted them, his eyes widening in a mix of fear and hope. "A human? And a dragon?" he called out, his voice distorted by the water but still comprehensible. "Have you come to aid us?"

Jerica nodded, fighting to keep her voice steady as she took in the full extent of the destruction. "We're here to help in any way we can. What … what happened here?"

The merman's face crumpled with grief. "The storms … they were like nothing we've ever seen. Our homes, our gardens, everything … destroyed in mere moments."

Nuri swam forward, her powerful tail propelling her gracefully through the water. "We've heard of similar devastation across the realms. Tell us, what might be causing these unnatural storms?"

The merfolk exchanged nervous glances before another, an older female with silver-streaked hair, spoke up. "There have been … whispers. Of a dark power, called the Eye of the Storm, rising in the depths. Some say they've seen shadows moving where no shadows should be."

Jerica nodded, even as she felt a chill run down her spine, one that had nothing to do with the cold water surrounding her. She looked at Nuri, seeing her own unease reflected in the dragon's eyes.

"We'll help you clear this debris," Jerica said, pushing her growing dread aside. "And then, if you're willing, we'd like to hear more about these rumors."

As they set to work, Jerica couldn't shake the feeling that they were swimming into something far more dangerous than they had anticipated. The Eye of the Storm, the Thunder King … what additional terrors awaited them in the depths of this ravaged sea?

* * *

Hours later, Jerica and Nuri pushed through the churning waters. The devastation they'd witnessed in the merfolk village had only strengthened their resolution to save these people, but the journey ahead seemed more daunting with each passing moment.

Nuri, do you think the Thunder King knows we're coming?

The water dragon's sinuous neck twisted gracefully as she turned to face Jerica. *It's possible. Emerus Dinty has spies everywhere. We must remain vigilant.*

Suddenly, a powerful current caught them both off guard, sending them tumbling through the water. Jerica's heart raced as she momentarily lost contact with Nuri and struggled to breathe.

Nuri! She reached for the oron stone in her pocket. Its tri-colored segments pulsed with energy, steadying her in the chaotic waters.

Hold on, Jerica! Nuri's telepathic voice cut through the panic as she swam beneath the kai and made their connection whole again. *Use the stone to anchor your—*

Her words were cut short as a massive shape hurtled toward them from the murky depths. Jerica's eyes widened in terror as she spotted rows of razor-sharp teeth.

Megalodon! Memories of ancient sea beasts from her studies flooded her mind.

Nuri's tail lashed out, creating a powerful vortex that pushed the prehistoric predator back. *Jerica, the goblet! Use it to create a barrier!*

Jerica fumbled for the jhorium goblet at her waist, her fingers trembling as she raised it before her. "Please work," she whispered, focusing her will on the glowing green artifact.

A shimmering field of energy erupted from the goblet, enveloping both Jerica and Nuri, who curled her long tail into a circle, just as the megalodon charged again. Its massive body slammed against the barrier, the impact sending shockwaves through the water.

It's working! Jerica felt both relief and disbelief. *But I don't know how long I can hold it!*

Nuri's eyes narrowed as she assessed their predicament. *We need to find a way past this beast. The currents here are too strong for us to outswim it.*

Jerica searched for a solution. The megalodon circled them, its ancient eyes filled with primal hunger. *Wait, I have an idea.* Her grip tightened on the goblet. *But it's risky.*

At this point, I'm open to suggestions, Nuri replied, her tail coiled and ready to strike if needed.

If I can use the goblet to create a tunnel of calm water, maybe we can slip past the megalodon and into those caverns over there, Jerica explained, gesturing to a rocky formation in the distance.

Nuri considered for a moment, then nodded. *The caverns look large enough. It's worth a try. On my signal, drop the barrier and focus on creating that tunnel. I'll do what I can to distract our prehistoric friend here.*

Jerica took a deep breath, steeling herself. They couldn't falter now. *Ready when you are,* she said, locking eyes with Nuri.

The water dragon's gaze softened for a moment. *You're braver than you know, Jerica. Now, let's show this overgrown fish what we're made of.*

Here goes nothing, Jerica mumbled, dropping the barrier and channeling all her focus into the goblet. A tunnel of eerily calm water began to form, cutting through the chaotic currents around them. Mere inches ahead of the huge monster, they slithered into the caverns.

* * *

Jerica and Nuri emerged from their hiding place an hour later, their bodies battered but their spirits unbroken. The megalodon's attack had pushed them to their limits, but it had also forged their partnership into something stronger, more cohesive.

That was … intense. Jerica's hands still trembled from the adrenaline and effort of staying astride Nuri's back while maintaining the barrier to block the cavern entrance. She noted new scratches marring the dragon's iridescent scales. *Are you alright?*

Nuri's mental voice resonated with a mix of exhaustion and pride. *I've weathered worse storms, my friend. But I must admit, your quick actions with that goblet saved us both. Your power is growing.*

Jerica felt a warmth bloom in her chest at the dragon's praise. *We make a good team. Now, which way to the third continent?*

As they swam, Jerica's mind wandered to the Thunder King and the destruction he had wrought. *Nuri,* she began hesitantly, *what do you know about this Emerus Dinty? About how he became … what he is now?*

The dragon was silent for a moment, her powerful tail propelling them forward. *Not much is certain,* she finally replied. *But there are stories. They say he was once a man of Gale, scorned and ridiculed as a young lad.*

You mean bullied? Jerica felt a wave of sympathy.

Until he found a sword of great power.

A sword? Jerica's brow furrowed. *Like the artifacts we're collecting?*

Perhaps, Nuri mused. *But twisted, corrupted by dark magic. It granted him strength, but at a terrible cost.*

Jerica shuddered, imagining the kind of man who, unable to put his bad past experiences behind him, would willingly go on to treat others badly. And to pay such a price for power. *And now he wants to enslave all the dragon realms.*

I fear that what we've seen is just the beginning. He won't stop until all of Andela bows to his will.

They swam near the water's surface for a while, each lost in their own thoughts. Suddenly, Jerica noticed a change in the water around them. An inexplicable chill ran down her spine. *Nuri, do you feel that?*

The dragon's movements slowed, her head swiveling as she scanned their surroundings. *Yes. The water ... it's too still.*

As they pressed forward, the eerie calm intensified. The usual sounds of marine life faded away, replaced by an oppressive silence.

Jerica's heart pounded in her chest as realization dawned. *We're getting close, aren't we? To the Eye of the Storm?*

Nuri's reply was grim. *I'm afraid so. And to the heart of the Thunder King's power. Steel yourself, girl.*

Suddenly, the water began to pulse with an otherworldly energy. Jerica's skin tingled, the hairs on her arms standing on end. She squinted through the murky depths, her heart racing as a massive shape began to materialize in the distance.

"By the gods," she breathed, her eyes widening in awe and terror.

Above them loomed a swirling mass of dark energy that seemed to devour the light around it. Bolts of purple lightning crackled across its surface, casting an eerie glow through the water.

And there, silhouetted against the pulsing maelstrom, stood a towering figure on a hilltop, with a fearsome sword at his hip. It could only be the Thunder King himself. Even from a distance, Jerica could feel his presence, the raw power that radiated from him in waves.

Jerica felt Nuri tense, the dragon's muscles coiling. *Nuri, how are we supposed to fight ... that?* She gestured toward the terrifying vortex of dark energy.

The Thunder King drew his sword, preparing to unleash its power on them, when Nuri dove deeper through the water, giving it all she could. Evil laughter followed.

Nuri, Jerica gasped, clutching the dragon's horns as they made a sharp turn, *I don't know if I can do this.*

"You can't escape, you fools!" As if to emphasize his point, a massive wave rose before them, threatening to crash down and separate them. Jerica's heart leapt into her throat, but before she could react, Nuri had already switched directions.

With a powerful surge, the water dragon launched them into the air, breaking through the surface of the sea. For a breathless moment, they were airborne, suspended between the raging ocean and the swirling vortex above.

In that instant, Jerica looked down and saw it—a flicker of fear in Emerus Dinty's eyes as he looked up at them. And suddenly, she understood.

"Nuri," she shouted as they plummeted back toward the water, "I know what we have to do!"

As they plunged beneath the waves once more, Jerica felt almost elated. The Thunder King wasn't invincible. He was afraid, as many bullies are. And that fear, that vulnerability, was the key to their victory. And at this moment, they needed a little time and space to form a solid plan to take advantage of his one weakness.

As Dinty raised his evil sword once more, Jerica raised the jhorium goblet, its green glow intensifying. As instructed, she placed the goblet to her mouth and called out a name.

Anahita!

Quicker than she could formulate the thought, the sea guardian appeared at their side and whisked them from the sea, to a new land. It was true. The third continent was a real place.

Chapter 4 — Rugged

Zeira's wings ached from hours in flight as she soared toward the looming mountain, its jagged peak piercing the clouds like a dagger. The young red dragon's heart pounded with a mix of willpower and doubt. She glanced at her companions—Gocri's massive white form cutting through the air, Sif's smoke-gray wings spread wide, and Jerica clinging tightly to her back.

"We're nearly there," Sif called out, her voice carrying over the rushing wind. "Everyone stay alert. This won't be easy."

Jerica leaned close to Zeira's head. "It's different than I imagined—the third continent. For some reason I thought it would be a misty paradise, warm and tropical."

"Because it's the land of smoke dragons?"

"I guess."

"It could be that their fragile form is ideal for these rugged mountains." Zeira swerved, her right wing narrowly missing one of the razor-sharp rocks that jutted from the ground at odd angles. Steep cliffs rose imposingly on all sides.

Sif led the way through a deep ravine, coming to a wide place beside a river, where—astoundingly—Nuri raised her head.

Zeira landed with a heavy thud, her claws scraping against the uneven stone. The others touched down beside her, their expressions grim as they peered upward at the hazardous landscape.

Jerica faced Nuri. "How did you—"

"Courtesy of Queen Salenthina. I've been bestowed with a rare talent among valthans, the ability to navigate smaller bodies of water. If a river or lake has even a small connection to the sea, I can traverse it. In certain instances, if there is water near the surface of the ground I can slither over that area as well—somewhat like a snake."

"A little fact you never mentioned ..." Zeira countered.

Jerica wanted details, to know how a dragon with a very long body could manage this skinny river, which surely must be no more than twenty meters wide. But there were more pressing concerns. She had to trust that Nuri knew what she was doing.

"Othos told us we would find answers here, on this continent. I hope he meant we would discover the place where Skellig is imprisoned. If we're going to confront the Thunder King, we could use our Spark friend's help."

"This place is very different than I imagined. I see now why it is called Rokke," Gocri said, his icy eyes narrowed. He snorted, a puff of frost escaping his nostrils. "But at least the sky is clear."

Sif was studying the terrain. "I know the area. We've come too far to turn back now. I believe we should press on."

Jerica nodded "We must proceed with caution. Sif, can you scout ahead and find the safest path?"

The smoke dragon dipped her head. "Of course. I'll be back shortly." With that, she took to the air, her form growing smaller as she disappeared into the crags above.

Less than ten minutes later, Sif was back. "Near the summit of this peak is an opening. If the legends of Rokke are true, the place has been used as a lookout point and encampment. It's quite possibly the place where they have Skellig imprisoned."

Jerica thought of Dym, Skellig's evil sire, and the fact that he was not well regarded in his home realm of Gale. It made a kind of sense that Dym might have connections in this new land, a place where he could imprison Skellig without encountering criticism for the act.

"We need to reach that summit," she announced. "Sif, you will lead the way. I will ride with Zeira. Nuri … I'm sorry. It doesn't look like this is a destination for you."

"Quite all right," said the water dragon. "I shall continue to scout the shoreline of this continent, in case we need an underwater escape route."

"Good idea."

They bade Nuri goodbye as Jerica climbed up to Zeira's neck. One by one, the dragons took flight. Sif, then Gocri, then Zeira.

As they began their treacherous ascent, the air currents became apparent, pushing them off their intended path, reaching jagged rocks outward, rocks that threatened to slice through scales and skin alike.

"This mountain seems determined to kill us before we even reach the top," Gocri declared.

As they rounded a particularly treacherous bend, a gust of wind knocked Jerica off her perch. Zeira's heart leapt into her throat as she lunged forward, catching the girl with her tail.

"Thanks," Jerica gasped, her face pale as she gripped the dragon's scales even more tightly.

Zeira nodded, her own pulse racing. "We need to be more careful. Perhaps we should find a place to rest for a moment."

"No time," Gocri rumbled from behind. "I smell a storm brewing. We must reach shelter before it hits."

Sif's head snapped up, her eyes widening. "A storm? Here? That can only mean one thing …"

"The Thunder King," Zeira finished, a chill running down her spine despite the heat of her inner fire. "He knows we're coming."

The group exchanged worried glances, the gravity of their situation sinking in. They had come so far, faced so much, but the true test still lay ahead. As clouds began to build, Jerica fought to quell the fear rising within her.

"We can't give up now," she said, as much to herself as to the others. "Whatever comes, we face it together. For Andela."

Gocri's massive white form surged ahead, his glacial scales glinting in the dimming light as he navigated the treacherous terrain. Despite his size, the Frost dragon moved with surprising grace, his powerful wings flexing as he flew from one jagged outcropping to another.

"Sif, over here," he called back, his voice a low rumble that seemed to vibrate through the rocks beneath them. "I can sense a path ahead that should lead us closer to the summit."

Sif landed on a pinnacle and eyed a narrow crevice snaking up the mountainside. Her giant gray wings folded tightly against her body as she concentrated, her form shimmering and shrinking until she resembled a wisp of a dragon, no larger than a house cat.

"I'll scout ahead," she said, her voice now a soft whisper on the wind. "My smaller form can squeeze through places the rest of you can't reach."

As Sif darted into the crevice, Gocri paused on the peak she had just abandoned, his icy breath forming small crystals in the air as he spoke. "Be careful, Sif."

I always am, came the faint reply from within the rock.

Zeira, with Jerica aboard, landed on the next peak over. Gocri turned his attention back to the path, his pale eyes narrowed in concentration. *The air grows colder the higher we climb,* he mused. *It reminds me of home in the Region of Bliss.*

Do you miss it? Jerica wanted to know, her breath coming in short gasps as she realized the lack of oxygen at this altitude.

Gocri's expression softened for a moment. *Sometimes. But Queen Freriss entrusted me with this mission. I won't let her down.* He paused, a hint of pride creeping into his voice. *She calls me 'Dren' now, you know—it's an endearment. After what happened at the Frozen Falls when I was a lad of only six centuries.*

Before Jerica could respond, Sif's voice entered their

telepathic conversation. *I've found a safer route! Follow me!*

The smoke dragon reappeared, her form undulating as she guided them toward a hidden path winding up the mountainside. As they flew directly above it, Jerica couldn't shake the feeling that they were being watched. She glanced at the others, wondering if they felt it too.

As they rounded a bend, Sif pointed to the ground, then led the others to land beside her. "We'll need to cross this clearing and there's a chamber on the other side." The group found themselves facing a dense thicket of thorny vines and twisted branches. The vegetation was so thick it seemed impenetrable, blocking their path entirely.

Zeira's eyes narrowed, a determined glint flickering in their fiery depths. "Stand back," she grunted, her voice low and rumbling. The young dragon from Blaze stepped forward, her scales glowing with an inner heat.

"Zeira, wait—" Jerica started, but it was too late.

With a rumble in her gut, Zeira unleashed a torrent of flames from her rear end. The fire engulfed the vegetation, turning the thicket into a blazing inferno.

Jerica shielded her face with her arm. "Little overkill there, Z."

"Yeah, maybe." If possible, the red dragon seemed to blush.

"I got this," Gocri said, stepping forward to blast the fire with a shot of icy breath.

As the flames died down, Zeira turned to the group, a hint of pride in her voice. "Path cleared. Let's move."

Jerica stepped forward, her eyes wide with a mix of awe and concern. "That was ... impressive," she said, her gaze darting between Zeira and the smoldering remains of the thicket. "But won't that alert the Thunder King to our presence?"

Zeira's confidence faltered for a moment. "I ... I didn't think of that," she admitted, her tail swishing nervously. "I just wanted to help."

Jerica placed a reassuring hand on Zeira's talon. "It's okay. We'll just have to be extra careful from here on out." She turned her attention to the mountain looming before them, the summit now shrouded in clouds. Her grip on the magical goblet tightened, its green glow reacting to her touch.

"How are you holding up?" Sif asked, noticing the intensity in Jerica's eyes.

Jerica took a deep breath, her fingers tracing the intricate designs on the goblet. "I'm ... managing. This goblet, it's like it has a mind of its own sometimes. I can feel its power growing the higher we climb on this mountain."

"Is that a good thing or a bad thing?" Zeira questioned, her head tilting in curiosity.

"I'm not sure," Jerica admitted, her brow furrowing. "But I do know we need its power to face the Thunder King. I just hope I'm strong enough to control it when the time comes."

Sif turned to the group. "We'll need to tuck our wings as we enter the chamber inside the mountain. It's supposed to be large, but—"

"Maybe not dragon-sized. We get it."

As they began to move through the cleared path, Jerica's thoughts tumbled with doubts and fears. What if she couldn't master the goblet's power? What if she let everyone down?

"Jerica," Zeira's voice cut through her thoughts. "You're not alone in this. We're all here, fighting together. We believe in you."

Jerica managed a small smile, touched by the dragon's words. "Thanks, Zeira. I just wish I had your confidence sometimes."

Zeira let out a snort, a small puff of smoke escaping her nostrils. "Me? Confident? After I just potentially alerted the Thunder King to our presence? I'm terrified most of the time."

"You hide it well," Jerica chuckled, feeling some of the tension ease from her neck.

As they continued toward the passageway, Jerica squared her shoulders and prayed they would find Skellig here. Soon, the dark opening of a large cave appeared.

A sudden gust of wind whipped around them, carrying with it an eerie chill that made Jerica shudder. She looked up, her eyes widening as she took in the scene just above them.

Dark, roiling clouds swirled ominously around the

mountain's peak, their edges tinged with an unnatural purple hue. Thunder rumbled in the distance, a low, menacing sound that seemed to reverberate through Jerica's very bones.

It seemed the Eye of the Storm had reached this continent too.

"By the ancient scales," Sif whispered, her smoky, serpentine form coiling tighter. "It's as if the mountain itself is trying to ward us off."

Zeira snorted, a small flame escaping her nostrils. "The Thunder King's work, no doubt. He won't make this easy for us."

Jerica felt a surge of anger at the mention of their enemy. "Emerus Dinty," she spat, the name tasting bitter on her tongue. "He's up there, thinking he's untouchable. But we'll show him the true power of unity between humans and dragons."

As if in response to her defiance, a particularly loud crack of thunder split the air, causing the group to flinch instinctively.

"We need to move," Gocri urged, his wings rustling restlessly. "The longer we stay here, the more time he has to prepare."

The dragons tucked their wings and entered the dark opening in the rock.

"Watch your step," Zeira warned, her voice barely above a whisper. "We have no idea what lies ahead."

Jerica nodded, her eyes scanning the ground for any signs of danger. The air grew thinner as they climbed, and a creepy stillness settled over them, broken only by the occasional rumble of distant thunder.

Sif, who had taken on a smaller form to better navigate the narrow paths, suddenly froze. "Wait," she hissed. "I smell something … off."

Gocri's nostrils flared as he tested the air. "Magic," he growled. "Dark and potent."

Zeira's heart pounded. "Could it be a trap?"

"Possibly," Jerica replied, her eyes narrowing. "Or it could be residual energy from the Eye of the Storm. Either way, we need to be extra cautious."

They proceeded with even greater care, each step measured and deliberate. Jerica's mind whirled with possibilities. What if they were walking into an elaborate trap? What if the Thunder King was simply toying with them?

As they rounded a sharp bend, Gocri suddenly threw out a wing, blocking their path. "Look," he said, nodding toward a seemingly innocuous patch of ground. "See how the stones are arranged?"

Jerica squinted, noticing for the first time the unnatural pattern. "It's too perfect," she realized. "Like it was placed there intentionally."

"A pressure plate, perhaps," Sif suggested. "Designed to trigger who knows what kind of nasty surprise."

Zeira nodded grimly. "Good catch, Gocri."

As they carefully skirted the potential trap, Jerica couldn't help but marvel at how seamlessly dragons and humans worked together. She turned to thank her teammates.

But her words died in her throat as they entered a large, central chamber in the mountain. Was this the prison that held their friend? But they had no chance to discuss it, or even to look around. Before them stood an imposing barrier of swirling, inky darkness. It pulsed with malevolent energy, completely encasing what must be the source for the Eye of the Storm.

"No," Zeira breathed, her eyes wide with disbelief. "This can't be."

Jerica felt as if all the air had been sucked from her lungs. "How?" she choked out. "How could he have known, and how could he create a storm inside a mountain? It's—"

Gocri's tail lashed in frustration. "We've come too far to be stopped now," he boomed. "There must be a way through."

Sif, who had reverted to half her full size, shook her head. "That barrier ... it's unlike anything I've ever seen here in Rokke. The magic is so dense, so corrupted."

Jerica's mind desperately searched for a solution. She looked down at the goblet in her hands, its soft glow seeming pitifully inadequate against the overwhelming darkness before them.

"Maybe ..." she started, her voice trembling slightly.

"Maybe the jhorium can penetrate it? Or at least weaken it enough for us to break through?"

Zeira turned to her, hope flickering in her eyes. "It's worth a try. But Jerica, be careful. We don't know how the barrier might react."

Jerica nodded, swallowing hard. She took a tentative step forward, raising the goblet. As she did, the barrier seemed to pulse more intensely, as if sensing a threat.

"Here goes nothing," she whispered, steeling herself for whatever might come next. She closed her eyes, focusing all her will on channeling the power of the jhorium.

The goblet grew warm in her hands, its glow intensifying. Jerica felt a surge of energy course through her, and she directed it toward the barrier with all her might.

For a moment, nothing happened. Then, with a sound like shattering glass, a small fissure appeared in the dark energy. Jerica's heart leapt, but her elation was short-lived. Almost immediately, the crack began to seal itself.

And then rocks began to break loose from the walls and roof of the cavern.

Chapter 5 — Misled

We have to get out—now!" Gocri's deep voice allowed no room for argument.

Three dragons and one human female rushed back the way they had come. It was all the dragons could do to tighten themselves down to fit through the tunnel. But in record time they were on the outside again, barely ahead of the collapsing chamber behind them.

Jerica stumbled near the edge of a precipice but Zeira caught her before she could fall, steadying her with a gentle wing. Together, they soared downward, off the mountain, to a wide clearing below.

"Holy grompers—that was close. I'm sorry," Jerica whispered, tears of frustration stinging her eyes. "I thought ... I hoped ..."

"You did your best," Gocri said, his voice uncharacteristically gentle. "We all did. But it seems the Thunder King was one step ahead of us this time."

"What about Skellig?" Zeira asked in a very small voice.

"We were misled." Gocri's tone was bitter. "There was no prison inside the mountain. I'm not placing blame, Sif. We thought the stories were legitimate too. But our friend was never here."

Sif's eyes blazed. "This isn't over," she declared. "We'll find him yet, some other way."

"You're right, Sif. We can't give up," Jerica said, her voice growing stronger as she spoke. "Emerus Dinty, this stupid *Thunder King*, might think he's won, but he doesn't know us."

All at once, a deep, menacing chuckle echoed across the mountaintop. The air crackled with electrical energy, raising the hair on her arms, sending a chill down her spine. From the swirling shadows cast by the storm overhead, a large human figure emerged.

Emerus Dinty, the Thunder King, stepped into view in the clearing. His enormous frame seemed to dwarf the nearby trees as he leapt onto a large, flat rock. A wicked smile played across his lips, his eyes gleaming with cruel satisfaction as he surveyed the group.

"Well, well," he drawled, his voice as ominous as distant thunder. "What have we here? A band of meddling fools thinking they can challenge my power?"

Jerica stood her ground, acutely aware of Gocri and Zeira flanking her protectively. Sif had shifted to a larger form, her scales bristling.

The Thunder King's gaze settled on Jerica, his smile widening. "And you, little one. Did you truly believe that paltry goblet could breach my defenses?"

Jerica's fingers tightened around the magical artifact. "We won't let you destroy Andela," she declared, her voice steadier than she felt.

Emerus threw back his head and laughed, the sound reverberating through the air. "Destroy? Oh no, you misunderstand. I intend to reshape it. To mold this land into something greater, more powerful—under my rule, of course."

He began to pace, his massive form radiating barely contained energy. "Imagine it. A world where the strong truly rule, where power is the only currency that matters. No more of this tiresome cooperation between dragons and humans. I will harness the might of the valthans, the Sparks, and the Frost dragons. I can bend the elements to my will!"

Jerica felt a surge of anger at his words. "You're insane," she spat. "Andela thrives *because* of our unity, not in spite of it."

The Thunder King's eyes flashed dangerously. "Unity? Oh, you mean the way the various tribes have been warring for a year now? Pathetic. They fight because I want them to. And when their strongest have been decimated, I will step in and show everyone how it's done, how a true leader operates."

He raised his hand, and a bolt of lightning arced from his fingers, striking the ground at Jerica's feet. She stumbled back, heart pounding.

"Your little quest ends here," Emerus Dinty declared, his voice dripping with arrogance. "Run back to your hovels while you still can. Or stay, and witness the dawn of a new era—one where the Thunder King reigns supreme!"

As he spoke, the dark clouds above churned more violently, flashes of lightning illuminating his imposing silhouette.

Jerica watched the Thunder King's display of power. The glimpse of fear she had detected before—every trace was gone now. The air crackled with electricity, sending tingles through the limbs. She glanced at her companions, noting the mix of awe and fear on their faces. Gocri's massive form seemed to shrink, while Sif had instinctively shifted into a smaller, more defensive shape. Even Zeira's fiery demeanor had dampened, her previous bravado replaced by wide-eyed shock.

"By the ancient scales," Gocri rumbled, his voice barely above a whisper. "I've never seen such raw power."

"You'd better believe it, Icy Pants."

Jerica felt a chill run down her spine. If even the mighty Gocri was shaken, what hope did they have?

The Thunder King's laugh boomed across the mountaintop. "Finally, you begin to understand. Your meager alliance is nothing compared to my might!"

As if to emphasize his point, he raised his hand again, and the ground beneath their feet trembled. Jerica stumbled, struggling to maintain her footing.

Taking a shaky breath, Jerica looked down at the glowing green chalice in her hands. Its light pulsed, almost in rhythm with her racing heart.

"What's this? Are you ready to hand over the jhorium implement to me?" the Thunder King's mocking voice rang out.

Jerica tucked the goblet beneath her tunic and shook her head.

"The little girl thinks she can stand against me? How adorable."

Jerica's eyes snapped open, anger flaring within her. "I am more than just a little girl," she declared, her voice stronger than she felt. "I am Jerica Barille of Cael, and I will not let you destroy our world!"

"Brave words," Emerus sneered. "But words are all they are. You have no idea of the forces you're dealing with, child."

Jerica stood taller, meeting the Thunder King's gaze. "Maybe not," she admitted. "But I know what's right. And I know that together, we're stronger than any one tyrant could ever be."

As she spoke, she felt her companions straighten beside her, their steadfastness strengthening. The Thunder King's eyes narrowed.

"You dare to challenge me?" he roared, raising his enchanted sword. "Then face the consequences of your foolishness!"

Lightning arced from the blade, hurtling toward Jerica. In that moment, time seemed to slow. She raised the jhorium goblet instinctively, and to her amazement, the lightning curved around her, drawn to the glowing chalice.

As the goblet absorbed the energy, its green glow intensified. Jerica felt the power coursing through her, raw and untamed.

"Impossible," the Thunder King whispered, his confident facade cracking.

Once again, she spotted that tiny flicker of weakness

within their foe.

The Thunder King's face contorted with rage, his eyes blazing with a mixture of fury and disbelief. He raised his enchanted sword once more, its blade crackling with barely contained energy.

"You think your little trick changes anything?" he snarled, his voice dripping with contempt. "I am Emerus Dinty, the Thunder King! I've conquered realms and bent dragons to my will. Oh, you naive little fools," he sneered. "You have no concept of true power. Allow me to demonstrate."

With a swift motion, he plunged his sword into the ground. The mountain trembled, and dark clouds swirled overhead, throbbing with unnatural energy.

Sif, in her smaller form, clung to Zeira's wing. "We need to retreat!" she shouted over the growing rumble. "We're not prepared for this!"

Jerica's thoughts tumbled, and she realized with a sinking heart that Sif was right. They weren't ready to face this level of power.

Guys, we need to regroup!

The others nodded, and Zeira extended a wing so Jerica could climb onto her back. Within moments the dragons began leaping into the air, taking off to the sounds of the Thunder King's laughter.

Jerica's thoughts boiled as they descended past the treacherous slopes. They had underestimated their enemy, and now they were paying the price. But as the sound of the Thunder King's mockery faded behind them, a new resilience began to take root.

"We'll find another way," she mumbled, more to herself than her companions. "We have to."

* * *

The sky erupted in a furious tempest as dragons clashed with storm creatures—monstrous creatures made of swirling storm clouds—their roars drowned by deafening thunder and shards of lightning. Skellig's yellow scales flashed amid the chaos, his black wings slicing through the turbulent air.

Sparks crackled around his talons as he dove at one of the creatures in the gale-force winds.

At the eye of the maelstrom stood the Thunder King, his mighty form silhouetted by flashes of electricity arcing across the sky. With a sweep of his enchanted sword, he summoned a barrage of lightning bolts that rained down upon the dragons. Jerica stepped into its path.

Then she snapped awake.

"What hap—" The scent of roasting meat wafted toward her and her stomach growled. She rubbed her eyes and looked up to see Sif standing over her. Someone had found a cloak and draped it over her. She pulled it tighter.

"Are you hungry?"

Her stomach rumbled again, the clear answer to Sif's question.

"We understand that humans prefer their meat cooked," Zeira offered, pointing toward the campfire on the beach.

"Thank you. Yes, we do." Jerica sat up, cross-legged, ignoring the traces of unknown blood on her benefactor's talons.

"You were restless in your sleep." Gocri tossed a long bone away, far from the firelight. "Dreaming?"

"Yes. Skellig was in the dream." Jerica accepted the slab of charred meat from Sif and took a bite. It was nothing to compare with her mother's hedgehog stew, but she was too hungry to be particular. She sent a grateful smile toward her companions. "Have you guys been discussing what we should do next?"

Zeira looked toward the sea, where the moon cast a long silver reflection across the black water. "Nuri, are you still here?"

The sleek blue valthan raised her head and slithered partway out of the water. "I am. Has our sleeping princess awakened?"

"Hey—I was exhausted. I didn't sleep that long, did I?"

"In human time … about twelve hours. It will be daylight again soon." Zeira gave her a toothy smile, compassionate for a dragon.

"Twelve hours! No way!" Jerica chomped down another

bite of the meat, which was tasting better and better.

"You are correct. You were exhausted." Sif dipped her head, gently nudging Jerica's knee. "And don't let them tease you. We each had several short dragon-naps, between taking turns at foraging."

Jerica let out a contented sigh. "I really did need the rest. So … back to my question. Have you considered what we should do next?"

"We must renew our efforts to find Skellig," Zeira said, looking toward Nuri for validation.

"Absolutely." Jerica licked her fingers. "Othos strongly suggested that here on the third continent would be the place to find him. Nuri, you've been scouting along the coastline. Do you have any likely locations mapped out?"

"The local valthans have not suffered the indignities that my population in Hythos did. I have sent several of them out on the mission of listening for rumors, finding out if anyone has heard of a yellow Spark dragon prisoner, or his awful sire, Dym. This is the smallest of the continents. If they are in this region, we should soon know something."

Jerica wiped her hands on the cloak and stood. "Where did this garment come from, anyway?"

"Many possessions have been cast aside as tribesmen flee the various areas. Gocri found this one for you."

"It might come in handy. I'll use it until we find the owner." Jerica stared out to the horizon, where the sun had cast the clouds in shades of pink and orange. A gentle breeze came off the water.

"No sign of that horrible Eye of the Storm," Sif commented. "Do you suppose the … you-know-who … has left the continent?"

"We should be so lucky. I wouldn't count on it." Jerica forced the dark memories aside. "Now. About Skellig. Where should we look?"

"King Myrdaynth said he had been imprisoned. So, we must locate some kind of fortress, I would think." Zeira began to stomp out the campfire, but Gocri pushed forward and instantly froze the small flames with his icy breath. "Okay, that works too."

Nuri had a faraway look on her face, but she quickly snapped her attention back to the group. "I've been in telepathic communication with the local valthans. This bit of land where we sit is a peninsula. To the west is a rocky shoreline with a settlement of sorts. Among the structures is one that might be described as a fortress."

"How shall we get there?" Jerica was eyeing a dense forest in that direction.

"I shall swim along the coastline."

"And you will get there ahead of us all," Gocri proclaimed. Nuri's speed in the water was legendary.

The water dragon nodded, a smug little smile on her face.

"The rest of us can surely fly above the forest," Jerica declared, eyeing her usual perch on Zeira's back. "Do we have any idea how far away this settlement is?"

"Thirty leagues by water is what they've told me."

"Over the land should be shorter, right?" Jerica was trying to envision a U-shaped piece of land, and the water dragon would need to swim three sides of it.

Zeira extended a talon for Jerica to mount, then the girl climbed her scales until she was seated. One by one, the dragons launched themselves into the air. Nuri had already disappeared below the waves.

"Race you to the other side!" Jerica called out.

Chapter 6 — Doubts

The forest blurred into a green haze as Zeira pumped her wings, branches whipping past below them. Her lungs burned with each ragged breath, heart hammering against her ribs. Behind her, Gocri's massive white body glided along easily, while Sif darted playfully between treetops in her smoke form. Jerica clung to Zeira's back, the girl's fingers digging into the red dragon's scales.

All at once, the wind picked up and the sunshine faded.

Uh-oh. Not this again. Jerica's thoughts reached the others.

A rumble of thunder sounded behind them. Zeira's stomach dropped. The Eye was getting closer.

"I am *not* up for another battle with this guy," Jerica shouted over the wind.

Zeira gritted her teeth. Their new leader was right, but even though yesterday's confrontation had diminished them, what choice did they have?

"Just a little farther," Zeira called back. "I see a ravine

ahead where we can—"

"WHERE YOU CAN WHAT, LITTLE DRAGON?"

The booming voice seemed to come from everywhere at once. Zeira faltered mid-flight, nearly sending Jerica tumbling. Gocri split off, trying to create a more diffused target for the madman. Sif shrunk herself to the size of a feather, but her airspeed immediately dropped. She drifted over to Jerica and settled on the girl's shoulder.

The Thunder King's mocking laughter rolled through the trees. "Hide? Cower? Make your pathetic plans to stop me?"

Zeira felt a surge of white-hot anger. How dare he? After everything he'd done, everything he'd taken from the creatures of this land. She opened her mouth, a blistering retort on her tongue—

"Don't engage," Gocri rumbled, ice crystals forming on his breath. "It's what he wants."

Zeira swallowed her words, but couldn't quell the fury burning in her chest. She glanced at her companions. Gocri's massive talons were clenched, frost creeping up his legs. Sif quickly shifted back to her dragon form and banked to the left, eyes narrowed to slits as she scanned the skyline. And Jerica … the girl's face was pale, her jaw set in a hard line as she gripped the glowing goblet.

"Aww, has the little red one lost her fire?" The Thunder King's voice dripped with false concern. "And here I thought you dragons were supposed to be fierce. Tell me, how does it feel to know you've failed? That everything you love will soon be mine?"

"You know nothing of love," Sif snarled, smoke curling from her nostrils. "Only power and greed."

A bolt of lightning struck a nearby tree, spraying them with burning debris. Zeira banked hard, shielding Jerica with her wing.

"POWER IS LOVE!" The Thunder King roared. "And soon, all of Andela will love me. Will worship me as their god-king. And I will have it all, starting with that little bauble your human pet carries."

Under the borrowed cloak, Jerica's grip on the goblet tightened. "Never," she whispered, but there was a tremor in the girl's voice.

For a moment, Jerica's doubts threatened to overwhelm her. How could they hope to defeat someone so powerful? Someone willing to destroy everything in his path? She was just a young villager. What right did she have to lead this group?

But then she felt Zeira's powerful wings, saw Gocri's icy gaze, the defiance radiating from Sif's very being. *They* believed in her. Trusted her.

No. She couldn't let the Thunder King's words poison her mind. Couldn't let him win.

Gocri poured on a burst of speed, feeling a familiar fortitude building in his core. "We need to split up," he called to the others. "Zeira, take Jerica and head east. Sif and I will draw his fire."

"But—" Jerica started to protest.

"Trust me," Gocri said, meeting the girl's eyes. The dragons trusted her—she needed to trust them. After a moment, Jerica nodded.

As Sif swooped away, Zeira allowed herself a small, fierce smile. The Thunder King wanted fire? She'd give him fire.

With a roar that shook the treetops, Zeira whirled in mid-air. A burst of flame erupted not from her mouth, but from her hindquarters, searing through the forest canopy.

"Come and get us, you pompous windbag!" she hollered.

As she and Jerica veered away from the others, Zeira's heart pounded with a mixture of fear and exhilaration. They might be outmatched, but they weren't beaten. Not as long as they had each other.

And fire. Lots and lots of fire.

The Thunder King's laughter boomed across the sky, chilling Zeira to her bones despite the heat of her own flames. "Foolish dragons," his voice rumbled. "You think you can stop me? I will reshape Andela to my liking, mine its treasures for my own, and your precious realms will crumble beneath my feet!"

As if to prove his statement, the Eye of the Storm whirled, darker and stronger.

Zeira's heart clenched. She glanced at Gocri, seeing her

own horror reflected in his icy eyes.

"He can't mean—" Gocri began.

"Oh, but I do," The Thunder King interrupted, his voice dripping with malice. "The jhorium will be mine, and with it I'll forge a weapon to bend reality itself. Your forests will burn, your glaciers will melt, and your people will serve me or perish!"

A cold fury ignited in Zeira's chest. "Never!" she roared, unleashing another burst of flame from her rear.

Suddenly, the air filled with an ear-splitting screech. Six Spark dragons, black with glowing yellow stripes, their scales glinting, burst through the forest canopy.

Now! Jerica conveyed to her team.

Gocri exhaled sharply, his icy breath crystallizing the air. Three of the Spark dragons froze in mid-air, plummeting to the forest floor.

Zeira twisted, corkscrewing through the air. Fire erupted from her, spinning in all directions, creating a dazzling, deadly display. The remaining black dragons shrieked as flames licked their scales.

Jerica's voice came through, strong and clear as she gripped the jhorium goblet: *I'm sending shields up!*

Shimmering green barriers sprang into existence, deflecting the Thunder King's lightning bolts. Sif darted between the magical shields, shifting from dragon to bird to mist, confounding their attackers.

As Zeira dove to avoid a Spark's wing talons, she looked back at Jerica. The girl's face was set in fierce concentration, her hands wrapped around the glowing goblet. They were holding their own.

But for how long?

The Thunder King's laughter boomed across the battlefield, sending chills down Jerica's spine. The air crackled with electricity as he raised his arms, his eyes glowing an unnatural blue.

"Enough of these games," he snarled. "Behold the true power of the storm!"

The sky darkened abruptly to an ugly purple-black, clouds swirling into a whirlwind above. Lightning arced between the clouds, and with a deafening crack, a massive creature emerged. It was like a dragon made of pure lightning, its body crackling with energy, eyes blazing white-hot.

"By the fires of Blaze," Zeira gasped, her wings faltering for a moment. "It's a completely new storm creature."

Gocri's voice carried on the wind. "We can't fight that thing! We need to retreat!"

The storm creature let out a thunderous roar, sending a shockwave through the air. Trees bent and snapped under its force.

"Jerica!" Zeira called out. "Can you shield us?"

The young girl's face was pale, her hands shaking as she gripped the goblet. "I-I don't know if I can hold it against that!"

Sif, back in her dragon form, swooped low. "We need to go, now!"

With a heavy heart, Jerica made the call. *Everyone, fall back! Head for the ravine to the west!*

As they fled, Zeira felt the heat of lightning strikes at her tail. The storm creature pursued, its roars shaking the earth. Frustration and exhaustion warred within her as they pushed themselves to their limits.

Finally, they reached a narrow canyon, and collapsed on a rocky outcropping, chests heaving. The storm creature passed overhead, not seeing them.

Zeira slumped against a boulder, her scales still smoking slightly. Jerica stood on her back and looked around "Is … is everyone alright?"

Gocri nodded weakly, but his eyes were distant. "Physically, yes."

Jerica sat down heavily, the goblet clutched to her chest. Her voice trembled as she spoke. "I couldn't maintain the shields. I felt the power, but it … it scared me. I was afraid I would lose control. And I lost my cloak, guess it blew away somewhere."

Zeira wanted to reassure her, but her own insecurities choked the words in her throat. Instead, she stared out at the darkening sky. This encounter with the Thunder King had been so much worse than before.

Jerica's eyes darted between her companions, taking in their weary expressions. "Where's Sif?" The smoke dragon wasn't among them.

Then they saw a gray-white streak heading toward them.

Sif felt a searing pain tear through her left wing. The world spun as she plummeted, her smoke form dissipating in wisps.

"Sif!" The collective cry of her companions echoed in her ears as she struggled to regain control.

Through blurred vision, Sif saw the ground rushing up to meet her. With every ounce of strength left in her battered body, she willed her smoke form to solidify. She hit the earth hard, tumbling across the rocky terrain before coming to a stop.

Pain radiated through her entire being. Sif tried to rise, but her left wing hung limply at her side, useless. She could taste blood in her mouth, the metallic flavor mixing with the acrid scent of her own charred scales.

"Sif!" Jerica called out, leaping off Zeira's back and running toward the prone form. "Can you move? We need to get you out of here!"

Sif gritted her teeth, forcing herself to stand despite the agony. "I ... I can manage," she gasped, her voice weak but resolute. "Don't worry about me. Focus on the Thunder King!"

"He and his storm creature are gone—for now." Jerica's reassurance did little to hide her thoughts. Sif's injury had shaken them, the reality of their vulnerability sinking in.

Her fingers touched the glowing green surface of her goblet, its faint warmth a comfort against the chill of despair threatening to overcome them. She took a deep breath, surprising herself with the steadiness in her voice.

"We may be battered, but we're not broken," she said. "Remember when we were in Cael? You chose to trust a village girl with the jhorium, to create a strange magical artifact. That trust is why we're here now, fighting for Andela."

Gocri's scales rustled as he shifted, his eyes brightening slightly. "You're right. Skellig wouldn't want us to give up. He believed in our cause."

"And once we get him out of wherever he's being held, he'll be right at our sides once more."

Jerica re-tied the jhorium goblet to her belt, and reached into her pocket, pulling out the oron stone. Its healing power had worked before. With Gocri's help, Sif sat up. Her left wing hung limply and she cringed when she tried to move it.

"Hold still. Hopefully, not all of my magical abilities were affected just now." Jerica gently felt the wing until she determined which bone was broken. She held the oron stone between her palms until it warmed and glowed—red, blue, and green—then placed it against the injured spot. Holding it gently against the skin, she felt the power of the stone seep into the dragon.

Within minutes, Sif's grimace turned into a smile. "That's amazing." She carefully tested the wing, lifting it from her side, flexing it.

Gocri and Zeira watched, transfixed, as Sif spread the wing to its full extent.

"Don't try any quick moves just yet. Sif, do you think you can transform into a smaller size? Maybe you and I can both be riders for the next leg of the journey."

Sif nodded, then transformed from her dragon form into her human shape; she could have been Jerica's little sister. She placed a hand on Jerica's arm. "All set."

Jerica felt a warmth spread through her chest, chasing away some of the doubt. "Thank you," she whispered, her voice growing stronger. "All of you. We've come too far to give up now."

"Speaking of coming far … Nuri is surely at the coast now, gloating over how much faster she reached the destination than we did," Gocri reminded.

Zeira straightened, her eyes regaining their fierce gleam. "You're absolutely right. Do you think the Thunder King is out of the region now?"

Jerica gave it some thought. "The oron stone … it's connected to the land itself, right? What if we could use it to locate a weakness in the Thunder King's defenses?"

Zeira tilted her head, staring at the stone in Jerica's hand. "It's possible. The oron is attuned to the natural energies of Andela. Great power, such as what we've seen from our enemy, often leaves … ripples, so to speak. If we can detect those ripples…"

"We might find a way to counter them," Sif finished, nodding approvingly.

A sudden gust of wind swept through their makeshift hideout, scattering leaves and sending a chill down Jerica's spine. She gripped the oron stone tighter, its warmth a stark contrast to the growing unease in her chest.

"We need to move," Zeira asserted, her scales bristling. "Before the Thunder King's forces return. I can smell them on the wind."

Gocri nodded, his icy breath creating a fine mist as he spoke. "Agreed. We've lingered too long already."

Jerica climbed onto Zeira's back and watched Sif do the same with Gocri. "All right. To the coast, and Nuri."

Fire dragon, ice dragon, and two human-sized passengers took off into the cloudy sky.

In the distance, a crack of thunder rumbled, followed by Emerus Dinty's taunting voice. "Did you think you could hide from me forever, mortals? I can smell your fear!"

Jerica's blood ran cold. "He's found us," she hissed.

"Fly, Zeira! Fly for all you're worth!" Gocri roared, as the two dragons went into maximum speed.

Fumbling with the goblet, Jerica focused her will, drawing on the magical energy within it. A shimmering wall of force erupted behind them, rendering them invisible.

"The shield won't hold for long," she warned, already feeling the strain. "Hopefully long enough to get us to the coast where at least we'll have the help of the valthans."

It felt like forever, but in reality was probably little more than ten minutes, when Jerica spotted the heavenly blue of the sea. Zeira and Gocri were already aware, and they took the most direct course.

Ahead, a huge weathered stone structure loomed, half-hidden by vines and moss. Without hesitation, they landed beside it. Although the sky ahead was a clear blue, behind them, the ominous clouds continued to roll in.

"A building? How will we—?"

Jerica pointed to one wall that had completely crumbled. "Maybe there?"

Zeira folded her wings and ducked her head and was able to step through the opening. "Gocri will never make it. He's too large."

"But I know how to disguise myself," he reminded. To prove it, the large ice dragon crouched to the ground, pulled his long neck inward, and draped his wings to the sides, until he resembled nothing more than an extra-lumpy bit of sand. One blue eye winked at them and then closed. He was invisible.

Sif, in her child-sized human form, jumped off his back and joined those inside the structure. With some creative rearrangement of the surrounding vines, they hoped they, too, were well hidden. They found themselves inside an ancient stone structure, which, aside from the broken wall they'd come through, seemed fairly intact. There was a wooden door at the opposite end of the great hall.

Jerica slumped against a crumbling wall, her chest heaving. "That ... was too close," she gasped, her fingers still clutching the goblet.

Zeira's scales glimmered in the dim light filtering through cracks in the ceiling. "We can't stay here long," she rumbled, her voice tinged with worry. "The Thunder King won't give up so easily."

As if on cue, a booming laugh echoed from outside, sending shivers down Jerica's spine. His voice carried through the stone, dripping with malice.

"You think you can hide from me?" he taunted. "I am the storm that will reshape Andela. Your wretched resistance is nothing but a dying breeze."

Sif clenched her small fists. "Do you think he can break in?"

Jerica closed her eyes, focusing on the energy of the oron stone. An idea crystallized in her mind, equal parts terrifying and exhilarating. She opened her eyes, meeting the gazes of her companions.

"I have a plan," she whispered, her voice steadier than she felt. "But it's dangerous, and I'll need all of you."

As Jerica outlined her strategy, a tremor shook the structure. Dust and small stones rained down from above. The Thunder King's forces were trying to break in.

Jerica's heart pounded. She reached for the oron stone, and placed it inside the goblet. As she prepared to channel its power, a blinding flash of light erupted from the stone.

In that moment of brilliance, a vision seared itself into Jerica's mind: The Thunder King, his enchanted sword sparking with dark energy, standing before a swirling vortex of storm and lightning.

The light faded, leaving Jerica gasping and wide-eyed. The others stared at her in concern.

"Jerica?" Zeira prompted, worry evident in her voice.

Jerica looked up, her expression a mix of fear and fierce doggedness. "I have an idea how to stop him," she whispered. "But we'll have to face the heart of the storm itself."

The walls around them shook. Through small cracks, they could see the ominous clouds coiling away, retreating. For now.

Jerica knew the future of Andela hung in the balance, and the true battle was still ahead of them.

Chapter 7 — Elowen

Jerica stared at the goblet and the tri-colored stone. "Come on," she urged. "You've got to have some secrets left to share. We need to find a way to stop Emerus before he enslaves every dragon in the realm."

A soft knock at the door interrupted her thoughts. Jerica quickly tucked the artifacts away, instantly leery.

"I am a friend. Do not be afraid," came a soft female voice.

Both dragons shrugged. *I can become a warrior very quickly, if needed*, Sif communicated.

Zeira sniffed the air. *I do not detect danger.*

Jerica stepped over to the door and edged it open. The door creaked, revealing a stooped figure wrapped in a faded blue cloak, using a walking stick. As the stranger stepped into the room, Jerica caught a glimpse of piercing silver eyes beneath the hood.

"Who are you?" Jerica demanded, her hand instinctively

moving to her belt. "What do you want?"

The figure chuckled, a warm, rich sound that seemed at odds with their mysterious appearance. "Peace, young one. I mean you no harm." Gnarled hands reached up to lower the hood, revealing the weathered face of an elderly woman. Her silver hair was pulled back in a loose braid, and her eyes sparkled with wisdom and mischief in equal measure.

"My name is Elowen," the woman said, leaning on her wooden staff. "And I believe I may have some answers to the questions that plague you."

Hope flared as Jerica thought of their search for Skellig. Othos had promised that there were answers on the third continent … Her eyes narrowed. "How could you possibly know what questions I have?"

Elowen's lips quirked into a knowing smile. "The winds whisper many secrets to those who know how to listen. And they've been quite chatty about a young girl with extraordinary gifts and an even more extraordinary destiny."

Despite her suspicion, Jerica felt a flicker of optimism ignite in her chest. "You know about the Thunder King? About the ancient magic?"

"I know many things, child," Elowen replied. She looked about the crowded space.

"I can wait outside," Zeira said, backing toward the hastily constructed wall of vines and breaking through. *Gocri and I will summon Nuri. If you need help, just utter the words.* She sent a meaningful look toward Sif, as well.

Elowen breathed softly, settling herself into a nearby chair with a soft groan. "It is quite a large chamber when not filled with a fire dragon, is it not? Now, where were we? Ah—my knowledge of the true nature of the Eye of the Storm and its connection to the power Emerus Dinty so desperately craves."

Jerica paused. This was exactly what they needed—someone who understood the forces they were up against. But caution held her back. "How do I know I can trust you? For all I know, you could be working for the Thunder King himself."

Elowen's eyes hardened, a flash of steel beneath the

kindly exterior. "If I served that tyrant, do you think you'd still be standing, child? The oron stone you carry would be in his hands, and your village would be nothing but ashes."

Sif bristled, but in the form of a human child, her annoyance came across as a pout, more than anything else. The old woman's words sent a chill down Jerica's spine, but she stood her ground. "Then prove it. Tell me something only someone who truly understands the ancient magic would know."

A long moment of silence stretched between them as Elowen studied Jerica's face. Finally, the old woman nodded, as if coming to a decision. She leaned forward, her voice dropping to a whisper.

"The jhorium goblet you crafted is more than a simple magical artifact, Jerica. It holds a key—a key to unlocking the true power of the oron stone. And that power, when combined with the Eye of the Storm, has the potential to reshape the fabric of our world."

Jerica's breath caught in her throat. The two artifacts *had* reacted powerfully when they touched. The implications of Elowen's words were staggering. "But ... how can we possibly—"

Hope surged through Jerica, chasing away the despair that had clouded her thoughts. She leaned forward eagerly. "You can teach me? You can show me how to harness this power?"

Elowen's expression grew serious. "I can, child. But the path ahead is fraught with danger. The magic you seek to wield is ancient and unpredictable. Are you prepared to face the consequences of such power?"

Jerica hesitated, doubt creeping in. But then she thought of her family, her village—all the innocent people and dragons who would suffer if the Thunder King wasn't stopped.

Her jaw set with fortitude. "I am. Whatever it takes, I'll do it. The Thunder King has to be defeated, no matter what."

A slow smile spread across Elowen's face. "Very well, then." The elderly magician stood, turning to a dark corner of the large room. "This old edifice may seem to be ready to fall, but it contains many surprises."

She pressed two of the stone blocks at once, and a doorway appeared. "Come."

Shall I summon the others? Sif asked.

Not yet. Stay here and keep our mental connection open.

"Good idea," Elowen said with a mischievous grin. "One can never be too careful."

"You know about my mental connection with the dragons?" Jerica seemed stunned.

"I know many things, young one."

Jerica followed Elowen down a short flight of steps and through winding corridors, her heart racing with anticipation. The old mage's robes whispered against the stone floor as they descended deeper into what seemed like the heart of the hillside. She raised her walking stick to light candles along the way.

"The knowledge you seek is not easily gained," Elowen warned, her voice echoing in the narrow passage. "Are you certain you're prepared for what lies ahead?"

Jerica's hand instinctively went to the pouch at her hip. "I have to be," she replied, her voice steady despite her nerves. "Too much depends on it."

They emerged into a vast, circular chamber with mysterious light emanating from its domed ceiling. Towering bookshelves lined the walls, stretching up into the shadowy heights. Ancient tomes and scrolls filled every available space, their spines bearing titles in languages Jerica couldn't begin to decipher.

"By the Ancients," Jerica breathed, her eyes wide. "I've never seen so many books in one place."

Elowen chuckled, a dry sound like crackling parchment. "This is but a fraction of the knowledge our order has accumulated over the centuries. The secrets of the ancient magic are hidden within these texts."

Jerica approached the nearest shelf, running her fingers reverently over the spines. "Where do we start?"

"That," Elowen said, fixing Jerica with a piercing gaze, "is up to you. The path to understanding is different for each seeker. What does your heart tell you?"

Jerica closed her eyes, concentrating. She thought of the

jhorium goblet, of the oron stone, of the Thunder King's insatiable desire for power. Slowly, she opened her eyes and scanned the shelves. A slim volume bound in deep green leather caught her attention.

As she reached for it, Elowen's hand shot out, grasping her wrist. "Are you certain?" the old mage asked, her voice low and intense. "Once you begin this journey, there is no turning back."

Jerica met Elowen's gaze unflinchingly. "I'm certain. Whatever it takes to protect my people and the dragons, I'll do it."

Jerica carefully lifted the green leather-bound book from the shelf, her fingers tingling as they made contact with its worn surface. As she opened it, the binding crackled, releasing a musty scent that tickled her nostrils. The pages, yellowed with age, were covered in intricate symbols and diagrams that seemed to shimmer in the soft light.

"What is this?" Jerica whispered, tracing a finger over a particularly complex glyph.

Elowen leaned in, her eyes gleaming. "That, my dear, is the language of the ancients. It speaks of the essence of magic itself."

As Jerica turned the pages, the air around her seemed to thicken, charged with an energy she could almost taste. The oron stone in her pocket pulsed warmly, as if responding to the book's power.

"I feel … something," Jerica said, her voice filled with wonder. "It's like the magic is alive."

"Because it is," Elowen replied, a hint of pride in her voice. "Magic is not just a tool, Jerica. It's a living, breathing force that flows through everything."

Jerica's brow furrowed in concentration as she studied a diagram depicting swirling energies converging on a central point. "This reminds me of the Eye of the Storm," she mused. "Is there a connection?"

Elowen's eyebrows shot up. "Very perceptive. Yes, storms are one of the most powerful conduits of magical energy in our world. But understanding its true nature … that's the key to unlocking your potential."

"I assume the books must remain here, but may I take notes?"

Elowen produced a quill and paper. As the hours passed, Jerica immersed herself in the ancient texts. The soft scratch of quill on parchment and the occasional rustle of turning pages filled the air. Gradually, connections began to form in her mind, pieces of a vast puzzle slowly coming together.

"Elowen," Jerica said suddenly, looking up from her notes. "I think I understand. The jhorium, the oron stone, the Eye of the Storm—they're like ... focuses for different aspects of magic."

Elowen's eyes sparkled. "Go on."

Jerica's excitement grew as she explained her theory. "The jhorium represents creation, the oron stone balance, and the Eye ... pure, raw power. If someone could control all three ..."

"They would be unstoppable," Elowen finished gravely. "Which is precisely why the Thunder King must never succeed in his quest."

Jerica shivered as the full implications hit her. "But that means ..."

"It means, my dear," Elowen said, placing a gnarled hand on Jerica's much younger one, "that you may be the only one who can stop him. Your connection to the jhorium and the oron stone is no coincidence. You have been chosen for this task."

And she'd thought her friends simply voted her in.

She thought of her family back in Cael, of the dragons who had become her allies. The responsibility felt immense, but instead of crushing her, it filled her with more courage than ever.

"I won't let them down," Jerica said, her voice steady and resolute. "I'll master this magic, whatever it takes."

Elowen smiled, a fierce pride in her eyes. "Then let us continue. The path ahead is long and fraught with danger, but I believe in you, Jerica Barille. You have the potential to change the fate of our world."

Elowen pulled two more books from the shelves and they bent their heads over the ancient tomes once more. Jerica knew that her journey was only beginning, but for the first time since facing the Thunder King, she felt hope blossoming in her chest.

The candles flickered, casting dancing shadows on the walls of the hidden chamber, as mentor and student delved deeper into the mysteries of ancient magic, preparing for the battles to come. From time to time, one of the dragons checked in on her, keeping their mental connection brief. *I am well,* Jerica answered each time. And she discovered that she meant it.

The passage of time lost all meaning, until after several days of study and numerous lessons, Elowen closed their current text with a thump.

"And now … you've mastered days of book learning. Now it's time to put it into practice." They walked the corridors, climbed the steps, and walked out into the fresh air, Elowen leading the way.

Jerica stood in the center of a small clearing, lifting her blonde hair off her neck, her eyes blinking at the light. The jhorium goblet gleamed in her left hand, its gentle green glow soothing her. In her right, the oron stone thrummed with energy, its tri-colored segments flickering like a distant storm.

"Focus, Jerica," she told herself. "You can do this."

She closed her eyes, drawing on the knowledge she'd gleaned from the days of intense study. The ancient magic stirred within her, a wild, untamed force that both exhilarated and terrified her.

Slowly, she raised the goblet. "*Aeris volantem,*" she intoned, her voice barely a whisper.

For a moment, nothing happened. Then, a gentle breeze swirled around her feet, picking up leaves and twirling them in a mesmerizing dance. Jerica's eyes flew open, a gasp of delight escaping her lips.

"I did it!" she exclaimed, her face breaking into a wide grin. "I actually created a breeze and made the leaves fly!"

But her triumph was short-lived. As quickly as it had appeared, the breeze died away, and the leaves drifted to the ground. Jerica slumped.

"Don't be discouraged," came Elowen's voice from the

edge of the clearing. She stepped forward, her eyes twinkling. "That was an excellent first attempt."

Jerica shook her head, frustration creeping into her voice. "But it wasn't enough. How am I supposed to confront the Eye of the Storm if I can barely conjure a breeze?"

Elowen's expression turned serious. "The path to mastery is long and arduous, young one. But I have a challenge for you—one that will test not just your magical abilities, but your courage as well."

Jerica straightened, her curiosity piqued. "What kind of challenge?"

She pointed to a towering oak at the far end of the clearing. "At the top of that tree is a nest. In it, you'll find a single feather from a storm dragon. To truly harness the power of the ancient magic, you must retrieve that feather."

Jerica's eyes widened as she looked up at the massive tree. Its lowest branches were easily thirty meters off the ground. "But ... how am I supposed to climb that?"

"You're not," Elowen replied with a mysterious smile. "You must use the magic you've learned to reach the top. Remember, Jerica—the ancient magic is more than just words and gestures. It's about will, intent, and the courage to push beyond your limits."

Jerica swallowed hard, her grip tightening on the jhorium goblet. "What if I fall?"

"Then you must trust in your abilities to catch yourself," Elowen said. "This is the next step in your journey, Jerica. Are you ready to take it?"

For a moment, Jerica hesitated. The tree loomed before her, an impossible obstacle. But then she thought of her village, of her family, of all that was at stake. She took a deep breath and nodded.

"I'm ready," she said. "There's no other choice."

Jerica approached the base of the oak, her heart pounding. She closed her eyes, focusing on the energy flowing through her body and into the jhorium goblet. The ancient words Elowen had taught her whispered through her mind.

"Ascendere," she purred, willing herself upward.

Nothing happened.

Frustration welled up inside her, but Jerica pushed it aside. She took another deep breath and tried again, this time visualizing herself rising through the air.

"*Ascendere!*"

A faint tingling sensation spread through her limbs, and for a moment, she felt lighter. But then gravity reasserted itself, and she remained firmly on the ground.

"Come on," Jerica whined, gritting her teeth. "I can do this."

She tried again and again, each attempt leaving her more exhausted than the last. Sweat beaded on her brow, and her arms shook from the effort of holding the goblet aloft.

"Why isn't it working?" she cried out in frustration.

Elowen's voice floated to her from across the clearing. "Remember, Jerica. The magic responds to more than just words. What drives you? What fuels your drive?"

Jerica closed her eyes, thinking of the Thunder King and the threat he posed. But most of all, she thought of the power within herself, the power she knew was there, waiting to be unlocked.

"I am more than just a village girl," she whispered to herself. "I am the wielder of the jhorium goblet. I am the keeper of the oron stone. And I will not be defeated by a tree."

Jerica raised the goblet once more. "*Ascendere!*"

This time, the magic responded. A rush of wind swirled around her, and Jerica felt her feet leave the ground. She gasped, her eyes flying open as she rose through the air.

"I'm doing it!" she cried out in elation. "I'm actually flying!"

But her joy was short-lived. As she neared the first branches, her concentration wavered, and she began to fall.

Panic seized her. "No, no, no!"

Instinctively, she thrust out her hand, the one not holding the goblet. To her amazement, a shimmering platform of energy materialized beneath her feet, halting her descent.

Jerica stared at the translucent surface in wonder. "Did I … did I just create that?"

"Well done!" Elowen called up to her. "You're beginning

to understand. The ancient magic is limited only by your imagination and will. Now, keep going!"

Emboldened by her success, Jerica pressed on. She alternated between floating and conjuring magical platforms, like stairsteps, slowly but surely making her way up the massive oak. With each obstacle overcome, her confidence grew.

Finally, after what felt like hours, Jerica reached the top. There, nestled among the highest branches, was a small nest. And in it, just as Elowen had said, lay a single iridescent feather.

As Jerica reached out to grasp it, a sudden gust of wind nearly knocked her from her perch. She clung to the branch, her heart racing.

"Don't give up now!" Elowen's voice drifted up from far below. "You're so close!"

Steeling herself, Jerica stretched out her arm once more. Her fingers brushed against the feather, and in that instant, a jolt of energy surged through her body.

Visions flashed before her eyes—swirling storm clouds, flashes of lightning, the beating of massive wings. She saw the Eye of the Storm, a swirling vortex of raw magical power. And at its center, she saw herself, wielding both the jhorium goblet and the storm dragon's feather.

The revelation hit her like a thunderbolt. "The goblet and the feather," she gasped. "They're connected. They're both conduits for the ancient magic!"

As the vision faded, Jerica found herself settling gently back on the ground, the feather clutched in her hand alongside the goblet. Elowen stood before her, a proud smile on her face.

"You've done it, Jerica," the mentor said. "You've taken the first step toward truly understanding the ancient magic. But remember, this is just the beginning. The path ahead will be challenging, but I believe you have the strength to see it through."

Jerica nodded, a burning gleam in her eyes. "I'm ready," she said, her voice steady and sure.

She sensed movement and turned toward the west. Her team was there! Zeira, Gocri, Sif … even Nuri … all waited at the edge of the clearing. All wore proud expressions. "Well done, little one," Gocri said. "Your days of tutelage have been rewarded."

Elowen held up a hand. "We have one final lesson."

And we have information you'll want to know—about Skellig.

As Elowen led her back toward the ancient library, Jerica sent a questioning glance to her comrades. What had they learned about Skellig's imprisonment?

* * *

This was to be her final day of lessons, she realized. Inside the library, Jerica rose to her feet, the jhorium goblet in one hand and the storm dragon's feather in the other. A surge of energy coursed through her veins, making her skin tingle with newfound power. She turned to Elowen, her eyes shining with a mix of excitement and pride.

"I can feel it," Jerica said, her voice barely above a whisper. "The connection between these artifacts, the ancient magic … it's like nothing I've ever experienced before."

Elowen nodded, her expression serious. "With great power comes great responsibility, Jerica. The Thunder King will stop at nothing to obtain what you now possess."

Jerica's jaw clenched at the mention of Emerus Dinty. "Let him try," she said, her voice hard. "I won't let him hurt anyone else. Not my family, not the dragons, not anyone."

She paced the room, her mind racing with possibilities. "We need a plan," she mused aloud. "Something he won't expect."

"What are you thinking?" Elowen asked, watching her young apprentice closely.

Jerica paused, her gaze falling on the glowing oron stone resting on a nearby table. "The Thunder King knows about the goblet," she said slowly. "But he doesn't know about the storm dragon's feather or the full potential of the oron stone. We can use that to our advantage."

She turned to face her mentor, her eyes alight. "I need to practice combining the power of all three artifacts. If I can master that, we might have a chance against him."

Elowen nodded approvingly. "A wise strategy. But remember, Jerica, the Thunder King is not to be underestimated. His sword is enchanted with powerful dark magic, and he has many of the Spark dragons and valthans under his control."

Jerica's expression darkened at the reminder of the enslaved water dragons. "All the more reason to stop him," she said firmly. "We'll free the valthans and put an end to his reign of terror once and for all."

As she spoke, the artifacts in her hands seemed to vibrate with energy, responding. Jerica took a deep breath, feeling the seriousness of the challenge ahead. But instead of fear, she felt a growing excitement.

"When do we begin?" she asked Elowen, her voice eager.

The old mage smiled, a glint of pride in her eyes. "We've already begun, my dear. But the real test lies ahead. Are you ready to push yourself beyond your limits?"

Jerica nodded without hesitation. "I'm ready for whatever it takes."

As she spoke those words, a distant rumble of thunder echoed outside.

"Tomorrow," Elowen said, her voice grave, "we begin your final preparations. Rest well tonight, Jerica. You'll need all your strength for what lies ahead."

Jerica tucked the oron stone into one pocket, the dragon feather into another. She suddenly realized how weary she felt.

As Jerica lay on the small bed inside the stone chamber that night, sleep eluded her. She couldn't help but wonder what the Thunder King was planning, what forces he might bring to bear against her and her allies. Elowen had spoken of his having dark magic, provided with the help of an evil magician. Who was that sorcerer?

And did either of them have a hand in Skellig's imprisonment? She had put those worries aside for a few days, but now the urgency was back. She and her team needed to get their friend back before his situation became any more dire.

As she finally drifted off to sleep, her last conscious

thought was of all those counting on her. "I won't let you down," she whispered into the darkness, a promise to herself and to all those she fought to protect.

Chapter 8 — Prisoner

A chill whipped Jerica's hair as she peered over the ridge, her eyes scanning the desolate landscape below. The third continent lay before them, a barren expanse of rocky terrain and scraggly vegetation. A thousand meters away, a foreboding structure loomed on a hilltop overlooking the sea—the prison where Skellig was held captive.

Jerica turned to address her companions. "You did your homework well."

"Homework?"

"An assignment to do outside of school … Uh, never mind."

"I get the idea," Zeira said. "You had your lessons indoors, while we worked on this assignment."

"And you, Miss Jerica, did your *homework* well," Sif added.

Jerica sent them all a smile. "Once you described this horrible prison, Elowen helped me locate a diagram for the interior." She only hoped it was halfway accurate.

Beside her, Gocri yowled low in his throat, his massive dragon form tense with anticipation. "Then let's not waste any more time. Every moment we delay is another moment Skellig suffers at the hands of his dreadful sire."

Jerica nodded, her jaw set. As she opened her mouth to reply, a voice called out from behind them.

"Hold there, friends! I hope you're not planning on storming that fortress without me."

The group whirled around to face the newcomer. A tall, lean young man with dark hair flopping across his forehead strode toward them, a roguish grin playing at his lips despite the gravity of the situation. He wore neutral brown trousers and tunic, and a sword hung in a scabbard at his side.

"Who are you?" Jerica demanded, her hand instinctively moving to her waist.

The man held up his hands in a placating gesture. "Peace, my lady. I'm Hamish Aldebrand, and I'm here to help."

Gocri's eyes narrowed. "Aldebrand? Related to Zebulon the Seer?"

Hamish's grin widened. "The very same. I see my father's reputation precedes me."

Jerica studied the newcomer warily. There was something disarmingly amiable about his manner, but she couldn't afford to let her guard down. "And why exactly should we trust you?"

Hamish's expression sobered. "Because I've been fighting against the Thunder King's tyranny for months now. I've seen firsthand the devastation he's wrought across this land, the way he's turned dragon against dragon, realm against realm. And I won't stand idly by while he continues to divide and conquer."

There was a fire in Hamish's eyes that spoke of genuine passion and conviction. Jerica found herself wanting to believe him, but caution held her back.

"How did you find us?" she pressed.

Hamish chuckled. "Let's just say I have my ways. When you've been operating with an underground resistance movement for as long as I have, you learn to keep your ears open. Word travels fast when a group of humans and dragons start making their way across the continent."

Gocri rumbled thoughtfully. "And how exactly do you propose to help us?"

"Well," Hamish replied, his eyes twinkling with mischief, "I happen to have intimate knowledge of that fortress's layout and defenses. Not to mention a few tricks up my sleeve that might just come in handy for a prison break."

"How do you know—"

"As I said, sources." His expression became serious. "Reliable sources who have more to lose than you do, should I betray them."

Jerica exchanged a glance with Gocri. The Frost dragon's expression was unreadable, but she could sense his uncertainty mirroring her own. They needed all the help they could get, but trusting a stranger was risky.

After a moment of tense silence, Jerica made her decision. "Alright, Hamish. You can come with us. But know this—if you betray us in any way, you'll wish you'd never crossed our path."

Hamish's grin returned, though there was a hint of respect in his eyes now. "Wouldn't dream of it, my lady. Now, shall we go rescue your dragon friend?"

As they set off toward the prison, Jerica pondered. She couldn't shake the feeling that Hamish's arrival would change everything. Whether for better or worse remained to be seen.

The group moved swiftly and silently across the rugged terrain, using rock formations and vegetation to conceal their presence—the dragons gliding low on silent wings, the humans scouting the terrain constantly. Below the imposing walls, at the base of the cliff, the sea churned violently; Nuri was there, keeping watch. If their information was correct, somewhere within those imposing walls, Skellig was waiting for them. Jerica only hoped they weren't too late.

"So," Hamish's voice broke through her reverie, pitched low to avoid detection, "what's the plan once we reach the fortress? I assume you have one beyond 'charge in and hope for the best'?"

Jerica shot him a withering glare. "Of course we have a plan. We're not amateurs." Although she privately admitted that breaking out prisoners was a new game.

Hamish held up his hands in mock surrender. "Just checking. No offense meant."

Zeira spoke up. "We plan to use our telepathic connections with Skellig to pinpoint his exact location within the prison. From there, we'll infiltrate using a combination of stealth and distraction."

Hamish nodded approvingly. "Not bad. But you might want to consider the guard rotations. They change every two hours, with a brief window of vulnerability during the shift change."

Jerica's eyebrows rose despite herself. "You really do know a lot about this place."

A shadow passed over Hamish's face. "Let's just say I've had reason to study it closely. The Thunder King has taken much from many of us. And your friend isn't the only dragon imprisoned inside."

There was a story there, Jerica realized. One that spoke of personal loss and a depth of motivation she hadn't initially credited to the charismatic stranger.

As they crept closer to the fortress, the group fell into a tense silence. Jerica's mind whirled. There were so many potential pitfalls. Skellig was counting on them—and now, all the captured dragons were. Failure wasn't an option.

Suddenly, Hamish threw out an arm, halting their progress. "Wait," he whispered. "Look there."

Jerica followed his gaze to a small outcropping of rocks not far from the fortress walls. As she watched, two shadowy figures darted between the boulders, moving with practiced stealth.

"Scouts," Hamish whispered. "Those human soldiers are the Thunder King's eyes and ears. We'll need to take them out quietly if we want any hope of maintaining the element of surprise."

Jerica nodded grimly. "Zeira and I will handle it. You stay here and keep watch." She expertly climbed upon the dragon's back.

As she and Zeira soared forward, Jerica couldn't help but feel a twinge of admiration for Hamish's quick thinking and observational skills. Perhaps his arrival truly was the stroke of luck they needed to pull off this seemingly impossible rescue.

She pulled the jhorium goblet into her hands and uttered the spell: *"Ascendere!"* The two humans' shrieks were lost to the wind as they levitated upward and blew away on the breeze. Zeira kept Jerica close enough to the scouts to keep them airborne until they were more than a league from the fortress. She lowered them gently to two meters above the ground. When they dropped, stunned, neither appeared ready to jump right back up.

Hamish's eyes widened as he watched Jerica's return, her fingers tracing the intricate patterns on her jhorium goblet. The air around her shimmered with an otherworldly energy.

"By the ancient winds," he breathed, his voice a mixture of awe and excitement. "You possess true magic, don't you? I've never seen anything quite like it."

Jerica met his gaze, her expression a blend of wariness and curiosity. "You can sense it?"

Hamish nodded emphatically. "My father taught me to recognize the signs. But this … this is something extraordinary. The power you wield could be the key to turning the tide against the Thunder King."

Before Jerica could respond, a searing pain lanced through her mind. She gasped, stumbling slightly. Zeira, Gocri, and Sif wore intent expressions.

Zeira, Gocri? Is anyone there? Jerica—my kai … Sifula? Anyone?

"Skellig, is that you?" she whispered aloud, causing Hamish to look at her with concern. *We're all here. Where are you?*

The dragon's mental voice was weak. *Deep … beneath the fortress … enchanted locks, sapping our strength … other dragons. They're suffering, Jerica. Some may not last much longer.*

Jerica's heart leapt as she relayed the information to Hamish. "We need to move fast. They're restrained by magic."

Hamish's expression hardened. "We'll need to combine our strengths. Your magic, my knowledge of the fortress … we might just have a chance."

Jerica couldn't shake the feeling of Skellig's desperation. The usually proud and powerful Spark dragon had sounded so vulnerable, so defeated. She clenched her fists.

Hold on, Skellig, she thought fiercely. *We're coming for you. All of you.*

Ten minutes later, Jerica's eyes widened as they stood at the base of the imposing structure. The prison loomed against the darkening sky, its stone walls stretching impossibly high, crowned with jagged battlements. Watchtowers punctuated the perimeter at regular intervals, their flickering torchlight casting long, ominous shadows across the barren ground.

"By the gods," Zeira breathed, her massive red form crouched low beside Jerica. "It's like a fortress from the old tales."

Jerica nodded, swallowing hard. "How are we supposed to get past those walls?" she whispered, watching as armored guards patrolled the ramparts, their movements precise and vigilant.

Hamish crept forward, his eyes narrowed in concentration. "We'll need to be clever," he intoned. "Brute force won't work here."

"No joke," said Sif.

Gocri rumbled softly, his icy breath misting in the air. "Perhaps we could create a distraction? Draw their attention away from a weak point?"

"That could work," Sif agreed, her gray wings rustling as she shifted. "I could use my smoke to obscure their vision, give us cover to approach."

"What if I could use the goblet to disrupt their magical defenses?" Jerica suggested. "Create a gap in their coverage?"

Hamish's eyes lit up. "Brilliant, Jerica! Combined with Sif's smoke, that could give us the opening we need."

Zeira nodded, her earlier uncertainty replaced by pure grit. "And once we're inside, I can use my fire to clear a path if needed."

As they continued to plan, Jerica thought about the enormity of what they were about to attempt. It frightened her, but Skellig's desperate plea steeled her resolve.

"We can do this," she said firmly, meeting each of their gazes in turn. "We have to. For Skellig and all the others trapped inside."

Hamish placed a reassuring hand on her shoulder. "Indeed we can, young Jerica. Now, let's go over the plan one more time. We'll need perfect coordination if we're to pull this off …"

Hold on, Skellig. We're coming.

* * *

Jerica crouched in the shadow of a massive stone pillar, the jhorium goblet clutched tightly against her chest. Gocri and Zeira were on the ramparts, each using their special talents to disable the guards. She wasn't sure if she felt more sorry for those being frozen or those being singed.

Sif, for her part, had shrunk herself to the size of a young griffin so she could traverse halls and doorways along with Jerica and Hamish. The nauseating stench of Sif's most odorous black smoke billowed across the moat and drawbridge, obscuring their approach. Jerica could hear the guards coughing.

The water in the moat churned. *I am not rising up until that cloud goes away,* complained Nuri.

Just be ready to deal with any of the guards who don't run away on their own, Jerica instructed.

"Now," Hamish whispered urgently, his breath hot against her ear.

Swallowing hard, Jerica thrust the goblet forward, channeling her magic through the ancient artifact. A pulse of energy rippled outward, colliding with the prison's defenses. For a heart-stopping moment, nothing happened. Then, with a faint shimmer, a gap appeared in the portcullis. She concentrated, widening the space until the iron bars simply melted away.

"It worked!" Sif whisper-cheered, her smoky gray scales glinting in the dim light. "Let's move!"

They slipped through the opening, Jerica's legs trembling as they entered the fortress proper. A corridor opened before them, a labyrinth of shadows and flickering torchlight.

"Left or right?" Sif asked, her form shifting and condensing as she took on a more humanoid appearance.

Hamish closed his eyes, brow furrowed in concentration.

"Left," he declared after a moment. "I sense a concentration of magical energy in that direction."

As they crept forward, Jerica almost panicked. *What if we're too late? What if Skellig's already—*

Her thoughts were cut short by the sudden echo of footsteps. "Guards!" Hamish whispered urgently.

Without hesitation, Sif expanded her smoky form, enveloping the group just as two armed figures rounded the corner. Jerica held her breath, certain the pounding of her heart would give them away.

The guards paused, peering into the haze. "What's this?" one grumbled. "Damned fogbank must have moved in again."

"Let's check it out," the other replied, taking a step forward.

Jerica felt Sif tense beside her, ready to unleash the noxious version of her smoke. But before the dragon could act, Hamish said something under his breath. A faint shimmer passed over the guards' eyes, and they suddenly turned, marching back the way they had come.

"A simple misdirection spell," Hamish explained as Sif's smoke dissipated. "But we must hurry. It won't last long."

They pressed on, navigating the twisting corridors. Twice more they narrowly avoided detection, once by ducking into an alcove as a patrol passed, and again when Jerica used the goblet's energy to disable a magical alarm seconds before they would have triggered it.

"We're close," Hamish whispered as they approached a heavy iron door. "I can feel the dragon magic beyond, although it's fairly weak."

Jerica reached out with her mind, searching for any trace of Skellig. *There!* A faint flicker of familiar consciousness. "He's here, behind these doors," she confirmed, her voice tight with emotion.

As Jerica moved to direct the combined energy of the goblet and the oron stone toward the lock, a sudden cry echoed from behind them. "Intruders! Sound the alarm!"

Jerica's blood ran cold as she whirled to face the new threat, the jhorium goblet glowing ominously in her grasp. They were so close. They couldn't fail now.

"Quickly!" Hamish urged, his hands already weaving another spell. "Get that door open. I'll hold them off!"

As chaos erupted around them, Jerica silently prayed they hadn't come this far only to fall at the final hurdle.

The combined spell finally melted through the lock. The iron door creaked open, revealing an enormous, cavernous chamber filled with rows of huge cages. The sight that greeted them made her gasp, her hand flying to her mouth in horror.

Dragons of all sizes and colors were crammed into spaces far too small for their massive bodies. Many bore visible wounds; their scales dull and lifeless. The air was thick with the harsh smell of stale air and despair.

"By the old gods," Hamish whispered, his usual bravado faltering.

Jerica's eyes frantically scanned the cages, searching for a familiar yellow form. "Skellig!" she called out, her voice cracking. "Where are you?"

A weak rumble echoed from the far corner. "Jerica … here …"

She raced toward the sound, the others close behind. Skellig lay curled in a cage barely large enough to contain him, his once-vibrant scales now a sickly pale yellow. His black wings were tattered, and angry red welts marred his hide.

"Oh, Skellig," Jerica choked out, tears streaming down her face. She reached through the bars, her fingers gently brushing his snout. "What have they done to you?"

Skellig's eyes, though dulled with pain, fixed on her with recognition. "You came," he rasped. "I knew … you would."

Sif grumped, her tail lashing angrily. "We need to get them all out. Now."

Hamish nodded grimly. "Agreed. Jerica, can you use the goblet to boost my magic? We'll need all the power we can muster to break these enchanted locks."

Jerica wiped her eyes, determination replacing her shock. She raised the jhorium goblet, its green glow intensifying. "Whatever it takes," she said firmly.

As Hamish began chanting, Jerica felt the goblet's power surge through her. She directed it toward Skellig's cage, visualizing the lock shattering. With a resounding crack, the metal bars twisted and fell away.

Skellig stumbled out, leaning heavily against Sif for support. "The others," he wheezed. "We must ... save them all."

"We will," Jerica promised, her voice like steel. She turned to the rest of the group. "Everyone, focus your efforts. We're not leaving anyone behind."

They spread out, working feverishly to free the imprisoned dragons. Jerica moved from cage to cage, channeling the goblet's power to amplify Hamish's spells. With each freed dragon, the energy level rose.

As the last cage fell open, a deafening roar shook the chamber. The liberated dragons, emboldened by their newfound freedom, unleashed their fury. Fire, ice, and lightning crackled through the air as they vented years of pent-up rage.

Skellig, drawing strength from the collective dragon magic, straightened to his full height. His eyes blazed with renewed purpose. "It's time," he rumbled, "to show my evil sire the true meaning of power."

Jerica nodded, the oron stone in her pocket pulsing in harmony with the jhorium goblet. She felt a profound connection to Skellig and the other dragons, their shared willpower coursing through her veins.

"Let's get you out of here," she said, her voice ringing with authority far beyond her fifteen years. She knew that this moment—this union of human ingenuity and dragon might—would change the course of their world forever.

She turned to Skellig. "How did they get you all into this place? There must be an entrance larger than the one we came through."

"There is, in the side of the cliff by the sea. My own wonderful sire brought me here, himself." Electricity sparked from his wing talons, decimated as they were, as he thought of the monstrous Dym.

As the group moved toward the exit, a chilling laugh echoed through the chamber. Jerica froze, her hand tightening around the goblet. Skellig's wings rustled nervously, and Sif's breath misted in the air.

"Did you really think it would be that easy?" a silky voice purred from the shadows.

Hamish stepped forward, his face a mask of shock. "Lydia? What are you doing here?"

A slender woman with raven hair emerged from a hidden alcove, her eyes glittering with malice. "Oh, Hamish," she sighed, "always so trusting. The Thunder King sends his regards."

Jerica's mind clicked. "You're the one who's been feeding information to the enemy," she realized aloud, her voice quavering.

Lydia's smile was razor-sharp. "Clever girl. Yes, I've been playing both sides. And now, I'll be taking that goblet."

Skellig groused, positioning himself between Jerica and the traitor. "You'll have to go through us first."

"With pleasure," Lydia hissed, raising her hands. Dark energy crackled at her fingertips.

A fire dragon's voice cut through the tension. "We don't have time for this! Guards will be here any second!"

As if on cue, shouts and the clang of armor echoed from the corridor beyond.

"Sif!" Jerica called out. "A diversion, please?"

The smoke dragon nodded, her form already shifting. In seconds, she had transformed into a perfect replica of the Thunder King himself.

"This way!" Sif roared in the king's booming voice, charging toward the sounds of the approaching guards.

Chaos erupted. Gocri arrived and unleashed a blast of frigid air, coating the floor in treacherous ice. Zeira and Skellig spread their wings, providing cover as the group made a mad dash for freedom.

Jerica clutched the goblet to her chest, her heart pounding. She could feel its power humming, responding to the surge of adrenaline coursing through her veins.

"Hamish!" she shouted over the din. "Can you seal the passages behind us?"

The young man nodded grimly, his earlier shock at Lydia's betrayal hardening into something new. He vocalized a string of arcane words, and the stone walls groaned and shifted, collapsing in their wake.

They ran through winding corridors, the sounds of pursuit growing fainter. Jerica's lungs burned, but she pushed on, drawing strength from the dragons around her.

Suddenly, they burst into open air, a rocky ledge with a long drop to the sea. The deep night sky extended above them, studded with stars. Looking up, Jerica allowed herself to hope.

Then, a volley of arrows whistled through the air. Zeira roared in pain as one grazed her wing. Skellig retaliated with a blast of lightning that lit up the side of the fortress, scattering their attackers.

"We need to get airborne!" Gocri shouted. "It's our only chance!"

"Will Skellig be strong enough—"

"I can make it," the yellow dragon declared.

Jerica hesitated, looking at Hamish. The dragons could fly to safety, but what about them?

As if reading her thoughts, Sif swooped down, back in her normal dragon form. "Climb on!" she urged. "I can carry you both!"

With no time to argue, Jerica and Hamish scrambled onto Sif's back. The smoke dragon's powerful wings beat the air, and they were aloft, joining the others in a desperate dash for freedom.

Arrows continued to whistle past them, but with each passing moment, the prison fortress grew smaller and the arrows fell harmlessly to earth. Jerica allowed herself a shaky breath, her grip on the goblet finally relaxing.

They had done it. Against all odds, they had rescued Skellig and the others, who had scattered in all directions. She hoped they would all make it to their homelands. But as the wind whipped through her hair, Jerica knew their trials were far from over. The Thunder King now knew the extent of their power. Lydia would no doubt report everything she'd seen.

As they soared into the night, leaving the prison far behind, Jerica's mind was already racing with plans for their next move. The real battle, she realized, was yet ahead of them.

Zeira wanted to push herself to fly faster, but Skellig couldn't keep up in his weakened state. The cold night air stung her eyes, but they weren't safe yet.

"We need to find cover!" she shouted over the wind. "The Thunder King's forces could still be in pursuit!"

Skellig, flying close beside her, nodded grimly. "There's an island off the coast. It's mountainous and rugged. We might find shelter in the caves."

As they changed course, Jerica's voice called out from Sif's back. "Wait! I'm sensing something through the oron stone. It's … it's like a warning."

Zeira's stomach churned with anxiety. "What kind of warning?"

"I'm not sure," Jerica replied, her brow furrowed. "But it feels urgent. Like we're heading into danger."

Hamish leaned forward, his eyes scanning the horizon. "Look there!" he pointed. "Those lights in the distance. They're moving too fast to be natural."

Zeira squinted, her dragon vision piercing the darkness. She saw them too—pinpricks of light streaking across the sky, heading straight for them.

"Airships," Gocri gasped.

Jerica had a chilling reminder of the horrendous Cerebus machine Emerus Dinty had invented for the purpose of mining jhorium. The mind who created that could easily conceive of flying machines with which to kill dragons.

"The Thunder King must have alerted his entire fleet."

"We can't outrun them forever," Sif said, her voice strained from the efforts of changing her form several times and now carrying two humans. "And we can't fight them all."

Jerica tried to think. They were exhausted from the prison break, low on resources, and now faced with an impossible choice. "We need to split up," she said, the words tasting bitter in her mouth. "It's our only chance."

"No!" Skellig protested. "We just got back together. We can't separate now!"

"We have to," Jerica insisted, though it pained her. "Hamish and I will go with Sif and Gocri. Head for the island."

Zeira broke in. "Skellig and I will lead the airships away."

"But—" Jerica began to argue.

"There's no time!" Zeira cut her off. "The goblet and the oron stone are too important. We can't let them fall into the Thunder King's hands. Skellig and I will find you when it's safe."

With heavy hearts, they began to diverge. As Sif and Gocri peeled away with their human cargo, Zeira looked at Skellig. His yellow scales seemed healthier now, in the moonlight, his black wings showing up against the star-filled sky. But despite the boost in energy he'd received from Jerica and the jhorium, he was nowhere near his full strength yet.

"Are you ready for this?" she asked, trying to mask the tremor in her voice.

Skellig's eyes met hers, filled with a mix of fear and hope. "No," he admitted. "But we don't have a choice, do we?"

Zeira shook her head. "Let's give them a chase they'll never forget."

"On the bright side, they'll run out of whatever fuel they use long before we do."

She hoped that was true.

As they banked sharply to the east, Zeira's mind whirled with possibilities. How long could they keep this up? Where would they go? And what new dangers awaited their friends in those treacherous mountains?

The airships grew closer, their engines roaring in the night. Zeira took a deep breath, steeling herself.

* * *

Jerica clung tightly to Sif's smoke-gray scales as they soared through the night sky, the wind whipping her blonde hair. She felt torn between the urgent need to escape and the gnawing worry for Zeira and Skellig.

"We need to find shelter," Hamish's voice carried over the rush of air. "There's a cave system in those mountains on the island. It should provide adequate cover."

Sif banked slightly, adjusting their course. Jerica felt the dragon's muscles tense beneath her.

"What if it's a trap?" Jerica shouted, her mind conjuring images of the Thunder King's forces lying in wait.

"We don't have much choice," Hamish replied grimly. "Those airships won't give up easily. We need to get out of sight while we plan our next move."

As they flew over the water, the island in sight, Jerica looked down. She spotted a trail of bubbles, a sure sign Nuri was racing just below the surface, heading in the same direction.

"I hope we made the right decision," she voiced. "I hope Nuri isn't swimming into the same trap that we could be heading for."

Sif's voice rumbled through her body. "Nuri is amazing underwater. And Zeira and Skellig are formidable. They'll find a way back to us."

The dragon's words were meant to be reassuring, but Jerica couldn't shake the dread settling in her stomach. She closed her eyes, reaching out with her mind, searching for that familiar spark of connection with the others. But there was nothing—only an unsettling void where their presence should be.

As they crossed the shoreline and descended toward a narrow opening in the mountainside, Jerica's grip tightened. "Be ready for anything," she warned, gripping Sif's scales to keep her balance.

The cave mouth loomed before them, a gaping maw of darkness. Jerica took a deep breath, steeling herself for whatever challenges lay ahead. They had escaped one danger, but were they flying right into another?

Chapter 9 — Cavern

Jerica paced the dragon's lair, nervously running her hands through her blonde hair. She'd managed to get her team to safety and all back together again, and now the cavernous chamber buzzed with tension, its stone walls amplifying every anxious whisper. Hamish stood near the entrance, his tall frame casting a long shadow.

Skellig lay curled against one wall, exhausted. His color looked better, but she could tell his prison ordeal, followed by the frantic flight to ditch the airships, had taken a toll. He would need rest before they dared risk another confrontation with the enemy.

Hamish's dark eyes met hers, his usual smile replaced by a grim set to his jaw. "We need to get back to the first continent, our homeland."

"Because ...?"

"That's the only known source of jhorium, and that's what Emerus Dinty is after. Don't you see? He's come here because you came here. If he can't mine his own jhorium he assumed it would be easier to take yours."

"Well, that's not happening."

"Right. What I'm suggesting is that back home we have allies who can help."

Skellig raised his heavy head. "There are also enemies … my sire, for one."

"Dym has returned to the first continent?"

"Aye. The moment he dropped me into that godforsaken prison. He will be in the Spark region, working to help the Thunder King rise to power." The yellow dragon shifted his injured leg to a more comfortable position. "To defeat Dinty, you will also need to defeat Dym."

"Are you okay with that?" Jerica wanted to know. "He is your sire …"

"Not anymore. I feel nothing but loathing for that evil dragon after seeing his part in imprisoning all those dragons, and what he's done to Andela." He tucked his head under a wing and went to sleep.

"You and I," Hamish said, "we have no concept of what it must be like to have a father who treats us that way. I met Hallis on my last visit to Cael. Your father and mine … they are honorable men. Skellig never had that experience."

His mention of her father made Jerica think of her mother and sister and the villagers of Cael. Her eyes prickled and she nodded, understanding.

"He's right." Zeira crouched inside the cavern entrance, watching both inside and out. "Skellig has a kind heart. His sire does not."

Hamish stood straighter. "Travel between continents is time consuming, and time is something we lack if we hope to defeat this evil human and his cadre of soldiers and pack of dragons-gone-bad. It took me months to make the journey. We must set out immediately, if we have any hope."

Jerica gave a sly grin. "We have a better way. I will coordinate it with Nuri." She turned to the rest of the group. "Everyone should rest now, while there's a chance."

Gocri grumbled a little, but settled into a corner and tucked his wings. Sif, who had transformed to a puppy-sized version of herself because of the crowded space, curled up next to Hamish. Zeira kept her position near the entrance, but she did close her eyes.

Jerica tiptoed out and made her way quietly through the boulders, down the slope to the sea. She mentally reached out to Nuri and outlined her plan. Then she raised the goblet to her mouth and summoned Anahita.

* * *

Jerica stood at the edge of a withered forest, her heart aching at the sight before her. The air hung heavy with an unnatural stillness, broken only by the occasional crackle of dried leaves falling to the ground.

"What, in the name of the gods, has happened here?" she whispered, her fingers unconsciously reaching for her belt.

Skellig landed beside her with a soft thud, his yellow scales still somewhat dulled by his recent experience. "The Thunder King's power grows by the day," he rumbled, black wings folding against his sides. "Look there."

Jerica followed his gaze to a nearby stream. What should have been a vibrant, rushing waterway was now little more than a trickle of murky liquid. As she watched, a small deer approached cautiously, only to recoil as if struck when its muzzle touched the water.

"Even the animals can sense the corruption," Hamish observed, his voice tight. "How long before there's nothing left to save?"

Zeira, Gocri, and Sif exchanged looks. None seemed to have an answer.

Jerica closed her eyes, reaching out with her senses. The once-vibrant region responded with silence. "We need to act fast," she said, opening her eyes. "But how do we counter destruction this powerful?"

Skellig's tail lashed in agitation. "With luck, the other captured Spark dragons will make their way back home. Their combined power might be enough to—"

"How long do you think it will take for the Thunder King to get back here?" Zeira wanted to know. "Maybe we have some time to visit the villages and find out what they need?"

Hamish shifted his weight from one foot to the other. "I wouldn't count on it. You traveled to the third continent and back with magical assistance. He most likely can do something similar."

"And every moment we wait, his power grows stronger," Jerica decided. "Perhaps we could lure him into a trap."

The others stared at her in horror. "Bring him to us?" Sif asked.

Jerica shook her head. "Not yet. We aren't ready. I'll need to give this more—"

Before she could finish the thought, a chilling howl echoed through the dying forest. Jerica spun around, her heart thudding as she caught sight of glowing red eyes peering from the shadows.

"We're not alone," she whispered urgently. "The Thunder King has corrupted some of the animals as well."

Skellig's wing talons crackled with electricity. "We should move. This is no place to linger."

As they took to the air, Jerica's thoughts would not slow down. The task felt enormous, but she refused to let despair take hold. Somehow, they would find a way to restore balance to Andela—no matter the cost.

The dragons instinctively flew toward the sea, landing on a stretch of open shoreline. Jerica thanked them as she and Hamish climbed down from their rides. "We need to get Nuri's input too. The valthans have been every bit as devastated by this monster as every other region of Andela."

Nuri, are you here?

Of course. The sleek blue water dragon rose and pulled herself partway onto the smooth sand.

Jerica reported the damage they'd observed—the withered forest, the toxic stream. "It's like what has happened in the valthan home waters. I'm worried for all the people, the dragons, and other creatures here."

"Every moment we delay, the Thunder King's power grows stronger," Nuri observed. "Word among the remaining healthy valthans is that he has already left the third continent, shortly after we did."

Hamish nodded grimly, his dark hair falling across his forehead as he leaned forward. "We were afraid of that. We need to act now, before it's too late."

The dragons stirred restlessly, looking toward Jerica. Skellig, the eldest of the group, fixed her with his piercing gaze. "What do you propose, young one?"

Jerica took a deep breath. "We need to divide our forces. Some of us should focus on gathering intelligence about the Thunder King's movements, while others work on building our defenses by recruiting the villagers and others to help."

Hamish stepped forward, his lean frame radiating confidence. "I agree. We should play to our strengths." He turned to address the group. "Skellig, your knowledge of the region makes you our best scout. Can you and Gocri survey the eastern territories?"

The lightning dragon inclined his massive head. "Spark and Ice. Consider it done."

Jerica considered their other options. "Zeira," she said, addressing the fire dragon, "your flames could help protect vulnerable villages from the corrupted beasts. Would you be willing to set up a defensive perimeter?"

Zeira's eyes gleamed. "I'll burn any who dare threaten the innocent."

As Jerica and Hamish continued to assign tasks, she felt a surge of pride in their makeshift team. Despite the dire circumstances, they were united in their goal.

"What about me?" asked Nuri, her watery blue scales shimmering with anticipation.

Jerica smiled, an idea forming. "Your ability to manipulate water could be crucial. We need you to try and restore some of the dried-up rivers. It won't solve everything, but it might buy us some time and resources."

Hamish nodded approvingly. "Good thinking. And what about us, Jerica?"

She brushed her fingers over the goblet, feeling its power hum at her touch. "We need to find a way to use the jhorium against the Thunder King. It's time we took the fight to him."

Hamish's eyes widened. "That's incredibly risky. Are you sure?"

Jerica met his gaze, her expression firm. "We don't have a choice. The longer we wait, the stronger he becomes. We need to strike while we still can. But first we must survey the situation. Sif, you don't have an assignment yet, and I need a favor."

"Anything."

"In your natural size and form, you could easily carry both Hamish and me. Will you take us around to scout the land?"

In response, Sif extended a foreleg, giving them a ladder of scales to climb to her broad back.

The storm-ravaged landscape lay below them as they soared above withering forests and dried-up lakes, above villages where the gardens lay in ruins and the people were nowhere to be seen.

"It's worse than I imagined," Jerica gasped, her voice barely audible. She spoke to Sif. "Can you sense anything?"

"There's an unnatural charge in the air. The Thunder King's recruits have been everywhere."

Jerica nodded, closing her eyes and reaching out with her magical senses. The land's pain washed over her in waves, making her gasp. "It's like … like the earth is crying out for help."

"Where do we start?" Hamish asked, a wrinkle appearing between his eyebrows.

Jerica opened her eyes, a fearsome drive blazing in their depths. "We follow the pain. The areas where the Thunder King's power is strongest will be where the land suffers most."

As they ventured deeper over the damaged terrain, Jerica's connection to the jhorium goblet intensified. She could feel it resonating against the corrupted energy around them, almost as if it were trying to purify the land.

"Sif," Jerica called out, "can you use your senses to help me pinpoint the areas of highest concentration? I think the goblet is reacting to the Thunder King's power."

Hamish tapped her on the shoulder, nodding his head to the east. The well-known silhouettes of Skellig, Gocri, and Zeira were coming toward them. When they came alongside, Jerica used their shared telepathy to fill them in on what they'd observed so far.

It's the same in the regions we observed, Zeira told her.

I feel like the goblet wants to help us heal the land. Skellig, can you use your lightning senses to show me where the worst of the damage is?

The Spark dragon nodded, his yellow scales gleaming despite the gloom. *Of course. It's the least I can do to make up for my sire's treachery.*

As Skellig released controlled bursts of lightning from his wing talons, Jerica focused on the goblet's response. Suddenly, it pulsed with an intense emerald light.

"There!" she exclaimed, pointing to a withered grove of trees. "The corruption is strongest in that direction."

As they landed beside the grove, the air grew thick with malevolence. Jerica's skin crawled as soon as her feet touched the ground, and she could sense the others' discomfort as well.

"It's like walking into a nightmare," Hamish muttered, his hand instinctively moving to the sword at his side.

Jerica steeled herself, raising the goblet. "We need to see if we can cleanse this area. It might give us insight into how to counter the Thunder King's power on a larger scale."

She closed her eyes, channeling her energy into the jhorium goblet. As she did, she felt a fresh surge of power, different than she'd experienced before. The goblet's glow intensified, bathing the wasted grove in pure, green light.

"Jerica," Skellig's voice cut through her concentration, tinged with awe. "Look!"

She opened her eyes to see the withered trees slowly coming back to life, their branches reaching toward the sky as leaves unfurled. The air seemed cleaner, lighter.

"It's working," she breathed, excitement filling her. "But this is just a small area. How can we possibly cleanse all of Andela?"

Hamish placed a reassuring hand on her arm. "One step at a time, Jerica. This is a start, and it's more than we had before."

As the group marveled at the rejuvenated grove, Jerica's mind went over the possibilities. The jhorium goblet was indeed powerful, but was it enough to stand against the

Thunder King's growing threat? And at what cost would this power come?

She clutched the goblet tighter, its comforting warmth a stark contrast to the chill of uncertainty that raised goosebumps on her arms. Would she be able to harness this power and face the Thunder King head-on?

A bone-chilling roar echoed through the newly revitalized grove, shattering the momentary peace. Jerica's heart leapt into her throat as she spun to look around, the jhorium goblet clutched tightly to her chest.

"Corrupted beasts. I encountered them daily in the prison fortress," Skellig griped, his yellow scales bristling as he positioned himself protectively in front of Jerica. "The Thunder King's handiwork, no doubt."

Through the mist that still clung to the edges of the cleansed area, Jerica could make out dark, twisted shapes advancing out of the woods. Her breath caught as she glimpsed glowing red eyes and gnashing teeth.

"We need to move ..." Hamish urged, already backing away. "Jerica, can you use the goblet again?"

She gripped the goblet and concentrated. Nothing happened. She shook her head, frustration mounting. "I-I don't know how. It just happened before, I'm not sure—"

A massive, corrupted bear burst through the tree line, its fur matted and oozing a foul, dark substance. Skellig didn't hesitate, spreading his wings toward the beast with a thunderous roar of his own. Lightning crackled from his wing talons, striking the bear and sending it reeling.

"Jerica, focus!" Skellig called out as his sparks grappled with the monstrous creature. "You have the power within you. Trust in it!"

Closing her eyes, Jerica tried to reconnect with the energy she'd felt before. The goblet hummed in her hands, but the power remained elusive. "I can't do it!" she cried, panic rising in her chest.

"Yes, you can," Hamish's steady voice cut through her fear. "Remember the teachings and why we're here. Think of your family, your village. Think of all of Andela counting on us."

Images flashed through Jerica's mind—her parents' worried faces, her sister Theresa's kind smile, the villagers of Cael looking to her with hope. She thought of Skellig, risking his life to protect them, and of the other dragons who had placed their trust in her.

Taking a deep breath, Jerica opened her eyes and raised the goblet. This time, she didn't try to force the power. Instead, she let it flow through her, a conduit between the jhorium and the corrupted land.

Green light exploded outward, washing over the twisted creatures advancing on them. The bear Skellig fought let out an agonized howl as the corruption melted away, leaving behind a disoriented but normal animal. Other beasts fled, their red eyes dimming as they disappeared into the forest.

As the light faded, Jerica swayed on her feet, suddenly exhausted. Gocri was at her side in an instant, supporting her with his strong body.

"That was incredible," the dragon breathed, genuine admiration in his voice. "You're growing stronger every day, Jerica."

She managed a weak smile, leaning against his scales. "I couldn't have done it without you all. Your faith in me … it makes me stronger."

Hamish approached, his expression a mix of pride and concern. "We make a formidable team, that's for certain. But we can't linger here. The Thunder King will have felt that surge of power. We need to keep moving."

Jerica nodded, straightening up despite her fatigue. "You're right. We have to stay ahead of him." She looked at Skellig. "Are you ready for whatever comes next?"

The Spark dragon's eyes glinted with a fierce loyalty. "Always, Jerica. Whatever storms we face, we face them together."

As they set off, airborne once more, deeper into the heart of Andela's corrupted lands, Jerica felt a warmth in her chest that had nothing to do with the jhorium goblet—the bond between her and the dragons grew stronger daily. She only hoped it would be enough to stand against the Thunder King's relentless pursuit of power.

* * *

The dense, twisted forest beneath them suddenly gave way to a vast clearing, and Jerica's breath caught in her throat. Before them stood an imposing structure of weathered stone, its crumbling spires reaching toward the stormy sky like gnarled fingers.

"By the ancient winds," Gocri breathed, his icy scales bristling with anticipation as he and the other dragons sought nearby landing places. "I've never seen anything like this in all my centuries."

Sliding down from Zeira's back, Jerica approached the ruins cautiously, her hand instinctively reaching to touch the jhorium goblet. As she neared, strange symbols carved into the stone began to glow with an eerie green light, almost in time with her heartbeat.

"It's reacting to the goblet," she whispered, her voice a mixture of awe and trepidation. "This place … it must be connected to the jhorium somehow."

Hamish stepped forward, his eyes narrowed as he studied the intricate markings. "These runes, they speak of an ancient power. One that predates even the oldest dragons."

"You can read them?"

"Oddly, yes. I'm not sure how. I was never the most brilliant scholar."

Skellig snorted, a small spark of lightning dancing between his wing talons. "Nothing is older than dragonkind."

"Perhaps not," Jerica mused, running her fingers along the glowing symbols. "But this feels … different. Primordial, almost."

As her hand touched the outline of a particular rune, a rumbling echoed through the clearing. The ground beneath their feet trembled, and with a grinding of stone against stone, a hidden entrance revealed itself at the base of the ruins.

Jerica exchanged a look with her companions, her heart racing. "Well," she said, a nervous laugh escaping her lips, "I guess we're meant to go inside."

Sif lowered her head, eyes gleaming as she shrunk herself

to the size of a large human, complete with broad shoulders and well-developed muscles. "I'll lead the way. If there are any nasty surprises waiting for us, I'd rather they meet me first."

Skellig and Zeira stood guard at the entrance, united. "No intruders will get past us."

"Nor me," said Gocri, preparing to take flight for aerial surveillance.

As they ventured into the darkness, Jerica pulled out the oron stone, its tri-colored glow casting dancing shadows on the ancient walls. The air grew thick with dust and the history of untold centuries.

"Look at these murals," Hamish whispered, gesturing to elaborate paintings that adorned the corridor. "They seem to depict a great battle … dragons and humans fighting side by side against some unseen force."

Jerica studied the images, her brow furrowed. "It's like nothing I've ever seen in our history books. This must predate even the oldest records."

As they delved deeper, the passageway opened into a large chamber. At its center stood a pedestal, upon which rested an object that made Jerica's heart skip a beat—a sword, its blade seemingly forged from pure jhorium.

"By all that flies." Sif rustled her wings nervously. "Is that what I think it is?"

"It must have been here since olden times." Jerica approached the sword, her hand outstretched. As her fingers neared the hilt, visions flooded her mind—flashes of an ancient battle, a terrifying darkness held at bay by the combined might of dragons and humans wielding jhorium weapons.

She gasped, stumbling back. "I … I saw something. The sword, it showed me …"

"What did you see?" Hamish asked urgently, steadying her.

"A war," Jerica whispered, her eyes wide. "A war against darkness itself. And this sword … it was the key to victory."

Sif's eyes narrowed, a low rumble in her throat. "If that's true, then we can't let the Thunder King get his hands on it.

It's exactly what he wants. With it, he'd be unstoppable."

Jerica nodded, a new calm settling over her. "You're right. But maybe … maybe we can use it against him. Turn his own quest for power into his downfall."

As she reached for the sword once more, the chamber trembled, dust raining from the ceiling. A distant boom echoed through the ruins, sending a chill down Jerica's spine.

"We're not alone," Hamish warned, drawing his own weapon.

Sif crouched, ready to change into any form needed for battle. "Whatever's coming, we face it together. Jerica, take the sword. It has chosen you."

With a deep breath, Jerica grasped the hilt of the jhorium weapon. As it came free from the pedestal, a surge of power coursed through her, ancient knowledge flooding her mind. She turned to face the entrance, the sword glowing brilliantly in her hand.

"Get ready," she said, her voice steady despite her pounding heart. "I have a feeling our real challenge is just beginning."

Jerica's mind scrambled to process the flood of new information. She turned to Hamish. "We need to act fast. The sword showed me the Thunder King's weakness."

Hamish leaned in as he studied the glowing jhorium blade. "What did you learn?"

"His power comes from corrupted ley lines. A dark magician with great powers created the connection that allows Dinty to access them," Jerica explained, her voice low and urgent. "These murals on the walls have shown me approximately where to find them, although the lines themselves are invisible. If we can locate and then purify them using this sword, we can cut off his source of dark magic."

Hamish seemed pensive. "That's a solid start, but how do we get close enough without being obliterated?"

Jerica bit her lip, considering. "We'll need a distraction. Ley lines are energy. Skellig's lightning abilities could be key. If he and the other dragons can create a storm to rival the Thunder King's, it might draw his attention long enough for you and me to reach the central ley line nexus."

Hamish nodded, a wry smile playing at his lips. "Risky, but it just might work. We'll need to time it perfectly, though."

"And what about Emerus himself?" Sif wondered. "Even with his power source compromised, he's still a formidable opponent."

"And he probably still has the evil magician on his side," Hamish cautioned.

"True. But one thing at a time, okay?" Jerica's grip tightened on the sword. "That's where this comes in. Once the ley lines are purified, the sword should be able to absorb and redirect his remaining power. But ..." she hesitated, "it'll require getting dangerously close to him."

Hamish gave her a reassuring smile. "We'll all be right there with you, Jerica. You won't face him alone."

As they continued to refine their plan, a sense of purpose settled over the group. The enormity of their task was daunting, but the alternative—allowing the Thunder King to control the land and plunge Andela into eternal darkness—was unthinkable.

"We should move out soon, before our enemy learns of our discovery here," Sif suggested, twitching with anticipation. "I'll gather the other dragons and brief them on their roles."

Jerica nodded, her heart pounding. "This might be our only chance. We have to make it count."

As they prepared to leave the ancient chamber, Hamish caught Jerica's eye. "Are you ready for this?" he asked softly as he bent to cover the jhorium sword with a spell to obscure its color.

Jerica took a deep breath. "Yes," she replied, her voice steady despite the tremor in her hands.

The group emerged from the ruins, with the first light of dawn breaking over the horizon.

"No time like the present." Jerica hoped her voice conveyed optimism.

As before, the dragons took flight, with Jerica and Hamish riding aboard Sif. Skellig's job was to locate the ley lines by sending exploratory bursts of lightning that would, with luck, illuminate them.

As they crested the final hill, more devastation of the Thunder King's influence stretched out before them. The valley was now cracked earth with little evidence of the lush grasses once there. Zeira circled an almost-dry lake bed, pointing down. And there was Nuri!

At Jerica's instruction, Sif immediately landed beside their valthan friend.

"I had hoped to find you. I cannot stay," Nuri breathed. "There is much danger ahead."

"We're discovering that. We are hoping to locate some nearby ley lines," Jerica said. "Would you know anything—"

Nuri shook her head. The water dragon didn't look well, her color faded and her movements weak.

"These waters are polluted," Sif said, sniffing the lake. "You need to get back to the sea, as quickly as possible."

Nuri nodded and swam, circling back toward a river that must have once fed the lake abundantly with water from the nearby mountains.

Be well, friend. Jerica sent the message, with little hope that it would work. She clutched the goblet and repeated the words. Nuri appeared to swim a little faster, unless Jerica only imagined it.

In the distance, dark storm clouds roiled ominously over a foreboding fortress, their substance a murky greenish-gray.

Zeira landed beside Sif, her scales gleaming like fresh blood in the eerie light. "I don't like this."

Jerica placed a comforting hand on the red dragon's muscular neck. "According to the murals, the ley lines are somewhere near this place," she murmured, her eyes fixed on the fortress.

Suddenly, a bone-chilling screech echoed across the valley. The group froze, exchanging alarmed glances.

"That ... that sounded like Skellig," Hamish whispered, his face pale.

Zeira's eyes widened in horror. "No," she breathed. "It can't be. How could they—"

Before she could finish, the sky erupted in a dazzling display of lightning. A massive, form emerged from the fortress, electricity crackling along its wings.

Jerica's blood ran cold as realization dawned. "By the gods," she gasped. "It's him!"

As the monstrous, lightning-wreathed dragon swooped closer, Jerica feared their carefully laid plans had just been shattered. They now faced not only the Thunder King but also their own friend and ally. Had Skellig really been twisted into a weapon against them?

"What do we do now?" Zeira asked, her voice trembling with fear and anguish.

Jerica gripped her new sword tightly, her mind racing. Their mission had just become infinitely more complicated, and the consequences of failure even more dire. As Skellig drew nearer, she knew they had mere moments to act.

The choice they made in the next breath would determine everything.

Chapter 10 — Soldiers

Lightning flashed all around the yellow and black dragon, and then Jerica saw it—vivid green beams of light traversing the air.

Behold—your ley lines, my lady. Skellig actually winked at her. He had come through for them!

Jerica leapt into action, pulling the jhorium sword and praying this crazy idea of hers would work. *Sif! Get me to that spot, where the three lines meet—fast!*

The smoke dragon dipped her right wing and put on all the speed she could muster. But the lines simply vanished. There one minute and gone the next.

Jerica stared. Skellig came to a stop in mid-air, his wing talons emitting only tiny, fizzling sparks now. Sif circled once more. But no one could see the ley lines now.

Jerica glanced over her shoulder. Through gaps in the trees, she caught flashes of gleaming armor and raised weapons. The Thunder King's forces were closing in.

Suddenly, Skellig's voice cut through. "Look! Up ahead!"

Jerica snapped her attention forward. Through the tangle of vegetation, she spotted a flash of weathered stone, perhaps two kilometers from the huge fortress they had left earlier, more than a league from the oncoming soldiers. Her heart leapt.

"Everyone, this way!"

Sif veered sharply to the right, leading the group toward the crumbling structures barely visible through the overgrowth. As they drew closer, Jerica could make out thick pillars and moss-covered walls, the ruins of some long-forgotten civilization, now reclaimed by nature.

"Are you sure about this?" Sif asked, doubt clear in her tone. "It could be a dead end."

"We don't have much choice," Jerica replied grimly. "It's our only chance to lose them."

They burst through a curtain of dried-up vegetation, into a small clearing. Before them loomed the entrance to the ruins—a massive stone archway, its surface etched with faded symbols. Thick roots snaked across the opening, as if nature itself was trying to keep the ruins' secrets.

Jerica found herself breathing heavily. "Quickly, inside! Skellig, Sif—can you use your abilities to cover our tracks?"

The two dragons nodded, immediately setting to work. As the others hurried into the ruins, Jerica hung back, scanning the forest behind them. The soldiers were veering toward the north, but were still less than a league away.

Jerica faced her group. "Everyone take cover! Now!"

The large dragons settled, blending themselves into the surrounding landscape. She and Hamish scrambled through the archway, ducking under low-hanging vines, followed by Sif who was now the size of a house cat.

Inside, cool shadows enveloped them. The air was thick with the musty scent of age and decay. Jerica's eyes struggled to adjust to the dim light filtering through cracks in the stone above.

"What now?" Hamish whispered, his voice echoing slightly in the vast chamber.

Jerica stood very still, considering the options. "We need

to go deeper, find a place to hide until we're certain they are gone." She turned to the tiny Sif. "Can you sense any dangers ahead?"

Sif closed her eyes, concentrating. After a moment, she shook her head. "Nothing immediate. But there's … something. An energy I can't quite place."

"We'll have to risk it," Jerica decided. "Hamish, see if you can make anything of these markings. They might give us a clue about what we're dealing with."

As Hamish examined the walls, Jerica found her thoughts drifting to their nemesis. What drove Emerus Dinty to such lengths? How had a man once ridiculed become the fearsome Thunder King?

Jerica? Zeira's soft voice broke through her musings. *The soldiers are much closer now. What if … what if we can't stop them?*

We have to, she answered firmly. *Hold your places everyone.*

A human shout from outside made them all freeze. "Spread out! Search every inch of this hillside!"

Jerica paused, running her free hand along the rough stone surface near the archway. As if in response, the oron stone in her pocket pulsed with warmth. Jerica gasped, pulling it out to find all three segments glowing faintly.

Hamish sent her a questioning look. She pocketed the stone and touched a finger to her lips, signaling silence.

"What about these old ruins?" came another shout, this time much closer.

Jerica could almost feel the energy of the soldiers, smell their sweat on the air that wafted through the archway.

"Don't bother with that old place. We searched it two days ago."

"All right then, men, move onward!"

Jerica slowly let out her pent-up breath. When she pulled the oron stone out of her pocket again, it was glowing more fiercely than before.

"What is it?" Hamish asked, studying the stone's behavior.

"I'm not sure," Jerica sputtered. "But I think it's reacting to something here. Come on."

She forged ahead, the stone's glow intensifying with each step. Less than twenty meters on, they came to a heavy wooden door covered with carvings. Jerica pulled the new sword from her belt and touched the tip of it to the forged metal handle on the door.

"Oh, my …" Hamish touched her elbow and she looked upward, where he was staring.

Hidden among the carved designs of fruit and vines and plants appeared words: **Three dragon scales to enter.**

"Okay … what on earth does that mean?" She turned to him with questioning eyes.

Hamish took a deep breath. "My father once told me about something like this." He stepped forward to examine the lock on the heavy door. "Yes. Very much like this. I'll be right back."

He dashed back in the direction they'd come.

"Wait—" But he was gone. She prayed he wouldn't be caught by the soldiers, but he returned in less than a minute. And he was holding three dragon scales—a red one, a yellow one, and an icy white one.

"How did you—"

"Don't ask." He placed the yellow scale on top of the red one. "Okay, I begged them from our friends. But you knew that."

She nodded. "I guess I knew that …"

"The good news is that the soldiers have moved on without finding our hiding place. They've passed over the hill now and are out of sight." Now he placed the white scale under the red one. When it touched, the three clicked into place with an audible snap, and the little scale-sandwich began to shift its shape.

"A key! How did you—Never mind." Jerica watched as he inserted the key into the lock on the heavy door.

It turned and the door slid open without a sound. She and Sif exchanged a look of amazement. The door opened into a vast chamber, its ceiling lost in darkness above. Ancient pillars, worn smooth by time, lined the perimeter.

"By the First Flame," Sif breathed. "What is this place?"

Jerica's gaze was drawn to the far wall, where intricate carvings covered every inch of stone. "Look," she said, raising the jhorium goblet. In its green glow, the etchings seemed to come alive—dragons in flight, villages of humans, forests and rivers. Then there were storms raging, and at the center, a figure crowned in lightning. The wall depicted the history of Andela.

"The Thunder King?" Hamish suggested.

Jerica approached the wall, transfixed. As she neared, the oron stone blazed brightly, its light mingling with that of the chalice. The carvings began to shimmer, revealing hidden symbols beneath.

"This is it," she breathed. "The magical clue we've been looking for. The key to understanding the Eye of the Storm. If we know who created it, we may be able to defeat it."

"You don't believe Emerus Dinty created the Eye, do you?"

"Not at all. He had magical help of some kind. Remember? We heard there was an evil magician behind all this." Whatever secrets these ruins held, she would uncover them. "Show me," she whispered, pressing her palm against the cold stone. "Show me how to save our land."

Hamish stepped forward, bending to examine the carvings. "Fascinating," he gasped, tracing a finger along an intricate swirl. "These aren't just decorative. They're a code, a message left behind by the ancients."

Sif shifted restlessly, her small wings glinting in the dim light. "What does it say? Can it help us defeat the Thunder King?"

Hamish's brow furrowed in concentration. "It's about the Eye of the Storm, says it is a powerful artifact that grants its wielder control over the elements."

"Yeah, we kind of knew that."

Hamish paused, his expression darkening. "But there's a cost. The more power one draws from it, the more it corrupts the user."

Jerica nodded. "Makes sense. That explains the Thunder King's madness. But how is he connected to it; how does he control it?"

"The Eye isn't just an object," Hamish continued, his voice hushed with awe. "It's a living entity, seeking a host. It chose Emerus Dinty, bonding with him, feeding off his ambition and greed."

Sif snorted, a small puff of smoke escaping her nostrils. "Great. So, we're not just fighting a power-hungry tyrant, but some ancient, parasitic artifact too?"

Jerica placed a reassuring hand on the dragon's neck. "We'll find a way, Sif. We have to."

Suddenly, Sif's head snapped up, her nostrils flaring. "Wait. I smell something … old. Really old."

The small dragon moved purposefully around the chamber, her keen senses guiding her. She stopped at a seemingly blank section of wall, tapping her talons gently over the surface.

"There's something here," she said, her voice tinged with excitement. "A hidden compartment, I think."

Hamish joined her, examining the wall closely. "Clever," he remarked. "See these tiny indentations? They're pressure points."

"How do we activate them?" Jerica wanted to know.

Hamish walked back to the wall he had been studying. As Jerica looked on, his finger traced the symbols, his lips moved, memorizing something. Then he walked back to the indentations Sif had discovered.

With deft fingers, he pressed them in a specific sequence. A soft click echoed through the chamber, and a section of the wall slid away, revealing a small, dusty alcove.

Jerica's breath caught in her throat as she peered inside. Ancient scrolls, their edges crumbling with age, lay nestled alongside strange artifacts of gleaming metal and cloudy crystal.

"By the flames," Sif whispered, her eyes wide. "What are these?"

Hamish carefully lifted one of the scrolls, unrolling it with reverent hands. "Knowledge," he said softly. "The kind that could turn the tide of this war."

Jerica's fingers trembled as she unfurled one of the ancient scrolls, her eyes darting across the faded script. Suddenly, she gasped, her heart racing. "This … this can't be real," she whispered, her voice a mix of awe and disbelief.

"What is it?" Hamish asked, leaning in closer.

Jerica swallowed hard, her mind reeling. "It's a spell," she explained, her voice growing stronger with each word. "A spell that could weaken the Eye of the Storm and sever the Thunder King's connection to it."

The chamber fell silent, her words hanging in the air. Sif's scales rustled as she shifted nervously. "Are you certain?" the small dragon asked.

Jerica nodded, her eyes never leaving the scroll. "Elowen taught me how to read spells. It's all here. The incantation, the required elements ... even a warning about the risks involved."

Skellig, who had been keeping watch near the entrance, turned his head. "Risks?" he rumbled, his voice traveling through the dimly lit chamber. "What kind of risks?"

Pushing the thought aside, she refocused on the scroll. "The spell requires immense power," she explained, her voice hushed. "It could drain the caster completely, leaving them ... vulnerable."

Hamish frowned, pushing his hair off his forehead. "And I'd wager that's not the only danger," he mused. "The Thunder King won't take kindly to someone trying to strip away his power."

Jerica nodded grimly. "No, he won't," she agreed, thinking of Emerus Dinty's fearsome reputation. The image of his enormous tyrannical presence, radiating menace, flashed through her mind. She suppressed a shudder.

"But we have to try, right?" Sif insisted, her voice filled with tenacity. "We can't let him continue to terrorize Andela, to threaten everyone we love."

Jerica met the dragon's earnest gaze, feeling a swell of affection for her loyal companion. "You're right," she said softly. "The risk is worth it, if it means we can stop him."

She looked down at the scroll again, her mind racing. The chalice she had created of jhorium, the oron stone with its three glowing segments, the newly acquired sword, and the knowledge contained in these ancient texts—all the pieces were falling into place.

"We have a chance," Jerica said, her voice growing stronger. "A real chance to end this."

She thought of her village, of Cael and her family. Of the valthans, the Spark dragons who had been made stone-like by suspended animation, and all those who had been imprisoned with Skellig. Of all the innocent people suffering under the Thunder King's reign of terror.

She felt a surge of hope. They had come seeking answers, and they had found so much more. They finally had found a way to fight back.

A sudden chill swept through the chamber, and the light from the jhorium goblet flickered ominously. Jerica's skin prickled with goosebumps as she sensed an unseen presence lurking in the deeper parts of the chamber.

"Something's not right," she whispered, her eyes darting around the room. Skellig was no longer standing watch at the entrance.

Sif reacted instantly. With a low growl, she exhaled a thick plume of gray mist that swirled around the group, coalescing into a shimmering dome.

"Stay close," Sif commanded, her voice tense. "My barrier will shield us from whatever's out there."

Jerica watched in awe as the smoke solidified, forming an impenetrable wall between them and the rest of the chamber. Through the haze, she could make out shifting shapes in the darkness beyond.

"What are they?" Jerica asked, her heart pounding.

Hamish shifted his weight and drew his sword. "Ancient guardians, perhaps. Or something the Thunder King's men left behind to deter intruders."

Protected within Sif's smoky cocoon, Jerica pulled out the oron stone, watching its tri-colored segments.

"We can't waste this opportunity," she said, her voice steady despite her fears. "I need to try something."

With trembling fingers, Jerica knelt and placed the oron stone beside the chalice of jhorium. The green glow of the jhorium intensified, resonating with the stone's power. She then carefully positioned the jhorium sword between them, completing a triangular formation.

"What are you doing?" Hamish wanted to know.

Jerica took a deep breath. "The scroll mentioned amplifying magical energies. If I can channel the power of these artifacts together ..."

She closed her eyes, focusing on the tingling sensation in her fingertips. As she concentrated, she felt a warmth spreading through her body, a current of energy flowing from the artifacts into her very being.

"It's working," she gasped, her eyes flying open. The oron stone's segments were now blazing with light, and the chalice seemed to hum with power. "I can feel it—it's like nothing I've ever experienced before."

Sif's smoky head tilted in curiosity. "Be careful, Jerica. Power like that can be intoxicating ... and dangerous."

Jerica nodded, trying to maintain her focus as the energy surged through her. "I know. But we need every advantage we can get against the Thunder King. If I can master the spells ..."

She trailed off as a particularly loud thud echoed from beyond their protective barrier. The shadows seemed to press closer, hungry and menacing.

"We should move soon," Hamish warned. "Sif can't maintain this barrier forever."

Jerica gritted her teeth, pushing herself to channel more of the artifacts' powers. She had to master this. The fate of Andela might depend on it.

As the energy flowed through her, Jerica caught glimpses of possibility—visions of herself wielding magic beyond her wildest dreams. But with that promise came a warning, a whisper of the corruption that such power could bring.

She thought of the Thunder King, of how his quest for dominion had twisted him. "I won't let it consume me," Jerica vowed silently. "I'll use this power to protect, not to destroy."

With a final surge of concentration, Jerica felt something click into place within her. The flow of energy stabilized, no longer threatening to overwhelm her but instead settling into a steady, controlled current.

She opened her eyes, a newfound confidence radiating from her. "I think I've got it," she announced, carefully gathering the artifacts. "We should go. There's still so much to learn, but at least now we have a fighting chance."

Sif nodded, lowering the misty barrier. "Ready when you are. But stay alert—we don't know what's waiting for us out there."

Jerica's gaze swept across her companions, their faces illuminated by the flickering light. "The Thunder King won't fall easily, even with these new tools at our disposal."

Hamish's eyes gleamed with the excitement of a new challenge. "The spell you discovered, Jerica—it's the key. But we'll need to get close enough to him, in order to use it."

As the group began gathering their belongings, preparing to leave the relative safety of the ruins, Jerica carefully packed the artifacts, wondering what challenges awaited them beyond the sanctuary of these ancient walls.

They emerged from the ancient ruins as Skellig rose from his crouched position. He seemed stronger, Jerica noted thankfully. He took a look down toward the forest below and let out a mournful cry. "The land … it cries out in pain, worse than ever. Can you feel it, Jerica?"

She nodded, her eyes glistening with unshed tears. It was true. Since the passing of the soldiers, the plants and waterways appeared more desiccated than before.

Hamish stepped forward, even his youthful face seeming weathered. "This is why we fight," he said, his voice gruff with emotion. "To restore what was lost, to heal these scars."

Zeira's keen eyes scanned the horizon, her lithe form tense with anticipation. "We should move," she warned. "The Thunder King's patrols could return."

Gocri stretched his wings, ready for flight. Jerica straightened her spine, drawing strength from the others. "You're right. We can't linger here." She turned to address the group, her voice steady. "Every withered tree, every scorched field—it's a reminder of what's at stake."

"Jerica," Hamish called, interrupting her thoughts.

She turned to him. "You read the runes in there. What do you recommend as our next move?"

"The Caverns? You make the call."

She took a deep breath, centering herself. "Right. We head for the Whispering Caverns that connect the Crystaline Sea with the land of the region," she replied, her voice growing stronger with each word. "According to a book I found in Elowen's library, legend says they amplify magical energies. If we can harness that power and direct it toward both land and sea at once ..."

"We might just have a chance of saving both," Zeira finished, a fierce grin spreading across her face. "And I know the way."

Chapter 11 — Getaway

Unfortunately, their newfound optimism was short lived. A horde of corrupted beasts awaited at the bottom of the hill, their eyes glowing an unnatural crimson. Twisted creatures with matted fur and razor-sharp claws, their bodies pulsed with dark magic.

"Not this again!" Zeira shouted.

Skellig's yellow form tensed beside her, his injuries from their previous battle still evident in the way he favored his left side. But anger blazed in the old Spark dragon's eyes as he spread his midnight-black wings.

"Stand your ground!" he bellowed, his voice carrying over the din. "We've faced worse than this rabble!"

Zeira wished she shared his confidence. Her gaze darted to Jerica and Hamish, the two humans looking impossibly small and fragile in the face of the oncoming horde. She felt a surge of protectiveness, mingled with uncertainty. How could she keep them safe when she could barely protect herself?

"Zeira, focus!" Sif's sharp command cut through her spiraling thoughts. Back in her full size, the smoke dragon's massive gray wings unfurled as she positioned herself at the front of their group. "Remember our plan. We fight as one!"

Skellig's wing talons began to spark and crackle, drawing Zeira's attention. Despite his injuries, raw power emanated from the ancient dragon as he raised his wings high.

"Brace yourselves!" he roared.

With a deafening crack, bolts of brilliant blue-white lightning erupted from Skellig's talons. They arced through the air, striking the lead beasts with pinpoint accuracy. The corrupted creatures howled in agony as electricity coursed through their twisted forms, their bodies convulsing before collapsing to the ground in smoking heaps.

Jerica gasped, awed by the display of elemental fury. But her amazement quickly turned to alarm as she realized the lightning wasn't just striking their enemies—it was forming a crackling barrier of energy around their group.

"Skellig, what are you doing?" she cried, wincing as the air itself seemed to vibrate with power. "You're still injured!"

The Spark dragon's eyes were bright with pain and exertion, but his voice remained steady. "Buying us time," he gritted out. "This won't hold them for long. A plan—anyone?"

Hamish stepped forward, the new sword gleaming as he gripped it tightly. "I can help hold them off. My father taught me more than just scholarship."

Jerica's mind raced. She was supposed to be their leader. How had she let these horrid creatures get the jump on them? The beasts beyond Skellig's barrier howled and clawed at the crackling energy, their corrupted forms pressing ever closer. Sif came to her rescue with an idea, using smoke and fire. It seemed as plausible as anything, at least it would give them time to take to the air and escape.

"Now, Sif!" Jerica shouted.

The massive smoke dragon unleashed a torrent of thick, black smoke that engulfed the corrupted beasts, their snarls turning to choked gasps as they struggled to breathe.

They watched in awe as Sif's smoke rendered the beasts

immobile, their twisted forms collapsing to the ground. But she knew they didn't have much time.

"Impressive," Skellig wheezed, his wings trembling from the effort of maintaining the barrier.

"Good job. Now I've got them." Zeira steeled herself, feeling the familiar heat building within her core. With a deep breath, Zeira channeled all her fiery energy into a blazing inferno. She felt the flames surge through her body, gathering at the base of her tail before erupting in a massive torrent of fire.

The blaze shot forth, igniting Sif's smoke and creating a wall of searing flame that incinerated the immobilized beasts. The heat was so intense that Zeira could feel it singeing her scales, but she pushed through the pain, focusing on clearing a path for their escape.

Skellig's eyes were wide with awe. "That was ... quite something, Zeira."

Sif nodded in agreement. "You've grown stronger," she observed.

Zeira felt a wave of exhaustion wash over her, but she extended a foreleg so Jerica and Hamish could take their places. "We can worry about that later," she said, her voice hoarse from the exertion.

"Right now, we need to move. More of them are surely coming."

The acrid stench hung heavy in the air, making Jerica's eyes water and her throat burn. She coughed, struggling to breathe through the thick haze that surrounded them. The young girl's blonde hair was matted with sweat and grime.

She reached for the jhorium goblet and felt her energy return. The new sword, safely tucked at Hamish's side, held a similar glow. Each of the dragons seemed poised for action.

"Be ready!" Jerica shouted to her companions, her voice carrying an authority beyond her years.

She raised her arms, fingers splayed wide, and a powerful gust of wind erupted from her palms. The sudden tempest whipped around them, clearing away the lingering smoke and debris. As the air cleared, she could hear her friends gasping in relief, finally able to breathe freely.

"Ready to take flight? We're off to the Whispering Caverns!"

"By the gods, Jerica!" Hamish exclaimed, his dark hair flying in the wind as he turned to her with a mixture of awe and his characteristic devilish grin. "When did you learn to do that?"

"All part of my schooling with Elowen," she said with a blush.

But before Zeira cleared the ground, four more of the corrupted beasts rushed at them from behind, grabbing the tip of Zeira's wing in their massive jaws. Hamish swung his leg over and slid down the dragon's side, meeting the four creatures with the jhorium sword drawn.

Jerica watched as Hamish engaged the first beast, his blade a blur of motion. He ducked under a massive paw swipe, retaliating with a swift strike that left the creature howling in pain. Two more beasts converged on him, but Hamish seemed to anticipate their every move, his father Zebulon's mystical teachings clearly evident in his fighting style.

Jerica couldn't help but marvel at the transformation. Gone was the scholarly young man who had spent countless hours poring over ancient tomes in the capital's library. In his place stood a warrior, moving with a grace and precision that spoke of hidden depths.

"Should we help him?" Jerica asked, her hand hovering over the jhorium goblet, ready to unleash its power if needed.

Zeira shook her head. "Watch," she rumbled, her voice filled with quiet admiration. "The son of Zebulon is more than capable."

As if to prove Zeira's point, Hamish executed a dazzling spin, his green blade catching the sunlight as it arced through the air. In one fluid motion, he dispatched the remaining beasts, their forms crumpling to the ground.

Breathing heavily, Hamish turned back to the group, his impish smile making a reappearance. "Well," he said, wiping his blade against his pants, "that was invigorating. Shall we press on?"

Jerica couldn't help but laugh, the tension of the moment broken by Hamish's casual bravado. As he mounted the dragon's back once again, she felt hopeful. They would soon be out of this desolate valley and onward to the Whispering Caverns, where she planned to practice and enhance the magic she'd studied. With its help, they could set up their own confrontation with the Thunder King rather than letting him and his minions continue to surprise them.

The moment of victory was short-lived. Skellig suddenly faltered. His massive yellow form swayed, wings drooping as if they'd become too heavy to bear.

"Skellig!" Jerica cried, her heart leaping into her throat.

The Spark dragon's eyes, usually bright, were now dulled with pain. He opened his mouth as if to speak, but only a weak rumble escaped before he dipped back to the earth below. With a thunderous crash that shook the ground, Skellig collapsed.

The others landed immediately and Jerica rushed forward, her hand instinctively reaching for the oron stone. But before she could act, a gray blur swept past her.

Sif, her smoke-like form billowing and reforming, reached Skellig first. Without hesitation, she expanded her form, massive wings unfurling like storm clouds. In one fluid motion, she enveloped Skellig, creating a protective cocoon around his prone form.

"Stay back," Sif's voice resonated from within the smoky barrier. "He needs space."

Hamish, still gripping his bloodied sword, stepped closer to Jerica. "Will he be alright?" he asked, his bravado replaced by genuine concern.

Jerica bit her lip, her eyes fixed on the smoke-shrouded dragons. "I don't know," she admitted. "With all he's been through … he must have been hurt more than we realized."

Inside the protective barrier, Skellig's labored breathing echoed. Each intake of air sounded like a struggle, reminding Jerica of the fierce battle they'd just endured.

"Skellig," Sif's voice was gentle. "Rest now. You're safe."

A weak rumble responded, barely audible. "Sif … I … I'm sorry. I should be stronger than this."

"Hush," Sif admonished, her smoky form rippling with what seemed like concern and fondness. "You fought bravely.

Your mother would be proud."

At the mention of his mother, Skellig's breathing seemed to ease slightly. Jerica felt a pang in her heart, remembering the Spark dragon's complicated family dynamics.

"Do you think …" Jerica whispered to Hamish, "do you think Skellig's injuries have something to do with what happened when he vanished? When the bad guys took him?"

Hamish's jaw tightened. "It's possible. Who knows what they did to him while he was their prisoner."

As they watched, helpless, Sif's protective barrier pulsed with an ethereal golden light and a soothing scent of something herbal. It was as if the essence of her smoke was infusing Skellig with strength.

"Sif," Skellig's voice came again, stronger this time. "Thank you. I … I've never had anyone shield me like this before."

The smoke dragon's response was gruff, but tinged with warmth. "Well, get used to it. We're in this together now, Spark dragon."

Jerica felt a surge of hope. The bond between dragon and human was powerful, but seeing the connection between these two vastly different dragons was equally inspiring. Zeira's scales glimmered in the fading light, her tail lashing with nervous energy.

Jerica stood up tall. "We can't stay here. The Thunder King's forces could return at any moment. We need to press on, find somewhere defensible."

"But Skellig—"

"I know," Zeira cut in, her tone softening slightly. "We're all exhausted, all injured. If we don't keep moving, we're easily attacked."

Sif's smoky form billowed in agreement. "The young one's right. We've no choice but to push forward."

Zeira felt a flicker of pride at Sif's words, but it was quickly overshadowed by memories. She'd never imagined herself as a leader, especially not of such a diverse group. The insecurity that had plagued her since Skellig's capture threatened to resurface, but she pushed it down ruthlessly.

"Jerica," Sif said, turning to their young human. "Can

you do anything for Skellig's wounds as we move?"

Jerica nodded, her blue eyes shining. "I … I think so. My magic's been growing stronger. I can try to heal him on the go." She'd been holding the oron stone, warming her hands with it.

As if in response to her words, Jerica's hands began to glow with a soft, soothing light. She placed them gently on Skellig's flank, and the Spark dragon let out a low rumble of relief.

"It's working," Skellig said, his yellow scales seeming to brighten slightly. "I can feel my strength returning."

The human girl's face was a mask of concentration, her blonde hair falling across her face as she channeled the magic into him.

"You're doing great, Jerica," Gocri encouraged, his gruff voice warm with pride. "Just pace yourself. We've got a long way to go."

"Do you think you can fly?" Jerica asked Skellig.

"I shall stay beneath him, in the air," Sif suggested. "If he becomes fatigued and needs a place to rest, he can settle onto my back."

"And I'll ride on his neck, with the oron stone's healing powers at the ready," Jerica assured them.

As the group took to the air, Zeira took point, her senses on high alert for any sign of danger. She could feel the heat building in her core, ready to expel a blast of fire at a moment's notice. The thought of using her unique ability—expelling fire from her rear end—brought a fleeting smile to her face. It wasn't the most dignified power, but it had saved them more than once.

"Zeira," Skellig called out weakly from behind her. "I … I'm sorry I got captured. I should have been stronger."

Zeira felt her heart clench at the pain in his voice. She glanced back, meeting Skellig's eyes. "It wasn't your fault," she said firmly. "We're just glad to have you back. And when we face Dym and the Thunder King, we'll make them pay for what they did to you."

As they pressed on above the rugged terrain, Zeira's mind went to thoughts of her mother, Gynnyth, and the strength of the Phoenix caste. She thought of Fire Lord Darazok Aeogan and the faith he'd placed in her.

"We'll make it through this," Zeira whispered. "We have to."

Hamish's keen eyes scanned the craggy landscape below, one hand always on the hilt of his sword. The scholarly son of Zebulon had never imagined he'd be in such a perilous situation, but his father's teachings had prepared him well. Every shadow, every shifting rock caught his attention as he maintained his vigilant watch for any storm or any creature that might become airborne and pursue them.

"Anything out there, Hamish?" Jerica called, her voice taut as she continued to tend to Skellig's wounds.

He shook his head, dark hair falling across his forehead. "Nothing yet, but we can't be too careful. The Thunder King's minions could be anywhere."

As if on cue, a low rumble echoed through the ravine. Hamish's grip tightened on his sword, his mind racing through the mystical knowledge he'd gleaned from his father. "Everyone, stay alert," he warned, his usually jovial face set in a grim straight line.

Behind him, Skellig stirred. The Spark dragon's yellow scales gleamed dully in the fading light as he struggled to remain flying. Hamish turned, concern evident on his face.

"Skellig, are you sure you're okay?" he asked, eyeing the dragon's injuries.

Skellig's black wings unfurled slightly farther, a spark of electricity dancing between his talons. "I'll be fine," he moaned.

Hamish nodded, understanding the importance of their mission. He couldn't help but admire the dragon's resilience, especially knowing the complex relationship Skellig had with his own father. It made Hamish grateful for Zebulon's guidance and support.

"Just don't push yourself too hard. Rest against Sif if you need to," Hamish cautioned, offering a small, crooked smile. "We need you at your best when we face the Thunder King."

Skellig's eyes met Hamish's, a flicker of gratitude passing between them. "I won't let you down," the dragon promised.

"Not again."

As if the mention of their enemy's name conjured something, a piercing shriek came from below.

"We can't afford to check it out," Jerica declared. "Let's press on."

As they continued to move forward, Jerica worried, especially about Skellig's weakened state. She glanced down at the yellow dragon's head, noting the pain in his eyes despite his labored breathing.

"How are you holding up, Skellig?"

The Spark dragon managed a wry smile. "I've been better," he admitted. "But don't worry about me. I've faced worse in my twelve hundred years."

Chapter 12 — Tension!

The barren wasteland seemed to stretch endlessly, a sea of cracked earth and jagged rocks beneath a bruised sky. Jerica kept an anxious eye ahead, even as she continued to apply oron magic to Skellig's injuries.

Where's the sea? How much farther to the caverns?

Zeira whirled around, her scales bristling with frustration. "I do not know. Okay? I just don't know!"

Jerica immediately felt terrible. She hadn't realized their telepathic channel was open.

Sif's massive gray wings unfurled as she loomed beside the smaller red dragon. "It's a natural question, Zeira. We're all just a *little* bit tired."

Gocri's rumbling voice cut through the tension. "Both of you, calm yourselves," the Frost dragon urged, his icy breath misting in the air. "This infighting serves no one but our enemies."

Gocri was right, but the situation pressed down on Zeira

like a physical force. The image of Skellig, when he vanished during his sire's attack, haunted her dreams, a constant reminder of how badly she'd failed the last time.

"We've been fleeing for weeks," Sif interjected. "Our efforts have amounted to nothing but exhaustion and defeat."

The smoke dragon's words struck a chord within Jerica. She'd been thinking the same thing, though she'd been afraid to voice it aloud. What if all their struggles were for naught? What if they were simply delaying the inevitable?

"Perhaps ..." Skellig's voice was barely above a whisper, his yellow scales dull with fatigue. "Perhaps we were never meant to win this war."

A hush fell over the group, the Spark dragon's words hanging heavy in the air. Jerica felt a chill run down her spine, colder than Gocri's frosty breath. She wanted to deny any thought of defeat, to rally her companions with words of hope. But doubt gnawed at her heart, insidious as the Thunder King's storm creatures.

"No," Zeira said, her voice hoarse. "I refuse to believe that. We were chosen for a reason. Our regions, our people, they're counting on us."

Sif snorted, a plume of black smoke rising from her nostrils. "Pretty words, Zeira. But words won't stop the Thunder King's lightning bolts or his armies of beasts and storm creatures."

Zeira's claws flexed, itching to lash out at someone. But she forced herself to remain calm, knowing that giving in to her anger would only prove Sif right.

"Then what do you suggest?" she asked, struggling to keep her voice level. "That we give up? Abandon our homes and our families to the Thunder King's wrath?"

"Ladies, please." Hamish kept his voice calm. "Bickering amongst ourselves is not the answer. There is no turning back now, so we have to work together."

Gocri shifted uncomfortably, his massive form casting long shadows in the fading light. "We've lost so much already," he groused. "How can we hope to stand against such power?"

Zeira suddenly felt a flicker of sympathy for the Frost dragon. She knew he was thinking of his home in Bliss, of

Queen Freriss and the subjects he'd sworn to protect. As she was thinking of Blaze and her own kind. "I apologize. My words were uncalled for."

"Gocri and Hamish are right. We must stand together," Jerica said firmly, drawing herself up to sit tall. "We've got each other, and the strength of our regions behind us. We can't give up now, not when so much is at stake." What she was careful not to say was that they'd been outmatched at every turn.

A distant rumble sounded.

Skellig's head snapped up, his dull scales summoning energy. "Storm creatures," he hissed, lightning dancing between his wing talons.

Jerica's heart pounded as she scanned the horizon. Dark shapes were moving against the bruised sky, growing larger with each passing moment.

And then she spotted a glimmer of moonlight on the ocean, no more than four or five leagues ahead.

"We're almost there," she promised. "Quickly! Bear to the right."

Nuri, are you there? Nuri can you hear me?

No response.

Nuri, we're going to the Whispering Caverns. If you can hear me, meet us there. The gods be willing that you can.

I can, came the response.

Jerica felt a little embarrassed that her last, desperate thought had been transmitted, but she was thrilled to hear their friend's valthan voice.

One by one, the dragons soared downward to land on a wide, sandy beach, the stormy cloud formations now on the far horizon behind them. Only meters away stood the smooth rock formations that formed the Whispering Caverns. Suddenly, the softly lapping waves of the Crystaline Sea erupted in foamy crests. Their valthan comrade pulled herself up on the shore.

Nuri's sinuous form coiled tighter, her blue scales quivering with barely contained agitation. Jerica noticed that her color, as Skellig's, had faded noticeably. Her eyes, usually calm as deep ocean waters, now churned with inner turmoil.

She turned to face the group, her voice carrying the same weary dejection the rest of them were feeling, as she filled them in on the valthans' desperate situation under the sea. "I feel that I need to be in Hythos, supporting my queen."

Jerica stepped forward, her slight human form dwarfed by the majestic creatures surrounding her. She walked over and placed a hand on the scales of Nuri's slender neck.

"Nuri," Jerica began, her voice steady despite the gravity of the situation. "I understand your dilemma. But remember why we're here. The Thunder King threatens not just the land, but the seas as well. If we fail—"

Nuri's usual calm demeanor cracked. "But while we struggle here, my people suffer. I can feel their pain, their fear, calling to me across the waves."

Jerica's hand instinctively went to the oron stone in her pocket. Its tri-colored segments—red, blue, and green—seemed to pulse. She took a deep breath, centering herself.

"We need you, Nuri," Jerica said, her voice gaining strength. "Your speed, your knowledge of the waters—they're invaluable to our cause. And think of what your absence would do to our unity, our strength as a team."

Gocri rumbled in agreement. "The human speaks truth, water-sister. Your departure would leave a void not easily filled."

Nuri's form undulated; her internal conflict visible in every ripple of her scales. "And what of the void I leave in my own realm?" she asked, her voice barely above a whisper.

Jerica stepped closer, placing both hands on Nuri's cool, smooth scales. The contact sent a shiver through her, a reminder of the vast differences between them, yet also of the bond they'd forged.

"By staying with us, by fighting the Thunder King," Jerica said, her eyes locked with Nuri's, "you're protecting your people too. Every victory we achieve here ripples out to all the realms. Your presence makes those victories possible."

Skellig, who had been unusually quiet, suddenly reared up, his yellow scales glinting in the dim light. "While we bicker, the Thunder King's forces grow stronger. Our indecision is his greatest weapon!"

The Spark dragon's outburst sent a jolt through the group. Jerica felt the hair on her arms stand on end, sensing the electric charge building in Skellig's wing talons.

"Skellig's right," Zeira said, her voice tight with frustration. "We're letting our personal struggles cloud our judgment. Every moment we spend arguing is a moment Emerus Dinty uses to strengthen his hold on the realms."

As if summoned by the mention of his name, a distant rumble shook the air. The dragons tensed, their heads swiveling toward the sound.

"Storm creatures, again," Sif hollered, her scales bristling.

Jerica's heart leapt as she saw dark shapes on the horizon, growing closer. "Quick! To the caverns."

With almost a singular push, the five dragons leapt into action. Hamish rode along on Sif's back, while Jerica clung to Nuri's dorsal fin and plunged into the water. It took only moments to reach the Whispering Caverns and seek shelter inside.

Nuri swam through the opening where the sea met the cavern. "The water continues until it meets with a river," she informed Jerica. "Most valthans prefer the open water, but I have come here sometimes, for the quiet."

Quiet? Jerica immediately noted the sound of wind whistling through the rocks. Apparently there were porous openings, and that must be the reason for the name. Although the wind was anything but *whispering* now.

Nuri deposited her human cargo on a sandbar. The other dragons arrived and were able to get far enough inside the cave's depths to be out of sight. Skellig settled on the soft sand, while Zeira and Gocri chose rocky outcroppings. Sif shrunk herself to a more manageable size and perched cozily on the sand near Skellig.

"We need to stay here long enough for Nuri and Skellig to heal," declared Hamish. "When the enemy engages us, we must have everyone at full strength."

Heads nodded, all around. Zeira peered out through the opening. "Once it becomes fully dark outside, Gocri and I will venture out and obtain food. There are some tasty night creatures in these parts."

Jerica nudged Hamish and uttered, "Unless you like raw meat, it would be good to start a little fire."

"Got it." He proceeded to pick up small sticks of driftwood.

An hour later, Nuri had snagged herself a decent-sized grouper and the others had returned with jaws and talons gripping a variety of game. Jerica turned her back on the distribution of the prizes until Hamish assured her he'd got a nice little piglet, skinned and roasting on a spit he'd fashioned from the sticks.

Dragons apparently did not sit down together for a meal. Each of them had chomped down the critter of their choice before the humans' dinner was barely charred. Which was fine with Jerica—she didn't especially share the joy of watching that whole process. As she and Hamish tended their meal, Zeira and Sif tossed the few uneaten bones out the cave entrance.

"Tell us more about this place," Gocri asked, once the humans had begun picking morsels from their own dinner.

"What I learned from the ancient scrolls we found is that these caverns have the reputation of enhancing magic. I will take some time to apply the spells I memorized and the magic I learned in my lessons with Elowen."

Jerica hoped her words would be accepted, would bring positivity back to the group, but it seemed that, with their bellies full, the others were back to griping. Zeira and Skellig, in particular, were proving themselves to be avid debaters.

Skellig's yellow scales bristled as he shifted in place, his black wings rustling uneasily as Zeira brought up a desire to rush back out and renew the battle. "Fight, yes, but at what cost?" His voice crackled with tension, like the lightning he could summon from his wing talons. "Every encounter weakens us further. How long before we're too exhausted to even defend ourselves?"

Zeira's tail lashed in frustration. "Would you have us give up, then? Retreat to our respective realms and hope the Thunder King's wrath passes us by?"

"Of course not," Skellig snapped, sparks dancing along his wing edges. "But we need a strategy beyond simply hurling ourselves at every storm creature that crosses our path."

Gocri rumbled in agreement, his voice gravelly with fatigue. "Skellig has a point. We're spread too thin, reacting instead of acting."

Sif's silver eyes narrowed. "And what would you suggest? We can't exactly knock on the Thunder King's door and ask him to kindly stop his conquest."

As the dragons bickered, Nuri remained silent, her sinuous blue form coiled tightly. Her gaze drifted toward the distant horizon, where she knew the vast ocean lay. The pull of the water called to her, a siren song of home and familiarity. She could almost feel the cool embrace of the waves, the comforting presence of her fellow valthans.

But as she looked back at her dragon companions, Nuri felt a different kind of tug. These weren't just allies in a war; they had become her family. She thought of Jerica, the human girl who had brought them together, who had shown such unwavering faith in their abilities.

"Please, guys. Arguing with each other will get us nowhere. We need to pull together, and we need to coordinate with the other realms," Nuri said suddenly, her voice cutting through the argument. "My people, the valthans—they could provide intel on the Thunder King's naval movements. And Skellig, surely your kin in Gale could offer insight into his storm magic?"

Skellig's expression darkened at the mention of his homeland. "My sire would sooner side with the Thunder King than aid us."

"But your mother," Nuri pressed, remembering Skellig's daily communications with her. "She might be willing to help, even if only in secret."

Jerica's eyes lit up. "Nuri's right. We've been fighting this war in isolation, but we're not alone. There are allies out there, if we're willing to reach out."

As the group considered this new perspective, Nuri felt the conflicting desires within her intensify. The urge to dive into the depths and rally her own people warred with her commitment to this mismatched family of dragons. She knew that her speed in the water could be a crucial asset in gathering information and coordinating with other realms. But the thought of leaving, even temporarily, filled her with an unexpected sense of loss.

Nuri's narrow skull dipped as she wrestled with her decision. Her spiraled horns caught the fading light from the campfire, casting intricate shadows on the cave walls. "I ... I could go," she said hesitantly. "I could swim to the valthan cities, speak with the four queens. But ..." She trailed off, her eyes meeting each of her companions in turn.

Jerica stepped forward, placing a gentle hand on Nuri's sleek scales. "But you're worried about leaving us," she finished softly.

Nuri nodded, her light-blue fin rippling. "We've come so far together. The thought of not being here, of something happening while I'm gone ... You don't know how worried I was when you were inland and I could not find you."

Skellig, despite his earlier frustration, moved closer to Nuri. "Your speed in the water is unmatched. If anyone can gather the intel we need quickly, it's you."

"He's right," Zeira added, her voice softer now. "And we'll be here when you return. All of us."

As Nuri looked at her fellow dragons, she saw the same conflict in their eyes that she felt in her heart. In the distance, they heard the rumble of another approaching storm. Without needing to say it, they banked the fire and settled down, out of sight of the cavern's entrance, hoping the night would pass without incident.

Chapter 13 — Woodsman

Jerica couldn't sleep, so she found a private area of the cavern and practiced her magic all night. When Hamish appeared in the morning, searching for her, she had mastered spells for levitating and for rendering herself invisible. She startled him by demonstrating both.

"Nuri's anxious to leave," he informed her. "Says there is one region where most of the valthans are unharmed. She can probably recruit some of them, for when the battle starts."

Jerica nodded. "Agreed. She should go. I want you to keep carrying the jhorium sword. I have the goblet and the stone."

"It *would* be smart to spread our resources." He took the treasured sword and handed her his own, a fine blade but with none of the magical properties of the other. She added his scabbard to her belt, and the two of them walked back to the main chamber where the dragons were waking and stretching their muscles.

Skellig appeared much better today, his scales held a healthy sheen. When his wings flexed they exhibited no soreness or limitations. Nuri, too, had regained her shimmering blue. The meal and a night's rest had brightened the spirits of Zeira, Sif, and even Gocri.

"Are we ready to see how many recruits we can find?" Jerica asked.

She stepped out of the cavern and watched Nuri's sleek blue form disappear beneath the waves. The valthan's departure left a hollow ache in Jerica's chest. She hoped Nuri would locate Anahita and receive help from her in saving the valthans.

Then she turned her attention toward the land. Where trees had stood with withering leaves, now there were only barren trunks and broken branches. The sky was a flat, ominous gray—not the roiling threat she'd seen in the Eye of the Storm, but nasty-looking nonetheless.

"I didn't want to tell you," Hamish said, standing at her side. "The storm that was building up last night—"

"We weren't ready to fight it," Jerica whispered to herself, her voice barely audible over the gentle lapping of waves on the shore. "I wasn't ready."

She squeezed her eyes shut, trying not to imagine fallen comrades, villages reduced to ash. But those visions persisted.

"Jerica … it would have been foolish to tackle last night's threat."

"If only I had mastered the magic sooner …"

Jerica's hand drifted to the pouch at her waist, feeling the comforting heft of the jhorium goblet within. The magical artifact she had forged seemed to beat with latent energy, as if sensing her turmoil.

"What good is this power if I can't protect anyone?" she asked the empty glade, her words tinged with bitterness. She didn't want to admit how personally she had taken the arguments between the dragons yesterday, how deeply she felt she had been a poor leader.

A stiff breeze whistled through the scorched trees, carrying with it the salty tang of the sea. Jerica lifted her head, her gaze drawn to the horizon where Nuri had vanished.

"At least the valthans are safe for now," she mused, a

flicker of relief penetrating her gloom. "Nuri will keep them hidden until …"

Until what? Until she could somehow turn the tide against the Thunder King's forces? The very thought seemed ludicrous.

She let out a harsh laugh, devoid of humor. "Some chosen one I turned out to be. I can't even figure out how to properly defend a grove of trees. What am I missing?" she wondered aloud, frustration evident in her furrowed brow. "There has to be a way to unlock the full potential of our artifacts."

"I'll get everyone ready to leave." Hamish placed a hand on her arm, gave a squeeze, then walked away.

"I'm just a village girl," Jerica voiced to herself. "How am I supposed to lead anyone against the Thunder King? He has an army of enslaved humans and dragons, and far more experience. What do I have? A glowing cup and a rock."

As she sat there, her father's words came back, from what felt like a lifetime ago:

"Ye have a gift, lass," Hallis had told her, his eyes shining with pride as she presented him with the newly forged goblet. "A talent beyond mere craftsmanship. Ye have magic in yer veins, whether ye know it or not."

She stood—taking a deep breath, squaring her shoulders, picking at a charred piece of wood near her feet.

"I can't give up," she declared to the weather-beaten glade, her voice growing stronger with each word. "Too many are counting on me."

She paused, leaning against a gnarled tree trunk, its bark rough against her palm. The scent of scorched earth and saltwater filled her nostrils, a stark reminder of the battles they'd endured. Jerica closed her eyes, trying to center herself, but doubt crept in like a persistent shadow.

"What if—" she whispered, her voice barely audible above the leaves rustling on the ground. The oron stone in her pocket warmed, as if responding to her uncertainty.

Jerica pulled out the stone, its tri-colored segments glowing faintly. She turned it over in her hands, remembering the raw power she'd felt when she'd first activated it.

The memory of Emerus Dinty's latest threat echoed in

her mind. His voice, dripping with derision, had promised retribution if she didn't hand over the jhorium. The thought sent a shiver down her spine.

Jerica straightened, her fingers tightening around the oron stone. "But I have a team of good-hearted dragons, and we have our magical artifacts. I'm the only one who can control my own doubts," she reminded herself. "It all has to count for something, right?"

She began walking again, her steps slow but steady. As she emerged from the tree line, Jerica caught sight of her companions waiting beside the cavern entrance. She tamped down her doubts.

"Are we ready?" She gave her words an edge of bravado. "Let's see who we can recruit to help us win this war." She marched over to Zeira, climbing and taking her familiar seat atop the fire dragon's red scales.

Hamish now wore the jhorium sword at his side, and was already in his place upon Sif's back. Jerica felt her spirits rise. At least they were doing something for the people and creatures of Andela.

One by one, the dragons launched themselves into the murky air, taking care to stay within sight of each other. They flew for more than an hour before Zeira sighted a small village below. When she conveyed the information via their mental connection, four dragons began a squadron-like descent into a wide field beside what was probably the town hall.

The main building's stone walls were standing, but the thatched roofs of nearly all the homes were gone. Fields that once held crops were decimated, and the farm animals roamed free, looking lost and confused.

"This place is so much like Cael," Jerica moaned.

Zeira turned her head to look up at her passenger. "It doesn't mean the same fate has befallen your town. Hold onto hope."

Jerica patted the scaly dragon and slid off her back. A man with a heavy beard, carrying an axe, was approaching. She knew the type.

"Hello, woodsman. I come from Cael, in the northeast." They exchanged enough pleasantries to establish their authenticity, and then Jerica took the time to introduce each of the dragons and Hamish.

"We travel the region in search of others who will help us defend Andela from the Thunder King."

"Aye. Our leaders have been having this same conversation. So far, we have two dozen hearty men and quite a number of archers." He scuffed one boot along the ground. "Um, those archers are elves. If that matters to ye."

Jerica shook her head. "Anyone willing to fight the Thunder King's soldiers is a welcome addition."

Hamish tilted his head toward one of several large trees that had been stripped bare. From a hollow place in the trunk stepped a slender being with luminescent skin. Her pointed ears and long, silky blonde hair gave her away as one of the elves Thorne had mentioned. Slung over one shoulder was a quiver of arrows. She reached into the hollow and pulled out a beautifully carved wooden bow.

"Meet Lyra," Thorne said.

"We and our dragon friends are looking for—"

"I heard." Lyra's voice was almost musical. "Count me in. Along with all of our skilled archers … and a few who are known more for their magical abilities than their accomplishments with a bow." She smiled playfully and let out a high whistle.

From trees, hedges, and behind buildings came dozens of elves of many sizes and shapes. The pointed ears were their common feature. They approached the group, showing no fear of the dragons.

"See? We stand ready."

"It's going to be dangerous when the battle begins," Hamish said. "Are you sure—?"

"Sure that we can handle ourselves in a battle situation? Yes." Every elf's features were set with solidarity for the cause.

"Thank you, everyone." Jerica thought of one more thing. "How shall we communicate, when either of us sees trouble?"

Lyra looked at the scabbard at Hamish's side. "Is that jhorium?"

Jerica nodded, instinctively touching the pouch at her

own waist. She saw Lyra's eyes shift to it.

"Use the power of the jhorium to send a signal. It will be received by all the creatures of our land. Trust me."

Jerica thought of a spell Elowen had taught her, where she would hold the goblet high and direct its radiant power outward. "We will do that."

"And now we should move on," Hamish suggested. "We need to visit each of the dragon realms, to find out how they have fared, and to see how much help we can count on."

"Use the goblet," Lyra advised. She met Jerica's eyes straight on. "You are a kairie, correct?"

Stunned that an elf knew this, Jerica could only nod.

"From a central location—say, somewhere around Genesia—you should be able to meld your power with that of each dragon, and that of the goblet. To the leader of each realm, put forth your request. They will hear you." She said it with such authority that Jerica couldn't help but believe her.

"Then we are off to Genesia."

They were airborne once again when a voice came into Jerica's head. *Does anyone know where Genesia is?*

The dragons twisted their necks, looking around at one another. From the back of Zeira, Jerica glanced toward Hamish, aboard Skellig this time, and saw that he was grinning.

Someone knows …

You lot haven't studied much Andelan geography, have you? He took a full two minutes to relish their puzzlement.

Genesia is a small province—well, relatively small—at the intersection where Bliss and Gale meet the borders of Blaze. Come on, guys. It's the home of the sol dragons, genesians … *Get it?*

Othos may be there! Jerica couldn't keep the excitement out of her voice.

If we're lucky. He could be a big help in this mission of ours.

Hamish proceeded to direct the flight. Hours later, he pointed out a landmark mountain in the distance. *That's our destination.*

Through the murky sky they could tell the sun was getting low, and as they descended through the mist, they caught sight of the ground.

This area hasn't been attacked! Jerica's surprise was evident.

Kind of makes sense. Emerus Dinty may think he's the biggest bull in the herd, but even he knows not to mess with the sol dragons.

She nodded. It made sense. She extended her senses to try and reach Othos, calling out to him mentally and verbally. But there was no response. A ripple of fear went down her spine. If something had happened to the most powerful dragon of all ...

No. She wasn't going there.

Is there a place in this region that's considered the center? she asked Hamish. *As close to all the other regions as we can possibly get?*

He nodded. *That's where we're going.* He tapped Skellig on the neck and pointed. Ten minutes later, a lovely green glade appeared. The lack of burned trees and destruction instantly lifted their spirits. They landed, touching the green grass and breathing the clean air.

"Who do we contact first? Suggestions?" Jerica wanted to know.

"We could try my homeland, Blaze. Darazok Aeogan is the Fire Lord. My mother is Gynnyth of the Phoenix caste." Zeira seemed a little embarrassed. "They're very powerful."

"Good idea." Jerica pulled the goblet from its pouch on her belt, polishing the gleaming green metal on the sleeve of her tunic. "Shall we reach out to the king first, or maybe ease into it by talking with your mother?"

"Why don't you open the communication in the way you feel is best." Jerica held the goblet aloft, aiming the mouth of it toward Blaze, while keeping one hand in contact with Zeira's right foot.

The red dragon took a deep breath and called out: "Gynnyth of the Phoenix caste? Mother? It's me, Zeira."

A warm voice immediately came back, seemingly broadcasting from the mouth of the jhorium goblet. "Zeira, it's wonderful to hear your voice, my dear. Have you found your kai?"

And then some. But Zeira kept the explanation quick and to the point.

"We need the help of the king, Mother. Will it be all right to reach out directly, do you think?"

"Darling, the king is right here with me."

Zeira looked at the others in the group, clearly a little self-conscious.

"We are at a meeting of the high council, discussing ... I assume you've heard what's going on?"

"That's the reason for our call. May Jerica please speak to the king?"

When a male voice quickly responded, Jerica spoke for the group. "Darazok Aeogan, we are honored to speak with you."

"Is this pertaining to the reign of terror by that so-called Thunder King? How can I help?"

"It is." She explained their mission to recruit dragons from each of the realms to unite against the tyrant.

"Of course. We have lost many, I shall warn you. Dozens of dragons have been imprisoned, held on an island off the coast. But among those who remain, nearly all of them will certainly join the battle."

"Thank you. I can't tell you what this means—"

"To all of us, young one. I have heard from other leaders, and every realm is affected. You are a very brave girl, taking on this challenge."

Jerica blushed. "You have a way to reach all the other leaders? At the same time?"

"More or less. Each of us has reported attacks, as they happen. This Dinty fellow cannot be everywhere at once, although he has apparently recruited huge numbers of humans and other creatures to do his bidding. His reach is surprisingly thorough—and terrifying."

"May I, um, *we* contact each of them, make certain our connection is working? That way, when the Thunder King attacks the next time, we will be ready to respond with force."

"Certainly." Darazok Aeogan's words echoed as they broke the connection.

"Quickly, let's finish getting this set up." Jerica rushed to Gocri's side and laid a hand on his frosty foreleg.

The goblet did its magic once again, and she was soon speaking with Queen Freriss. She quickly gave the same explanation as with Darazok, and the Queen's response was an unqualified promise of support. "We are pleased to see all the dragon regions working together, dren."

Gocri and Jerica exchanged a look, unsure which of them the endearment was meant for. But it didn't matter. They had two of the five regions on their team. Within the hour, Queen Chrys of Rokke had promised the smoke dragons' support, as well.

Jerica walked over to Skellig. "What do you think? Will your homeland's king go along?"

Skellig shook his head. "I am uncertain."

"I understand. Dym will make it difficult."

"He is allied with Dinty, and I would be very cautious about revealing anything of our strategy."

"Your mother? I know you remain in contact with her …"

Skellig shook his large head. "I am cautious about confiding. Dym can easily break through her reserves."

"Okay, is there another leader, one who can be trusted?"

"Lord Myrdaynth is the king, but I do not trust him."

Jerica remember Myrdaynth's uncaring attitude and the fact that he had reneged on a promise. "Any other ideas?"

"We might try reaching out to my … I'm not sure of the word. To humans, it would be a … cousin, I think?"

Hamish couldn't help chuckling. "You have a cousin?"

"We were not nest-mates, but there was a kinship between our mothers. We played together as dragonlets, and stayed close through the centuries."

"You know his state of mind, whether he is or is not sympathetic to Dym or Emerus Dinty?"

"He most definitely is not."

Jerica laid a hand on the edge of his shiny black wing and raised the goblet. "Let's give it a try."

"Konungr of Spark—do you hear me?" Skellig boomed.

"Skellig, you old gromper! What's going on?"

Jerica could instantly hear the old friendship in the two Spark dragons' teasing ways. Before they could get into long tales of their childhood adventures, she tapped Skellig's wing and raised an eyebrow.

"Oh, right." Skellig introduced her and let Jerica take over to explain the situation.

"It's extremely important that none who are sympathetic

to Dym or the Thunder King know what we are doing, gathering forces to fight them," she finished.

"Old Myrdaynth is useless," Konungr said. "He has participated in the capture of dragons, only to turn around and apologize to the citizens. The old guy is getting … I don't know what humans call it. Addle-minded or something?"

"Senile, it sounds like. Well, for our purposes, that's just fine. Keep him in the dark as you recruit those you can trust. We shall watch for our opportunity and then call in all our forces."

Konungr assured her that would be the case. Then they broke the connection. She wished Nuri were nearby, but this place was simply too far inland. On the bright side, she knew the water dragons were in good hands with Anahita to assist them.

"Jerica, that was brilliant," Hamish said as the group split up, the dragons off in search of another meal. "That goblet is like an extension of your will—the connection is that strong."

"Can I share a story?" At his nod, she spoke of a memory that flickered to life in her mind, vivid and warm. She was back in her father's workshop, the familiar scents of metal and fire enveloping her. Jerica could almost feel the heat of the forge on her skin, hear the rhythmic clanging of hammer on anvil.

"'Focus, J,' my father said. 'The jhorium is rare and wit' a temperament. It be requirin' a steady hand and an unwaverin' will.' I can see myself standing before the blazing forge, sweat is pouring off my forehead as I carefully poured the molten jhorium into the mold. That green, glowing liquid seemed alive with an otherworldly energy.

"I did it," Jerica whispered. "I forged the goblet when everyone said it couldn't be done. If I could master jhorium, I can lead us to victory against the Thunder King."

Hamish reached out and took her hand. "You can. You will."

As he walked away, preparing to make camp for the night, she pulled out the oron stone, its tricolored segments glowing faintly in response to her touch. "I have power of my own," she said, her voice growing stronger. "It may not be flashy magic, but I'm learning that it's real."

Jerica turned back toward the camp. "We're not finished yet," she declared to the empty glade. "The Thunder King hasn't seen what we're truly capable of. I hope."

A soft rustle in the nearby foliage caught Jerica's attention. She turned, her hand instinctively reaching for the sword at her hip, only to relax as a familiar yellow form emerged from the shadows. Skellig, his black wings folded tightly against his body, approached her with silent grace.

"Skellig," Jerica breathed, happiness washing over her. The Spark dragon's presence was a balm to her agitated soul. "I'm so happy to see how well you are recovering."

He paused before her, his ancient eyes seeming to peer into the depths of her being. Without a word, Skellig lowered his head and gently nudged Jerica's shoulder, a gesture of silent support that spoke volumes.

Jerica's composure crumbled. She wrapped her arms around Skellig's neck, burying her face in his scales. "I don't know if I can do this. One minute I think I'm strong and the next minute all my doubts return," she whispered, her voice muffled. "Everyone's counting on me, but what if I'm not strong enough?"

Skellig rumbled softly, a sound that vibrated through Jerica's body. He didn't speak—he was a dragon of few words—but his presence alone offered comfort. They stood there for a long moment, girl and dragon, united.

Finally, Jerica pulled back, wiping her eyes. "Thank you," she said, managing a small smile. "I needed that."

Skellig tilted his head, his gaze never leaving her face. Jerica found herself settling onto a nearby log, and the dragon curled up beside her, his body a shield against the cool forest air.

"I keep thinking about my village," Jerica said softly, her fingers absently tracing patterns on Skellig's scales. "About my family. Do you think they're safe? The Thunder King …"

She trailed off, unable to voice her deepest fears. Skellig shifted closer, offering silent reassurance.

"I know you understand," Jerica continued. "It can't be easy, with Dym being the way he is."

At the mention of his sire, Skellig's muscles tensed briefly. Jerica immediately regretted bringing it up. "I'm sorry," she said quickly. "I shouldn't have—"

Skellig shook his head, cutting off her apology. His eyes met hers, and in that moment, Jerica felt a deep connection between them. Two souls, each bearing tremendous expectations.

"We're quite the pair, aren't we?" Jerica said with a wry smile. "A girl with a magical goblet and a dragon who can shoot lightning. Old TK won't know what hit him."

Skellig snorted, a puff of smoke curling from his nostrils in what Jerica could have sworn was amusement. She laughed, the sound light and genuine for the first time in days.

Skellig's golden eyes shifted to the pocket of Jerica's tunic, where the oron stone rested. With a gentle nudge of his snout, he drew her attention to it. Jerica's hand instinctively moved to the pocket, feeling the familiar contours of the stone through the fabric.

Skellig rumbled softly, his gaze intense as he watched her withdraw the stone. In her palm, the three segments flared apart and back together, throbbing with an inner light.

Jerica's brow furrowed. "I still don't *fully* understand its power. How am I supposed to use it against the Thunder King?"

The Spark dragon tilted his head, then slowly extended one of his wing talons. A faint crackle of electricity danced along its edge, reminding Jerica of his formidable abilities.

"Right," she said, nodding. "Power isn't always about understanding. Sometimes it's about trusting your instincts."

As if in response to her words, the oron stone's glow intensified. Jerica gasped, feeling a surge of energy course through her body. It was both exhilarating and terrifying.

"Each time we've encountered Emerus Dinty I've been so focused on what I can't do," she said, her voice gaining strength. "Maybe it's time I started believing in what I *can* do."

With a deep breath, Jerica rose to her feet. Her legs felt steadier than they had in days, her posture straightening.

"We've lost so much," she said, her voice barely above a whisper. "But we're still here. We're still fighting. Thank you, Skellig," she said, reaching out to touch his scales. "For reminding me of who I am. Who *we* are."

Jerica turned and began walking back toward the camp, her steps purposeful and confident. Skellig padded silently beside her, his massive form casting a shadow that seemed to shield her from the world's troubles.

As they approached the clearing where the others waited, Jerica felt a subtle shift in the air. She paused, tilting her head skyward. The oppressive blanket of dark clouds that had shrouded them for days was beginning to thin, revealing a sliver of moonlight.

"Look," she breathed, a smile tugging at her lips. "The sky's clearing."

More than one of the dragons rumbled, a sound of approval that vibrated through the earth beneath their feet.

"Maybe it's a sign," Jerica mused, "that we're on the right path after all."

Hamish had built a cheery fire and the others had hunted down some food. Jerica took a deep breath and strode into the camp, her newfound confidence radiating with each step. The bustling activity around her paused as her companions turned to look, sensing the change in their young leader.

"Alright, everyone," Jerica called out, her voice clear and strong. "We've got a long day tomorrow, but I believe in us. In all of us."

She was no longer just the girl from Cael who had stumbled into this adventure. She was becoming the leader her companions needed, the adversary the Thunder King feared.

Chapter 14 — Ambush

By morning the mood had shifted. Tensions ran high and there had been some renewed bickering among the group. Zeira, in particular, seemed peeved at Jerica's new confidence and had stomped away about an hour ago. It was puzzling. Was the young dragon going through something like the hormonal changes adolescent humans did? What was with the mood swings? Quietly, Hamish assured her everything would be fine. When the danger became immediate again, they would pull together.

"I hope so. Without teamwork, we're dead."

"What's your plan?" he questioned. "Should we be moving out, trying to track down where Dinty is making his latest moves?"

Before Jerica could respond, a sound cut through the air—the snap of a twig, followed by the rustle of leaves. All heads whipped toward the source of the noise, the dragons instantly on alert.

"What was that?" Jerica whispered, her hand instinctively tightening around the oron stone in her pocket. Its warmth intensified.

Gocri's icy breath misted in the air as he spoke. "Something approaches. Or someone."

Sif's form shimmered, ready to shift at a moment's notice. "Friend or foe?" she hissed.

Jerica's nerves tightened. Had Zeira returned so soon? Or was it the Thunder King's forces, finally catching up to them? She thought of the jhorium goblet, safely hidden in its pouch. If it fell into the wrong hands ...

"Everyone, be ready," she ordered, surprised at the authority in her own voice. "But don't attack until we know what we're dealing with."

As the footsteps drew nearer, Jerica felt the rawness of her nerves. One wrong move could spell disaster for them all. She took a deep breath, steeling herself for whatever emerged from the shadows.

Suddenly, the forest exploded into chaos. Storm creatures burst from the undergrowth, their bodies crackling with electricity and eyes glowing an unnatural blue. They swarmed the clearing, surrounding Jerica and the dragons in a matter of seconds.

"Ambush!" Skellig roared, rearing up on his hind legs as lightning arced between his horns.

Zeira flew in and executed a perfect landing within the group.

Jerica's heart pounded in her ears as she spun, trying to take in the full scope of the attack. The storm creatures were everywhere—hulking, misshapen beasts with limbs that crackled and sparked. Their howls sent chills down her spine.

"Form a circle!" she shouted, tugging Hamish toward the center of the clearing. "Don't let them separate us!"

The dragons moved swiftly, despite their earlier disagreements. Gocri's massive ice-white form took up position to Jerica's left, while Sif's smoke-gray scales shimmered as she flanked her right. Skellig, still bristling with electrical energy, guarded their rear.

"Emerus must be getting desperate," Sif grouched, her

voice thick with smoke. "Sending his pets to do his dirty work."

A storm creature lunged at Gocri, its hind claws leaving scorch marks on the ground. The ice dragon retaliated with a blast of frost that froze the beast in mid-leap.

"Less talking, more fighting!" Skellig roared. He released a bolt of lightning that forked through the air, striking three creatures at once and sending them reeling.

Jerica ducked as a storm creature sailed over her head, its body trailing sparks. She couldn't help but marvel at the dragons' raw power, even as fear threatened to overwhelm her. "Watch each other's backs!" she called out. "They're trying to divide us!"

Sif exhaled a thick plume of smoke, obscuring a group of advancing creatures. "I can't keep this up forever," she warned. "There are too many of them!"

Jerica's mind went on alert. They needed a strategy, and fast. The storm creatures were relentless, dozens of them pressing in from all sides. She could feel the heat of their electrical charges, and smell the ozone in the air.

"Gocri, Skellig, Sif! See what you can come up with!" Jerica reached for the goblet as the others went into action.

The dragons moved in perfect synchronization, their earlier disagreements forgotten in the heat of battle. Gocri's icy breath formed a jagged wall around them, which Skellig immediately charged with crackling energy. Sif's smoke billowed outward, creating a disorienting fog.

For a moment, Jerica dared to hope they might gain the upper hand. But then she heard a sound that made her blood run cold—the unmistakable boom of thunder. Storm creatures began to break through their defenses.

"He's here," she whispered, her grip tightening on the jhorium goblet. "The Thunder King is coming."

Jerica's heart pounded as she felt the raw power of the chalice through her fingers. She knew what she had to do, even as fear threatened to paralyze her. Taking a deep breath, she raised the artifact high above her head.

"Everyone, tighten our group!" she shouted, her voice carrying over the relentless roars of the attackers. "I'm going to try something!"

The dragons converged around her, their massive bodies forming a protective circle. Jerica closed her eyes, focusing all her concentration on the goblet. She felt its energy coursing through her, a torrent of magical power.

With a huge groan, Jerica channeled the jhorium's power outward. A shimmering dome of energy exploded from her hands, expanding rapidly to envelop the entire group. The storm creatures slammed into the barrier, their electrical charges dissipating harmlessly against its surface.

"By the Flame," Skellig breathed, his eyes wide with awe. "How are you doing this?"

Jerica gritted her teeth, sweat beading on her brow. "I don't know how long I can hold it," she gasped. The strain was immense, like trying to hold back a tidal wave with her bare hands. "We need a plan!"

Zeira suddenly straightened. Her earlier doubts about Jerica seemed to evaporate.

"You've given us a chance," the red dragon whooped, her scales gleaming in the ethereal light of the barrier. "Now it's time we use it."

Without warning, Zeira reared back on her hind legs, her chest expanding as she drew in a massive breath. Jerica watched in amazement as the dragon's entire body began to glow with an inner fire.

"Cover your ears. And keep the barrier intact until I tell you!" Zeira roared.

A moment later, a jet of white-hot flame erupted from Zeira's rear, so intense that Jerica could feel the heat even through her magical barrier. But it wasn't aimed at the storm creatures in front of them. Instead, the fire shot backward, propelling Zeira forward like a living rocket.

The red dragon slammed into the barrier, which flexed but held. As she rebounded, with wings spread, she launched herself into the air, spinning in a tight circle just beneath the dome's apex.

"What are you *doing*?" Jerica cried, her arms shaking with the effort of maintaining the shield.

Zeira's only response was another deafening roar as she

unleashed her flame again, this time in a continuous stream. The fire formed a swirling vortex within the confines of the barrier, growing hotter and more intense with each rotation.

Jerica could feel the magic of her shield weakening under the combined assault of the storm creatures outside and the inferno within. But just as she thought she couldn't hold on any longer, Zeira shouted, "Now, Jerica! Drop the barrier!"

Without questioning, Jerica released her command to the goblet. The magical dome vanished instantly, and the fiery tornado Zeira had created exploded outward. Storm creatures were incinerated or flung away by the blast, leaving a wide circle of scorched earth around them.

As Zeira landed heavily beside her, panting from the exertion, Jerica couldn't help but laugh in disbelief. "That was … incredible," she gasped.

Zeira turned to her, and for the first time in days, Jerica saw respect in the dragon's eyes. "You're not so bad yourself," Zeira rumbled. "Perhaps I was too hasty in my judgment."

But before Jerica could respond, a booming voice echoed, chilling her to the bone. Hamish spun toward the sound and drew the jhorium sword.

"Impressive," it said, seeming to come from everywhere at once. "But your little light show is over. It's time you faced true power."

Jerica scanned the battlefield, frantically trying to locate the source of the ominous voice. The dragons formed a protective circle around the two humans, their scales bristling with anticipation.

"Stay alert," Gocri lumbered, his icy breath misting in the air. "This isn't over yet."

As if on cue, the remaining storm creatures surged forward in a renewed assault. But this time, something was different. The dragons and Jerica moved as one, their earlier discord forgotten in the face of shared peril.

Skellig crackled with electricity. "Jerica, boost my power!" he called out.

Without hesitation, Jerica gripped his talon with one hand and raised the glowing green goblet with the other, channeling its energy into the lightning dragon. His eyes blazed white-hot as he unleashed a blinding arc of lightning that forked and struck multiple storm creatures at once, reducing them to ash.

"My turn," Sif rumbled, her smoky form billowing. Jerica instinctively knew what to do, pulling the oron stone from her pocket and directing its blue segment toward her. Sif's smoke thickened, becoming an impenetrable, choking fog that engulfed a group of approaching enemies.

Zeira and Gocri exchanged a look, then shouted in unison, "Jerica, to us!"

Jerica felt a surge of pride at their trust. As the two dragons made contact with her, she raised both the goblet and the oron stone, its red and green segments keeping rhythm with her racing heart. As the magical energy flowed into Zeira and Gocri, they reared up on their hind legs, unleashing a devastating combination of fire and ice.

The contrasting elements spiraled together, creating a mesmerizing vortex that tore through the ranks of storm creatures. Steam hissed and ice crackled as the hybrid attack decimated their foes.

"We're pushing them back!" Hamish shouted, his voice hoarse but triumphant.

Indeed, the storm creatures were retreating, their numbers dwindling rapidly under the onslaught of the unified group. As the last of the enemies disappeared into the forest, an eerie silence fell over the battlefield.

Jerica lowered her arms, her legs trembling with fatigue. The dragons, too, showed signs of exhaustion—Zeira's flames sputtered weakly, while frost clung to Gocri's scales. Hamish kept his sword at the ready.

"Is it … over?" Sif asked, her smoky form dissipating slightly as she relaxed.

Skellig shook his head, sparks flying from his horns. "I don't think so. That voice … he's still out there."

Jerica nodded grimly, clutching the goblet and oron stone close. "We need to stay on guard." She knew that voice.

But even as she allowed herself a small smile at their teamwork, a chill wind swept through the clearing. The sky darkened ominously, and a low rumble of thunder echoed in the distance.

"I think our real battle is just beginning." Zeira said quietly, her eyes fixed on the horizon.

Jerica's heart sank as she surveyed her companions. The adrenaline of battle faded, leaving behind a stark reality of their injuries and exhaustion.

"We need reinforcements. I can't believe I didn't manage to call them up," Jerica said, her voice trembling slightly. She winced as she shifted her weight, feeling the sting of a gash on her leg. "Is everyone alright?"

Zeira snorted, a small puff of smoke escaping her nostrils. "Define *alright*," she remarked. "I feel like I've been trampled by a herd of thunder beasts."

"At least you're still standing," Gocri rumbled, his massive form sagging. "I'm not sure how much more ice I have left in me."

Jerica limped toward them, her hand still clutching the goblet. "We fought well together," she said, trying to inject some optimism into her voice. "We proved we can—"

"Can what?" Zeira interrupted, her eyes flashing. And her foul mood was back. "Nearly get ourselves killed? Exhaust our powers for a battle that might not even matter in the grand scheme of things?"

"Zeira," Jerica began, but the red dragon cut her off.

"No, Jerica. This isn't working. Look at us!" Zeira gestured with her wing, encompassing their battered group. "We're falling apart. And for what?"

The words stung, and Jerica felt tears prick at her eyes. "I thought … I thought we were in this together."

Hamish stepped forward. "We are. Don't forget that." But blood ran down his face and his shirt was ripped.

A heavy silence fell over the group, broken only by the distant rumble of thunder. Jerica looked from dragon to dragon, seeing the doubt and fear in their eyes. The unity they'd found in battle was crumbling once again, replaced by exhaustion and mistrust.

Suddenly, Gocri's head snapped up, his nostrils flaring. "Wait," he said, his voice tight with alarm. "Where's Skellig?"

Jerica's blood ran cold as she scanned the clearing. The

yellow Spark dragon was nowhere to be seen. "He was just here," she whispered, panic rising in her chest. "During the battle, he was—"

A deafening crack of thunder cut her off, and the sky above them erupted into a swirling mass of dark clouds. Eerie green lightning forked across the heavens, illuminating the forest in harsh, strobing flashes. The Eye of the Storm was back, full force.

A booming voice echoed through the air, seeming to come from everywhere and nowhere at once. "Missing your sparky little friend?" The accompanying laugh was deep and menacing. "Soon, you will all bow before the Thunder King!"

Jerica clutched the goblet tighter, her mind racing as she prepared to call in the promised reinforcements. They needed help now that one of their own was missing. As the storm raged overhead, she met Zeira's eyes, seeing her own fear reflected there.

"What do we do now?" Gocri asked, his voice barely audible over the howling wind.

Jerica opened her mouth to respond, but no words came. Had their adversary taken Skellig again? Could he survive this? For the first time since their journey began, she had no answer to give.

Chapter 15 — Trouble

The sky crackled with energy, dark clouds roiling overhead as hot lightning illuminated the faces of friends and foes alike. Jerica's muscles burned with exertion as she raised the goblet and put out the calls to their allies. "He's here! He's unleashed a ton of fighters—and he may have Skellig!"

Just then Zeira dodged another bolt of electricity, her wings lifting her into the air, amidst the chaos. All around them, fresh storm creatures swarmed, their ethereal forms flickering in and out of existence as they pressed their attack. Was there no end to this?

A faint voice came to Jerica, one she recognized as Queen Chrys, the leader of Rokke. *We're … in trouble … valthans … Your Nuri is—* And the transmission cut off.

"Gocri, to your left!" Zeira cried out, her voice cutting through Jerica's thoughts. The massive Frost dragon pivoted, his bulk belying his agility as he narrowly avoided a tendril of living lightning. Jerica's heart pounded in her chest as she tried to reach the other kingdoms.

A sharp pang of worry threatened to break her concentration. No! Focus. They need you.

"Jerica, use the goblet to disrupt their formation!" Zeira called out, her amber eyes scanning the battlefield for the young human girl. She spotted Jerica on the ground, her blonde hair flaring in the wind as she raised the jhorium chalice high.

"I'm trying!" Jerica shouted back. She turned the goblet toward the incoming enemy, dropping her attempts at communication for the moment. "Hamish! Use the sword!"

Zeira swooped low, her talons raking through a cluster of storm creatures that had been advancing on Jerica's position. The girl's eyes widened in gratitude.

"You can do this," Zeira encouraged, her voice softer now.

Jerica closed her eyes, concentrating again on bringing more fighters to their aid. Two more kingdoms reported being overrun, themselves, unable to send their volunteers. Zeira's movements brought her attention back to the sky.

Jerica gave up on the plea for help and took stock of her own group. Gocri was holding his own against a group of larger storm creatures. But where was Sif?

A rumble beneath her feet disrupted her thoughts as the ground erupted, revealing a terran dragon's serpentine form. Whatever. She would accept help from any of the realms. Storm creatures scattered in surprise, and Jerica seized the opportunity.

"Now, Hamish!" she shouted, signaling to him.

Hamish raised his sword, his eyes glowing with arcane energy as he began to chant. The air around them shimmered, and Jerica felt a surge of strength course through her body.

"Push forward!" she commanded. "We can't let them regroup!"

As one, the dragons and their human allies pressed their advantage. But even as they gained ground, a nagging doubt gnawed at the back of Jerica's mind. Where were Skellig and Sif?

A sudden shift in the air caught Jerica's attention, and she turned to see a massive storm creature materializing directly above Zeira. Time seemed to slow as Jerica realized she was too far away to intervene.

"Zeira, look out!" she screamed, as the dragon sped toward her.

Gocri's eyes narrowed as he witnessed a storm creature looming over Jerica. Without hesitation, he unleashed a blast of glacial breath. The freezing gust whistled past Zeira, crystallizing the air in its wake.

The storm creature, caught in mid-strike, froze solid. Its lightning-wreathed form became encased in a thick layer of ice and crashed to the ground.

Zeira's relief was palpable. "Gocri, you magnificent beast!" she called out, her wings settling as she landed beside Jerica. "Are you alright?"

Jerica nodded, her eyes wide. "Thanks to Gocri. I thought I was done for."

Gocri's chest swelled with pride, but his pale complexion remained focused. "We're not out of danger yet," he rumbled, his gaze sweeping across the battlefield. "There are still too many of them."

As if on cue, the ground beneath their feet began to tremble again. Zeira's first thought was an earthquake, but then she remembered—

The earth erupted in a shower of dirt and rock, revealing Sif in her terran form. The smoke dragon-turned-terran-turned-human emerged from the tunnel she'd created, her eyes gleaming.

"Surprise," Sif quipped. She turned to address the stunned storm creatures surrounding them. "Did you miss me?"

Before Jerica could formulate a response, the ground rumbled once more and, suddenly, fissures opened beneath the feet of the storm creatures. Chaos ensued as they stumbled and fell, their ranks thrown into disarray.

"Brilliant work, Sif!" Zeira called out. "Keep them off balance!"

As Sif continued to manipulate the earth, creating pitfalls and obstacles for their enemies, Jerica's mind went over tactical possibilities. We might just pull this off after all, she thought, a spark of hope igniting in her chest.

But even as they pressed their advantage, Jerica couldn't shake the feeling that this was just the beginning. The Thunder King was still out there, and he was not giving up.

A blinding flash illuminated the darkened sky, followed by a deafening crack that shook the air. Jerica's eyes darted to the source, her heart pounding as she witnessed Skellig's awesome power unleashed.

He was back!

The Spark dragon's yellow scales glinted in the eerie light as lightning arced from his wing talons, striking down a cluster of storm creatures. Their unearthly shrieks pierced the air as they disintegrated into wisps of vapor.

Skellig, on your left! Jerica switched to their mental connection over the din of battle.

The dragon pivoted, his black wings unfurling, and he launched another barrage of lightning. *I see them,* he grizzled, his eyes narrowing.

Jerica marveled at Skellig's precision and power. He fought with a ferocity that belied his recent injuries. She wondered briefly how he managed to channel such strength in the face of his personal struggles with his sire.

"Jerica, watch out!" Zeira's warning snapped her back to the present.

Instinctively, Jerica raised her jhorium goblet, its green glow intensifying as she focused her will. A storm creature lunged at her, its misty form coalescing into razor-sharp claws.

"Not today," Jerica proclaimed, channeling her power through the magical vessel. A burst of energy erupted from the goblet, enveloping the creature in green light. It writhed and twisted, its form distorting as the spell took hold.

Panting, Jerica called out to her companions, "The jhorium weakens them! Aim for the disoriented ones!"

Skellig roared in acknowledgment, his lightning strikes now targeting the creatures caught in Jerica's spell. The combined assault was devastating, each bolt finding its mark with deadly accuracy.

As she prepared to cast another spell, Jerica finally

understood the Thunder King's obsession with jhorium. If he ever got hold of it, the rest of the creatures in the land would be toast. The thought sent a shiver down her spine, even as she raised the goblet once more.

"Jerica, behind you!" Skellig's voice boomed.

She whirled around, her heart in her throat, to face a new wave of storm creatures bearing down on her position. She spotted Hamish across the chaotic battlefield, his dark hair practically standing on end as he ducked beneath a storm creature's crackling tendril.

"Gocri!" Hamish called out. "Their left flank is weakening. If you can freeze the ground beneath them, we can create a bottleneck!"

The ice dragon's eyes glinted with understanding. Gocri swooped low, his freezing breath coating the earth in a thick layer of ice. Storm creatures slipped and stumbled, their misty forms struggling to maintain cohesion on the treacherous surface.

Hamish's lips curled into a devilish smile as he watched the action. He raised his hands, holding the sword up, channeling the mystical energy his father had taught him to harness. "Sif! Can you create some earthen barriers to funnel them toward Skellig?"

The dragon nodded, her massive terran form already shifting as she burrowed into the ground. Moments later, jagged walls of stone erupted from the frozen earth, herding the disoriented storm creatures into a tight formation.

"Now, Skellig!" Hamish shouted, his lean frame taut with anticipation.

The lightning dragon didn't need to be told twice. A blinding arc of electricity leapt from his wing talons, plowing through the clustered enemies and reducing them to wisps of dissipating mist.

Zeira soared overhead. "Well done, Hamish! Keep it up!"

Hamish felt a surge of pride at the dragon's praise, but he pushed the feeling aside. There was no time for self-congratulation. His eyes scanned the battlefield once more, seeking the next strategic advantage.

"Jerica," he called out, spotting their leader wielding her

jhorium goblet. "If we combine your disorienting magic with my father's banishment incantation, we might be able to send some of these creatures back to their own realm!"

Jerica's eyes widened with realization. "Brilliant! Let's give it a try!"

As they moved into position, Hamish couldn't help but marvel at the synchronicity of their group. In this moment, dragons and humans were working together as if they'd trained for years. It was everything he'd dreamed of when he'd left home to join this fight. And he hoped their cohesion would hold, after the battle.

"Ready?" Jerica asked, her goblet glowing with barely contained power.

Hamish nodded, his hands already tracing the complex patterns of the banishment spell. "On three. One … two …"

A storm creature lunged at them, its form crackling with venomous energy.

"Three!" Hamish shouted, completing the final gesture as Jerica's spell burst forth from her goblet.

The combined magic enveloped the creature, warping the reality that surrounded it. With a sound like tearing silk, a rift opened in the air, and the storm creature was yanked back into another dimension.

"It worked!" Jerica exclaimed, her face flushed with exertion and excitement.

Hamish allowed himself a brief moment of satisfaction before turning his attention back to the battle. Zebulon would be pleased. "Let's see how many more we can send home," he said, his cute but devilish smile returning as he prepared for the next incantation.

"Watch your left, Hamish!" Sif's voice rumbled from beneath the earth.

He spun, narrowly avoiding a storm creature's attack. Without missing a beat, Skellig's lightning struck the creature, reducing it to mist.

"Thanks," Hamish called out, momentarily flushed with pride. This was where he belonged, using his knowledge and skills to make a difference.

Zeira's wings beat furiously, but a whirling mass of air and electricity materialized beneath her, sucking her downward. She roared in defiance, but the pull was too strong.

"Zeira!" Gocri's voice cut through the chaos. The young red dragon plummeted, engulfed by a swarm of storm creatures that seemed to materialize from the air itself.

Panic gripped Zeira's heart as razor-sharp claws tore at her scales. "I can't—" she gasped, her words cut short as electricity coursed through her body.

In that moment of desperation, a familiar icy blast cut through. Gocri's massive form barreled through the storm creatures, his freezing breath turning them to brittle statues that shattered on impact.

"I've got you," Gocri rumbled, catching Zeira mid-fall. His white scales glistened with frost as he set her gently on the ground.

Zeira panted, her legs shaky. "Thank you," she managed, locking eyes with her rescuer. "I thought I was—"

A deafening crack interrupted her, and they both whirled to see Jerica cornered by a colossal storm giant, its fist crackling with barely contained lightning. The Eye of the Storm seemed to be producing thousands of them, one after the other.

"Jerica!" Zeira cried.

In a blur of yellow and black, Skellig appeared between Jerica and the giant. "Not today, you overgrown thundercloud," he snarled, spreading his wings wide to shield the human.

The storm giant's fist came down with earth-shattering force. Skellig gritted his teeth, bracing for impact. Lightning exploded around them, temporarily blinding all of them.

When Zeira's vision cleared, she saw Skellig huddled, his wings smoking but still protectively curled around Jerica. The girl clutched her jhorium goblet, eyes wide with shock and gratitude.

"Skellig, are you—" Jerica began.

The Spark dragon managed a pained grin. "Just a little toasty, nothing to worry about." He winced as he stood, electricity still crackling across his scales. "Though I might need a moment to catch my breath."

"We need to regroup," Jerica gasped, her confidence

returning. "Gocri, can you create an ice barrier to give us some cover?"

The Frost dragon nodded, already moving to comply. As he began to form a protective wall of ice, Zeira turned to Jerica and Skellig.

"Are you both alright?" she asked, her voice laced with worry.

Jerica nodded, still clutching her goblet. "Thanks to Skellig. I've never seen anyone move that fast."

Skellig attempted to shrug nonchalantly, but couldn't hide a grimace of pain. "It's what any of us would have done," he said, his eyes meeting Zeira's. "We're in this together, after all."

Zeira felt a lump form in her throat. It was a quiet reminder that they shouldn't argue. Ever.

"Alright," she said, her voice growing stronger. "Let's show these storm creatures what happens when they mess with our family."

All around were determined nods, but the visible signs of exhaustion were evident on everyone's faces. Gocri's ice barrier provided a momentary respite, yet the relentless assault of the storm creatures continued to batter against it.

Hamish slumped against the icy wall, his breath coming in ragged gasps. "I don't know how much longer I can keep this up," he admitted, wiping blood from a gash above his eye. "My magic reserves are nearly depleted."

Sif emerged from the ground nearby, her terran form covered in dirt and grime. She reverted to one of her human shapes, wincing as she favored her left leg. "Those blasted creatures are getting smarter. They almost caught me in my last tunnel."

Jerica felt her own body protesting, muscles screaming from the prolonged battle. But she pushed the pain aside, focusing on the task at hand. "We can't give up now," she said, her voice hoarse but resolute. "Look out there—his army is weakening. We're making progress."

Through gaps in the ice barrier, they could see the battlefield strewn with the fallen forms of storm creatures. The once-overwhelming force had been reduced to a fraction of its original size.

Zeira peered through the ice, her eyes widening. "She's right," she breathed. "There's maybe a third of them left now."

Skellig straightened, grimacing as he flexed his injured wing. "Then let's finish this," he growled, electricity crackling around his claws. "I've got enough fight left in me for one last push."

Gocri rumbled in agreement, frost gathering around his muzzle. "As do I. We've come too far to falter now."

Jerica looked at each of her companions in turn, seeing the mix of pain and fighting spirit in their eyes. "Alright," she said, her voice low but fierce. "Here's the plan. Gocri, when I give the signal, bring down this barrier. Sif, I need you to create as much chaos as you can from below. Zeira, focus on weakening their defenses. Skellig, Hamish, and I will lead the frontal assault. Are we ready?"

The group nodded, steeling themselves for what was to come. Jerica took a deep breath. "On my mark," she said, raising her hand. "Three ... two ... one ... now!"

The ice barrier shattered, and they surged forward as one, their unified attack catching the remaining storm creatures off guard. Despite their exhaustion, despite their injuries, they fought with renewed vigor, each one drawing strength from the others.

Jerica's heart pounded as she narrowly dodged a bolt of lightning from a nearby storm creature. The air crackled with electricity, making her hair stand on end. She gritted her teeth, pushing through the pain of her injuries.

"Sif! Now!" she shouted, her voice hoarse from the constant yelling.

The ground beneath their feet rumbled ominously. Suddenly, fissures opened up, swallowing several creatures whole. Sif burst from the earth, her terran form covered in dirt and grime, eyes blazing.

"Nice work!" Gocri shouted, his massive dragon form swooping low. He unleashed a blast of freezing breath, immobilizing a group of enemies that had been closing in on Jerica.

Jerica nodded her thanks, raising the jhorium goblet high. "Cover me!" she called out, "I need a moment to cast!"

Skellig immediately moved to her side, electricity arcing between his claws. "I've got you," he screeched, striking down several approaching creatures.

Despite their progress, Jerica couldn't shake the feeling that something was wrong. The Thunder King hadn't moved from his position, watching the battle with an eerie calm that sent chills down her spine.

"It's too easy," she muttered to herself. "What's he planning?"

As if in answer to her thoughts, a deafening crack of thunder split the air, vibrating the ground beneath them. The remaining storm creatures suddenly retreated, forming a protective circle around their master.

"Fools!" The Thunder King's voice boomed, dripping with contempt. "Did you really think you could defeat me so easily?"

Jerica signaled for her companions to regroup. They gathered around her, battered and bloodied but still standing tall.

"What now?" Sif asked, her eyes never leaving the enemy.

Jerica took a deep breath, assessing their situation. "We finish this," she said firmly. "Together. We've come too far to back down now."

Hamish nodded, a wry smile on his face despite the dire circumstances. "Well, I always wanted to go out in a blaze of glory."

"No one's going out today," Jerica interrupted. But a nagging doubt lingered in the back of her mind.

What was the cost of this victory going to be?

She pushed the doubt aside, focusing on the immediate threat before her. The Thunder King stood atop a rocky outcropping, his enchanted sword crackling with otherworldly energy. His eyes, cold and merciless, locked onto hers.

"You've come far, little girl," he sneered, his voice booming over the din of battle. "But your journey ends here."

Jerica bristled at the threat, but she held her ground. "It's over, Emerus," she called back. "Your army is defeated.

Surrender now, and we can end this without further bloodshed."

The Thunder King's laughter was like rolling thunder. "Surrender? You fool. I am the storm incarnate! I do not yield!"

With a roar, he leapt from his perch, his sword arcing through the air toward Zeira, as he landed nearby. She barely managed to dodge, feeling the crackle of energy as the blade passed inches from her scales.

"Zeira!" Gocri's voice rang out. "We've got your back!"

The Ice dragon's freezing breath created a barrier between Zeira and the Thunder King, buying her precious seconds. Skellig's lightning struck from above, forcing Emerus to defend rather than attack.

Hamish caught sight of Jerica, who was kneeling on the ground, her hands clasped around her jhorium goblet, lips moving in a silent incantation. Whatever she was planning, they needed to give her more time.

"Keep him distracted!" Hamish shouted to the others. "Whatever it takes!"

Sif burst from the ground beneath the Thunder King's feet, nearly toppling him.

Emerus Dinty snarled, his face contorted with rage. "Enough of these games!" he roared. The sky above darkened and swirled ominously; the air grew charged with electricity.

"Everyone, take cover!" Jerica cried, but her warning came too late.

A blinding flash erupted from the Thunder King's sword, followed by a sharp crack. She felt herself thrown backward, her world spinning. As she struggled to her feet, her heart sank at the sight before her.

Her companions lay scattered across the battlefield, dazed or unconscious. Only Jerica and Gocri remained upright, her eyes now blazing with an inner fire as she raised her goblet high.

"It's ready!" Jerica shouted. "Gocri, now!"

The Thunder King turned toward Jerica, his sword raised for a killing blow. Their eyes met.

Chapter 16 — Frost

The clash of ice and thunder shook the very foundation of the earth, as Gocri and the Thunder King locked in mortal combat. The glacial dragon's massive form, resplendent with shimmering white scales, towered over the brawny human king. Yet Emerus Dinty, the self-proclaimed Thunder King, exuded an aura of evil power that sent chills, even through Gocri.

"You cannot hope to defeat me, dragon," Emerus snarled, his enchanted sword crackling with barely contained energy. "Surrender now, and I may yet spare your miserable life."

Gocri's eyes narrowed, his willpower burning like blue fire in their depths. "I will never yield to the likes of you, Thunder King. Your reign of terror ends here."

With a roar that shook the heavens, Gocri unleashed a torrent of frigid breath, the icy blast crystallizing the air around them. Emerus raised his sword, deflecting the attack from his body, but frost still crept along his armor, the metal groaning under the strain.

As they clashed again and again, Gocri knew he couldn't defeat the Thunder King alone, but if he could just buy enough time for the others to escape …

"Your ice is nothing but a feeble chill against my power," Emerus taunted, his sword slicing through the air and leaving trails of lightning in its wake. "I will crush you and all who stand against me!"

Gocri gritted his teeth, feeling the strain of the battle in every scale of his body. But he couldn't falter, not now. The faces of his friends, and of Queen Freriss, flashed through his mind, steeling his nerves.

"You may have strength, Thunder King," Gocri keened, his voice echoing with the power of ancient glaciers, "but you lack the heart of a true warrior. Your cruelty will be your downfall!"

With renewed vigor, Gocri unleashed another blast of his ice breath, this time aiming not at Emerus directly, but at the ground beneath his feet. The earth froze instantly, creating a treacherous landscape of jagged ice spires and slippery surfaces.

Emerus stumbled, momentarily caught off guard by the change in terrain. Gocri seized the opportunity, his massive tail sweeping low and fast, threatening to knock the Thunder King off his feet.

"Flee, my friends!" Gocri roared, although he didn't dare take his eyes off the enemy to see if they made it out. "I will hold him here!"

As he fought, Gocri's mind thought of his home in Bliss, of Queen Freriss's kind words and the trust she had placed in him. He couldn't let them down, couldn't let the Thunder King's evil spread any further.

"Your bravery is admirable, but futile," Emerus sneered, regaining his footing. "You sacrifice yourself for nothing. I will hunt them down, one by one, and you won't be there to protect them!"

The words cut deep, but Gocri refused to show weakness. Instead, he channeled his fear and anger into his next attack, summoning a blizzard that swirled around them, obscuring vision and biting at exposed flesh with needle-sharp ice crystals.

"You underestimate the strength of unity, Thunder King," Gocri declared, his voice steady despite the exertion of maintaining the storm. "Even if I fall here, others will rise to take my place. Your reign of terror will end, one way or another."

Gocri hoped it was true, that his friends would find a way to overcome the darkness that threatened their world. With every ounce of his strength, he fought on, determined to give them the chance they needed to escape and regroup.

The Thunder King snarled in frustration as another of his lightning bolts glanced off Gocri's icy shield. Dark energy crackled around him, his enchanted sword glowing an ominous purple. He advanced relentlessly, each step melting through the ice beneath his feet.

Gocri scanned the battlefield. Zeira was beginning to come around, after the stunning blow Dinty had dealt earlier. Skellig was on his feet, but rather unsteady. Jerica and Hamish were helping Sif.

"You think your pitiful ice can hold me back?" Dinty roared. "I've conquered realms, dragon. I've enslaved your water-dwelling kin. Your defiance is nothing but a fool's errand!"

Gocri's muscles trembled with exhaustion, his white scales dulled by the strain of battle. Yet, he stood his ground, ice crystals forming with each labored breath. "And you ... you think your stolen power makes you invincible?" he panted.

The Thunder King's eyes flashed dangerously. "Stolen? I earned this power! The weak don't deserve it."

Summoning another surge of strength, Gocri released a blast of frigid air, momentarily pushing Emerus back. But the effort left him gasping, his limbs heavy as lead.

I can't keep this up much longer, Gocri thought, desperately reaching out to Jerica and the others.

"Your friends have abandoned you, dragon," Emerus taunted, readying another attack. "They flee while you face your doom alone. How does it feel to be so utterly expendable?"

Gocri's heart clenched at the words, but he refused to let doubt take hold. "They haven't left me," he grimaced, risking another glance toward his comrades. Zeira was on her feet now. "They fight on, as I fight here. Every moment I keep you at bay is a moment they use to find a way to defeat you."

With a roar of rage, Emerus charged, his sword arcing through the air. Gocri barely managed to dodge, feeling the crackle of dark energy as the blade missed his neck by inches. The near miss sent a jolt of fear through him.

His ice-white scales glistened as exhaustion took its toll.

Emerus Dinty advanced, dark energy crackling around him forcefully. His eyes gleamed with malicious triumph. "Your precious ice is melting, dragon. Soon, you'll be nothing but a puddle at my feet."

Gocri summoned what little strength remained, sending a wave of frigid air toward his foe. But where before it had created a wall of ice, now it merely coated the ground with a thin layer of frost. The Thunder King laughed, a sound that chilled Gocri more than any winter wind.

"Is that all you have left? Pathetic," Emerus sneered, raising his enchanted sword. "I'll carve you up and use your bones to decorate my throne room."

Desperation clawed at Gocri's heart. He thought of his home in Bliss, of all that would be lost if he fell here. With a defiant roar, he lunged at Emerus.

His jaws snapped shut inches from Emerus's face, but the Thunder King's blade found its mark. It plunged deep into Gocri's chest, dark magic searing through him. He felt his body sway.

A hundred meters away, Zeira let out a heart-wrenching keen, while Skellig's wings drooped in shock. Even Hamish, usually quick with a quip, stood silent, his face ashen.

As Gocri's massive form crumpled to the ground, a palpable wave of despair washed over his allies. The proud glacial dragon, who had stood as their bulwark against the Thunder King's wrath, lay still and silent.

Emerus stood over his fallen foe, his laughter echoing across the desolate landscape. "Let this be a lesson," he called out to the group as he rose and vanished into the swirling cloud of the Eye of the Storm. "This is the fate that awaits all who dare to stand against me."

The hope that had sustained them through their trials seemed to evaporate like morning mist as they gazed upon Gocri's motionless form.

Jerica's legs gave way beneath her as she stumbled toward Gocri. Her vision blurred with hot tears, and she collapsed beside the glacial dragon's massive head. Her small hands trembled as they reached out to touch his cold scales.

"No, no, no," she whispered, her voice cracking. "Gocri, please. You can't … we need you."

The jhorium goblet at her hip held a faint green glow, as if sensing her distress. Jerica barely noticed, her mind awash with memories of Gocri's unwavering support, his dry humor, the way his ice-blue eyes would crinkle when he smiled.

"I'm so sorry," she choked out, pressing her forehead against his snout. "This is all my fault. If I hadn't insisted on facing the Thunder King now, if I'd listened to you about being more cautious …"

The anguish of their failure crashed down upon her, threatening to crush her spirit entirely. How would she face Queen Freriss in Bliss, all the people and dragons counting on them to stop Emerus. How could they possibly succeed now, without Gocri's strength and wisdom?

Jerica's fingers brushed against the oron stone. Its three colored segments remained dull and lifeless. She clutched it tightly, willing it to show her a way forward, but found no answers in its smooth surface. She held the stone against Gocri's wound, but nothing happened. No glow, no healing reaction.

"What do I do now?" she whispered, more to herself than to her friend's silent form. "How can I lead them when I've already failed so terribly?"

The sound of Emerus's laughter echoed in the distance, a chilling reminder of the danger they still faced. Jerica's grief gave way to a flicker of anger, then cold-blooded determination. She sat up straighter, wiping her tears with the back of her hand.

"No," she said, her voice stronger now. "I won't let your

sacrifice be in vain, Gocri. We'll find a way to stop that tyrant, I promise you that."

She placed a hand on Gocri's scales once more, her touch gentle but resolute. "Rest now, my friend. We'll carry on the fight in your name."

As Jerica stood, her legs still shaky, she felt their situation settle heavily upon her. The path ahead seemed darker and more treacherous than ever, but she knew she had no choice but to press on.

Zeira approached Jerica, her massive red form casting a shadow over the young girl. The dragon's eyes glistened with unshed tears, her usual fiery demeanor dampened.

"Jerica," Zeira rumbled, her voice thick with emotion. "We can't stay here. The Thunder King will return soon."

Hamish stepped forward, reaching for her hand as he knelt beside Jerica. "She's right. We need to move."

Jerica nodded numbly, her gaze still fixed on Gocri's lifeless form. "But we can't just leave him here," she whispered. "What—what do dragons do with their dead? Should we bury him?"

Hamish slipped an arm around her shoulders. "There's no time. I believe dragons want their bodies left in the open, for the elements to take care of them." He helped Jerica to her feet.

"His flesh will proudly feed others." Zeira's nostrils flared, a small puff of smoke escaping as she fought to control her emotions. "I ... I remember when I first met Gocri," she said, her voice trembling. "He was trapped in a block of ice, victim to one of the Thunder King's cruel spells. I used my fire to free him, and from that moment, our alliance was forged."

Others nodded, recalling their own memories of the Frost dragon.

"Othos," Jerica called out. "We beseech you, great celestial dragon. Please, care for Gocri's body. We ... we have no choice but to leave him behind."

The words caught in her throat, and she felt Skellig's nose press reassuringly against her shoulder. His touch steadied her, reminding her of the responsibility she bore as their leader.

Hot tears began to fall from Zeira's eyes, sizzling as they hit Gocri's still form. "He was so brave, so loyal. We can't let his sacrifice be in vain."

Hamish gave Jerica's hand a comforting squeeze. "We'll honor him by continuing the fight. It's what he would have wanted."

Jerica looked up at her companions, seeing the hope in their eyes despite their obvious despair. She took a deep breath, steeling herself. "You're right. We need to keep moving."

As they prepared to leave, Jerica cast one last look around the desolate wasteland. The barren landscape seemed to stretch endlessly in every direction, a stark reminder of the Thunder King's destructive power. The air was heavy with ash and the sooty smell of burnt vegetation, while the sky above remained an ominous, brooding gray.

"This place," Jerica whispered, "it's like hope itself has been drained away."

Hamish nodded grimly. "The Thunder King's influence grows stronger every day. We're running out of time."

Zeira's tail lashed in agitation. "Then we must press on, no matter how bleak things seem." But beneath the despair, a spark of something else burned, a fire fueled by the memory of Gocri's sacrifice and the unwavering support of her remaining companions.

Jerica's heart felt heavy as they walked away, each step a reminder of their loss and the monumental task ahead. The wind howled across the barren landscape, carrying whispers of the enemy's power.

"I can't help but wonder," she said, her voice barely audible above the gusts, "if we're just delaying the inevitable. Gocri was so strong, and yet ..."

Zeira's wings rustled as she moved closer to Jerica. "Strength isn't always about raw power. I want to say how sorry I am for my earlier words. I didn't mean to cause strife within the group."

Jerica nodded, accepting the apology.

Zeira continued. "Gocri's true strength was in his heart, his willingness to sacrifice everything for those he cared about."

Hamish nodded, his weathered face filled with grief. "Aye, and we do him a disservice if we give up now. Every step we take is a tribute to his memory."

As they crested a hill, the group froze. In the distance, another massive storm was brewing, dark clouds swirling ominously. Flashes of lightning illuminated the tempest, each bolt reminiscent of the Thunder King's devastating attacks.

Jerica's breath caught in her throat. "Again. He's coming for us."

The air crackled with tension as the group exchanged worried glances. They were exhausted, demoralized, and now faced with yet another battle. Skellig and Sif took flight, intending to scout the surrounding area, while the others would continue on foot.

"What do we do?" Zeira asked, her usual confidence wavering.

Jerica closed her eyes, remembering Gocri's unwavering courage in the face of certain doom. When she opened them again, there was a fire burning within.

As the storm approached, bringing with it the threat of their greatest challenge yet, Jerica couldn't help but wonder: would their unity be enough to overcome the Thunder King's terrifying power? Or would Gocri's sacrifice mark the beginning of the end, for them all?

Chapter 17 — Regroup

They crested a hill, seeing water in the distance. It was a stark reminder of how far across the land the battle had carried them, and how Nuri was out there somewhere, dealing with another set of problems, probably on her own. Jerica's earlier confidence quickly melted.

"I failed them," she whispered, her voice hoarse from screaming spells during the battle. "I failed them all."

A low rumble sounded behind her, and Jerica looked up to see Skellig landing nearby. His yellow scales were covered with soot and marred by fresh wounds, a testament to the ferocity of the battle they had just endured.

Young mage. Skellig's voice resonated in her mind, tinged with weariness and concern. "We must move on. It is not safe to linger here."

Jerica shook her head, her eyes burning with unshed tears. "How can we move on? Look around us, Skellig. We've lost everything."

The dragon's massive head lowered, bringing one golden eye level with Jerica. "Not everything, little one. We still have each other, and while we draw breath, there is hope."

A bitter laugh escaped Jerica's lips. "Hope? What hope is there when the Thunder King's forces have laid waste to half of Andela? When we couldn't even protect a single village?"

She reached into her tunic, pulling out the jhorium goblet. Its green glow seemed muted, as if it too were affected by the despair that permeated the air. "What good is this if I can't use it to save anyone?"

Skellig's tail swished, stirring up eddies of ash. "The goblet's power is not diminished, Jerica. It is your belief in yourself that wavers."

Jerica's fingers tightened around the goblet's stem, feeling the familiar thrum of magic within it. "I don't know if I'm strong enough for this, Skellig. I never asked to be a mage, to bear this responsibility."

"Few who are worthy of great power ever ask for it," Skellig replied, his voice gentle despite its rumbling depth. "It is thrust upon them, and they must rise to meet it."

Jerica closed her eyes, remembering the faces of her family back in Cael. Her father, Hallis, working tirelessly at his foundry. Her mother, Nyssa, always ready with a warm embrace. Her sister, Theresa, and brother-in-law, Vyler, the baron who had always believed in her potential.

"You are so wise. And you're right. I can't let them down," she whispered to Skellig. "I can't let Andela fall."

The dragon's warm breath washed over her as he exhaled. "Then stand, young mage. Stand and face the challenges that lie ahead."

With a deep breath, Jerica pushed herself to her feet, her legs shaking but holding firm. She looked out over the ruined landscape once more, but this time, she forced herself to see beyond the destruction. In her mind's eye, she saw the land as it had once been, as it could be again.

"We need to regroup," she said, her voice gaining strength. "And we need to try contacting Nuri again."

Skellig nodded, a spark of approval in his ancient eyes. "Good. We will need every ounce of courage in the days to come."

To their right, Zeira and Sif were soaring low over the land, watching for signs of life, villages that might have survived the onslaught.

Jerica and Hamish climbed onto Skellig's back, settling at the base of his long neck. As the dragon spread his wings, preparing to take flight, she allowed herself one last look at the battlefield below.

"I swear," she grunted, "I will not let this be the end of Andela. The Thunder King will rue the day he unleashed his forces upon our land."

With a powerful leap, Skellig launched them into the air. As they soared above the devastation, Jerica felt a flicker of hope rekindling in her heart. And she, Jerica Barille of Cael, would see it through to the bitter end.

Zeira's crimson wings beat rhythmically as she soared through the ashen sky, her scales glistening with an eerie sheen in the fading light. Below her, Sif glided in her smoke dragon form, her gray body almost indistinguishable from the haze that cloaked the ruined landscape.

"We should retreat," Zeira called out, her voice wavering. "There's nothing left for us here."

"Agreed." Sif dipped a wing and flew alongside. "The sea is ahead. I see Skellig in the distance." The two picked up speed to catch up. Soon, they sensed Jerica's voice.

Nuri ... please ... answer me. Jerica's thoughts filtered through, fragmented and fading.

Zeira turned her head toward Sif. "Jerica's still trying to reach the valthan dragons. What if ... what if they've fallen too?"

Sif's expression hardened. "We can't assume the worst. Not yet."

But doubt gnawed at them both. The flew together in silence, conserving their waning energy.

* * *

Jerica stood at the water's edge, letting the violent gray waves crash over her boots. They had found refuge in a rocky, protected area and rested for two days. After an additional day's travel, they'd arrived at the sea.

Nuri! Please, if you're out there, answer me! We've lost … the land is torn apart. We need you!

But only silence greeted her plea. Jerica's shoulders sagged.

"What if they're all gone?" she breathed to Hamish, her voice barely audible. "The valthans, the dragons from other realms who were to be our backup, our last hope … what if the Thunder King has defeated them too?"

His expression was grim. No doubt he was also thinking of his own home and family, uncertain what was going on throughout the realm.

The thought sent a chill through her body, colder than the ash-filled wind that howled around them. Jerica clutched the goblet tighter, its warm glow the only comfort in a world that seemed to have abandoned all hope.

She shook off the feeling when she spotted Zeira and Sif flying toward them. Both dragons stumbled slightly as they landed, their exhaustion evident. Jerica realized the two had been arguing. Again.

"And what good is an oath if we're all dead?" Sif snapped, smoke curling from her nostrils. "We can't win this fight. Not anymore."

Zeira whirled on Sif, eyes blazing. "So you'd have us run? Hide in some distant land while the Thunder King destroys everything we love?"

"I'd have us live!" Sif roared, her form rippling as she struggled to maintain her draconic shape. "What use are we to anyone if we're all slaughtered?"

Skellig turned to them and hissed between his teeth. "Stop this! We owe it to Gocri to keep fighting. He wouldn't have given up."

"Gocri isn't here," Zeira said softly, her earlier fire dimming. "And that's on me." Her voice broke. "I failed him."

Jerica stepped forward—she had to say something to diffuse the situation. Suddenly, the jhorium goblet pulsed in her hands, warm and insistent. She gasped as a memory flooded her mind—clear and vivid as if she were living it again.

She saw Anahita, the guardian of the sea, standing before a gathering of dragons and humans alike. The sea queen's voice echoed in Jerica's mind: "Hope is not found in victory alone, but in the courage to keep fighting even when all seems lost. It is in these darkest moments that our true strength is revealed."

The vision faded, leaving Jerica breathless. She looked up at the dragons, their faces filled with doubt, some anger, and mostly fear.

"Wait," she said, her voice stronger than she expected. She repeated the words of Anahita. "Notice, please, that it's when we are bickering that the Thunder King swoops in and takes advantage. He may be human but he has a way of taking advantage of our most vulnerable moments. We cannot allow him to do that."

The faces around her softened as each dragon realized the truth she had spoken.

"We can't give up," Jerica continued, her voice trembling but growing stronger with each word. "Gocri ... he didn't die for nothing. He believed in our cause and he fought to the very end. We owe it to him to keep fighting. The Thunder King thinks he's broken us, but he's wrong. We're still here. We're still breathing. And as long as we are, we have a chance."

Zeira lifted her head, her scales shimmering in the fading light. "You speak bravely, villager from Cael. But bravery alone won't win this war."

"No," Jerica agreed, "but it's a start. Gocri showed us what true sacrifice looks like. We can't let that be in vain."

Skellig, who had been silent until now, rumbled deep in his chest. "The girl speaks truth. Gocri was ... he was my friend. My brother. I won't dishonor his memory by giving up now."

Jerica felt a flicker of hope ignite in her chest. She turned to face all three dragons, her slight frame dwarfed by their massive forms. "We've lost so much, but we're not defeated. The Thunder King may have won this battle, but the war isn't over."

Zeira's eyes softened as she regarded Jerica. "Perhaps ... perhaps you're right. We've come too far to turn back now."

Sif nodded, her earlier doubts fading. "If Gocri could see us now, he'd probably freeze us all for even thinking about giving up."

A chuckle rippled through the group, breaking the tension. Jerica felt a smile tug at her lips, remembering Gocri's frosty breath and the way his eyes would twinkle, even when he acted like the grumpy one of the group.

"We're stronger together," Hamish said, his voice filled with conviction. "The Thunder King may have his armies, but we have each other. We have our bond, our friendship. That's something he can never understand, or defeat."

Skellig lowered his massive head, bringing his eye level with Jerica's. "You've grown, little mage. Gocri would be proud to see you now."

Tears pricked at Jerica's eyes, but she blinked them back. "Then let's make him prouder still. Let's gather our forces and show the Thunder King what we're really capable of."

As one, the dragons roared their agreement, the sound echoing across the ravaged landscape and the open sea. In that moment, despite the overwhelming odds, despite the grief and loss in all of them, Jerica felt a spark of hope ignite within her heart. Her fingers brushed the oron stone and its tri-colored segments pulsed with energy.

"I have an idea," she announced, her voice steady despite the rapid beating of her heart. "The Thunder King's strength lies in his armies, but we have something important—the ability to strike from multiple fronts simultaneously."

"The fighters from the other regions…" Hamish supplied, with a glint in his eye.

"… Along with the elves, who are expert archers … and the woodsmen that Thorne was planning to recruit. And, I need to be smarter about how I'm using the magic I've learned."

Skellig cocked his head, curiosity gleaming in his ancient eyes. "Go on, little mage."

Jerica held up the jhorium goblet, its ethereal green glow casting dancing shadows across her face. "We've been using the goblet defensively, but what if we turn it into a weapon? A way to disrupt his forces from within?"

Zeira's scales rustled as she shifted closer. "How do you propose we do that?"

"The oron stone," Jerica explained, her excitement growing. "Its three segments—red, blue, and green—they're not just for show. Each color represents a different type of magic. If I can harness them through the goblet, we could create illusions, control the elements, maybe even influence minds."

"Influence minds? In what way?" Hamish wanted to know.

"Use these powers to get the word out to each of the realms at the same time. To attack Dinty and his minions before they attack us."

Sif's eyes widened. "That's ... that's incredible. But can you really do all that?"

Jerica took a deep breath, standing up straight. "I don't know. But I have to try. We all have to try everything we can."

Skellig was the first to speak, his voice a low rumble. "It's a risky plan, Jerica. But then again, nothing worth fighting for comes without risk."

Zeira nodded, her scales glinting in the fading light. "I've seen you grow from a timid village girl into a true leader. If anyone can make this work, it's you."

Sif, back in the smaller version of her natural form, bounced on her haunches, barely containing her excitement. "Let's do it! We'll show the Thunder King he messed with the wrong team!"

Jerica felt a surge of gratitude and affection for her dragon companions. She raised the jhorium goblet high, its glow intensifying as if responding to the collective harmony of the group. "Then it's settled. We'll use the cover of night to our advantage, striking at the Thunder King's forces when they least expect it."

Will that include the realms of the seas?

Nuri? Are you out there?

I'm right here.

The water swirled and then the blue water dragon pulled herself onto the sandy beach. "I heard something about harnessing the magic of the stone to communicate between the various regions."

"We hope so. But first of all, how are things in your world?"

Nuri's expression grew somber. "Not good. You saw the seabed, the devastation."

Jerica nodded, tilting her head toward the decimated forest behind them.

"Oh, no. It's the same here, now." Nuri's gaze circled the area, taking in the faces she saw. "Where is Gocri?"

When they informed her of his fate, her expression became angry. Her tail thrashed the water so violently it threatened to create a tidal wave.

"Nuri! Watch it."

"Sorry. I am unable to assimilate this information."

"We've all had a hard time with it." Jerica's voice cracked.

Nuri waited a long moment before speaking again. "Our queen had a visit from Anahita, and the queen promised to recruit as many able-bodied valthans as possible. If you can enhance communications to us, we are ready to stand with you, to make the sea an inhospitable place for that unspeakable man and his soldiers."

"We should keep our plans private and our movements quiet," Zeira said, stepping toward the water's edge.

Jerica nodded "Yes. The less we need to interact with anyone along the way, the better. We can't risk word of our approach reaching the Thunder King before we do."

And with that, Nuri dipped back into the sea.

* * *

Jerica stood atop a moss-covered boulder, pulling her blonde hair back from her face, eyes blazing. She and Hamish and the dragons had moved closer to the forested area for cover, even though most of the trees were mere skeletons of their former shapes.

"Okay, as we discussed, we can no longer wait for the Thunder King to make his next move. We must strike first, and strike hard."

Hamish stepped forward, his hand at the hilt of the

jhorium sword as he looked up at Jerica. "You mentioned a plan?" he asked, a hint of his devilish smile playing at the corners of his mouth.

"We'll divide into two teams," she explained, her gaze sweeping over the group. "Hamish, you'll work with Sif and Zeira. I'll partner with Skellig."

Zeira's wings rustled nervously, but Sif, in her human form, placed a reassuring hand on Zeira's leg. "We've got this," she said with a confident nod.

Jerica felt a swell of pride as she watched her friends rally together. This is what we need, she thought. Unity in the face of darkness.

"Our goal," Jerica continued, "is to experiment with combining our elemental powers. We need to create attacks so devastating that even the Thunder King won't be able to stand against them."

Hamish's eyes lit up with excitement. "Like mixing your jhorium magic with Skellig's lightning?" he asked, his scholar's mind already racing with possibilities.

Jerica nodded. "Exactly. And your mystical knowledge combined with Sif's smoke and Zeira's fire could be equally powerful. We need to rehearse some maneuvers."

As the group spread out to different areas for practice, Jerica caught Skellig's eye. The ancient yellow dragon regarded her with a mixture of respect and curiosity.

"Ready to make some magic?" Jerica asked, a hint of challenge in her voice.

Skellig's mouth curved into what could only be described as a dragon grin. "Always, young one. Though I warn you, my lightning isn't for the faint of heart."

Jerica laughed, feeling a surge of excitement despite the gravity of their situation. "Good thing I'm not faint of heart, then."

As they moved to a clearing nearby, Jerica could hear the others beginning their practice. The air crackled with energy as Hamish's mystical incantations mixed with the roar of Zeira's flames and the hiss of Sif's smoke.

Jerica raised the jhorium goblet, feeling its power coursing through her. "Alright, Skellig. Let's see what we can do."

The yellow dragon reared back, electricity dancing between his teeth. As he unleashed a bolt of lightning, Jerica channeled the jhorium's energy through the goblet, creating a swirling green and yellow light.

The combined forces collided in midair with a thunderous boom, sending shockwaves through the clearing. Trees swayed, the few remaining leaves scattering in the sudden gust of wind. Hamish and his group sent surprised stares in their direction.

Jerica stumbled back, her heart pounding. "By the gods," she whispered, staring at the scorched earth where their powers had met.

Skellig let out a rumbling laugh. "Not bad for a first attempt, little mage. Shall we try again?"

As they continued to practice, Jerica felt her connection to the jhorium deepening, her control becoming more precise with each attempt. She began to anticipate Skellig's movements, adjusting her own magic to complement his lightning strikes.

Across the clearing, she could see Hamish, Sif, and Zeira making similar progress. Hamish's face was a mask of concentration as he remembered the spells they'd discovered in the dusty alcove, then wove complex patterns in the air, guiding Sif's smoke and Zeira's fire into intricate, deadly formations.

Jerica turned to face Skellig once again.

"Are you ready?" Jerica asked, her voice barely above a whisper.

Skellig's wings twitched with anticipation. "As I'll ever be, young one."

Jerica took a deep breath, centering herself. She raised the goblet high, feeling the power of the jhorium coursing through her veins. At the same moment, Skellig spread his wings wide.

"Now!" Jerica cried.

A blinding surge of energy erupted from the goblet, arcing toward Skellig. The Spark dragon's wing talons crackled with electricity, meeting Jerica's power midair. The collision was explosive, sending stronger shockwaves through the clearing.

Jerica gasped, her eyes wide with wonder. "It's ... it's working!"

The combined energies swirled and danced, forming a vortex of green and yellow light. Skellig's voice rumbled with awe. "I've never felt anything like this before."

As it grew, Jerica felt a new connection forming between her and Skellig. She could sense his thoughts, his emotions, as clearly as her own. Together, they guided the swirling energy, shaping it, molding it.

With a shared thought, they released their creation. The vortex shot forward, carving a path through the forest. Trees splintered and the ground trembled as the devastating energy tore through everything in its path.

When the dust settled, Jerica and Skellig stood in stunned silence, staring at the destruction before them.

"By the ancients," Skellig breathed. "What have we done?"

Jerica's legs felt weak. She leaned against Skellig's massive form for support. "We've created something ... incredible. And terrifying."

From across the clearing, they heard a whoop of excitement. Hamish came bounding toward them, his dark hair splayed across his forehead, eyes wild with enthusiasm.

"That was amazing!" he shouted. "How did you do it?"

Sif and Zeira followed close behind, their expressions filled with awe.

"I've never seen anything like it," Zeira said, her earlier insecurity seemingly forgotten in the face of this new development.

Sif, in her dragon form, circled the area of destruction. "The power you two harnessed ... it's beyond anything I thought possible."

Hamish's grin turned devilish. "Well, now it's our turn to step up our game." He turned to Sif and Zeira. "What do you say, ladies? Shall we show them what we can do?"

Zeira nodded eagerly, while Sif let out a puff of smoke in agreement.

Jerica watched as Hamish, Sif, and Zeira practiced their combined attacks, their movements becoming more fluid and synchronized with each attempt. The air crackled with fiery energy, a testament to their growing power. As the sun began to dip below the horizon, painting the sky in hues of orange and purple, Jerica knew it was time to bring their training to a close.

"Everyone, gather around," she called out, her voice carrying across the clearing. "I can't express how proud I am of all of you," Jerica began, her voice steady despite the nerves fluttering in her stomach. "What we've accomplished here … it's nothing short of miraculous."

Hamish grinned, his eyes bright with excitement. "We're going to give that Thunder King a real shock, aren't we?"

Jerica nodded, a small smile tugging at her lips. "That's the plan. But remember, our strength isn't just in our individual abilities or even our combined attacks. It's in our unity, our trust in each other."

She glanced at Skellig, who nodded encouragingly. "The Thunder King may have his enchanted sword and an army of enslaved soldiers, but he stands alone. We have each other, and that's our greatest advantage."

Zeira lowered her head to meet Jerica's gaze. "Do you really think we're ready to face him?" she asked, a hint of uncertainty in her voice.

Jerica reached out, placing a hand on Zeira's warm scales. "I do. We've grown stronger than I ever thought possible."

As she spoke, Jerica felt the oron stone in her pocket pulse with energy. When she drew it out and looked at it, its three colored segments were glowing in unison. It was as if the stone itself was affirming her words.

"Tomorrow, we set out for the Thunder King's fortress," Jerica continued, her voice growing more resolute. They had only a vague sense of its direction, but had to trust they would be shown the way. "It won't be an easy journey, and the battle ahead will test us in ways we can't imagine. But I believe in us. I believe we can end his reign of darkness."

"For all the realms he's terrorized," Hamish added.

"For a future without fear," Zeira chimed in.

Skellig's eyes gleamed. "For the balance of all magic."

Jerica felt a lump form in her throat, overwhelmed by

the conviction in her friends' voices. She thought of her family back in Cael—her sister Theresa and brother-in-law Vyler managing the village in these uncertain times. She was fighting for all those villagers too.

"For all of us," Jerica said, raising the jhorium goblet high. "Together, we'll bring an end to the Thunder King's tyranny."

"Let's practice our moves a little bit more," Zeira suggested. The groups scattered again.

We're becoming a real team, a true force to be reckoned with, Jerica realized, watching as Hamish, Sif, and Zeira executed a particularly complex maneuver.

As darkness fell, Jerica called for a halt. The others gathered around her, their faces flushed with exertion and excitement.

"Today," Jerica said, her voice filled with pride, "we've learned a lot. What we've accomplished here—it's more than just combining our powers. It's teamwork."

Hamish nodded, his usual grin replaced by a look of strength.

Zeira, her earlier uncertainty gone, stood tall and proud. "I never thought I could do some of the things we did today," she admitted. "But with all of you ... I feel like anything is possible."

Sif let out a puff of smoke in agreement. "The Thunder King won't know what hit him," she declared.

Skellig, the oldest and most experienced among them, regarded the group with approval. "In all my years," he rumbled, "I've never seen a group come together quite like this. The Thunder King should be very, very afraid."

As night fell and the stars began to twinkle overhead, Jerica looked at her companions—human and dragon alike— and felt a surge of hope. The road ahead would be difficult, fraught with danger and uncertainty. But in this moment, watching the firelight dance across the faces of her friends, Jerica knew one thing for certain.

They were ready.

As the darkness deepened, they began to prepare for their journey. Jerica carefully packed the jhorium goblet and the oron stone, wrapping them in soft cloth to protect them. She couldn't help but marvel at how these magical objects had changed her life, transforming her from a simple village girl into a leader in this epic struggle.

Hamish approached her as she finished packing. "You know, when we first met, I never would have guessed you'd be the one leading us into battle against the most dangerous man in the realms," he said with a wry smile.

Jerica chuckled. "Believe me, I'm as surprised as you are."

"Well, for what it's worth," Hamish said, his tone growing serious, "I wouldn't want anyone else leading us. You've got a good head on you, Jerica Barille."

His words warmed her heart, chasing away some of the doubts that had been nagging at her. "Thank you, Hamish. That means a lot."

As they finished their preparations, a sense of anticipation filled the air. They gathered in a circle.

Skellig spoke up, his voice gravelly but filled with warmth. "Whatever happens in the coming days, I want you all to know that it has been an honor to fight alongside you. We face a formidable foe in Emerus Dinty, but we're well trained and we have powerful magic among us."

Jerica nodded, feeling a mix of anticipation and fear coursing through her veins. "Skellig's right. The Thunder King may have his enchanted sword and his army, but he's never faced anything like us before." She didn't bring up the evil magician they'd yet to encounter or dragons, the likes of Dym, who would fight alongside their enemy.

She looked at each of her companions in turn—Hamish with his unruly hair and cocky grin, Sif with her quiet strength, Zeira with her newfound confidence, and Skellig with his ancient wisdom. They were an unlikely group, but together, they were unstoppable.

"Get some rest," Jerica said finally. "Tomorrow, we face our destiny."

As they settled down for the night, Jerica clutched the jhorium goblet close to her chest. Its soft green glow was comforting, a reminder of how far she'd come and what she was fighting for. Tomorrow would put them all to the test.

Chapter 18—Stronghold

They set out early in the morning, before the first rays of the sun had shown themselves. Jerica traveled aboard Zeira's back, Hamish again with Sif. Their destination, the stronghold of the Thunder King was some fifty leagues away.

"I can't stop thinking about Gocri," Zeira said, her voice barely above a whisper. "The way he faced the Thunder King … it was so brave." Her golden eyes softened, a plume of smoke curling from her nostrils.

"Gocri's sacrifice won't be in vain. We'll find a way to stop Emerus Dinty and free the other dragons." But, deep inside, Jerica was thinking about how the Eye of the Storm kept growing and growing. And how Emerus would not give up until he had the jhorium.

Skellig's voice came through. *Look below, to the left. What's that?*

Jerica peered beyond Zeira's large form. Another ruined village met her gaze.

Should we land there and check it out?

What would we be able to do?

Hamish suggests we at least give it a look, Sif added.

Something told Jerica it would be a good idea.

Three dragons and two humans landed at the site. Jerica called out, hoping the inhabitants had merely taken cover and would come out to greet them. But nothing stirred.

As in other places they'd seen, most of the homes had suffered severe damage, but the largest building stood, mostly intact. Jerica and Hamish walked inside.

"It appears to be the town hall," she said.

"And these rooms on the left are a library. Perhaps the official archives."

"We could probably learn from the documents, but is it our right to search them? To take anything?" Her eyes scanned the shelves, where the enemy had done their damage. More than half the library's content was scattered over the stone floor.

"I think the residents of this place would be happy to be freed," Hamish decided. "If we discover anything that might help our mission, I wouldn't feel badly about borrowing it."

"Where should we start?"

"I'm going back outside. I'll ask the dragons to stand guard, to make sure we aren't taken by surprise with another attack, and to let any returning villagers know that we mean them no harm."

Jerica's gaze swept over the piles of ancient scrolls and tattered tomes scattered around them. She knelt on the dusty floor and picked up a book, setting it aside when she saw that the subject was agriculture. Others covered topics of grazing animals, some were about forging metals. As tempted as she was to read more on that subject, she set it with the others. They needed something that could help with their present situation.

As she unrolled a weathered scroll, dust motes danced in the air, carrying the musty scent of forgotten lore. Strange symbols covered the parchment, twisting and intertwining in mesmerizing patterns. Hamish wandered back into the room.

"What do you make of these?" she asked, tilting the scroll

so Hamish could see.

His eyes narrowed as he studied the cryptic markings. "They resemble the runes used by the ancient fire wizards of Blaze. See how this symbol looks like a flickering flame?"

Jerica leaned closer, her brow furrowed in concentration. "You're right! And this one here, it's almost like ... a storm cloud?"

Excitement rose in her chest as connections began to form in her mind. Could this be the key to understanding the Eye of the Storm? She grabbed another scroll, this one adorned with faded illustrations of swirling vortexes and lightning bolts.

"Hamish, look at this!" Jerica exclaimed, her voice echoing off the stone walls. "These diagrams ... they might be showing how the Eye draws its power!"

His keen gaze took in the intricate drawings. "We should show these to Zeira and the others. If the symbols are related to dragon lore, and *if* we can decipher them, we might find a weakness in the Eye's defenses."

Jerica's mind pieced together fragments of information, like a complex puzzle. "And if we find a weakness, we can exploit it. We can cut off Emerus's connection and leave him vulnerable!"

"That's the spirit! Now, let's see what other secrets these ancient texts hold."

Hamish searched the room, coming back with a sturdy cloth bag. "If the dragons can help us decipher these, we might have a much better chance against the Thunder King."

He dropped the scroll containing the fire and cloud images, along with two others Jerica had found, into the carry-bag and draped its strap across his chest. Outside, they found a sheltered spot and unrolled the scroll on a flat stone.

"The language is that of Blaze," Zeira confirmed, her eyes wide. "We must have crossed the border. I can't believe I didn't realize that."

"No matter—can you read it?"

"Of course." She peered closely at the scroll. "It would be helpful if you can unroll it ..."

Naturally. The scrolls had been created by humans,

for human hands to manipulate. Once they'd worked out a system for reading it, Zeira gave the printed parchment her full attention.

"Look at this passage," Zeira rumbled, her claw carefully indicating a series of intricate glyphs. "It speaks of a 'nexus of elemental forces' and a 'convergence of realms.' Could this be referring to the Eye of the Storm?"

Jerica leaned in, her heart pounding with excitement. "It must be! And here—what's this?"

"It mentions a 'binding ritual' that can be undone by … wait, what's this word?" Zeira squinted at the faded text, frustration mounting as the crucial information remained just out of reach. She huffed, a small jet of flame escaping her nostrils and briefly illuminating the scroll.

"Careful!" Jerica yelped, snatching the precious document away from the dragon's fiery breath. "Zeira! Did you see what you just did? Fire, and not from your … other end."

"I know! Amazing!" Zeira's scales then rippled with embarrassment. "My apologies. Sometimes I forget how fragile human artifacts can be."

Jerica managed a smile. "It's alright. We're so close, Zeira. I can feel it. The answer is here, hidden in these ancient words. We just need to find it before it's too late."

As she turned back to the scrolls, her brow furrowed, Jerica knew that the connection between fire and storm, as shown in the symbols, was somehow crucial. They had to figure out a way to break the link between the Thunder King and the Eye of the Storm. There was no other choice.

Jerica's fingers traced the cryptic language on the scroll, her forehead creased in concentration. Beside her, Zeira continued to read. The girl was learning that dragons were not quick readers.

"What if we combine this glyph with the one from the eastern tablet we found at the dusty alcove in the ruins?" Jerica mused, her blue eyes bright with excitement. She had made a tracing of it, and pulled that from her pocket now. "It could represent the Eye's connection to the elements, give us some idea of how this super-storm was originally formed."

Zeira hummed thoughtfully, her scales shimmering in the

dim light. "An astute observation. My mother once described something like that."

Jerica grinned. "That's brilliant, Zeira! Your knowledge of dragon lore is invaluable here."

The young dragon preened slightly, her earlier insecurities momentarily forgotten.

Suddenly, the dragon's claw froze over a particularly complex passage. "I can't ... I can't understand this part." She read the words aloud to Jerica, but the meaning wasn't clear to either of them.

Zeira's large eyes met Jerica's. "Perhaps we've reached the limit of our knowledge," the dragon admitted, her own confidence wavering.

For a moment, Jerica felt doubt. Were they truly capable of stopping the Thunder King? Had they come this far only to fail?

But then, her hand brushed against the jhorium goblet at her side, its familiar warmth grounding her. She took a deep breath, steeling herself. "No," she said firmly, meeting Zeira's gaze. "We can't give up now. Gocri's sacrifice, the fate of Andela—it all depends on us figuring this out."

Zeira's posture straightened, her earlier fire returning to her eyes. "You're right. This is just another challenge to conquer."

With a sigh, they turned back to the ancient texts. As they worked, Jerica couldn't help but marvel at how far they'd come—a village girl and a young dragon. And despite the earlier tension between them, they now stood united in a quest to save their world.

An hour later, Jerica stood up, her neck stiff from poring over the ancient texts. Hamish had walked over to join them.

His expression turned serious. "Let's think this through. What do we know about the Thunder King's strengths and weaknesses?"

Jerica began to pace, her fingers absently tracing the contours of the goblet. "Well, we know his power comes from that enchanted sword and his connection to the Eye of the Storm. But he's still human, vulnerable to physical attacks if we can get past his defenses."

"And the Eye itself?" Zeira prompted, her tail curling thoughtfully.

"It's a magical construct," Hamish mused. "Powerful, yes, but not invincible. If we could disrupt its energy source somehow …"

Jerica's eyes lit up. "We've been practicing together, combining our abilities to create something stronger … What if we used our combined power to create a sort of magical barrier? Something that could isolate the Thunder King from the Eye, disrupt his influence on it, even for a moment?"

She snapped her fingers. "Yes! And if we could do that while simultaneously attacking him physically …"

"We might have a chance of severing the connection permanently," Hamish finished, excitement evident in his voice.

"So … what does that mean? We somehow disrupt the elemental power of the Eye at the same time we physically attack Emerus Dinty?" Jerica sounded skeptical.

Zeira interrupted their strategizing. "Do you think we can really do this? Take on the Thunder King and win?"

Hamish was quiet for a moment, his expression thoughtful. "I believe we can," he said firmly. "Together, we're stronger than Emerus Dinty could ever imagine. And even though he has this grandiose idea of ruling the world, *we* have a cause worth fighting for."

"The jhorium, it's not just rare, it's conductive to magical energy. And we possess two jhorium artifacts. If we channel our powers through them while creating that barrier …"

"… we could potentially create a force strong enough to separate the Thunder King from the Eye!" Zeira finished, her tail lashing with enthusiasm.

The three exchanged glances, realization settling over them. Jerica felt a surge of hope, tinged with a cold, slender thread of fear.

"This could work," she breathed. "But Zeira, the risks …"

The dragon's expression sobered. "I know. We'll be putting ourselves directly in harm's way, and on his home ground. The Thunder King won't hesitate to strike us down if he gets the chance."

Jerica nodded grimly. "And there's no guarantee the goblet can withstand that level of magical energy. If it's destroyed, we would be completely vulnerable."

Zeira's voice was low as she added, "Not to mention, if our plan fails, we'll have revealed our strategy. We won't get a second chance."

A heavy silence fell between them as Jerica weighed the potential costs against what they stood to gain. She thought about what they had already lost under the Thunder King's growing power. Then she balanced that against what remained to be lost, if he persevered.

"It's worth it," she said finally, her voice steady despite the fear coiling in her stomach. "The fate of our world is at stake. We have to try."

Hamish nodded solemnly. Then he seemed to remember something. "We shouldn't stay here in this village much longer. The locals may have vacated in fear, but surely some of them will be coming back. And they may not be happy to find us here."

Jerica nodded. He was right.

"Skellig found a cave, less than an hour away. We can shelter there while we make our plans." He opened the cloth carry-bag and pulled out a rolled parchment. "Keep this—it's a map. The other items, the scrolls written in your language, Zeira … I should take them back into the library."

As they ascended into the sky and moved south, Jerica noticed for the first time that the region had conical mountains, many of which emitted plumes of smoke. Wide valleys were strewn with jagged black volcanic rock chunks. She thought it felt bleak, but Zeira let out a contented sound, almost a purr, a reminder that this was the Fire dragon's homeland.

Skellig led the way toward a particularly rugged peak, but at least it wasn't a volcano. As he crossed a ridge and dipped to the shady side of the rocky terrain, Jerica spotted the cave. It looked like a huge one, by human standards, but she supposed this was what dragons would consider an ideal nest.

With two quick bursts of lightning from his wing talons, the Spark dragon settled at the cave entrance. Sif followed, and Zeira came in right behind her. Their human passengers dismounted.

"Oh, I've missed the warmth of my homeland," Zeira commented, stretching her wings luxuriantly. "See the volcano on the horizon?"

"The one with fire shooting out the top?" Skellig wanted to know.

"That's Mount Zeiron. My mother chose my name based on it."

Hamish made a polite sound, but the others seemed unimpressed. "Gocri would have hated it," Sif observed, a tinge of sadness in her voice.

"Yes, I suppose he would. We can't all be as lucky as I am." Zeira said matter-of-factly.

Sif turned to the cave entrance, shifting to a smaller form of herself as she entered, to accommodate the others.

Hamish touched Jerica's arm. "While you and Zeira were poring over the scrolls, I did a bit of other research. I learned the location of the Thunder King's fortress. It's built upon a mountaintop in Gale. He calls the castle Thunderhaven."

"Oh, please." Jerica shook her head. "The ego of the man. Although I suppose Dintyville sounds … well …"

"Yeah. Doesn't have the same ring to it," Hamish agreed with a chuckle. Then he sobered. "I'm guessing the location in Gale accounts for the reason he recruited Skellig's sire, and others among the leadership there."

"Dym is important in Gale?"

"Why else would he have gotten away with attacking, kidnapping, and imprisoning his own son? I have a feeling he and this Emerus Dinty are two of a kind."

She nodded slowly. "Yes, I had that feeling as well."

"Let's find it on the map," he said, pulling the rolled parchment from his bag.

Inside the cave, the dragons had each claimed their own corners, Zeira nearest the entrance where she could take advantage of the hot outside air, which she had declared 'lovely.' Jerica and Hamish chose a flat spot in the center of the large cavern and Jerica unfurled the large parchment map, its edges curling slightly in the hot, humid air. Hamish pointed out the mountain which would be their destination. Jerica knelt beside the map, using the green glow of her jhorium goblet for light as she drew their planned route with her finger.

"If we approach from the southeast," she mused, her brow furrowed in concentration, "we can use the Towering Cliffs as cover. The rock formations there should mask our approach. And on the west lies the sea, which will probably prevent an escape by the humans, unless they have ships."

"Plus, if we're lucky, we might receive assistance from Nuri and her group." Hamish stared at the terrain layout.

"She does know how to take down a ship," Jerica observed, remembering.

Zeira lowered her massive head, her hot breath rustling the map's edges. "So true. But we'll need to time our arrival precisely. I have noted that the Eye of the Storm is most vulnerable during the new moon, when its power wanes."

"Good observation!"

Zeira smiled at Hamish's compliment.

Jerica nodded. She'd pulled the oron stone from her pocket, to hold down the edge of the curled map. Its tri-colored segments glowed faintly, as if sensing the importance of their planning. "That gives us a week to prepare. We'll need to gather our allies."

"The Phoenix caste," Zeira said, her eyes gleaming. "My mother, Gynnyth, said she could rally them. Their fire magic could be crucial in breaching the Thunder King's defenses."

As Jerica jotted down notes, a nagging worry gnawed at her. "Zeira," she began hesitantly, "what about the jhorium? The Thunder King wants it desperately. If we bring the goblet and sword, we risk—"

Her words were cut short by a loud *crack*. A burst of hot wind came through the cavern entrance, showering them with debris. Through the dust, a towering dragon emerged— orange and red scales gleaming like polished rubies, eyes blazing with fury.

"Karzoka Aeogan," Zeira gasped, instinctively curling her tail protectively around Jerica. "What are you doing—?"

"Ah. I heard you were here." The newcomer stepped

inside their sanctuary. "My father has been critically injured. In his place, I am now the Fire Lord of Blaze." The son of the king fixed them with a piercing stare.

Zeira cringed. This was one of the cruel dragons who had teased her mercilessly as a youngling. He was only a century older than herself. Surely, he had no business ruling the entire region of Blaze.

"Plotting against your own kind, Zeira?" he snarled. "Consorting with humans to overthrow the natural order?"

Jerica's heart hammered in her chest. Their careful planning teetered on the edge of ruin if the leaders of each realm would not back them up. She watched as Zeira's muscles tensed, knowing the young dragon was deeply conflicted about something.

"Karzoka," Zeira began, her voice steady despite the tremor Jerica could feel running through her body, "we seek only to protect Andela from—"

"Silence!" Karzoka roared, flames licking at the edges of his jaw. "You will abandon this foolish quest and return to your duties. The affairs of humans are beneath us."

Jerica's mind reeled. They couldn't afford to lose Zeira or the support of the Phoenix caste. With a deep breath, she stepped forward.

"Fire Lord," she said, forcing steel into her voice, "perhaps we can come to an arrangement. The power of jhorium could greatly benefit your people …"

Jerica's words hung in the air, the green glow of the jhorium goblet in her hand casting eerie shadows across the cave walls. Karzoka Aeogan's eyes narrowed, his gaze flicking between the human girl's face and the precious artifact.

Zeira tensed beside Jerica, her scales bristling with nervous energy. "Karzoka—"

"You will refer to me by my title," he hissed.

"My *Lord*," she said.

Hamish spoke up. "Please hear us out. What we propose could change everything."

The Fire Lord's nostrils flared, smoke curling from them as he considered their words. Finally, he nodded, a single, curt motion. "Speak quickly, then. My patience wears thin."

Jerica exchanged a quick glance with Zeira before launching into their plan. "Each of us has a crucial role," she explained, her voice growing stronger with every word. "Zeira's fire abilities will be key in breaching the Thunder King's defenses. The oron stone," she touched the three-segmented stone clutched in her hand, "will help us locate the exact point where his connection to the Eye of the Storm is weakest."

Zeira picked up the thread seamlessly. "And Jerica's mastery of the jhorium goblet will be our ace. It's the only thing capable of severing the connection completely."

As they outlined the rest of their strategy, Jerica could see the Fire Lord's expression shifting from skepticism to grudging interest. When they finished, silence fell over the cave.

"And if you fail?" Karzoka rumbled, his voice like the grind of stone-against-stone.

Jerica swallowed hard. "We've prepared for every contingency we can think of. But if the worst should happen ..." She trailed off, unable to voice the dire consequences.

Zeira stepped forward, her head held high. "If we fail, my Lord, I will return to face whatever punishment you deem fit. But we cannot stand idle while the Thunder King threatens all we hold dear."

Karzoka's gaze bore into them for what felt like an eternity. Finally, he exhaled a great plume of smoke. "Very well. You may proceed with your plan. But know this: the fate of Blaze rests with you. Do not disappoint me."

With a powerful beat of his wings, the Fire Lord departed, leaving Jerica and her team alone once more. As the dust settled, Jerica thought she heard Zeira utter a curse word.

She reached out, placing a hand on Zeira's warm scales. "What was that all about?" she asked. "I definitely sensed a history between you."

Zeira lowered her head, bringing her eyes level with Jerica's. She started to speak, then stopped and shook her head. "A childhood nemesis. I thought I'd long ago been done with him."

Skellig bristled. "If you want me to—"

"Not right now. We don't dare pick a fight with a realm leader at this point."

"Later then," Skellig settled back on the ground.

Zeira sent him an appreciative nod, and the team turned back to their plans to confront the Thunder King at his castle. And to do that, they would need to call upon all the resources at their disposal.

"Whatever comes," Jerica whispered, her fingers tightening around the goblet, "we can handle it."

Zeira's eyes glowed with fierce loyalty. "We can."

* * *

The sun sank below the horizon, casting long shadows across the mouth of the cave. It would soon be dark. Jerica's fingers trembled slightly as she touched the intricate patterns on the jhorium goblet, seeing its green glow intensify.

"Zeira," she called out, her voice barely above a whisper. "It's time."

The red dragon unfurled her wings, stretching them wide before padding over to Jerica's side. "Are you certain you're ready?" Zeira asked, concern evident in her reptilian eyes.

Jerica nodded, swallowing hard. "As ready as I'll ever be. The nights are dark now, and we must make our move soon—timing it with the new moon. We can't afford to wait any longer."

Together, they moved through the cave, rousing their allies. Jerica pushed aside the ache in her gut, focusing on the task at hand.

"Remember," she said, addressing the gathered group, her voice stronger now. "The Thunder King's power comes from the magic inside the Eye of the Storm. We sever that connection, we stand a good chance of defeating him."

A murmur of agreement rippled through the group. Jerica felt a swell of pride mixed with trepidation.

Zeira's warm breath tickled her ear as the dragon leaned in close. "You're doing well," she encouraged. "They believe in you."

Jerica managed a weak smile. "I just hope I don't let them down."

They stepped outside the cave, the distant rumble of thunder—a constant reminder of their enemy's presence—sent a shiver down her spine.

"Thinking of home?" Zeira asked, settling beside her.

Jerica nodded, her throat tight. "My family, Cael … it all seems so far away now." She touched her belt. "I never imagined when I created this goblet that it would lead to … all of this."

Zeira's tail curled protectively around Jerica. "You've grown so much since then. We both have."

As they flew from the cave entrance, out over the rugged land below, Jerica had a sudden thought. "Zeira, when we face Emerus Dinty … if things go wrong …" She hesitated, the words catching in her throat.

The dragon turned her head to look back at her kai, her eyes narrowed. "What is it?"

Jerica took a deep breath. "If it comes down to it, I want you to take the goblet and the stone and flee. Get them as far from the Thunder King as possible."

Zeira's wings flared, shock evident in her posture. "Absolutely not! I won't leave you behind!"

"Listen to me," Jerica insisted, her voice low and urgent. "These artifacts are too powerful to fall into his hands. Promise me, Zeira. Promise me you'll protect them, no matter what."

The dragon was quiet for a long moment, conflict clear in her eyes. Finally, she dipped her head in a reluctant nod. "I promise. But it won't come to that. We'll face him together, and we'll win."

Jerica managed a smile, hoping her friend couldn't see the fear behind it. "Together."

Chapter 19—Starlight

The vastness of the night sky enveloped the dragons as they soared through the inky darkness, their scales glimmering like diamonds against the backdrop of countless stars. The cool air carried with it the scent of distant storms. On Zeira's back, Jerica clung tightly, her small frame dwarfed by the dragon's massive body.

Zeira's wings beat steadily, each powerful stroke propelling them further into the unknown. To her left, Sif's silver scales shimmered like starlight with Hamish riding on her back, while Skellig's distinctive yellow form cut through the air on her right, his black wings invisible in the night. They'd instinctively left an empty spot for Gocri, their recent loss an unspoken burden that seemed to slow their flight.

We have a plan to summon the dragons of the realms, when we are ready. Jerica's voice came through to them. *But what about those in Gocri's land? Since our contact with the leadership depends upon my touch with a team member, how will we reach out to Bliss?*

I have an idea. Skellig sounded confident.

"Great Othos, we need your guidance," Skellig's deep voice rumbled through the night air. "We need additional help. Tell us what to do next."

Silence answered their pleas, broken only by the whisper of wind through their wings. Jerica's heart sank, doubt creeping into her mind. Had Othos abandoned them? Were they truly alone in this fight?

Maybe he didn't hear us, Sif suggested, her voice tinged with uncertainty. *Should we try again?*

Jerica leaned forward, her hair whipping in the breeze. "Not yet," she said, her voice barely audible over the rush of air. *I think ... I think I feel something.*

Zeira craned her neck, to catch a glimpse of the girl on her back. *What do you mean, Jerica? What do you feel?*

It's like ... a presence, Jerica replied, her eyes closed in concentration. *It's faint, but it's growing stronger. I think it's Othos.*

As if summoned by her words, a shimmering light appeared before them, coalescing into the form of the massive celestial dragon. Othos' ethereal body stretched across the sky, his wings spanning the horizon like a living aurora.

My children, Othos' voice resonated in their minds, a symphony of starlight and ancient wisdom. *I have heard your call, and I come to you in your hour of need.*

Jerica felt a wave of relief wash over her, mingled with awe at the celestial dragon's presence. "Great Othos," she began, but the words faltered on her tongue.

I know of your missing brother, Othos continued, his voice gentle yet powerful. *Gocri is at peace among the stars.*

Jerica's grip on Zeira's scales tightened, and she could feel the dragon's emotions roiling, through their connection, like a tempest. *Othos, we plan to storm the Thunder King's castle, to break his connection with the Eye of the Storm. It must happen within the next four days, and we need reinforcements. We devised a method to contact each of the region leaders, but we'll be unable to reach the dragons of Bliss without Gocri here with us.*

Ah. I do understand your dilemma.

Othos' form shimmered, and suddenly, Jerica found

herself immersed in a vivid vision. She saw a great ritual, dragons and humans working in harmony, their combined power flowing into a single point of light in the middle of a circle of stones. At the center of it all stood Jerica, wielding the jhorium goblet, channeling energies beyond mortal comprehension.

Othos' voice echoed through the vision. "Dragon and human, fire and spirit, united in purpose and power. This is what will defeat the Thunder King."

As quickly as it had appeared, the vision faded, leaving Jerica blinking in the starlight. Othos was gone. She glanced at her companions, seeing the same mix of wonder and confusion on their faces.

"Did you just see what I saw?" Jerica's voice was shaky.

Sif nodded, her silver scales catching the starlight. "A ritual of some kind. But how can we possibly harness that much power?"

"Together," Zeira said, surprising herself with the strength in her voice. "Just as Othos showed us. We must combine our strengths, our very essences."

Skellig snorted, two small sparks escaping his wing talons. "Ancient magic? It seems like a fool's errand."

"Do you have a better idea?" Jerica challenged, leaning forward on Zeira's back. "We've seen what the Thunder King can do. If this is our only chance to stop him, we have to take it. I trust Othos."

The girl speaks wisely, Othos' voice resonated once more, in their minds. *The path ahead is fraught with danger, but it is the only way to save your world from the Thunder King's tyranny. You have already hit upon the tyrant's secret fear, losing power by losing his connection to the Eye.*

"But where do we even begin?" Sif asked, her voice tinged with uncertainty. "We don't know how to perform such a ritual, or what we'll need."

Othos' voice remained strong. *One more component will be crucial for you to obtain—a fragment of storm-forged stone. Once you have that, seek out the ancient stones of Aethoria. There, and within the scrolls, you will find the knowledge you seek. But beware, for the Thunder King's forces will not stand idle. You must move swiftly and with purpose.*

As the last traces of Othos' presence disappeared, Jerica turned to the others. "Does anyone have a clue what a storm-forged stone is?"

Skellig nodded enthusiastically. "I do! It comes from a place where lightning strikes the earth repeatedly. There aren't many, but one of those places is where I used to play as a young dragonlet."

"Of course you did." Sif looked a little worried.

For a crazy moment Jerica wondered if she could simply send Skellig out to retrieve the special rock, but she quickly pushed that thought aside. It was too dangerous for the group to split up. Skellig had already been taken captive once, and they had no time to stage another rescue and put the team back together. It was all or nothing at this point.

"All right then, lead the way," she told the Spark dragon, her voice carrying across the night sky to her companions.

* * *

The ravaged forests of Andela gave way to craggy mountains. "There," Skellig called out, nodding toward a particularly rugged peak. "That's where we'll find the storm-forged stone."

Zeira banked sharply, her massive wings catching an updraft. "Are you certain? This place reeks of old magic and danger."

"I'm sure," Skellig replied. Othos' words had been clear. "The essence of storm-forged stone can only be found where lightning strikes the earth repeatedly. And that would be here, in the Chasm of Echoes."

As they approached the peak, the air crackled with electricity. Skellig let out a happy rumble. "Ah, home."

Zeira and Sif seemed less enchanted with the place, and the two humans were downright apprehensive.

"We don't have a choice," Jerica decided, her voice tight. "Othos said we must act quickly."

They landed on a rocky outcropping, the ground beneath their feet warm and humming with energy. Jerica slid from

Zeira's back, her legs wobbly after the long flight. She took a deep breath, steeling herself for what lay ahead.

"What now?" Zeira asked, her eyes scanning the forbidding terrain.

Jerica closed her eyes and touched the oron stone in her pocket. "Okay, Skellig, where is this place where the lightning has struck repeatedly?"

"There are good spots all around here."

As if on cue, a bolt of lightning split the sky, striking a jagged spire of rock not far from where they stood. The ground beneath their feet vibrated, causing Jerica to stumble back against Zeira's flank.

"Ah-ha, spotted one!" Skellig sounded way too happy.

He led them carefully across the uneven ground, the air growing thicker and more charged with each step. Jerica's skin tingled, the fine hairs on her arms standing on end. Another flash of lightning illuminated the valley, a little farther away this time.

"Oh my gosh, there!" Sif called out, gesturing with her snout. "Do you see it?"

Jerica squinted through the gloom. A small outcropping of rock glowed faintly with an inner light that matched the rhythm of the oron stone. "That's it," she breathed. "The storm-forged stone."

As they approached, a low rumble filled the air. At first, Jerica thought it was more thunder, but then she saw the ground shift and buckle. "Look out!" she cried, stumbling backward as the earth before them erupted.

A creature burst forth from the ground, its body a patchwork of stone and crackling energy. It towered over them, easily twice the size of Zeira. Lightning arced between its massive fists as it roared a challenge.

"By Othos," Skellig muttered. "A storm elemental. Of course it couldn't be easy."

Jerica's mind zipped through the options. They needed that stone, but how could they possibly overcome such a guardian? Her hand tightened around the jhorium goblet as an idea began to form.

"Zeira, Sif, flank it!" she called out. "Skellig, keep it

distracted. I have a plan, but I need time!"

As the dragons sprang into action, Jerica closed her eyes, focusing all her concentration on the goblet. She had created it, imbued it with magic she barely understood. Now, she prayed it would be enough.

The elemental creature shrieked, mixing with the dragons' roars and the constant rumble of thunder. Jerica blocked it all out, channeling her energy into the goblet. She felt it grow warm in her hands, then hot, then blazing.

"Jerica!" Zeira's voice cut through her concentration. "Whatever you're going to do, this would be a good time!"

Jerica's eyes snapped open. The elemental had Skellig's head pinned down, its fist raised for a crushing blow. Hovering above them both was a familiar jade green dragon.

Dym!

Skellig's sire let out a burst of maniacal laughter, clearly supporting the elemental rather than his own son. Without thinking, she thrust the goblet forward, willing it to act.

A beam of intense green light erupted from the goblet, striking the elemental squarely in the chest. For a moment, nothing happened. Then, with a sound like shattering glass, cracks spread across the creature's body. It let out one final, earthshaking roar before collapsing into a pile of rubble.

Dym's expression turned to one of pure fury. As Jerica prepared to aim the goblet's power toward him, the elder Spark dragon turned and dipped below the crest of the mountain, disappearing from sight.

Silence fell over the valley, broken only by the heavy breathing of the dragons and the distant rumble of thunder. Jerica lowered the goblet, her arms shaking from exertion.

"Well," Skellig said, shaking off debris as he climbed to his feet, "that was certainly spectacular."

"Skellig, your sire just came back and tried to kill you again," Zeira reminded.

Skellig uttered a growl in the direction where Dym had vanished, but gave no indication he wanted to follow, to retaliate.

Sif approached the glowing outcropping, now unguarded. "The storm-forged stone. We did it."

As Hamish carefully collected a fragment of the precious material, Jerica couldn't shake the feeling that this was only the beginning. They had overcome their first deadly obstacle, but at what cost? And what greater challenges lay ahead?

"One goal accomplished," she murmured, securing the stone in a pouch at her waist. "Let's hope the rest are easier."

Zeira snorted, a small puff of smoke escaping her nostrils. "Somehow, my friend, I doubt they will be. But we're with you, every step of the way."

Jerica nodded. As they prepared to take flight once more, she apprehensively cast one last look at the valley. The Thunder King's shadow loomed over everything, a constant reminder of what was at stake. And Dym was still out there—somewhere not far away.

"On to Aethoria," she said, her voice stronger than she felt.

The wind whipped around her as Zeira soared through the night sky, but Jerica remained still, lost in concentration, preparing herself for the upcoming ritual Othos had shown them in the vision. She took a deep breath, visualizing the magic as a vibrant green river coursing through her veins. Slowly, she opened her eyes, gasping as she saw tendrils of emerald light dancing around her hands.

"I … I think I'm doing it!" she exclaimed, a mix of excitement and disbelief in her voice.

Sif, flying close by, let out a low whistle. "I see it! Impressive, young mage. You're a quick study."

Jerica's cheeks flushed with pride, but she maintained her focus. "It's still difficult to control. How do I—" The light suddenly flared, causing Zeira to bank sharply to avoid the burst of energy.

"Careful there!" Skellig called out, his scales glinting in the moonlight. "We'd rather not become crispy dragon snacks."

Jerica winced. "Sorry, I didn't mean to—"

"No apologies necessary," Zeira interrupted, her tone gentle. "Learning to harness such power takes time and patience. You're doing remarkably well."

As they flew on, Jerica continued to practice, each attempt bringing more control and understanding.

"I've been wondering," Jerica said after a while, her voice barely audible over the rushing wind. "Why me? Why was I chosen for this?"

Skellig glided closer, his golden eyes fixed on her. "Destiny works in mysterious ways, little one. Perhaps it's not about being chosen, but about rising to meet the challenge when it presents itself."

Sif nodded in agreement. "You've shown courage and compassion beyond your years, Jerica. Those qualities, combined with your innate magical ability, make you uniquely suited for this task."

"It's true, Jerica," Hamish added, watching the exchange from his position on Sif's back. "My father speaks of destiny, a person's true purpose in life. This is yours."

Jerica fell silent, pondering their words. She wondered if Zebulon knew of this crucial mission when he said those things to his son.

As dawn broke on the horizon, casting the sky in hues of pink and gold, Zeira began their descent toward a dense forest where even the barren tree trunks afforded some measure of protection. "We should rest here for a while," she announced. "All of us need to regain our strength."

Once on the ground, Jerica stretched her stiff limbs, wincing at the soreness in her muscles. She watched as the dragons settled themselves, their massive bodies creating a protective circle around her.

"You've come a long way since we first met," Sif observed, her silver scales shimmering in the early morning light. "Remember how terrified you were of us?"

Jerica laughed, the sound bright and clear in the quiet forest. "How could I forget? I nearly fainted when Zeira first spoke to me."

"She was afraid we might eat her," Zeira told Hamish. "Even though we all know that humans don't taste good—at all."

"And now look at you," Skellig chimed in, his voice filled with warmth. "Riding dragons, wielding ancient magic, saving the world. Not bad for a village girl from Cael."

A lump formed in Jerica's throat as thoughts of her home

and family flooded her mind. "Do you think … do you think they're safe? My parents, Theresa, Vyler?"

Zeira's eyes softened with understanding. "The Thunder King's reach is vast, but not all-encompassing. We must have faith that they are well, and that our actions will ensure their continued safety."

Jerica nodded, blinking back tears. She reached for the oron stone, drawing comfort from its familiar bulk. "I miss them so much," she whispered. "But I know what we're doing is bigger than just me or my village. We're fighting for everyone."

"That's the spirit," Sif said, her tail curling around Jerica in a protective gesture. "And when this is all over, you'll have quite the tale to tell them."

As the group settled in for a brief rest, Jerica couldn't help but marvel at how far they'd come. She was glad the bickering had ended. The bonds between them had grown stronger with each challenge faced, each obstacle overcome. They were no longer just a girl, a scholar, and some dragons thrown together by circumstance, but a family forged in the fires of adversity.

Jerica closed her eyes, allowing sleep to claim her. In her dreams, she saw visions of a world free from the Thunder King's tyranny, a future worth fighting for. And she knew she would do whatever it took to make that dream a reality.

When she woke, a few hours later, her first thought was of their next duty, to perform the ritual that would break the Thunder King's connection to the Eye of the Storm and, with it, his control over the realm. She stood and made the announcement. "Today's journey to Aethoria could prove to be quite dangerous. I want everyone to be ready."

Zeira turned her head slightly, meeting the girl's gaze with one large, fiery eye. "Of course it's dangerous," she replied, a hint of her old confidence returning. "But we're dragons, and you're no ordinary human. Danger is what we do best."

Skellig let out a rumbling chuckle. "I'm with you, Zeira. To Aethoria and whatever lies beyond."

Sif nodded. "As am I. We started this journey together, and we'll see it through to the end."

Hamish gave her hand a squeeze and then the humans took their seats for the flight.

As the dragons adjusted their course, heading toward the mysterious stones of Aethoria, Jerica felt a glimmer of hope ignite within her. A band of blue sky showed through the ever-present clouds, as if the heavens were lending their strength to the unlikely band of heroes. They had lost much, but they had gained something too—unity that transcended the boundaries between dragon and human, something the land of Andela had been missing for a long time.

"Do you think the stone circle will be safe?" Jerica asked as they flew over the quiet, dead-looking land, the wind whipping through her hair.

Skellig's wings beat steadily beside her. "The Thunder King's forces have been spread thin searching for us. We shall hope they've not discovered the location."

"And if they have," Sif added with a fierce grin, "we'll just have to remind them why it's unwise to anger dragons."

Jerica clutched tightly to Zeira's scales, thinking about the vision Othos had sent. The ritual combining the life force of the dragons and the magic of Andela—it was their only hope, a fragile thread connecting them to the possibility of victory against the Thunder King.

But she felt little confidence in her ability to perform it.

She went over and over the vision in her mind, keeping it fresh, drawing new inspiration each time she went through the steps mentally.

They flew through the day and into the night, and when the prime constellation was at its zenith in the sky, Hamish pointed to the ground. Sif dipped a wing and soared down toward the circle of tall monoliths. Starlight reflected off a large body of water, barely thirty meters away. The sea.

And all at once, Jerica knew why Othos had sent them to this place. As the dragons landed, the water churned ferociously and a sleek blue head appeared.

"Did someone call for an extremely quick ride through the water?" Nuri's tail swished as she pulled herself up onto the shore.

"It's better than that," Jerica assured her. She proceeded

to explain to all of them what she'd learned about combining the life force of dragons with the magic of jhorium. "Come into the stone circle."

Nuri slithered toward them, in her newfound way, while the others walked the short distance to the stones.

"Hamish and I found some scrolls recently. The symbols shown in them, written in the language of Blaze, match with the message Othos gave us. Zeira, please give each of our team the words they will need to speak at the exact time the magic enters the jhorium goblet. Hamish, you will represent humankind during the ritual."

"All of humankind?" His face seemed to go a little pale.

Jerica nodded with a smile. "It's a big job but somebody's got to do it."

One by one, Zeira went to each dragon and explained the symbols and words they had found. And one by one Water, Fire, Lightning, and Smoke solemnly learned their roles.

Jerica stepped to the center of the circle. "The ritual," she began, her fingers absently tracing the intricate patterns on her jhorium goblet, "combines the life force of dragons with the magic of Andela. If we can perform it correctly, we can sever the Thunder King's connection to the Eye of the Storm."

Sif's wings faltered for a moment. "Our life force? That sounds ... dangerous."

"This could be dangerous," Jerica admitted, her face grim. "But it's our only hope. Without it, Emerus Dinty will become invincible. He has already informed us that he'll enslave more dragons, more people. He'll never stop. Remember, once we begin, we can't stop. No matter what happens."

Zeira's body tensed. "And if we fail?"

Jerica swallowed hard. "If we're still alive, we'll try again."

A heavy silence fell over the group, broken only by the whisper of wind across scales and horns. No one wanted to know the unspoken part of that answer.

Skellig was the first to speak. "Magic like that ... it's unpredictable. Unstable."

"Maybe so," Jerica countered, her voice rising with passion. "But what choice do we have? You've seen what the Thunder King can do. You've felt his power growing. We can't just give up!"

"She's right," Zeira said softly. "We've come too far to turn back now."

Nuri glided closer, her eyes shining with a mix of fear and eagerness. "I don't like it, but ... I trust you, Jerica. And I trust Othos. We must try."

Jerica felt a surge of gratitude toward the water dragon. She reached out, placing a hand on Nuri's neck. "I know it's asking a lot. I know the risks. But I believe in us—in all of us. We're stronger than Emerus Dinty could ever imagine."

Skellig snorted, a small puff of smoke curling from his nostrils. "But words won't save us from the Thunder King's wrath if this goes wrong."

"No," Jerica agreed, her hand moving to the oron stone. "But this might. And these," she added, lifting the jhorium goblet and pointing to the jhorium sword at Hamish's side. "We have tools he doesn't expect, power he can't fathom. We can do this."

Zeira turned her head, meeting Jerica's gaze with one gleaming eye. "I'm with you, Jerica. Whatever it takes."

"As am I," Sif added.

All eyes turned to Skellig. The old dragon huffed, a sound somewhere between amusement and resignation. "Well, I suppose if we're going to die, we might as well do it spectacularly. Count me in." He handed over the storm-forged stone.

"Hamish, on the count of three, raise the sword as you say the words Zeira gave you." Jerica felt lighter, even as a new responsibility settled in its place. They were committed now, for better or worse. As she placed the storm-forged stone in the center of the circle and began to raise the goblet, she silently prayed to Othos, to the stars, to whatever forces might be listening. "Guide us," she whispered. "Give us strength. And maybe, just maybe, give us a miracle."

She took a deep breath and could sense the others doing the same. "One ... two ... three!"

The goblet glowed more brightly than she'd ever seen it, lighting the stone circle and beyond. A surge of energy rushed upward from the storm-forged stone on the ground, through the base of the goblet. It was all she could do to hold onto it. She gasped, nearly dropping the artifact as visions of ancient power flooded her mind.

"Jerica!" Zeira's concerned voice cut through the chaos. "Stay focused!"

Gritting her teeth, Jerica channeled the wild energy coursing through her veins. The dragons began to glow, their life force intertwining with the ritual's magic. Streams of red, yellow, blue, and white light swirled around them, creating a vortex of power.

"I can feel him," Jerica said through clenched teeth. "The Thunder King. He knows what we're doing."

From kilometers away, she heard Emerus Dinty's voice in her head as he roared in fury. "No!" he roared, and she saw, in her mind's eye, his enchanted sword crackling with dark energy. "I will not be defeated by a child and her pet lizards!"

Jerica's arms shook with effort as she held the goblet aloft. Sweat poured down her face, mingling with tears of exertion. "It's working," she gasped. "I can see the Eye of the Storm. It's ... it's like a living thing, a darkness-filled thing."

The massive swirl of magic grew more intense, the air seeming to vibrate with power. Skellig let out a low groan of pain. "We can't hold this for much longer, Jerica," he warned.

Jerica's mind searched for the key to severing the Thunder King's connection. Then, in a moment of clarity, she understood. "The goblet," she whispered. "It's not just a conduit. It's a vessel."

With a cry, Jerica thrust the jhorium goblet into the heart of the magical vortex. The artifact's glow intensified, becoming almost blinding. Jerica felt as if her very essence was being pulled into the goblet, along with the combined life force of the dragons and the ancient magic of Andela.

"No!" The Thunder King's voice echoed across the land, filled with rage and desperation. "I am invincible! I am eternal!"

But Jerica could feel her connection to the spell weakening. With one final push, she poured every ounce of her will into the ritual. The goblet shattered, releasing a shockwave of pure magical energy that knocked Jerica off her feet.

And then, as warmth flooded her body, she knew the magic had worked.

An excellent job, my dear, came Othos' voice.

Sif's scales rustled. "Did … did we do it?" she croaked, struggling to sit up.

Zeira lowered her head, nuzzling Jerica gently. "Look," the dragon said softly.

In the distance, visible even from their vantage point, a dark tower crumbled. The Thunder King's fortress, once thought impregnable, was collapsing in on itself.

Sif let out a triumphant roar. "You did it, Jerica! The Eye's power is broken, and with it, the Thunder King's reign of terror!"

Jerica smiled weakly, exhaustion threatening to overwhelm her. "We all did it," she corrected. "Together."

Jerica's limbs felt like lead as she struggled to her feet, leaning heavily on Zeira's sturdy leg. The red dragon's scales were warm against her skin, a comforting contrast to the chill that had settled deep in her bones.

"We should … we should check on the others," Jerica mumbled, her vision swimming.

Hamish appeared at her side, his dark hair disheveled and his face smudged with dirt. "Easy there, hero," he said, offering a steadying hand. "You've done enough for one night."

Jerica nodded, a lump forming in her throat as she thought of all they had sacrificed to reach this moment. "Gocri," she whispered, her heart aching. "He should be here to see this."

Zeira's head drooped, her eyes closing briefly. "He gave everything so we could have this chance," the dragon said softly. "We won't let his sacrifice be in vain."

As they stood there, catching their breath, Jerica felt a jolt. "What about Skellig?" she asked suddenly, her eyes widening with worry. "If the Thunder King's power is broken, do you think …?"

"I am here," the yellow dragon assured her. "Undamaged."

"Nuri?"

A flash of electric blue flowed from the shoreline, up to

the standing stones. "Whew! That was intense, girl. I literally had to run for the water to cool off."

The others smiled at the valthan's comic expression.

Hamish nodded, his smile fading. "First things first, though. We need to secure whatever might be left of the Thunder King's fortress. Make sure he can't regroup or cause any more harm."

Jerica felt a wave of dizziness wash over her. The enormity of what they had accomplished—and what still lay ahead—was just now sinking in.

Zeira nudged her gently with her snout. "You don't have to do it all right now, Jerica," the dragon said softly. "You've done more than anyone could have asked. Rest. Heal. We could all use a breather right now."

As if on cue, Jerica's knees buckled. Hamish caught her before she could fall, scooping her up in his arms. "Right then," he said, his tone brooking no argument. "You're going to sleep for about a week, and then we'll sort out the rest of this mess."

Jerica wanted to protest, but her eyelids were already growing heavy. As Hamish carried her toward a makeshift camp they had set up before the ritual, she babbled, her head lolling against Hamish's shoulder, "We really did it."

The last thing she heard before sleep claimed her was Zeira's rumbling voice: "Rest well, little one. You've earned it."

As Jerica drifted off, the reality of their victory—and the price they had paid for it—settled over the group like a heavy blanket. They had won the battle, but she had a dark feeling that the war for Andela's future was far from over.

Chapter 20—Unshattered

Thunder roared overhead as Jerica's heart pounded in her chest. She ducked beneath the swirling dark energy, feeling its icy tendrils brush against her skin. All around her, chaos reigned.

"Watch out!" she cried, throwing up a shimmering magical barrier just as a bolt of lightning struck the ground where a dragon named Azurite had been standing moments before.

The sapphire-scaled dragon huffed in thanks, then reared back and unleashed a torrent of frost breath at the advancing storm creatures. Their misty forms solidified into jagged ice sculptures before shattering into a thousand glittering shards.

Jerica reached for the goblet but it was lying in pieces on the ground. The Thunder King stood atop a swirling black cloud silhouetted by flashes of lightning. With a dismissive laugh, he faced her.

"Foolish girl," he boomed. "Did you really think your

dreadful magic could harm me? I am the master of storms, the ruler of the skies!"

Jerica cried out, waking herself up.

"Bad dream?" Hamish asked, from his seat against a burnt tree trunk.

She nodded. "The worst. The jhorium goblet—"

Then she remembered. The goblet had shattered last night, during the ritual. What would they do without its power?

Hamish held something in his hands, which he extended to her now. "Repaired. But I'll need you to test it."

"How did you—?"

"Magic. I'll tell you, I had to work all night to find the right restoration spell. The goblet seems intact now, but I can't guarantee its magical power is still there."

As soon as Jerica took the object from his hands, it began to glow with its familiar deep green color. "This is promising, at least."

"Try an easy spell," he suggested.

She looked toward the small campfire they'd used, now gone cold. When she aimed the goblet toward the spot and envisioned flames, the cheery fire sprang to life again.

"Easy spell—check. How about something more difficult?"

They stood and walked to the edge of the clearing. A charred boulder the size of her father's workshop stood four hundred meters away. When she aimed the goblet toward it and uttered the words of the spell, she made sure to direct the energy outward, away from themselves. The boulder exploded into a dozen pieces, which rained down like a shower of baby elephants, but none came dangerously near.

"All right!" Hamish looked elated, as if he'd personally whacked the big rock into submission. "Um, good job, Jerica."

"What's going on?" Zeira inquired, stepping closer to them.

"Just making sure we have our best weapon ready."

"Speaking of which …" The Fire dragon preened a little. "Our reinforcements are on the way. When we storm the Thunder King's castle—or what's left of it—we won't have to go in alone."

"For now, we have help from Blaze and Bliss—what are their names again?"

Zeira raised her head and looked around. "Give me ten minutes, and I'll introduce you."

Two winged shapes appeared on the horizon and quickly cleared the distance, coming to land nearby. Zeira greeted the red one by name—Ember. "And you must be Azurite," she said to the other.

"I must be." The Frost dragon, a female, had much the same surly manner as Gocri. Jerica immediately felt a kinship. It was the dragon from her dream this morning.

Zeira introduced the two humans, plus Skellig, Sif, and Nuri, to the newcomers.

"I know what you're thinking," said Azurite. "Is this all we get? And the answer is, no. There are more coming. I have six more coming from Bliss. They will wait at the edges of your camp until the action begins. Five from Rokke have committed to be here. And, Ember, I believe you have ..."

"Twelve from Blaze. And we gave them the same instructions. Wait nearby until we give the signal. So, when does the action begin?"

Probably sooner than we'd like, Jerica thought to herself.

By midday, only two of the supplemental fighters had showed up, but Jerica was beginning to worry about waiting too long. Fighting in the dark, in the unfamiliar territory around the Thunder King's castle, would pose additional challenges they didn't need right now. She called out to all those present to gather around.

Sif gave the briefing. "This morning, in the early hours, I shifted myself to a much smaller size, in order to remain undetected, and posing as a feral cat I did a thorough reconnaissance of the Thunder King's lair." She turned to Jerica, her expression solemn. "Unfortunately, the portion of the castle that we saw crumbling last night ... that's only a small part of it. The entire compound is huge, and there is a large portion unharmed. Based on where I saw lights, smelled cook fires, and felt the presence of guards, most likely Emerus Dinty himself has found a safe haven."

"So, we didn't break his connection to the Eye of the Storm after all?"

Sif held up one foreleg. "I believe we did—or we weakened it dramatically. But it seems he has the ability to regenerate that connection. We want to move in before he has a chance to completely reestablish it."

All the dragons were nodding thoughtfully.

"Tell us the rest," Hamish suggested.

"On the far side of the mountain where his castle sits … I saw a storm cloud forming. It's small, at this point, but …"

It will only get bigger. No one needed to say it. They all understood.

"I want us to pair up, fighters with skills that can complement each other. Zeira and Azurite—you're a team. Hamish, you with the sword and Skellig with his sparks will made a strong team. Nuri—get as close as you can but stay safe. If you must be submerged in water, at least stay close to the shoreline where you can coordinate additional valthans to help." The fighters looked at their partners, sizing each other up, nodding in agreement with the arrangement. "Ember, I'd like you to come with Sif and me."

Sif described the layout of the castle once again, scratching a diagram on the dirt with a talon, pointing to the areas she felt would be most vulnerable. She pointed at a spot south of the castle. "The Eye is over here. If we can blast it hard and disable it, this will go a long way toward hampering Dinty and his efforts."

"Any questions?" No one spoke up. "Then we're off. Spread out. Watch each other's backs."

Zeira and Azurite took off first, heading toward the place where Sif had reported seeing the Eye.

Nuri wound her way up a river that had nearly dried up, and she valiantly managed to cover quite a distance. Jerica worried, but at least the waterway would lead the valthan back to the sea if necessary.

Skellig, with Hamish on his back, launched into the air, circling toward the castle on the opposite side to where Zeira was going. Hamish had the jhorium sword and Jerica prayed it would be sufficient to hold the enemy at bay, if not destroy them completely.

"Our turn," she said as the others became smaller in the distance. "Sif, Ember … let's do this!"

How's everyone doing? Jerica checked their telepathic network as soon as she was airborne.

Approaching the Eye of the Storm now, Zeira reported. *It's larger than Sif described, and growing.*

Not good.

Circling the castle, came Skellig's firm voice. *About a quarter of the walls are crumbled. We're going around to the intact side.*

There's more water in the river, nearer the castle. If I can find a way into their water system, I can really mess things up for this Dinty character.

Jerica chuckled at the water dragon's practical nature.

Be on alert, Sif said. *We're directly approaching the front of the castle.*

And there's Emerus Dinty himself, came Ember's response. *Look out!*

Before Jerica had fully focused on the human figure below, Ember let loose a deafening roar. The red-scaled beast dipped a wing, dropping in altitude as she unleashed a massive fireball at the Thunder King.

For a moment, Jerica's heart soared with hope as the flames engulfed their foe. But when they cleared, the tyrant stood unscathed, a cruel smile twisting his lips.

"Is that the best you can do?" he taunted. "Perhaps I should show you true power!"

At his gesture, the Eye of the Storm whirled up and over their heads, shooting bolts of lightning down from the sky. Jerica cried out in alarm, desperately weaving her magic to deflect the deadly strikes. But there were too many, coming too fast.

A bolt slipped past her defenses, a searing pain lancing through her side. She flinched backward, nearly dropping the precious jhorium goblet. Luckily, she had tied it to her belt again.

"Jerica!" Azurite's concerned voice cut through the din of battle. "Are you alright?"

She nodded grimly, sitting upright again. "I'm fine. Zeira,

can you and Azurite get a shot at him? Perform your fire and ice maneuver?"

As she spoke, Jerica's hand went to the oron stone. Its tri-colored segments pulsed with energy, reminding her of all they had sacrificed to get this far.

His booming laughter echoed. "Give up, little witch. You cannot hope to defeat me. Surrender the jhorium, and perhaps I'll grant you a quick death!"

Jerica's eyes narrowed, a fire igniting within her. "Never!" she shouted back defiantly. "We'll stop you, no matter the cost!"

With renewed energy, she channeled her magic through both the jhorium goblet and the oron stone. Tendrils of multicolored energy swirled around her, growing brighter and brighter until they erupted in a blinding flash.

His smug expression faltered as the wave of power slammed into him, momentarily disrupting his control over the storm.

Seizing the opportunity, Zeira and Azurite launched a coordinated assault. Fire and ice collided with the Eye in a spectacular explosion of elemental fury.

For a breathless moment, Jerica dared to hope they had gained the upper hand. But as the smoke cleared, the Thunder King emerged, battered but far from defeated. His eyes blazed with murderous rage as he raised his enchanted sword toward the swirling cloud that was the Eye.

He snarled. "You will pay dearly for that!"

The sky above turned an ominous, unnatural green. The air seemed charged with vicious energy as he prepared to unleash his most devastating attack yet.

Jerica steeled herself, her mind racing as she assessed their precarious situation. The Thunder King's power seemed to grow with each passing moment, his fury fueling the tempest that raged around them. She knew they needed a new strategy, and fast.

Azurite, Skellig! she called out mentally, not trusting her voice to be audible over the howling wind. *We need to break his focus. Flank him from both sides!*

The two dragons exchanged a quick glance before

nodding in unison. They split off, circling wide to approach the Thunder King from opposite angles. Jerica felt a surge of pride at their seamless coordination.

As the dragons maneuvered into position, Jerica raised her hands, once again channeling her magic through both the jhorium goblet and the oron stone. She focused on creating a shimmering barrier of energy around herself and her companions, hoping to buy them some protection against the Thunder King's inevitable next assault.

His laughter boomed across the land. "Your pathetic tactics are no match for my power!" he roared, swinging his enchanted sword in a wide arc. A bolt of lightning erupted from the blade, forking out to strike at Jerica and both dragons simultaneously.

Jerica gritted her teeth as the lightning slammed into the magical shield provided by the goblet. The barrier held, but she could feel it weakening under the onslaught. "Now!" she shouted to her draconic allies.

Ember and Azurite unleashed their elemental breath weapons in perfect sync. A stream of white-hot fire and a blast of freezing ice converged on the Thunder King from opposite sides.

For a moment, it seemed their strategy had worked. The Thunder King's concentration wavered as he was forced to defend against different attacks from multiple directions. But then his eyes flashed with vindictive glee.

"Is that the best you can muster? I can grow the Eye of the Storm to magnificent dimensions, you fools," he taunted, his voice dripping with disdain. With a sweep of his sword, he redirected the dragons' attacks back at them, amplified by his own dark magic.

Jerica watched in horror as Ember and Azurite were thrown backward by the force of the reflected assault. She could see the pain and exhaustion on their scaled faces.

"We can't keep this up forever," Azurite worried, struggling to regain her flight path. "He's too strong!"

Jerica searched for a new angle of attack. "We need to disrupt his connection to the Eye of the Storm so he can't make it any larger," she muttered. "But how?"

As if in answer to her question, he unleashed another devastating barrage. Lightning and freezing rain shot down from the skies, each bolt seeking to shatter Jerica's weakening defenses.

"You cannot hope to stand against me!" he howled. "I am the master of the storm, the rightful wielder of jhorium's power. Your resistance is but a petty disturbance!"

Jerica felt a flicker of doubt creep into her heart. But then she caught sight of Ember, the Fire dragon, battered but unbowed, still fighting at her side. Their unwavering loyalty steeled her commitment.

"We're not beaten yet," she declared, keeping her voice steady. "As long as we stand together, there's still hope."

With steady hands, Jerica began weaving a complex spell, drawing on every ounce of magical knowledge she had gained in their journey, the various spells she had learned from Elowen and practiced in the Whispering Caverns. She would find some way to turn the tide of this battle.

A blinding flash of lightning split the sky, passing mere inches from Jerica. As it struck the ground, it crackled and smoldered, the pungent smell of ozone rising to fill her nostrils. Sif flinched as she zigzagged defensively. Jerica lost her seat, her heart racing as she tumbled backward. Sif swooped low and caught her, narrowly avoiding the scorched earth.

"That was too close," Ember roared, her voice tinged with concern. The Fire dragon swooped low, unleashing a torrent of flames to create a momentary barrier between Jerica and the Thunder King.

Jerica's eyes widened. Spending all this time around Zeira, she'd forgotten that most dragons' flames came from their mouths, powerfully.

She watched as the Thunder King raised his enchanted sword, dark energy crackling along its length. "He's channeling the Eye's power through his weapon," she realized aloud. "If we could separate him from that sword ..."

Before she could finish her thought, the Thunder King let out a primal scream of rage. The sky above them darkened to an unnatural pitch, and a maelstrom of wind and lightning erupted around him.

"You dare to challenge my dominion?" his voice rumbled unnaturally loud. "I'll show you the true meaning of power!"

With a sweep of his sword, he sent a wave of crackling energy surging toward the group. Sif barely managed to sweep Jerica out of its path, the magical blast singing the tip of her tail as it passed.

"Thanks," Jerica gasped, her heart pounding. She could feel the Thunder King's desperation growing, his attacks becoming wilder and more unpredictable.

Ember circled overhead, unleashing bursts of flame to counter the lightning strikes. "His control is slipping," the dragon observed. "But that only makes him more desperate!"

Jerica nodded grimly. "We need to press our advantage, but carefully. One wrong move and we're finished."

As if to emphasize her point, a bolt of lightning struck a nearby tree, causing it to explode in a shower of splinters. The group scattered, dodging the deadly shrapnel.

The Thunder King's laughter echoed across the castle moat, tinged with a hint of madness. "You cannot hide from the storm! I am everywhere, I am all-powerful!"

But even as he spoke, Jerica noticed a flicker of uncertainty in his eyes. Despite his words of bravado, his connection to the Eye was weakening, and he knew it. She steeled herself for what was to come, knowing that the Thunder King's desperation would only lead to more devastating attacks.

"Get ready," she warned her companions. "This is far from over."

You've got that right. It was Skellig's voice.

She looked toward his position and her heart sank. Bearing down upon their Spark friend was his spiteful sire, Dym.

"Oh no, no, no, no!" She envisioned the last time, when Dym attacked Skellig and nearly killed him.

"Hamish! Use the jhorium sword—help him!" But her words were lost on the wind.

The elder dragon's jade green body zipped past Skellig, shooting a lightning bolt that struck his wing.

Jerica forced her mind to clear enough to send a coherent

message to the other dragons. *Skellig, get Hamish to use the sword. Everyone else, rush to their defense—now!*

She pulled the jhorium goblet from its pouch once more, gripping it, intending to form a protective shield around Skellig. But Dym zipped between them, cutting off her view to her friend and forcing Sif to make a defensive swerve.

"Okay then, you big green jerk. Take this!" She aimed the goblet at Dym and unleashed the shield. It surrounded him, forcing all his lightning bolts to stay inside. The older dragon roared his displeasure as he dodged a spark he, himself, had created.

The shield won't hold forever, Jerica warned the others. *Any ideas what we should do when it dissipates and he comes out madder than ever?*

You don't have to do anything. Skellig's voice sounded cold, completely without emotion. *I will handle this.*

But—

It's my place. Leave him to me. Turn your backs if you don't want to watch.

Skellig, please—he's your sire.

An abusive sire, to be sure. And no one has ever stood up to him.

Zeira and Azurite peeled away, turning their attention back to the castle and the sputtering Emerus Dinty below. It seemed the Thunder King didn't appreciate being ignored.

Jerica tried to reach out with her senses to Nuri, but the valthan didn't respond. She addressed Sif and Ember. *What should I do?*

But Sif had followed Zeira's lead and was leaving the two Spark dragons to fight their own battle. Jerica caught one last look at Hamish, still sitting astride Skellig. How could they simply fly away from *him*?

Overhead, the Eye of the Storm had grown larger, now covering more than half the sky, its color a frightening blend of purple and green, giving a sickly cast to everything below. As it continued to emit lightning bolts and strong winds, Jerica forced herself to focus on the bigger picture, the fact that she and her team were in a battle for their lives.

I'll try once more to break the connection between Dinty and the Eye, but I need you all to buy me some time.

Azurite, her scales shimmering with an ethereal light, nodded firmly. *We've got your back, Jerica. What's the plan?*

The Thunder King's voice boomed, "Your feeble attempts are futile! The storm bows to me alone!"

Ignoring his taunts, Jerica quickly outlined her strategy. *Ember, Azurite—use your elemental powers to create a diversion. Zeira, I need you to guard my flank. And Sif.* She locked eyes with the smoke dragon. *See if you can amplify my spell when I give the signal.*

She would have preferred to have Hamish and the jhorium sword for this last part, but her ally had worse problems of his own right now.

Ember swooped low, unleashing a torrent of flame that forced the Thunder King to stumble backward, while Azurite blasted the ground with ice. "Whatever you're planning, little mage," the dragon called, "do it quickly! We can't hold him off forever!"

Jerica nodded, raising the jhorium goblet high. She began to chant, her voice growing in power as its glow intensified. The air around her shimmered with arcane energy.

He roared in fury, sensing the threat. "You *dare* challenge my power?" He hurled a massive lightning bolt directly at Jerica.

Azurite intercepted the attack, catching the bolt in midair. The impact sent her reeling, but she held firm. "Hurry, Jerica!"

Jerica's chant reached a crescendo. She felt the Eye of the Storm's energy, its connection to the Thunder King wavering. With a final, powerful word, she thrust the goblet forward, sending a beam of pure jhorium energy straight at the tyrant's chest.

He howled as the beam struck him, his link to the Eye visibly fracturing. "No! This cannot be!"

"Now, Sif!" Jerica shouted.

The combined force of their power surged forward, further weakening the Thunder King's hold on the Eye. The storm cloud began to visibly shrink, losing mass every second.

Jerica caught a glimpse of Azurite's battered form. The dragon's scales were singed, her breathing labored. Yet, her eyes burned as they met her gaze. She sent a silent thank-you.

We've faced worse than this overgrown bully, Zeira rumbled, a wry smile twisting her features. "Remember the Chasm of Echoes?"

Jerica chuckled despite herself, thinking of their harrowing adventure to collect the storm-forged stone. *How could I forget? You nearly got us eaten by a rock formation.*

And you saved us with that brilliant light spell, Zeira countered. *Just like you'll save us now.*

Their banter was cut short as the Thunder King's roar shook everything around them. "Insolent whelps!" he wailed, crackling with barely contained energy. "I am Emerus Dinty, the Thunder King! I've crushed armies and subjugated realms. You think your pathetic band can stand against me?"

And suddenly, there was Hamish, in front of the castle drawbridge. He stepped forward, his sword gleaming. "We're not just standing against you," he shot back. "We're going to end your reign of terror!"

Jerica's head spun, looking for Skellig, wondering how Hamish came to be on the ground in front of the castle.

The Thunder King's eyes narrowed dangerously. "Bold words from a mere foot soldier," he sneered, from the ramparts above. "Perhaps you need a demonstration of true power!"

The tyrant raised his enchanted sword, and the storm clouds grew once again, swirling ominously. Jerica felt the hairs on her arms stand on end as the air charged with electricity. She knew they were pushing him to his limits, and that only made him more dangerous.

"Zeira! Ember!" Jerica called out. "Defensive positions!"

As the Thunder King ordered a barrage of lightning strikes from the storm cloud, Ember swooped low, shielding Hamish with her massive wings. Jerica's magic from the goblet coalesced into a shimmering dome, deflecting the worst of the assault.

Jerica gritted her teeth, pouring even more of her own power into maintaining their defenses. She could feel the strain on her body, her limbs trembling with exertion. But giving up wasn't an option. Not when they'd come so far, not when the fate of multiple realms hung in the balance.

"I won't let you hurt anyone else," Jerica said to the Thunder King. Images flashed through her mind—the enslaved water dragons, the devastated villages, the prison from which they'd rescued so many, the fear in the eyes of those who'd suffered under his tyranny. Each memory fueled her tenacity.

The Thunder King's attack intensified, his desperation palpable. "You cannot hope to match my power!" he roared. "I am the master of storms, the conqueror of realms!"

But even as he spoke, Jerica could see the cracks in his bravado. His movements were becoming erratic, his breathing labored. The Eye of the Storm pulsed erratically, its connection to the Thunder King becoming more unstable by the moment.

"He's weakening," Sif observed, her voice tight with concentration. "But so are we. We need to end this soon."

Jerica nodded, her mind racing. They were so close, but one misstep could spell disaster. She locked eyes with each of her companions in turn, drawing strength from their unwavering trust. "Sif, drop me down beside Hamish. We need to combine the power of both of our jhorium artifacts."

Moments later, standing united with Hamish, her fingers tightened around the glowing jhorium goblet. She raised her free hand, feeling its power thrumming through her veins. *Now!* she cried, her telepathic connection cutting through the chaos of the battle.

As if orchestrated by an unseen conductor, her companions moved in perfect harmony. Dragons unleashed torrents of elemental fury, their combined might crashing against his defenses. Jerica channeled her magic through both the goblet and the oron stone, weaving a complex tapestry of power that sought out the weaknesses in the Thunder King's connection to the Eye of the Storm.

Hamish held the jhorium sword aloft with one hand, weaving spells in the air with his other.

The Thunder King's eyes widened in disbelief as he felt his control slipping. "Impossible!" he roared, his voice tinged with fear for the first time. "I am Emerus Dinty, the Thunder King! I cannot be defeated by a mere girl and her pet lizards!"

"Yeah, you said that already," Hamish said under his breath. "Same old song."

Jerica gritted her teeth, pushing harder. "We're more than that," she called out to the man above them, her voice strained but determined. "We're family. We're hope. We're everything you've tried to destroy!"

As the dragons continued their attack, the Eye of the Storm flickered, its swirling energies becoming erratic. The Thunder King's face contorted in rage and panic. "No!" he screamed, raising his enchanted sword high. "I will not be denied!"

With a primal cry, he launched himself downward and across the castle moat, straight at Jerica, his blade crackling with dark energy. Time seemed to slow as Jerica watched the sword descending, knowing she couldn't dodge in time without breaking her concentration on the spell.

"Jerica!" multiple voices cried out in alarm.

In that heartbeat of terror, Jerica made a split-second decision. She poured every ounce of her remaining strength into the spell, even as the Thunder King's blade came within inches of her face.

A blinding flash erupted seemingly from all directions at once, accompanied by a deafening crack that shook the foundations of reality. Jerica felt herself being flung backward, her vision going white.

As consciousness slipped away, Jerica had only one thought: *Did we do it? Is it finally over?*

Chapter 21 — Reinforcements

"What happened?" Jerica slowly opened her eyes to find herself lying on the ground fifty meters outside the castle.

"Which part of it?" Hamish was at her side, kneeling, with gentle fingers checking her pulse. "Dym is no more. The Thunder King fled to the interior of his castle here, and I'm pretty sure Nuri knows something about that."

"Nuri is here?"

"She was in the moat when Dinty lashed out at you. Apparently, she made her way through the water channels that connect the castle to the river."

Jerica rubbed her temples, massaging the pain away. "I'll have to ask her more about that. And ... Wait—what! Dym is no more? You mean he's—"

"Yes. Gone for good. Skellig took care of it."

She felt a blank place in her heart. "How could he ...? His own sire?"

"Jerica, you and I are lucky to have had fathers who are good men. Not all of them are. You must believe justice has been done."

Skellig flew in and landed nearby, sensing Jerica's distress. With a gentle nudge of his steady nose, he said only one thing: "We shall not speak of it." Then he took off, joining Zeira and Azurite, who were checking on Ember.

Jerica got to her feet, wanting to run over to them, to console everyone, but Hamish put a hand on her arm to stop her.

"I didn't finish the whole story," he said. "Word has gotten out all over the realm and help is on the way, with more dragons arriving hourly. Thorne is bringing dozens of woodsmen with their enchanted axes, and Lyra's team of elven archers are already beginning to arrive."

Jerica nodded, processing it all. "You say Dinty has retreated into the castle?"

"Aerial surveillance tells us he has at least a hundred soldiers—those captive humans of his—gathered in the castle bailey. Somewhere within the keep he must have enough weapons stored to arm them all."

"We have to stop it! If hundreds of armed soldiers come pouring out at us, we won't be able to fight that."

"Jerica, hold on for one minute." He nodded toward the moat, where a slender blue head rose from the water. "Let's talk to Nuri first."

The two of them strode over to the edge of the moat and greeted Nuri warmly. "I understand you were responsible for sending that maniac running," Jerica said. "I'm impressed."

"Tell her the rest of it, Nuri."

The valthan preened a little. "I have a fairly good idea of the layout of the castle, from swimming through its waterways. It's amazing what you hear when you just float beneath the surface and listen."

"Do tell."

"Emerus Dinty has a chamber inside, something like a throne room I gather, although I haven't seen it. This is where he meets with the magician who created the Eye of the Storm."

"The magician's name?"

"Brakkis. He was standing in the entryway during Dinty's assault on you. Maybe you saw him?"

Jerica shook her head. "A little busy at that moment ..."

"Anyway, he's a weathered old man with scraggly gray hair and hands like claws, and he wears purple robes. I wanted to rise up and drag him into the water, but I got a better chance at Dinty."

"That's fine, Nuri. Your information is invaluable," Hamish said. "So, you think Dinty and Brakkis are in this throne room now?"

"Possibly. Or he might be in the grassy area inside the perimeter walls, gathering his troops."

"We'll figure that out. I can ask Zeira to fly over and check."

"The top two floors of the castle keep were demolished in our earlier attack," Hamish said, "but I'm guessing the lower floors are where he has the weapons stored. We should try to get inside and find out. Destroy or disarm the weapons if we can."

"I'll go. Sif can make herself smaller and the two of us can sneak around in there."

"Jerica ... it's too—"

"Hamish, I need for you to be out here, organizing the new arrivals and strategizing which of our fighters will be at the various locations. Please. Every time we think we've got this guy defeated, he manages to get away. We need to be completely organized."

He nodded, although he didn't look happy when she and Sif began their preparations to go inside on their own. Sif would become human-sized, and the two of them would ride on Nuri's back through the waterways, until they reached the center of the castle.

* * *

The stench of sulfur and decay clung to the air as Jerica and Sif crept through the winding corridors of the Thunder King's stronghold. Shadows danced on the obsidian walls, cast by flickering torchlight that threatened to reveal their presence at any moment. Jerica's heart thundered in her chest, each beat a reminder of the perilous task that lay ahead.

Sif had reverted to dragon form, a very small model of herself, for ease in traversing hallways and stairs, and yet she could be ready to grab Jerica and take flight if necessary. Her smoky scales shimmered faintly in the dim light. Jerica could sense the tension radiating from her companion as Sif's muscles coiled like springs beneath her armored hide.

"We're getting close," Sif whispered, her voice barely heard over the increasing rumble of thunder. "I can smell his foul magic growing stronger."

Jerica nodded, her fingers tightening around the glowing green goblet tied to her belt. The rare mineral pulsed with an otherworldly energy, as if sensing and remembering the encounters with this enemy. She took a deep breath, steeling her nerves.

"Sif," she rambled, "what if we're not strong enough? What if—"

The smoke dragon's eyes flashed as she cut her off. "We cannot afford to doubt ourselves now, young one. Remember why we're here. Remember what's at stake."

"You're right," she said, meeting Sif's gaze. "We have to succeed. For everyone's sake."

They pressed onward, their footsteps muffled in the dusty halls. As they rounded another corner, a massive set of iron-bound doors loomed before them, decorated with arcane symbols that seemed to writhe and twist in the torchlight.

Jerica's breath caught in her throat. "This must be it," she whispered. "The throne room, heart of his power."

The dragon's wings rustled restlessly. "Indeed. And beyond those doors, our greatest challenge awaits."

"Sif," she said, her voice barely a whisper, "I'm scared."

The ancient dragon's eyes softened as she regarded her human companion. "As am I, Jerica. But fear does not make us weak—it reminds us that we have something worth fighting for."

Jerica nodded, drawing strength both from Sif's words and the warmth of the jhorium goblet in her hands. She took a deep breath, centering herself as she had practiced countless times before.

"Together, then?" she asked, managing a small smile.

Sif's mouth curved into a dragon-grin, revealing rows of razor-sharp teeth. "Together, little one. We disable this little tyrant, bind him in magic, and separate him from his minions."

They approached the ominous doors. The air crackled with tension, making her skin prickle. The stones of the stronghold seeming to hold their breath, Jerica wove a simple spell with one hand, and the double doors swung open.

"Now, Sif!" she cried, raising the goblet high.

With a deafening roar, Sif unleashed a cloud of dark, noxious smoke while Jerica channeled her own power through the goblet. It pulsed with an otherworldly green light, weaving ropes of magical light.

"What's this?" the Thunder King seemed shaken, then his voice boomed. "You dare challenge me in my own domain?"

Sif's smoke intensified, combining with the energy from Jerica's goblet to create a dazzling tapestry of elemental forces. The air crackled and popped, filled with the scent of storms and magic.

"Hold fast, Jerica." Sif's small form trembled with exertion. "We must not falter!"

A bone-chilling laugh echoed through the chamber, and Jerica's blood ran cold as a figure materialized behind them—the Thunder King's evil magician, cloaked in purple robes, his gray hair standing out wildly around his hood.

Beside him stood the raven-haired woman from the prison. Lydia, the betrayer of the resistance. Jerica wanted to create a spell to slap the traitor's face, but she couldn't think of one at the moment.

"Your efforts are futile," the magician sneered, raising gnarled hands crackling with dark energy.

"Brakkis. At last we meet." Jerica's voice sounded far steadier than she thought it would.

"Jerica Barille. Such a child you are. It's almost a shame to—" But before the magician could unleash his spell, a blur of motion caught Jerica's eye. Several figures burst into the room—Hamish, his dark hair wild and his eyes blazing; Thorne and three other woodsmen with axes ready; and Lyra, leading four of her elven archers.

"Sorry we're late to the party," Hamish called out, a hint of his trademark grin visible despite the gravity of the situation. He brandished the jhorium sword.

Emerus Dinty's eyes took on a hungry look at the sight of it.

Sif's form shifted and writhed, clouds of dark smoke billowing from her as she advanced on Brakkis. "Your dark arts are no match for our combined strength!"

Lyra turned to her archers, who unleashed a barrage of golden-tipped arrows that forced the magician to stumble back. "For Andela!" she shouted.

As her friends engaged the magician, Jerica redoubled her efforts, pouring even more energy into the goblet. She could feel the magician's control wavering, even as her own power shuddered.

Sif's eyes met hers, filled with pride. *You are stronger than you know, Jerica Barille. Your heart is pure, your will unbreakable. Remember why we fight!*

The dim chamber exploded with light, and for a moment, time itself seemed to stand still. In that frozen instant, Jerica felt the scales tip, the balance of power shifting.

And then, chaos erupted.

Hamish darted to the left, his lean form a blur of motion as he ducked beneath a crackling bolt of Brakkis's dark energy. "Lyra, now!" he shouted, his voice carrying over the cacophony of battle.

The lithe archer responded instantly, her silken hair flashing in the light as her archers unleashed more arrows over Hamish's crouched form. The magician's eyes widened in surprise, his concentration faltering for a crucial moment.

Hamish rolled to the far side of the chamber, his hands glowing with mystical energy, his father's teachings flowing through him. "Thorne—now!" he cried, releasing a pulse of pure magic that intertwined with the woodsman's thrown axe.

Thorne's blade struck true, shattering the magician's hastily erected shield. The combined assault sent their foe reeling, his dark robes smoldering.

Meanwhile, Jerica gritted her teeth, her entire body trembling with the exertion of holding the Thunder King at bay. "Sif," she gasped, "I can feel it weakening!"

The smoke dragon blasted Dinty with more of her dark, noxious fumes. "Push harder, Jerica!" she urged, her ancient eyes gleaming. "We're close to breaking through!"

With a cry that seemed to come from deep in her soul, Jerica channeled every last ounce of her will into the goblet. The jhorium artifact blazed with blinding light, its power intertwining with sparks generated by the arrows of the archers. Jerica could feel the Thunder King's control wavering as their enemy edged toward an open doorway.

"Just ... a little ... more!" she cried through clenched teeth, pushing beyond what she thought possible, driving Dinty outside into the castle courtyard, following him. And then she felt something deep within her begin to shift.

The stronghold trembled; its foundations quaking as the elements spiraled out of control. Jerica's hair whipped around her face, static electricity crackling in the air. Through the chaos, she caught glimpses of her allies locked in their own battles.

Sif darted between pillars of crackling energy, her movements fluid and graceful. "Hamish!" she called out, "On your left!"

Hamish turned, his voice cutting through the din, chanting arcane words as he wove complex patterns in the air.

Opposite him, Brakkis was doing the same, his clawlike fingers tracing spells of his own making.

"Keep it up, everyone!" Hamish yelled, his dark hair plastered to his forehead with sweat. "We're disrupting the elemental balance!"

Outdoors, in the castle bailey, the Eye of the Storm swirled with dark energy and began to beat erratically overhead. Jerica could feel the connection between the malevolent element and its master weakening, fraying like a worn rope under too much strain.

"*No!*" The Thunder King roared, his voice laced with panic and fury. "What are you doing, you insolent child?"

Jerica gritted her teeth, sweat beading on her brow as she poured more power into the goblet. *Breaking your hold on the elements*, she hoped.

The Eye's pulsations grew less focused, its dark tendrils of energy lashing out wildly. Sif crouched protectively over Jerica, her wings a shield from the chaotic bursts.

"Stay with it," the dragon urged. "You're doing it, Jerica. The Eye is losing its grip!"

The Thunder King staggered, his once-imposing figure now hunched and trembling. The storm began to dissipate, revealing small glimpses of clear sky.

"Oh no, it's not! Not while I have an ounce of magic left in me!" Brakkis hobbled through the door of the chamber, out to the grassy area where Jerica was in the battle of her life.

She glanced behind him but there was no sign of Hamish or the woodsmen. What had Brakkis done to them? And in that moment, when her attention lagged, the evil old magician conjured one final spell. Sending a great lasso of green and purple energy skyward, he harnessed the Eye of the Storm and connected it back to Emerus Dinty.

Brakkis collapsed to the ground, his purple robes vibrating with tiny sparks of green lightning that gradually fizzled and died.

Chapter 22 — Resurgence

Dinty rose, standing tall once again, flexing his muscles, sending an evil glare toward Jerica and Sif.

Uh-oh. Sif's voice sounded tiny.

Overhead, the Eye of the Storm whirled again, whipping fallen leaves and other debris into a blinding fury.

Hamish! A little help here! Jerica's arms trembled as she struggled to redirect the goblet's power and to remain standing as Dinty paced toward her, driving her toward the broken place in the outer castle wall.

A deafening boom shook the earth. Jerica stumbled, nearly dropping the precious goblet. And then, at her side, appeared the welcome sight of red scales.

Zaroth, the eldest of the fire dragon fighters landed lightly on the grass. His deep voice rumbled. "The Thunder King won't give up so easily, but we will not either."

As if summoned by Zaroth's words, the wind began to howl. Rain lashed down in stinging sheets, obscuring Jerica's vision. She squinted through the deluge, barely able to make out the dragons' massive forms as Zeira and two other dragons defied the weather and flew in to join her.

Hamish has sent the archers and the woodsmen inside. If we can drive Dinty back into the stone keep, they can take him. Zeira's comforting voice came through the awful din. *Skellig has more Spark dragons on the way, as well.*

Lightning forked across the sky, illuminating the world in stark flashes. The dragons overhead roared in defiance as bolts struck their scales. Jerica's hair stood on end, electricity crackling in the air around her, and the dragons formed a protective circle, shielding her from the whirling storm cloud with their bodies. Wind buffeted their wings, threatening to tear them from the sky, yet they held formation.

"Fools!" Emerus Dinty grumbled. "Do you think you can defeat the Thunder King so easily? I control the elements themselves!"

To prove his point, a massive bolt of lightning arced down, striking mere feet from where Jerica stood. She jumped back, momentarily blinded by the flash. A noxious smell filled her nostrils.

Jerica realized, with growing dread, that he had almost backed her up to the portion of missing wall. Two missteps would send her tumbling to the jagged rocks far below and into the sea.

Just as despair threatened to overwhelm her, a familiar voice cut through the chaos.

Jerica! Dragons of the sky! Hold fast!

Nuri's sleek form burst from the churning waves below, followed by an army of sea dragons. Their sinuous bodies gleamed, even in the stormy light.

Nuri! Jerica cried, relief flooding through her. *You came back! Where are you?*

The water dragon's eyes gleamed with fierce pride. *I brought reinforcements. We're just below the battlements of the castle. Already, we have churned the sea to erode the ground this bastion stands upon.*

Jerica edged sideways, shouting at the Thunder King to distract his attention. "You'd better check the eastern walls—

your fortress is about to go under!"

Emerus Dinty's voice rang out again, tinged with surprise and a hint of fear. "What's this? More dragons to crush beneath my storms?"

Nuri's laugh was like the crash of waves on the shore. "You'll find us harder to crush than you think, Thunder King!"

With a series of sharp, barking calls, Nuri began to coordinate the sea dragons' attacks. They dove and leapt from the water, their movements precise and synchronized, churning the waves to unprecedented heights.

Through the broken perimeter walls, Jerica watched in awe as the sea dragons countered the Thunder King's storms with their own elemental might. They created walls of mist to diffuse lightning strikes and used powerful jets of water to disrupt the Eye's wind currents.

"Don't let up!" Nuri commanded. "Push forward! Show him the true might of dragon-kind!"

Inspired by the sea dragons' arrival, the sky dragons redoubled their efforts. Fire dragons breathed spouts of flame to evaporate torrential rains, while earth dragons summoned stone barriers to prevent Dinty's foot soldiers from approaching the castle.

The sea dragons surged forward, their scales gleaming like polished sapphires as they rode the crests of massive waves. With a thunderous crash, they brought the full force of the ocean to bear repeatedly against the Thunder King's defenses.

"Now!" Nuri screamed, her voice carrying over the din of battle. "Create the maelstrom!"

As one, the sea dragons dove beneath the churning waters. Jerica watched in awe as the sea began to swirl, slowly at first, then with increasing speed. A colossal whirlpool formed, its hungry depths threatening to swallow everything in its path.

"By the ancient scales," Jerica breathed, her eyes wide. "I've never seen anything like it."

You might want to move away from that wall, came Nuri's voice.

The fire dragon beside her rumbled in agreement. "The sea dragons' power is truly a sight to behold."

Lightning crackled overhead as the Thunder King fought to maintain control. "You think your parlor tricks can defeat me?" he roared, his voice booming across the open space. "I am the master of the elements!"

But even as he spoke, Jerica could see the strain on his face, hear the quiver in his voice. The whirlpool was disrupting his storms, pulling apart the dark clouds and dispersing his lightning strikes.

"It's working!" Jerica shouted to her dragon companions. "Now's our chance to strike!"

Without hesitation, the airborne dragons dove into action. Fire dragons unleashed streams of molten fury, their flames intensified by the updrafts from the whirlpool. Earth dragons hurled boulders with pinpoint accuracy, aiming for the Thunder King's stronghold.

Jerica's heart swelled with pride as she watched the dragons work in perfect harmony. The sea dragons' whirlpool provided distraction from the sky dragons' attacks, while the sky dragons' assaults kept the Thunder King unfocused from the growing threat below.

"Stay close!" Jerica shouted, her voice nearly lost in the cacophony. "We need to protect each other!"

As if in response, a massive ice dragon named Frost unfurled his wings, creating a crystalline barrier that deflected several lightning strikes. The ice crackled and hissed, but held firm.

"Well done, Frost!" Jerica called out, relief flooding her voice. But her reprieve was short-lived as she noticed the Thunder King's evil grin.

With a roar, he whipped another of his magical threads upward toward the Eye of the Storm, summoning a cyclone of devastating power. Debris whirled through the air, becoming deadly projectiles that threatened to shred dragon wings and puncture vulnerable hides.

Jerica clutched the jhorium goblet tighter, her heart racing.

"Blaze!" Jerica called to a nearby fire dragon. "We need a wall of flame to protect our flanks!"

As the dragons moved into position, the Thunder King's

laughter echoed through the air. "Your measly defenses are nothing against my might!" he taunted, hurling another barrage of lightning.

But this time, the dragons were ready. Their winds clashed with the Thunder King's cyclone, creating a deafening roar as the air currents battled for supremacy. Blaze's wall of fire rose high, incinerating debris before it could harm their allies.

Jerica watched in awe as her friends unleashed their elemental fury. Ice dragons created glittering shields, deflecting lightning bolts back toward their source. Earth dragons raised stone barriers, providing cover for their more vulnerable kin.

"No!" the Thunder King blared, his composure cracking as his attacks were thwarted. "This cannot be!"

But it was. The dragons, united in purpose, drove the Thunder King inside the sturdy stone keep. At the first set of stairs inside the impressive structure, Thorne and the woodsmen waited. Axes flew, one of them nicking the enemy's enchanted sword. Dinty nearly dropped it, but recovered at the last moment. He raced up the stairs to the second level, pursued by the elves' golden arrows.

Hamish, what's going on in there? Jerica's heart pounded as she surveyed the chaotic scene outside. The air still crackled with raw energy, both from the Eye's relentless assault and the dragons' fierce retaliation. Despite their earlier victories, she could see the toll the prolonged fight was taking on her allies. She climbed over a pile of strewn stones, a portion of the collapsed wall, to get a view below.

"Look!" Jerica exclaimed, pointing toward the Thunder King's ground forces. "They're retreating!"

Indeed, the once-imposing army was now in disarray. His human followers threw down their weapons, eyes wide with terror as they fled the castle.

Beside her, Sif's scales smoldered, smoke curling from her nostrils. "We have them on the run. Shall we press our advantage?"

Jerica hesitated, torn between the desire for victory and concern for her friends. "We can't let up now," she decided, her voice steady despite her racing pulse. "But be careful. Men like Emerus Dinty are most dangerous when cornered."

As if summoned by her words, a bellow of rage erupted from the heart of the storm. The Thunder King emerged at the ramparts of the stone keep. His eyes, wild with fury, locked onto Jerica.

"You dare challenge me?" he roared downward at her, raising his enchanted sword high. "I am the master of storms, the conqueror of realms! No mere girl and her pet lizards can stand against me!"

Jerica stood her ground, drawing strength from the dragons around her. "Oh, please, we've heard it all before. We are not your subjects, *Emerus*," she called back, taunting him with his true name. "And we will never bow to your tyranny!"

"Pet *lizards*? I don't think so," Zeira muttered. "Anyone here feel like a lizard? Let's show this pathetic human what we're made of."

Jerica grinned. *It doesn't pay to insult a dragon.*

In perfect unison, Nuri unleashed a blast of water toward the castle while Ember breathed a stream of white-hot flame. The elements collided midair, creating a scalding cloud of steam that engulfed the Thunder King's position.

Emerus Dinty's enraged roar cut through the fog. "You think your silly games can conquer me?" he snarled, emerging from the mist, his enchanted sword emitting an eerie blackish light.

"Don't care for the steam bath, Dinty?" roared Azurite. "How about we cool you off?" She let forth with a massive blast of icy breath that instantly froze the steam cloud and pelted hailstones down on the Thunder King.

Gocri would be so proud, thought Jerica.

Emerus staggered but didn't fall, not even when Skellig swooped in with lightning bolts aimed at the now-icy flooring beneath the enemy's feet. Dinty's eyes, burning with hatred, found Jerica. "You'll pay for this insolence, girl!" he howled, raising his sword to the sky.

Dark clouds swirled from the Eye of the Storm overhead, crackling with barely contained energy. Jerica's stomach dropped as she realized what was coming.

"Everyone, brace yourselves!" she cried out, her voice tinged with desperation.

Lightning erupted from the heavens, a blinding web of destruction aimed directly at the dragons. But before it could strike, a massive wave rose from the sea, deflecting it. The lightning struck the water, sending electrical currents rippling across its surface.

Nuri surfaced at the rocky shoreline, water streaming from her iridescent scales. "Thought you could use a shield," she said with a wink to Jerica.

Jerica's relief was palpable. "Perfect timing," she breathed. "Everyone! Together!" Her voice carried a power that surprised even her.

What followed was a spectacle unlike anything Jerica had ever witnessed. Fire and Ice, Earth and Spark, fresh water and salt—all the elements converged in a swirling vortex of raw power.

At the center of it all stood the Thunder King, his face a mask of disbelief and growing fear. His sword, once a symbol of his invincibility, now seemed paltry against the onslaught of draconic might. As the elemental maelstrom engulfed Emerus Dinty, Jerica allowed herself a moment of hope. *Could this be it?* she wondered. *Have we finally defeated him?*

Then, his expression changed and a deep, menacing laugh cut through the silence. Jerica's blood ran cold as the mist parted, revealing the enemy, still standing tall, his enchanted sword glowing once again with an otherworldly light.

"Fools," he snarled, his eyes wild with a mixture of rage and triumph. "Did you really think your pathetic display could defeat me?"

With a swift motion, he raised his sword high. The entire sky darkened ominously, and Jerica felt the air crackle with energy.

"Brace yourselves!" she shouted to the dragons.

As if in response to her words, a blinding bolt of lightning struck Emerus's sword. The Thunder King's laughter grew maniacal as the energy coursed through him, his body seeming to grow larger, more monstrous with each passing second.

By the gods, Jerica thought, *what have we unleashed?*

"You want power?" Emerus roared, his voice distorted and inhuman. "I'll show you true power!"

The air around them began to swirl violently, as a huge cyclone, and Jerica felt herself being lifted off her feet. She desperately reached out, managing to grasp onto Zeira's scales. She watched in horror as Emerus, now a towering figure of pure elemental energy, raised his sword once more.

"This world will bow to me," he roared, "or it will burn!"

The last thing Jerica saw before the world exploded into blinding light was the determined faces of the dragons around her.

And then, everything went dark.

Chapter 23 — Mocked

The oron stone pulsed warmly in her palm, its tri-colored segments glowing faintly as if recovering from the confrontation. Jerica clasped it, drawing from its warmth, unsure how it had come to be in her hand.

Beside her, Skellig's massive yellow form tensed, his black wings rustling with nervous energy. "Jerica, wake up," Skellig's voice was barely above a whisper, laced with concern. "We could still turn back, find another way—"

"No," Jerica sat up, her voice steadier than she felt. She looked around. "Where—?"

"We're outside the castle. That last blast sent everyone flying. You and I landed just outside the crumbling part of the wall."

She craned her neck to see past his massive form.

"Don't look down. We are barely perched upon this rock. It's a straight fall into the sea."

"Okay, then." She patted her sides, seeing with relief that

the jhorium goblet was still tied to her belt. She took a deep breath, filling her lungs with the electric air. As she exhaled, a strange calm washed over her, replacing the fear. The oron stone seemed to hum in response, its glow intensifying. "I suppose we move forward—if we can figure out where that is."

Skellig nodded.

"Besides," she added, managing a wry smile, "I doubt your mother would approve of us running away now."

Skellig snorted, a small jet of lightning escaping his nostrils. "True enough. She'd never let me hear the end of it."

"So, where are the others?"

"I am not certain about everyone. Nuri and her fellow valthans dove deeply, I believe. Zeira, Sif, and Azurite were on the opposite side of the castle. They are either still within the fortress walls, or they may have exited in the same manner we did."

"Blown away?"

He nodded. "But alive. I have been in telepathic contact."

"Hamish? The woodsmen and the elves? Do we know their condition?"

"I do not."

"And the Thunder King?"

Skellig tilted his head to the west.

Emerus Dinty, the Thunder King, stood atop the ramparts of the castle keep, his form silhouetted against the force of dark energy, the Eye of the Storm, the source of his power, Jerica realized with a shudder. Dinty had cleverly directed its power away from himself, and he remained unharmed.

"So," the Thunder King's voice boomed, filling the air. "The little village girl thinks she can challenge me in my own domain." His laughter was like rolling thunder, menacing and mocking. "How quaint."

Jerica's grip on the oron stone tightened, its warmth spreading up her arm and suffusing her body with strength as she climbed aboard Skellig's back and they hopped easily over the wall, into the relative stability of the castle grounds, away from the treacherous sea below. From the windows of the castle keep, she could hear repetitive pounding sounds; she hoped it was the axes of the woodsmen, chopping through the hatch door, coming for Dinty's position on top.

She met the Thunder King's gaze unflinchingly, her voice clear and strong as she replied. "I'm more than just a village girl, Emerus Dinty. And I'm here to end your reign of terror."

The Thunder King's eyes narrowed, focusing on the glowing stone in her hand. "Ah, the oron stone. I see you've learned a few tricks since our last encounter." His lips curled into a sneer. "But your little tricks won't save you or your precious Andela."

"They're not tricks," Jerica countered, sliding down from the dragon's back.

Skellig remained protectively close to Jerica, electricity crackling along his wing talons. "Your time is over, Thunder King," the dragon blared. "Release the captives and surrender, or face the consequences."

Emerus Dinty's laughter echoed once more, but this time there was an edge of uncertainty to it. "Surrender? I think not." He raised his arms, dark energy coalescing around his hands. "I'll crush you both and take that stone for myself. Then nothing will stand in my way!"

Jerica felt a surge of power as the oron stone blazed with light, its three segments pulsing in harmony with her heartbeat. In that moment, she knew with absolute certainty that she could—and would—defeat this tyrant.

"You're wrong, Emerus," Jerica said, her voice resonating with newfound authority. "Your reign ends here. For Andela, for the dragons, and for all those you've hurt—I *will* stop you."

She raised the oron stone high above her head, its three segments—red, blue, and green—glowing with an otherworldly light. The stone pulsed with ancient energy, sending waves of warmth cascading through her body.

"By the power of earth, sky, and sea," Jerica recited, remembering the words of the spells she had learned from Elowen, her voice steady despite her racing heart, "I call upon the spirit of Andela to break the chains of tyranny!"

As the words left her lips, Jerica felt a profound connection to the land beneath her feet. The stone's vibrations intensified, resonating with the essence of Andela itself. She gasped as visions flooded her mind—lush forests, soaring mountains, and vast oceans, all teeming with life and magic.

Emerus Dinty's face contorted with rage. "No!" he roared, his voice booming like thunder. "I will not be undone by a mere child!"

The Thunder King thrust his arms forward, unleashing a torrent of dark magic. Storm creatures—writhing masses of shadow and lightning—materialized around him, their hollow eyes fixed on Jerica.

"Jerica, watch out!" Skellig cried, his wings unfurling protectively.

But Jerica was already moving. She ducked and rolled, narrowly avoiding a bolt of crackling energy. The oron stone never left her grasp, its glow intensifying with each passing second.

"Is that the best you can do, Thunder King?" Jerica taunted, her newfound confidence surging through her veins. "I thought you were supposed to be all-powerful!"

Emerus snarled, hurling another barrage of dark magic. "Insolent brat! I'll teach you the meaning of true power!"

Jerica leapt and twisted, her movements fluid and precise. She could feel the oron stone guiding her, enhancing her reflexes and agility. A storm creature lunged at her, its claws raking the air where she had been moments before.

"Skellig, now!" Jerica shouted, diving behind a rocky outcropping.

The dragon unleashed a blast of lightning, scattering the storm creatures. Jerica used the momentary distraction to focus her energy on the words of magic once more.

"You can't hide forever, girl," Emerus heckled, stalking toward her hiding place. "Give me the stone and the goblet, and I might consider sparing your miserable life."

"Why do you want them so badly, Emerus?" she called out, her voice echoing off the castle walls. "Is it because deep down, you know you're not as powerful as you pretend to be?"

The Thunder King roared. "How dare you—"

Jerica seized the opportunity. Standing tall once more,

she placed the stone in the jhorium goblet, darting from her cover and focusing all her will into the two artifacts. Their light blazed even brighter, forcing Emerus to shield his eyes.

Lightning crackled around Emerus, his eyes blazing with unbridled rage. The air grew thick with suppressed energy, making Jerica's skin tingle. With a terrifying bellow, the Thunder King hurled a massive bolt of electricity directly at her.

Jerica's instincts kicked in. She jumped to the side, feeling the heat of the lightning singe her hair as it passed. The bolt struck the castle wall behind her, sending rocks and debris flying. She jammed the oron stone back into her pocket, where she felt—

It was the storm dragon's feather, the one Elowen made her retrieve during her training. She clutched it in the palm of her right hand, while her left held onto the goblet.

"You insolent child!" Emerus roared.

Jerica felt a jolt of energy, running from the palm of her hand, through her body, and into the earth at her feet. The ground beneath Jerica's feet began to tremble violently. Cracks spider-webbed across the ground, glowing with an ominous red light. She stumbled, struggling to maintain her balance.

Gritting her teeth, Jerica tightened her grip on the dragon feather. She closed her eyes, channeling every ounce of her will into the artifact.

"I won't let you win," she whispered.

The goblet's glow intensified, bathing the air in iridescent light. Jerica felt a surge of power coursing through her veins, more powerful than anything she'd experienced before.

"Look up!" one of the dragons called out.

Jerica's eyes snapped open. Above them, the Eye of the Storm began to flicker. Its inky blackness started to fade, replaced by patches of clear sky.

"No!" Emerus howled, his face contorted with fury and fear. "Brakkis!"

But the evil magician was gone, his purple robes lying on the ground in an inert pile.

Jerica allowed herself a small smile as she concentrated her willpower on the feather and the goblet. "It's working," she thought.

Emerus's eyes blazed with a manic intensity as he raised his arms skyward. "You think you've won, girl?" he snarled, his voice echoing through the cavern. "I am the Thunder—"

In a blinding flash, Dinty's form began to elongate and distort. Jerica watched in horror as the tyrant's body dissolved into pure energy, streaming upward toward the faltering Eye of the Storm.

"What's happening?" Jerica cried out, her grip tightening on the dragon feather.

Skellig answered grimly. "He's merging with the Eye itself. It's his last desperate gambit."

Jerica's heart pounded as she watched Emerus's essence intertwine with the swirling mass of air above. The Eye pulsed with renewed vigor, its dark energy crackling with malicious intent.

"You *cannot* stop me now!" Emerus's voice boomed from the sky, seeming to come from everywhere at once. "I am the storm, the thunder, the essence of chaos!"

Jerica gritted her teeth, feeling doubt creep into her mind. How could she possibly defeat an enemy who had become one with the source of his power?

"Don't give up, Jerica!" Zeira's encouraging roar snapped her back to focus. "What about the storm-forged stone—we still have it! Let's use both!"

Not taking her eyes off the storm cloud, Jerica let go of the goblet and slipped her fingers beneath the wristband on her forearm, where she wore the mark of the kairie, and slipped out the stone she had forgotten she was carrying. She carefully passed it to Zeira.

Together now!

Taking a deep breath, Jerica pulled the oron stone from her pocket once more, then raised it and the feather above her head. Zeira extended her neck and held up the other stone in her teeth. "I am Jerica Barille of Cael," she shouted, her voice ringing with newfound confidence. "And I will not let you destroy our world!"

The oron stone's light intensified, its three segments now brilliant. Jerica felt as if the essence of Andela was flowing through her.

Above, the Eye of the Storm writhed and twisted, Emerus Dinty's furious face occasionally visible in its depths. "You cannot hope to match my power!" he raged.

But Jerica stood firm, channeling every ounce of her will into the magical artifacts. Cracks began to appear in the Eye's surface, spreading like a spiderweb across its dark expanse.

"*No!*" Emerus's voice was filled with panic now. "This is impossible!"

With a final, earth-shattering crack, the Eye of the Storm shattered. Fragments of dark energy exploded outward, dissipating as they fell. And with them, the essence of Emerus Dinty, the Thunder King, scattered to the winds.

Chapter 24 — Aftermath

As the last echoes of the explosion faded, Jerica pocketed the magical feather, her arms trembling with exertion. "Is it … is it over?" she asked, her voice barely above a whisper.

The stench of smoke and charred dragon scales hung heavy in the air as they surveyed the devastation. Zeira dropped the storm-forged stone to the ground. Her scales, once a vibrant crimson, were now dulled with soot and blood. She gripped her side, each breath sending a sharp pain through her ribs, a reminder of the brutal battle they had just endured.

Nearby, Skellig lay sprawled on his side, his yellow scales marred by angry red gashes. His black wings, usually so majestic, were crumpled. The Spark dragon's eyes were closed, his breathing shallow and labored.

Sif was barely recognizable. Her gray form seemed to flicker and waver, as if she might dissipate at any moment. Tendrils of dark smoke leaked from her nostrils with each exhale, a sign of her depleted energy.

Jerica's gaze drifted toward the sea, where Nuri and the other water dragons, their sleek blue bodies glistening with an oily sheen, huddled together at the water's edge. Even they, who had fought from that distance, bore the marks of battle.

"We … we did it," Zeira croaked, her voice hoarse from roaring. "But at what cost?"

Sif's form solidified slightly as she turned to face Zeira. "We're alive. That's what matters."

A sudden realization hit Jerica like a bolt of Skellig's lightning. "Wait … where's Hamish?"

Panic gripped her heart as she scanned the battlefield, searching for any sign of the tall, dark-haired young man who had become such an integral part of their team. His absence was a glaring void in their battered group.

"Hamish!" Zeira called out, ignoring the pain that flared in her chest. "Hamish, where are you?"

The other dragons stirred at her cry; their own exhaustion momentarily forgotten in the face of this new concern.

Skellig forced himself to his feet, his wings dragging in the dirt. "I don't see him," he moaned, his yellow eyes darting across the landscape.

Nuri slithered further onto the shore, her narrow skull swiveling as she searched. "He was with us when the storm got really nasty," she said, her voice tinged with worry. "Could he have been thrown clear?"

Jerica considered the possibilities, each more terrifying than the last. She had believed him to be in the tower, the castle keep, along with the woodsmen and elves, but clearly he was not. They had already vacated that space. Had Hamish been captured? Injured? Or worse? The thought of losing him after everything they'd been through together was unbearable.

"We have to find him," she declared, forcing herself to stand despite the protest of her battered body. "Spread out. Search every crevice, every shadow. He has to be here somewhere."

As the dragons began to move, each wincing with pain but driven by concern, Zeira closed her eyes and reached out with her other senses. She inhaled deeply, trying to catch Hamish's scent amidst the overwhelming odors of battle.

"Come on, Hamish," she muttered under her breath. "Where are you? Give us a sign."

The silence that answered her plea was deafening. Jerica fought back the despair that threatened to overwhelm her. She couldn't give up. Not now. Not after everything they'd sacrificed.

"Keep searching!" she called out to their companions who were leaving the evil castle in a stream. "He's counting on us. We won't leave him behind."

As Jerica limped forward, searching the area for any clue, she couldn't help but reflect on how much Hamish had come to mean to her—to all of them. His quick wit, his unwavering courage, his belief in their cause. "Hold on, Hamish," she whispered.

Jerica's legs buckled beneath her, the oron stone slipping from her trembling fingers as she collapsed to the scorched earth. The world spun violently, her vision blurring as the last remnants of her strength evaporated.

"Jerica!" Zeira's panicked roar cut through the haze. The ground shook as the dragon lumbered toward her fallen form.

Sif's voice, usually melodic, was strained with worry. "What's happening to her?"

Jerica tried to respond, to reassure them, but her lips refused to form words. Casting repeated spells had drained her completely, leaving her a hollow shell. She felt gentle talons carefully turning her over.

"Her heartbeat is weak," Skellig rumbled, his usual gruffness tinged with concern. "The magic … it's taken too much from her."

Nuri's cool scales brushed against Jerica's forehead. "She's burning up. We need to cool her down, quickly."

Through half-lidded eyes, Jerica saw the water dragons gathering around her, their long necks intertwining as they conferred in hushed tones.

"Hold on, little one," Zeira murmured, nuzzling Jerica's cheek. "You've done so much. Don't you dare give up now."

Jerica wanted to tell them not to worry, that she just

needed rest, but darkness was creeping in at the edges of her vision. Her last coherent thought was of the goblet, of its green glow.

As her eyes drifted shut, Jerica became aware of a change in the air. The oppressive atmosphere that had pressed down on them for so long began to lift. A gentle breeze caressed her face, carrying with it the scent of rain-washed earth and new beginnings.

She felt a new presence nearby.

Sif's gasp drew Jerica back from the brink. "Look! The clouds ... they're breaking up!"

Jerica forced her eyes open, blinking away the fog. Above them, where the roiling mass of dark clouds had once dominated, were light, wispy clouds. Even these were slowly dissipating, torn apart by ribbons of golden light. Shafts of sunlight pierced the gloom, illuminating the battered landscape in a warm glow.

"I think it's over," Skellig breathed, his voice filled with awe.

Zeira's forehead creased a little. "He can't come back?" Her words sent a little jolt of worry through everyone.

As the clouds continued to retreat, a brilliant rainbow arced across the sky, its vibrant colors a stark contrast to the devastation below. The air felt lighter, cleaner, as if the atmosphere had been purged of the Thunder King's malevolence.

Jerica felt a surge of hope rise within her, giving her the strength to stand and look around. But the memories of all the times Emerus Dinty had managed to come back, to attack again, hung at the back of her mind.

As Jerica's thoughts hovered there, the ground beneath them began to tremble. The dragons tensed, their scales bristling, but Jerica felt a strange calm wash over her. She knew, somehow, that this was not a threat.

Suddenly, the air shimmered and warped, like heat rising from sunbaked paving stones. A colossal form materialized before them, so vast that Jerica had to crane her neck to take it all in. Othos, the ancient genesian dragon, had arrived.

His scales gleamed like polished gemstones, each one

reflecting the newborn sunlight. His wings, when unfurled, seemed to touch the edges of the sky. Jerica felt her breath catch in her throat at the sight of him.

"Othos," she whispered, awe coloring her voice.

The great dragon's eyes, deep as the ocean and just as ancient, fixed upon her. When he spoke, his voice brought comfort rather than fear.

"Jerica Barille," Othos intoned, "you have done what many thought impossible. You have vanquished the Thunder King and brought hope back to Andela."

"He's really gone?" Jerica felt her cheeks flush with a mixture of pride and humility. "I couldn't have done it without them," she said, gesturing to the dragons around her. Relief flooded through her, but it was quickly overshadowed by concern. "But at what cost? Look at us, we're all …" she gestured weakly at the battered dragons around her.

"Fear not," Othos rumbled. "Your wounds, both seen and unseen, shall be healed."

He turned his gaze to the other dragons, particularly Skellig, who stood with his black wings half-spread, yellow scales dimmed and tired.

"You have all fought bravely," Othos continued. "And now, let me ease your burdens."

The great dragon began to shrink, his form condensing until he stood before them, still towering but no longer impossibly vast. He approached Zeira first, placing a gleaming talon upon her head.

Golden light flowed from Othos into Zeira, suffusing her entire body. Jerica watched in amazement as the fire dragon's wounds closed, her dull scales regaining their fiery luster.

Zeira's eyes widened in wonder. "I … I feel renewed," she gasped. "As if the battle never happened."

One by one, Othos moved among the dragons, his healing touch restoring their strength and vitality. Jerica marveled at the transformation, seeing her friends whole once more.

When Othos finally reached her, Jerica felt a moment of trepidation. "Will it … will it hurt?" she asked, hating how small her voice sounded.

Othos's eyes crinkled with kindness. "Only the pain leaving your body, young one."

As his talon touched her forehead, Jerica gasped. Warmth flooded through her, chasing away the bone-deep exhaustion and mending her battered body. It felt like being embraced by sunlight, like diving into a cool stream on a hot day, like coming home after a long journey.

When it was done, Jerica stood, marveling at the absence of pain. "Thank you," she breathed, looking up at Othos with gratitude shining in her eyes.

The ancient dragon nodded, a hint of a smile playing at the corners of his mouth. "You have all done well," he said, his gaze sweeping over the assembled dragons. "But remember, this victory is but the first step on a long road. Andela will need your strength and wisdom to rebuild, in the days to come."

Jerica squared her stance, feeling a new sense of purpose. "We're ready," she declared, looking to her companions for confirmation. They nodded, their unity evident in their postures.

Othos's approval was palpable. "Then let us begin the work of healing our world," he said, his voice filled with hope and promise.

The ancient dragon began to glow, a soft, golden light emanating from his scales. It spread outward, enveloping each of the humans, elves, and dragons in turn. Jerica watched in amazement as cuts sealed, bruises faded, and the weariness seemed to lift from her companions.

Skellig, who had been favoring one of his wings, suddenly stood tall, his eyes bright with renewed energy. "By the winds of Gale," he exclaimed, flexing his wings. "I feel as though I could fly for days!"

Jerica couldn't help but smile at the Spark dragon's enthusiasm. She turned back to Othos, a question forming on her lips. "What about the oron stone?" she asked, holding up the tri-colored gem. "It seems … dimmer now."

Othos lowered his great head until his eye was level with Jerica. "The stone has served its purpose, young one. Its power is not depleted, merely resting. In time, it will regain its strength—as will you all."

Jerica nodded, her fingers curling protectively around the smooth surface. She thought of her village, of her family, wondering how they had fared, with Dinty's soldiers everywhere in recent weeks. As if reading her thoughts, Othos spoke again.

"Your home is safe, Jerica. The Thunder King's defeat has lifted the shadow from all of Andela. Those humans who fought with him have now renounced the attachment. It's as if they were under a spell and have now awoken."

Relief flooded through her, bringing unexpected tears to her eyes. She blinked them away, turning to face the vast expanse of land stretching out before them. The other dragons gathered around her, forming a protective semicircle.

"It's beautiful," Zeira announced, her fiery scales glowing as she faced the sunlight.

"And it's ours to protect," Skellig added, his voice firm with renewed purpose.

"We've won a great victory," Jerica said, her voice carrying clearly in the crisp morning air. "But our work isn't done. In order to heal, to rebuild, Andela will need all of us." Jerica nodded, feeling the next new responsibility settle onto her—but it wasn't a burden. It was a calling; one she was ready to answer.

She looked at each of her dragon companions in turn, seeing the same determination reflected in their eyes. "Are you with me?"

The dragons' response was immediate and resounding. Roars of affirmation filled the air, a chorus of loyalty and unity that seemed to make the sky vibrate.

Othos watched this exchange with approval. "You have grown much, Jerica Barille," he said. "From a village girl helping in her father's foundry to a true leader of dragons and humans alike."

Jerica felt a swell of pride at his words, but also a flicker of uncertainty. "I still have so much to learn," she admitted.

"As do we all," Othos replied, wisdom gleaming in his ancient eyes. "But you have taken the first, most crucial step—you have brought hope back to Andela. The rest will follow."

As the sun climbed higher in the sky, bathing the land in golden light, Jerica stood tall among her dragon allies. The oron stone rested in one pocket, the storm dragon feather in the other, reminders of the power they had harnessed together. Before them lay Andela, scarred and somewhat broken, ready to be rebuilt.

"Well," Jerica said, a smile tugging at her lips, "shall we begin?"

"I appreciate your enthusiasm but there is one more thing," Othos said.

"We ... we really did it, though?" she asked, hardly daring to believe.

"Indeed." Othos's massive head dipped in a nod, his eyes, like twin suns, focusing on her. "However, I did mention that there is one more thing."

He turned toward the north, where a shimmering glow lit the horizon. "My friend, Anahita, is not only the guardian of the seas," he began. "She protects the skies as well, keeps the stars in their proper places in the firmament."

The shimmering glow grew, a soft light moving toward them, until they could see that it was, indeed, the vast form of Anahita. She set her feet gently on the earth, just beyond Othos, opening her cloak to set something before her.

A hush fell over the group as Othos turned his attention to the still figure lying motionless on the ground. Jerica's breath caught in her throat as she recognized Gocri's emaciated form. The once-mighty glacial dragon looked like a mere shadow of himself, his white scales dulled and his body frighteningly thin. Anahita had transported him, lovingly and safely.

Othos lowered his massive head, his eyes glowing with an otherworldly light. "Gocri," he intoned, his voice resonating with power. "Return to us."

A shimmering aura enveloped Gocri's body, vibrating with ethereal energy. Jerica watched, her heart pounding, as color slowly seeped back into the frost dragon's scales. His chest began to rise and fall with steady breaths, and a low groan escaped his lips.

"Can it be?" Jerica whispered, her voice thick with emotion. She took a tentative step forward, hardly daring to believe what she was seeing.

Gocri's eyes fluttered open, confusion giving way to recognition as he took in his surroundings. "What … happened?" he croaked, his voice weak but unmistakably alive.

Tears sprang to Jerica's eyes. "Gocri! We thought you were … we thought …" She couldn't finish the sentence, overwhelmed by the miracle before her.

The frost dragon attempted to sit up, his movements still shaky. "Easy, dren," Othos rumbled, using Queen Freriss's term of endearment. The celestial dragon touched Gocri's forehead, in the same way he had touched the others. "Your strength will return in time."

As Gocri regained his bearings, Jerica's attention was suddenly drawn to movement at the edge of the clearing. Her heart leapt as she recognized the tall, lean figure emerging from the shadows.

Hamish.

His dark hair was disheveled, in wild array across his forehead as he scanned the area with frantic eyes. When his gaze finally landed on Jerica, relief washed over his features. Without hesitation, he broke into a run, closing the distance between them in long strides.

He's alive. He's okay. He came back. The emotions threatened to overwhelm Jerica, but she forced herself to remain composed.

As Hamish drew near, Jerica noticed the tension in his muscles, the worry lines around his eyes. His usually mischievous smile was nowhere to be seen, replaced by a look of genuine concern.

"Jerica," he called out, his voice hoarse. "Are you—I was afraid …" He trailed off, clearly struggling to articulate the feelings.

"You're all right!" Three dragons said it at once. Jerica smiled, relieved.

"I am, indeed," Hamish said. The jhorium sword still hung from his belt, its scabbard battered and torn.

"Nuri said you were helping the valthans. I thought you were still in the castle, all that time."

"Nuri's words are true. Did you like the little whirlpool we conjured?" His cheeky grin was back.

"That was your work?"

"Well, sixteen valthans, whipping their tails in unison, is what got it started. This baby here," he said, patting the sword, "this is what amplified their efforts."

Hamish looked up, noticing how the clouds were nearly all gone.

Jerica nodded, trying to reassure him. "I'm okay, Hamish. We all are, thanks to Othos." She gestured to the celestial dragon, who regarded Hamish with a knowing look.

Hamish's eyes widened as he took in Gocri's return, and then the massive form of Othos, then darted back to Jerica. "What about the Thunder King?" he asked, tension evident in his voice.

"Gone, completely vanquished," Jerica confirmed, a small smile tugging at her lips despite her exhaustion. "But there's so much more to tell you. So much has happened ..."

Hamish closed the distance between them, his lean frame towering over Jerica as he gently placed his hands on her upper arms. His dark hair lay over his forehead, and there was that familiar, devilish smile.

"You did it," he breathed, his eyes shining with admiration. "I knew you would."

Jerica felt a warmth spread through her chest, a mixture of pride and something else she couldn't quite name. "*We* did it," she corrected, reaching up to squeeze his hand. "All of us, together."

As if on cue, the dragons began to gather around them. Zeira, her scales gleaming once again, nuzzled Jerica's side. Sif and Skellig flanked Hamish, their massive forms creating a protective circle around the two humans. Even Gocri rose to his feet and made his way to the group.

Jerica embraced the emaciated frost dragon. Finally, their team felt complete again. "Thank the gods," she whispered into his chilly scales.

You're welcome!

Jerica looked around, alarmed at the large, booming voice. Othos and Anahita had both disappeared.

Chapter 25 — Renewal

They made their way north, away from the ruined castle with its terrible memories, toward the forest, where leaves were already beginning to sprout on the trees. The woodsmen, elves, and other dragons had all left for their home regions, everyone hoping against hope that Emerus Dinty had not figured out some way to come back into power.

At least, for now, the land felt peaceful. Othos' assurances that Dinty was really and truly gone went a long way toward their peace of mind. Hamish had gathered enough wood for a campfire; Zeira lit it (from her mouth, this time—her skills were improving). Skellig had come up with some meat for roasting, although no one said they were hungry.

"It seems we owe you both a great debt," Zeira rumbled, her voice filled with gratitude. "Jerica, creating the jhorium goblet. And Hamish, your knowledge proved invaluable."

Hamish shook his head, his expression turning serious. "No debt is owed. This was our fight too. The Thunder King threatened all of Andela, humans and dragons alike."

Jerica nodded in agreement. "What now?" she asked, looking from Hamish to the assembled dragons. "How do we even begin to rebuild?"

Skellig, his voice a low rumble, spoke up. "We start with what we know. The Thunder King's influence spread far, and there may still be pockets of resistance, both dragon and human, that we may need to deal with. Hopefully we can rally them to the cause that is for the good of the entire realm."

"My father's teachings," Hamish interjected, his eyes lighting up. "He spoke of ancient alliances between dragons and humans. Perhaps it's time to renew those bonds."

Jerica felt a surge of love for her country. "And the jhorium," she added, thinking of the glowing green chalice and the sword that had played such a crucial role in their victory. "We need to understand its full potential, and ensure it never falls into the wrong hands."

As the group continued to discuss their goals, Jerica couldn't help but marvel at the scene before her. Dragons and humans, standing side by side as equals, united in their desire to restore Andela to its former glory. It was a far cry from the simple life she had known in the village of Cael, but she wouldn't have it any other way.

"We have a long road ahead," Sif observed, her keen eyes scanning the horizon. "But I believe we've proven that we can overcome any obstacle."

Hamish nodded, his hand finding Jerica's and giving it a reassuring squeeze. "We've already achieved the impossible," he said, his voice filled with quiet confidence. "What's a little rebuilding compared to that?"

Jerica laughed, feeling a newfound lightness. Yes, the task ahead was daunting, but surrounded by friends, she felt ready to face whatever challenges lay ahead.

"We've won a great victory," she said, her voice carrying across the gathering. "But our work is far from over. As Hamish suggested, we have a chance to build something truly remarkable—a world where dragons, other creatures, and humans coexist in harmony."

Skellig, his yellow scales gleaming in the fading light,

nodded in agreement. "It won't be easy," he rumbled, electricity crackling between his wing talons. "There are centuries of mistrust to overcome."

Jerica turned to the Spark dragon, noting the determined set of his jaw. "You're right, Skellig. But if anyone can bridge that gap, it's us. We've already proven that dragons and humans are stronger together."

Hamish leaned forward from his seat on a large rock in front of the fire, his eyes alight with excitement. "Think of the possibilities," he said, gesturing expansively. "Dragon riders soaring through the skies, human healers working alongside dragon shamans, shared knowledge and resources benefiting all our peoples."

As Jerica listened to Hamish's words, her mind filled with visions of the future. She imagined soaring over Andela on dragonback, exploring hidden corners of the land and uncovering long-lost secrets. The thought sent a shiver of anticipation down her spine.

"There's so much we don't know about this land," she mused aloud. "Ancient ruins, forgotten magic … who knows what we might discover?"

Zeira, her scales shimmering with an otherworldly light, dipped her head in agreement. "The old stories speak of wonders beyond imagination," she said, her voice tinged with excitement. "Perhaps it's time we sought them out."

Jerica felt a growing sense of anticipation. "Whatever comes next," she said, her voice firm, "we face it as one, united in purpose and spirit."

A chorus of agreement rose from the assembled group, a harmony of human voices and dragon rumbles. As the last light of day faded, giving way to a star-studded sky, Jerica looked up at the familiar constellations and felt a sense of peace settle over her. Tomorrow would bring new challenges, new adventures, and new discoveries. And she couldn't wait to face them all.

Epilogue

The village square of Cael erupted in a cacophony of cheers and applause as Jerica stepped onto the wooden platform, her heart pounding. Hundreds of faces beamed up at her, their eyes shining with adoration and gratitude. The jhorium goblet in her hand gave off an ethereal green glow, casting glimmers across the eager crowd.

Jerica's gaze swept over the sea of people, her chest tightening with emotion. She spotted her father, Hallis, his weathered face creased with pride, and her mother, Nyssa, dabbing at her eyes with a handkerchief. Beside them stood her sister, Theresa, arm-in-arm with Baron Vyler Dartmoor, both grinning from ear to ear.

She had learned that, during the onslaught, they had gathered the villagers of Cael and taken everyone to a safe place while the Thunder King's soldiers tromped through, ravaging their fields. Similar stories of heroism had come out in nearly every village she'd visited.

A young girl with braided pigtails pushed through the crowd, clutching a bouquet of wildflowers. "For you, Miss Jerica," she said shyly, offering up the colorful blooms.

Jerica knelt down, accepting the gift with a warm smile. "Thank you, little one. These are beautiful."

As she straightened, an elderly man hobbled forward, leaning heavily on a gnarled cane. In his free hand, he held a small wooden carving of a dragon. "I've been working on this since we heard the news," he said, his voice quavering. "It's not much, but I hoped it might remind you of your brave companions."

Jerica's throat tightened as she carefully took the carving, running her fingers over the intricate details. "It's perfect," she whispered. "Thank you so much."

More villagers surged forward, presenting her with everything from baskets of fresh bread to hand-knitted shawls. Jerica accepted each gift with genuine gratitude, her arms soon overflowing.

Baron Dartmoor stepped onto the platform, raising his hands for silence. The crowd's excited chatter died down as he spoke. "People of Cael, we gather today to honor a true hero. Jerica Barille, through her courage, wisdom, and extraordinary gift, has saved our world from darkness. Jerica, we owe you a debt that can never be repaid."

The crowd erupted in cheers once more. Jerica felt her cheeks flush, a mix of embarrassment and pride washing over her. He's giving me too much credit, she thought. I couldn't have done any of this without the elves, the woodsmen, and … the dragons.

As if reading her thoughts, Baron Dartmoor gestured for her to speak. Jerica took a deep breath, stepping forward. The crowd fell silent, hanging on her every word.

"Thank you all, for this incredible welcome," she began, her voice strong despite her nerves. "But I cannot accept this honor alone. The true heroes of this tale are my dragon companions." She gestured toward the group standing at the edge of the clearing. "Skellig, Gocri, Sif, Zeira, and Nuri, over there in the village lake. And Hamish, son of Zebulon, whom many of you know."

A murmur rippled through the crowd at the mention of the dragons' names. Jerica pressed on, her passion growing with each word.

"Without their bravery, their wisdom, and their unwavering friendship, our world would still be shrouded in darkness. They taught me the true meaning of unity and the incredible power of working together."

Jerica's eyes met Zeira's, the young red dragon who had struggled with self-doubt but had found the courage to lead when it mattered most. "Even in our darkest moments, when all seemed lost, we never gave up on each other. That bond, that loyalty, gave us the strength to overcome every obstacle in our path."

She looked at Skellig, the ancient yellow Spark dragon, and his complicated relationship with his sire. "We all face challenges, conflicts that seem insurmountable. But when we stand together, supporting one another, there is no adversity we cannot overcome."

Jerica's voice rang out across the square, filled with conviction. "The lesson I learned on this journey is one I hope we can all take to heart. Our differences, be they between human and dragon or simply between neighbors, are not weaknesses. They are the very things that make us stronger when we unite."

She raised the jhorium goblet high, its green light washing over the rapt faces before her. "This goblet represents not just the banishing of darkness, but the dawn of a new era. An era where all creatures work side by side, where friendship and understanding bridge even the widest divides."

Tears pricked at Jerica's eyes as she concluded, "I stand before you not as a hero, but as a reminder of what we can achieve when we open our hearts to one another. The real magic, the true power to change our world, lies within each of us and within the bonds we forge with those around us."

As Jerica's final words hung in the air, a moment of stunned silence fell over the crowd. Then, as one, they erupted into thunderous applause. Cheers and whistles filled the air, along with cries of "Long live Jerica!" and "Hail the dragon friends!"

Jerica's family rushed onto the platform, enveloping her in a group hug. Her father's strong arms wrapped around her, his voice gruff with emotion as he whispered, "I've never been more proud, my girl."

Her mother kissed her cheek, tears streaming down her face. "You've grown so much, Jerica. Your words ... they were beautiful."

Theresa squeezed her hand tightly. "You've changed everything, little sister. The world will never be the same."

As the celebration continued around her, Jerica drifted toward her dragon companions. She hoped they could somehow sense the impact they had made, the way they had inspired not just her, but an entire village—perhaps an entire world—to embrace unity and friendship across all boundaries.

The green light of the jhorium goblet pulsed steadily in her hand, a reminder of the incredible journey she had undertaken and the even greater adventures that surely lay ahead.

Jerica's heart swelled with a bittersweet ache as she approached her dragon friends. Skellig, Gocri, Sif, and Zeira stood in a semicircle. Nuri pulled herself to the edge of the lake and raised her neck toward her companions, their scales glimmering in the fading sunlight. Jerica placed a hand on Skellig's rough hide, feeling the warmth radiating from within.

"I ... I don't know how to say goodbye," Jerica whispered, her voice thick with emotion.

Skellig lowered his massive head, his golden eyes meeting hers. "Then don't, little one. This isn't goodbye. It's simply until we meet again."

Gocri snorted, a puff of steam rising from his nostrils. "We've faced so much together. That bond can never be broken."

Jerica's fingers tightened on the jhorium goblet. "I'll never forget what you've all done for me, for all of us."

Nuri's fins rustled as she stepped forward. "And we shall carry the memory of your bravery with us always, Jerica Barille."

Tears welled in Jerica's eyes as she moved from dragon to dragon, embracing each one. When she reached Zeira, the youngest of the group, she paused.

"You taught me so much about courage, Zeira," Jerica said softly. "I hope you know how strong you truly are."

Zeira's scales flushed a deeper red. "It is you who showed us the strength of humans, Jerica. We are all changed because of you, and you will always be my kairie."

As Jerica stepped back, she felt a presence beside her. Hamish stood there, his dark hair laying over his forehead, a mixture of excitement and nerves apparent on his face. Behind him stood his father, Zebulon the seer, a gentle man whom Jerica had only recently become acquainted with.

"It's time," Hamish said gently.

Jerica nodded, taking a deep breath. She turned back to the dragons, her chin held high despite the tears streaking her cheeks. "May the winds always be at your backs, my friends. Until we meet again."

With a final wave, Jerica watched as Nuri dipped below the water's surface and swam away, then the other dragons spread their wings and took to the sky, their forms growing smaller against the setting sun. She allowed herself a moment to feel the loss, the vacancy in their departure before squaring her shoulders and facing Hamish.

Zebulon shook hands with his son and brought Jerica into a fatherly embrace as he wished them well.

"Ready for our next adventure?" she asked, a hint of her old mischief sparking in her eyes.

Hamish's smile was equal parts devilish and determined. "I've been ready since the moment I met you, Jerica Barille."

As they walked toward the village gates, packs slung onto their backs, Jerica couldn't help but marvel at the path that lay before them. The oron stone hummed softly in her pocket, giving off its latent energy. Somewhere along the way, the storm dragon's feather was lost, but she now had the spell to retrieve another one, should the need arise.

"Do you really think we can do this?" she asked Hamish, her voice low. "Unite the tribes, bring peace to Andela?"

Hamish's hand found hers, giving it a reassuring squeeze. "If anyone can, it's you. You've already done the impossible, remember?"

Jerica's fingers tightened around the jhorium goblet.

"*We've* done the impossible," she corrected. "And we'll do it again, together."

As they passed through the gates, the cheers of the villagers fading behind them, Jerica felt the wisdom of those she had met along the way. The road ahead would be long and fraught with challenges, but with Hamish by her side and the memory of her dragon friends to guide her, she knew they could face anything.

The world stretched out before them, a canvas of possibility waiting to be painted with hope and unity. Jerica took her first step into that future, ready to write the next chapter in the story of Andela.

* * *

As Zeira soared over the craggy peaks of Blaze, the familiar heat of her homeland embraced her like an old friend. The young dragon's scales gleamed a vibrant red in the late afternoon sun, a stark contrast to the ashen clouds billowing from the nearby volcanoes. She felt a surge of pride as she approached the central gathering place of her clan, her heart pounding with anticipation.

Landing gracefully on the obsidian platform, Zeira was immediately surrounded by a crowd of dragons, their eyes wide with awe and admiration. Among them, she spotted familiar faces—dragons who had once mocked her insecurities and doubted her abilities. Including Karzoka Aeogan, her tormentor. But he hung back at the edge of the crowd, not meeting her eyes. Clearly, he was no longer pretending to rule the region. She felt grateful that his father had recovered.

"Zeira!" a voice boomed. It was Fyrax, another of her most vocal critics from the past. "We heard tales of your bravery. Is it true you faced the Thunder King himself?"

Zeira met his gaze steadily, her voice calm but firm. "We all did what was necessary to protect our world, Fyrax. Every dragon, every human played their part."

A murmur of respect rippled through the crowd. Fyrax lowered his head in a gesture of deference. "We were wrong about you, Zeira. You've brought honor to Blaze."

Before Zeira could respond, she heard her mother's voice. "My daughter!" Gynnyth cried, pushing through the throng of dragons.

As her mother approached, Zeira braced herself for the usual barrage of concerned questions and protective admonitions. Instead, Gynnyth simply nuzzled her daughter's neck, her eyes shining with pride.

"You've grown so much," Gynnyth whispered. "I always knew you were destined for greatness, but I never imagined ... I'm sorry if I ever held you back."

Zeira felt a lump form in her throat. "You never held me back, Mother. You gave me the strength to fly."

As night fell over Blaze, Zeira found herself perched on a high cliff, gazing out over the fiery landscape. Her thoughts drifted to Jerica and Hamish, imagining their journey to help the villages and regions across Andela. She wondered about Skellig, hoping against hope that the Spark dragon had fully recovered from the torture of his captors and the death of his sire.

"What challenges await them?" she mused aloud. "And what role will we dragons play in this new world they're building?"

The future awaited her, as vast and unpredictable as the skies she loved to soar. And for the first time in her life, Zeira felt truly ready to face whatever it might bring. She had faced her fears, proven her worth, and found strength she never knew she possessed.

With a deep breath, Zeira spread her wings, preparing to take flight into the star-studded night. As she launched herself into the air, she felt a familiar warmth building in her gut. With a mischievous grin, she let loose a burst of fire from her rear end, painting the sky with a trail of crimson flame.

"For Andela," she whispered to the wind. "For friendship. For the future we'll build."

And as Zeira soared higher, her fire lighting the way, she knew that whatever challenges lay ahead, they would face them, working side by side to forge a brighter tomorrow.

Fan Submissions

Thanks to the help of some fans & readers, several characters in this book have some unique names!

Salenthina — Brett Gable
Finnry — Mechelle Salyers
Vanze — Vance Schollmeyer
Skellig — Kate Craven
Doolan — Elizabeth Davis
Gocri — Robert Allen Chalk
Zeira — Caryl Nantze
Akainu, Dym — Andrew Dyer
Sifula, Hamish — Carol Minot
Nuri — Nicki Jones
Myrdaynth — Justin Morgan
Darazok Aeogan — Kimberley Richardson
Brenin Draig — Claire Jones
Zebulon — Jennifer Salmon
Aldebrand — Mechelle Salyers
Konungr — Yuliya Mulvaney
Brakkis — Justin Morgan
Ligeia — Julie Granger

Jeff & Kinsey the corgi

Note from the Publisher

As many of Jeff's fans know, he passed away very unexpectedly in 2023, while working on this, his third Dragons of Andela book. His original plan was to create five books in the series, one based on each of the dragon characters. Sadly, that was no longer possible. When his wife located two chapters and several pages of handwritten notes and gave them to us, we at Secret Staircase Books decided to enlist the help of a ghost writer to finish the book, turning the series into a trilogy. We hope you like the result.

Jeffrey M. Poole lived in picturesque southern Oregon with his wife Giliane, and their dog, Kinsey the corgi. He is the best-selling author of the cozy mystery series Corgi Case Files and of the fantasy series Bakkian Chronicles, Tales of Lentari, and the Dragons of Andela. Jeffrey was a member of Mystery Writers of America, and Science Fiction & Fantasy Writers Association. Fans and readers can still follow him online on Facebook, or on his personal blog, where a list of all his published titles can be found. His free monthly newsletter is still being published, with personal tidbits from Giliane and news about the books, especially whenever there are deals or freebies. You can get a free short story by subscribing.

In every book, Jeff always extended his thanks to his readers, for giving his books a chance when there are literally hundreds of thousands to choose from. In his words, "Thanks for being there, guys! It means the world!" We also extend our thanks to those who contributed character names, and to the beta readers whose input has been invaluable: Sandra Anderson, Susan Gross, and Paula Webb.

As his publisher, we know that the worlds and stories in his books will live on forever. Rest in peace, Jeff.

Mystery
CORGI CASE FILES
Case of the One-Eyed Tiger
Case of the Fleet-Footed Mummy
Case of the Holiday Hijinks
Case of the Pilfered Pooches
Case of the Muffin Murders
Case of the Chatty Roadrunner
Case of the Highland House Haunting
Case of the Ostentatious Otters
Case of the Dysfunctional Daredevils
Case of the Abandoned Bones
Case of the Great Cranberry Caper
Case of the Shady Shamrock
Case of the Ragin' Cajun
Case of the Missing Marine
Case of the Stuttering Parrot
Case of the Rusty Sword
Case of the Secret Staircase (short story)
Case of the Unlucky Emperor
Case of the Ice Cream Crime
Case of the Hobbit Heist

For all the latest news on Jeff's books, scan the QR code to get his free email newsletter!

www.ingramcontent.com/pod-product-compliance
Lightning Source LLC
Chambersburg PA
CBHW021504110726
47899CB00001BA/291